THE EMPIRE WARS

THE EMPIRE WARS

BOOK ONE

AKANA PHENIX

BLACK
STONE
PUBLISHING

First edition: 2024
ISBN 979-8-212-91357-7
Young Adult Fiction / Fantasy / General

Version 1

Blackstone Publishing
31 Mistletoe Rd.
Ashland, OR 97520

www.BlackstonePublishing.com

To every precious human lost to genocide.
You were loved, you are treasured,
and you will be eternally remembered.

War makes men.
  —Maxim of the Allied Force Military

TABLE OF CONTENTS

PREFACE

The Empire Wars is a dystopian-fantasy novel and completely fictional. As in all stories about genocide, graphic violence, human exploitation, extreme intolerance, abuse of power, and blatant inhumanity are portrayed. This book is best suited for people in their late teens and older. There are several references to real genocides that have occurred throughout human history, and all of humanity should be aware of our collective global past and present and be cautious of our possible futures to prevent those genocides' repetition around the world. Many lives have been lost. Families broken. Children killed. Cultures erased. The effects of which still remain with us all today.

As I researched history, I noticed documentaries, books, and movies dedicated a high focus to the Aryan race ideology—blond hair, tall stature, and blue eyes—their physical markers for "superiority." It launched theories and rhetoric that pervaded other countries—and I felt compelled to write about the inescapability of its history. And why it remains.

A separate inspiration was Get Out and its social commentary. The movie details the experience of an isolated Black character, at times the only Black character. A familiar experience I sought to explore as well.

On a personal note, some of my family members were killed in genocide, and both of my grandmothers were teen brides married to older men. These topics are also depicted in the book, but I have chosen not to include a large age gap. However, these issues still occur in real life.

While I've done my best to approach these subject matters with care, some readers may be sensitive to these on-page depictions. I want every reader to be safe. Please follow your heart and trust your limitations.

Welcome to *The Empire Wars*.

THE ALLIED FORCE MILITARY

HEAD COMMISSIONS OF HUNTING

PLEASE BE ADVISED THAT ALL SELECTED PREY HAVE CHOSEN TO CONTRIBUTE TO A GLORIOUS HUNTING TRADITION IN OUR MILITARY HISTORY.

ANY ATTEMPT BY THE PUBLIC TO INTERFERE IN ANY CAPACITY WILL BE CONSIDERED TAMPERING AND IS PROHIBITED.

VIOLATORS ARE SUBJECT TO IMMEDIATE EXECUTION.

THE NATION'S REPUBLIC APPRECIATES YOUR FULL COOPERATION.

PART ONE:
THE SNIPER HUNT

CHAPTER 1

LOCATION: THE TRAEGER ISLAND WAR CAMP

EAST SECTOR

"Take off your clothes."

I choke on a train of words. "What?"

"Take off your clothes, and step onto the weight scale," the sergeant instructs me.

The lively crowd of attendees falls silent. My jaw drops; I'm convinced he's using crude humor until I see the serious faces of the armed soldiers. There is nothing subtle about their black tactical uniforms and rifles. The sergeant smiles warmly, as if that will be encouraging. As if any of this is normal.

Voices, whispers, all hush in one dramatic drop.

A knot fuses in my gut.

"We only ask the best to be measured," he promises me. A pale hand lands on my shoulder, squeezing it. "We wouldn't invite you if you weren't vitally important." His voice is clear and crisp, well trained. With the public's eyes watching him, he's not the militant brutalizer we all fear in the fields.

Right now, an artificial smile wraps his face.

My heart pounds. Rapidly.

I'm trapped in the adult sector. Surrounded by full-grown men.

My dirty-blond hair sticks to my cheeks. Exposed, I drag it behind my roughened ears. On-screen, my field-green eyes are blown wide with fear. Nudity has never been a tradition in the Great Hunt; none of the participators have ever been required to remove their clothes first to weigh themselves. *Take off my clothes? In front of everyone?*

I wait for him to retract his order. But the sergeant remains cordial. "The audience is prepared to view the main attraction. Please, proceed."

The cameras and buzzy lights are bright, hot, shoved in our faces. Ready to record.

I'm first in line.

I take a shaky step forward. My lungs squeeze in my chest as I panic.

My breath comes fast. My blood freezes at the idea of stripping out of my brown sack work dress and displaying my bare skin in front of thousands of people. Revealing my sweat-soaked body to strangers.

Slowly, my nails snag on my tan shorts, pulling them down to my ankles. But as I step out of the threadbare shorts, my body numbs again. *I can't strip out of my dress. I can't.*

Shame inflames my cheeks and ears. "Head up to the stage." The sergeant's scarred palm presses my spine forward. But my blood screams in my ears. *Keep the dress on. It's all you have left, Coa.*

Gooseflesh breaks out across my skin. *This can't be real.*

But it is real. My sleep barracks have been chosen for the week. This is the Great Hunt. Where the Arctic soldiers will hunt down the foreign laborers in the fields, and vacationers fly to the island to watch. If one laborer dies in the soldiers' hunt, the rest of their family is executed. In front of everyone.

The competition begins at the weigh-in, held in a bullring where instead of bullfights, there's a sand pitch with a dazzling silver stage in the middle and massive luxury seating areas that envelop the ring.

Meanwhile, the poor victim is broadcast on several huge screens for thousands to view.

It's competitive because the soldiers will open fire on us when the Great Hunt begins, and therefore we'll need to sprint for the heavy-duty shelters made of reinforced steel. The catch is there are only two of these shelters, and each will only fit two or three people inside of it.

Everyone will need to kill for a spot inside. Otherwise, they'll be shot dead if the snipers find them.

Terror grips my throat.

Every family must select one person. The *right* person—their lives depend on it. If that person fails, parents, sisters, brothers, and children will be butchered afterward in wholesale slaughter.

My forehead is still sticky with my older sister's kisses. *British pilots will save us—any day now. You need to fight for the littlest ones—Rabbit and Buckthorne. They need us.*

But my body stays frozen in shock.

"I promise, it's only ceremonial." The sergeant's soft voice enters my ears. He sounds friendly, warm. As if he isn't a man who orders executions as if they are canteen dinners. As if he doesn't watch each gassing with a sickening smile of pride. "It's painless. Every Hunt should begin with getting to know our laborers inside and out."

Inside and out.

Kømmand Sergeant Thorleiv Arcus is a man of plastic civility. His silky, perfect blond hair was combed and styled just for this event. Normally, he would be overseeing the fields, staining his gloves with our sweat and tears. "Visitors are here to witness historical traditions. You are the male fans' favorite blond."

You're the male fans' favorite blond.

I fold my arms to cover myself, but it's insufficient—I feel their gaze latch onto my chest anyway. I tell myself none of this will change me. My bright-green eyes and my spread of golden freckles will always be the same. My quirky, odd feet will always be the same. I will still be white passing, not white. Even my slightly full lips will remain the same. No matter what will happen to me.

But my gut instinct knows better.

Cornered, I observe my chaotic surroundings.

The sports complex is jammed with pale people, thousands of tourists crammed outside and inside the bullring. Screaming children charge through the outer complex, stampeding through congested lines of concession-stand customers. A crush of teens swarms the butcher stands, fighting off seagulls stealing their greasy steaks and sausages. Packs of shoppers argue over fan T-shirts. Masses of people fill up the tiered seats inside. The richest people in the cushy front-row seats are close enough to see everything, every hair on my body, every cut on my lips, every fleck of dirt on my cheeks, and cheaper seats at a distance are stocked with more regularly dressed people who need to squint to even see the screens. The bullring is huge.

But it's claustrophobic, somehow, thousands of eyes glued to my face, their attention hot on my body. Fully focused. It reeks of a rancid steak house.

All at once, the smells of smoked meat, unwashed skin, and beer malt hit my nose.

Right now, numbers spin on-screen, and my heart stops when I'm only in the first digit in value. *One.*

"Your rank's lower than expected," the sergeant remarks, frowning slightly. "There's always the weight scale to help you out. I'm certain you'll increase in the ranks if you weigh more than you look."

My mouth turns as dry as salt.

Cameras are rammed in front of me. Hot lenses glare straight into my eyes.

Take off your clothes. I war with my mind. *No. Stay clothed at all costs. Even if you die, die with honor.*

Days ago, my sleep barracks were safe. We're right near the burial fields, where the diseased and executed bodies are dumped, so we're often forgotten. That safety doesn't exist anymore.

Every synapse fires, urging me to run.

But the entire military base, which doubles as a forced-labor camp and contains this sports arena, is surrounded by high-security walls edged with barbed wire, and near the entrance are six rows of bronze sleep barracks, symbolizing the total loss of freedom.

Victims starve openly here, their hope extinguished by the soldiers, who crack down on every minor offense. Right now, even though the camp has turned into a tropical destination for tourists, human remains stain the soldiers' polished boots.

Even the sergeant's boots.

Amusement lives in the eyes of the man before me. "Don't tell me I accidentally stepped on your blood during the barrack raids, did I? How coarse of me, if I did."

"No, sir."

"Good. I'd hate to harm any of the livestock." He smiles.

Livestock. That's what his perverse men call us—we're either livestock or talent. The talent are privileged—dancing girls for the soldiers' beer halls, performers for the vacationers, concentration camp musicians prodded and beaten for pleasure by the drunk militants from time to time. But mainly well fed.

Well groomed. They are allowed to bathe on weekdays.

The rest of us are human livestock. Used for labor, grunt work, cleaning, killing.

We only bathe on Sundays, breathing in our own filth, sleeping in mud-splattered sheets, afflicted by diseases and infections from the harsh conditions.

In the eyes of these men, we are either food or entertainment for them and the tourists. Provisions or amusement. Talent that is brutalized for exploitation. Food that can be killed, burned, discarded.

As disposable as their own clothing.

"Thank you for participating. The other barrack girls cried for hours." He smiles wider.

Suddenly, a violent rage cracks inside my psyche at his chuckle. The girls I've slept next to, packed side by side for years, are tormented at his request; none of them are ever expected to survive this.

His remorseless mockery. It changes everything. My *sisters* were some of the girls that cried.

"Kill me." I bare my teeth at him. "Kill me. Now." *Cut him, Coa. Rip his trachea out.*

An aggressive protectiveness spikes inside of me for the honor of our barrack. I've wrestled wildcats, cougars, and king snakes for scraps of meat to live on. Right now, he's the murderous wolf in front of me. I've killed dangerous wolves before.

"What a bold statement!" The sergeant laughs, sliding his arm around me, and thousands of fans holler and whistle. The air becomes sticky with their attention. "Are you positive?"

"I am. Kill me right now." My teeth grit. I refuse to remove my eyes from his, challenging him.

"After I give the order, you can't change your mind," he warns me, speaking very slowly, as if I'm very young or brainless. "Do you need another second? Everyone tastes fear every now and again."

"I don't taste fear." Fear is alien to me right now through the pure anger coursing through my veins. I couldn't recognize it if I tried.

I know his people. The Arctic, known as the Allied Force, is a militarized nation. Located near the North Pole, it obliterated every other nation in the Arctic Circle to gain full control of the entire Arctic. Its military structure is unrivaled, its strategies annihilate whole continents, and its specialized technology is undefeatable.

When the world collapsed, the Allied Force seized advantage. It was the only nation prepared.

It could have saved other nations when the world fell.

However, the Allied Force does not believe in foreign countries. Citizens are permitted to kill anyone they suspect of having foreign blood. All foreigners, if not killed outright, are sent to forced-labor camps. Their boastful citizens believe in their homeland's superiority. According to them, their birthright is to be the only country left on earth.

Afterward, they will rebuild the earth in their militarized Arctic image. And they are nearly finished.

Most of the world's population is now dead. No military can exceed theirs. No population can withstand them. It is the reason why America and Britain were forced to combine their resources and reserves, uniting to form the North Transatlantic Empire. They are the last empire left standing on earth. Other than the Allied Force itself.

The Alvorada Empire can't be considered a real empire—it's a mess of refugee colonies. Vulnerable. Helpless. A mass of evacuees who barely escaped with clothing, spare coins, and their lives.

No one will save us.

My heartbeat gallops in my chest. *Kill me. Kill me. Kill me. Now.*

My family is full of orphans, strays, and runaway children. We don't stand a chance. We can't possibly survive this—but we can at least die together.

I know why we're here as foreigners. These forced-labor camps are designed for propaganda—masculinity rituals for Arctic young men. A symbol of their historical past. A salute to their future.

Centuries ago, the Allied Force was nearly driven to extinction, its population depleted by the severest winter conditions on earth. The most extreme frozen temperatures to ever exist, but still their men persisted. And overtook the world.

This hunt is a paean to their nation's resilience. A promise of their future glory.

A cloudless sky blankets a crowd of fans. They are grandly unified, wearing clothes printed with their Arctic nation's flag of dark battle-axes and stark-white mountains. Nationalist banners surround the compound. Silver supremacy pins adorn shirts, dresses, boots. I know they're all eager to watch my murder.

I know—but I do not care.

Kill me. Kill me. Kill me. Now. It's a war chant in my head now. *Kill me before I kill everyone in sight.*

"It's only for a few moments." The sergeant's husk-heavy voice breaks my thoughts again. The pine smoke pinches my nostrils. His voice is almost sweet, audibly entertained. "It will be over before you know it. Don't be foolish, livestock."

His warm condescension bleeds in my ears.

Now I'm insolent. A ferocious urge to protect my sisters, my brothers, and our pride surges inside of me all over again. My mouth constricts in defiance. "I am Coa Rangecroft—*not livestock*—and I demand you kill me now. Would you rather I do it for you? Take a knife to cut my own throat?"

Amusement drains out of his eyes. A dangerous tension increases in his terse silence. As his silence intensifies, I fear they will rip my clothes off for me.

I'm the youngest one they've ever had.

"We will kill you. Shoot you straight to death. You understand that outcome, right?"

"Yes." I don't swallow my words and beg at their feet for forgiveness. They'd *love* to see that. A girl kissing his polished boots and apologizing over and over. My teeth grind. I'd punch his teeth out first.

He has no idea I will take him with me. Any way I can.

We will die together.

"A pity," he responds at last. His mouth's hard bitten. "You seemed the sharpest in your barrack. This will be excruciating then."

Drying his calloused hands with a spare rag, the sergeant asks charitably, "Any final words?"

"No. No last words." I shake my head. There's no turning back. Everything is already lost. The wilderness where I grew up was desolated. My whole commune is gone.

They took everything from me. Now I will take everything from *him.*

I will kill us both.

As soon as his back turns, I prepare myself. In case my elegant, proper oldest sister is in the crowds watching me, I smooth the wrinkles from my dress like she taught us.

I scrub out the water stains with my nails to look as presentable as possible. I keep my odd feet together. I fix a few stray hairs, then lift my jaw to prepare for my first-ever murder of a man.

Like my older brother, Hucket, taught me, I distribute even weight on both my feet to balance my fighting stance.

The sergeant signals to the soldiers on the perimeter to take aim. On-screen, crimson dots appear on my throat, indications of the guns about to end my life.

A stab of last-second terror hits me. Hot and bitter.

"Enjoy your final moments. Afterward, we'll massacre your section."

My smile falters. He knows those words drew blood. He continues.

"We will proceed from youngest to oldest and slaughter all your barrack mates in your name."

That last part was intended to cut straight to the bone. Right inside of me. I lose balance, swaying with the gravity of his cold-blooded words.

"Do you know what happens after the massacre?" he asks casually. He sabotages my determination with a wry smile. His actual smile, a nauseating one of sadistic pleasure the tourists have never seen before, appears across his face.

Visceral images of my siblings' innocent faces bludgeoned in cold blood blister against my eyelids. I whip my head, trying to wrench them out of my mind. But he goes on. The gruesome scent of molten flesh. Scorched hair. He affects a bored tone. "It lasts for weeks. Not their bodies, of course, their stench from the incinerators."

I tear off my boots and socks without thinking.

I loathe myself for the small cry in my throat. How tiny my voice sounds.

Desperately, I peel open the black knife straps on my thighs. *Hurry. Move fast.*

"Wait . . ." A dry whisper is suffocated in my trachea. "Let me . . ." Regret throttles me as my words tangle.

Apologize, Coa. Get on your knees and apologize. I gather the words and try to gain the cowardice to surrender myself. Meanwhile, I expect him to gloat. *Of course, you changed your mind.* But instead, the sergeant has already moved on. As simply as ordering fresh oysters for dinner, he arranges the order to put my whole family to death. *Wait!*

My windpipe shrivels. *"Hold on!"*

The final kill order is given out loud.

I swallow thickly, breathless, preparing to let out a primal scream. "W—!"

As the words are crushed in my teeth, an older boy—tan skinned and green eyed—begins to shed his clothes, snatching the attention of the soldiers and triggering gasps from the front-seat viewers.

An athletic body, bold in the sun, steps forward. He's intimidatingly handsome. Captivating. He resembles the sergeant and most of the audience: sandy-blond hair, white but healthy skin. But it's clear by his tan he's been out in the broiling sun more than they have.

His chiseled jaw gives him an overconfident appearance, and his nose is bent, like danger and blood sport are second nature to him. His posture is powerful, his stature easily six feet two, maybe more. Sunlight catches his messy, curly hair, turning it gold. His untamed waves of blond tangle in his unsettling green eyes. We make sudden eye contact. Intensely.

What's he doing? The soldiers advance toward the stage. He's daring to ruin the kill shot, and the whole audience leans in, since it's deliciously early for a surprise double kill.

The crowds are palpably hungry to see it; you can feel it in the air. *They're going to kill him. Live.* He bounds up the platinum steps two at a time and strides past the black hunting flags flapping in the wind. He reaches into the gold bowls of previous Huntsmen's blood—mixed with chemicals to keep it from clotting—dips his palm in, and slams it over his wide chest, accepting the challenge.

Blood drips down his muscular abdomen.

All sound is sucked out of the crammed adult section, except his footsteps. He steps to the edge of the silver-plated platform. Right in front of the cameras crowded below him. Recording him.

Filming his broad shoulders, barrel chest, and powerful hairy legs.

It's completely quiet. We all hold our breath.

Eight more soldiers aim up, but the sergeant lifts his hand to stop them, narrowing his eyes. They watch the young man. We watch him.

He's calm. Without complaint, he peels off his dark briefs, the last piece of clothing on his toned body, and abandons it behind him. He doesn't seem to care that his whole body's exposed. He smirks at us and winks at me. His manhood is obvious between his healthy legs, and he has a lot to be proud of, inciting a new boisterous roar from the audience.

But something else catches my eye. His tanned back is marked with deep, gashing scars that make my own labor scars seem like roughhousing bruises.

He stands at the top of the polished steps, and I realize they didn't carve AGRE into his back—as is customary. FOREIGNER. They violently, aggressively slashed SEVRĘ into his bare skin: TRAITOR.

CHAPTER 2

Not missing a beat, the sergeant follows him—and the young man plasters on a shamelessly flirty smile for the crowds. I can barely breathe, waiting for a barrage of gunshots to end his life. "Son, your spine is made of tungsten. How courageous of you."

"How good of you to nominate me in the first place, Arken. Sharp thinking."

His voice is an attractive rumble. Deep. Laughter warms the whole sports complex, now ripe with a brand-new anticipation. *He's going to be gunned down. Naked!* Shoppers stop purchasing souvenirs at stands; derisive socialites stop scoffing with disgust at our filth-covered rags; older teenagers crowd around the barriers that keep the underaged out of the adult sector. All watching him.

Except for the sergeant. His eyes remain on the crowds.

"What's your name, compatriot?" The sergeant clasps the naked nominee on the bare arm. But it's clear they already know each other. *Arken.* It's a nickname that in Allied Force Vikarian means *the butcher.*

The outdoor sunlight bathes the young man's skin in aurum, adorning his dark-blond hair like a gilded laurel.

Fans eat up his bold move, shouting all at once for his attention. But the nominee trains his eyes on me, and I feel a spike of electricity. He's menacingly good looking. A formidably handsome young man. "Hazen Creed."

A distant gunshot startles a flock of spur-winged geese into flight.

"Hazen Creed." The sergeant squeezes his bare arm. "You're incredibly brave for what you did. How old are you?"

"Eighteen."

"Eighteen. That explains the wild bravery." The sergeant draws a hearty laugh from the crowd. But the rest of us captives glower.

Hazen Creed *does* seem brave. Perfect for a lethal hunt like this.

Only a few can survive.

Raw savagery explodes inside of me in one blood-filled beat. As I'm an eighteen-year-old myself, I experience the gravity of the situation settling inside of me, and I appraise Hazen's body, his stance. I evaluate his ability to kill me if I'm distracted. He could end me and effortlessly move on, killing the next victim, earning the safety shelter for himself. But that can't happen.

What was I thinking, trying to die? I need to save us at every cost. My siblings are counting on me. I need to win this Hunt.

Right now, I have the advantage over citizens of other dead empires that lost a war to the Allied Force—I am a fireborn with dangerous hidden lightning right inside my blood. *I could kill him. I could win.*

There are no winners in war. But there's no point in dignity in the face of survival either. As much integrity as I want to hold on to, it's gone now—if they want me to be naked, I'll be naked. As long as I win the Great Hunt.

Almost no one outside Makari-Africa has had magic since the Middle Ages. As far as they know, it barely exists anymore. *These men don't know that I create natural fire. I will burn him alive.*

I blow white smoke from my nostrils like a bull. I reexamine Hazen. His body boasts of pure manhood—squared shoulders, roughened skin, sharp jawline. As if mocking my own girlish appearance.

He stares right at my peculiar bare feet, and I lean on my good foot to hide the shriveled one. My good foot is still odd shaped, bowed inward, but it's not half as bad as my left foot. I glare at the electric weight scales as my cheeks burn with heat, focusing hard to keep my eyes from noticing his tilted head of confusion.

Due to the severity of the damage to my feet, I should have difficulty standing or walking, but I've taught myself to stand for hours on them. I've trained myself to run for miles.

Right now, under Hazen's own feet are electric scales about to weigh him. *Let him be low ranked. Let him hit two or one.*

"Hazen Creed, tell us . . ." The sergeant pulls him forward, closer to the rabid onlookers. Hazen doesn't move, not even his eyes. His eyes are still on mine.

I don't break our gaze either. Pungent island wind blows over my nose.

He winks again, and it fills me with unfathomable fury, as if he believes I will die instead of him.

"As you hunt, what's a quote you'd prefer to stand by?" The sergeant's uneven mouth quirks. *How would you like to be remembered for your sacrifice?*

Hazen's going to die. Even if I have to rip through his liver with my teeth, he's a dead man now.

"Glory before fear," Hazen says, repeating a Great Hunt mantra. I've heard it all over the military base. *Glory before fear. Let glory lead you. Glory is destined.* His smirk widens. "Glory is destined for me in the Great Hunt."

He's unafraid and unflinching, as if daring me to try to kill him. Applause bursts for him in the vivacious audience. Older teenagers wave the Arctic's iconic flag colors—black, green, and brown—in overzealous support of him. Some even wave the white Victory Year flag as if he's the winner already.

I tune them out. *I can't let him get to the shelter before me.* Even a young man as fit as Hazen Creed knows a bullet-proof shelter is his best chance at surviving in the Great Hunt.

"Glory before fear. How perfect." The sergeant praises the fact that Hazen quoted Barritus, the founder of the Allied Force military. Barritus's warlike ivory statues are every-where, glowering over us in the fields. "May glorious history remember your name."

But before I can even think of Hazen Creed butchering me, I think of what these people will see when I'm naked. Hundreds of viewers across the compound will watch me strip off the sticky bandages wrapped tight around my chest; they'll see me slip off my brown potato-sack dress and expose my starved body to them. They'll see the sugarcane knife straps now loosened around my upper thighs. Empty of my fieldwork knives.

At this second, I don't care that these people will watch my dark-blond hair spill wildly over my naked waist, or notice how soft pink certain parts of me are. At this very second, I am ready to sprint to take off my clothes, impa-tient for my turn.

Prepared to secure my place. At all costs.

It hits me that this is how they get people to commit

atrocities. Right now, I'd kill everyone in front of me to return to my siblings alive.

The sergeant's men glare me down.

Most of the soldiers are called enforcers. But the sergeant created his own military force, with the lower rank called carnage men and the higher rank called slaughter men. They are his eyes. His ears.

His bullets.

You're lucky if the enforcers get to you first—they have standards and protocols. His carnage men are reckless, lawless—a danger to every victim within their proximity. But the slaughter men are the darkest threat—murder experts. Sadists. There's nothing left of you after their execution.

Focus. Gold confetti blasts across the packed labor camp. Night laborers will have to spend hours sweeping it clean, grateful they're not the ones sent to the burial fields.

"Hazen Creed is in," announces the sergeant, earning rapturous applause that cuts open my battered eardrums. The silver scale bursts into celebratory color, washing Hazen Creed's stark-naked frame in bright amber. My pulse spikes. "Welcome your first participator, Hazen Creed."

Focus, Coa.

"Ranked the highest number: seven."

Smiling in celebration, Hazen whispers inaudibly to the sergeant. *What is he murmuring?*

The sergeant frowns at me. Directly. *What happened?*

Without another word, Hazen descends the polished silver steps. He keeps his steady gaze on me, which is deeply intense, since eye contact alone is suffocating when someone's completely naked and staring right at you. I avoid gazing between his thighs, but I'm standing at the base of the steps, and his body needs to pass mine in order to return to his clothes by my feet. Hazen stands next to me in the dusty sand. I feel his bare skin brush against my own sweaty skin. His skin is dry; he didn't even break a drop of perspiration.

Inhaling his natural scent—earth and ocean—I try to keep track of every other part of him.

Particularly his scent, in case I'm sightless in the tangled jungle later. Rainforests contain dense canopies—clusters of heavy trees and ceilings of leafy branches—so there will be low visibility.

Ranks are meaningless, I tell myself. They give no advantages. A rank is only the military base's estimation of when the participator will die during the seven-day Hunt.

Almost no one lasts past five nights.

They believe I will be killed the first night. *One.*

Fine. Let them underestimate me. Hazen bends to pick up his abandoned clothes, and my ankles tangle in his dark shirt. My damaged foot stumbles as I try to step past it.

"Thank you for advancing forward. Sorry that I—"

"Don't apologize." Hazen stands back and straightens. Smiles. "I don't mind being naked. There's a rush of adrenaline to it." A flash of perfect white teeth.

That wink again.

He's being nice, I realize. He saved my life and just showed me how easy it was; all I have to do is copy. His cocksure smile widens. "Valor's luck to you."

I give a fake smile. "Valor's luck to you."

Hazen slips his clothes back on and buttons his black trousers, as though public showmanship doesn't particularly affect him. But his tense mouth and narrowed eyes betray him: he's furious.

"Hazen Creed! Hazen Creed! Hazen Creed!"

It's pure mayhem as the vacationers fanatically chant his

name and belt out their endorsement. Someone shoves me forward.

"Take off your clothes and step onto the weight scale."

Their eyes land on my raw face again. I practically sprint past the sergeant this time.

But he halts me at the silver platform, right at the base of the steps.

CHAPTER 3

"Nominee, are you capable of fire?" the sergeant mutters toward me under his breath, idly glancing in Hazen's direction. *How did Hazen know? How did he catch the thinnest, the whitest, of my smoke?*

"Fire tricks, mostly," I lie. Not exposing the fact I could incinerate him.

As if smelling the lie in my voice, he smirks. "Useful. Do you have a family? Parents?" *Anyone we could weaponize against you?*

"No. I don't have a family." I start pulling off my knife straps. "They're all dead."

"No immediate family?" the sergeant specifies, speaking in front of the entire war-camp complex at this point. Flocks of teens are now crammed around the signs outside that read *Restricted*, thirsty to know what's happening inside. Peeking over the barriers. Heaps of Arctic women rouge their lips as Hazen Creed, now clothed, returns to stand on the participators' end of the silver-plated stage. He winks at them. "You're certain?"

A bead of sweat lands on the silver stage as soon as I set my bare foot on it. "Yes."

The sergeant lowers his voice. "No parents? No cousins still alive? No siblings?"

Siblings. His gaze holds finality, as if he's spotted us at the canteens before. *His carnage men see everyone.*

My voice is firm. "Dead."

"Dead. All right then." His eyes hold a warning. "You will represent your nation. Make Hallowell proud."

Steady, Coa. Heat blasts across my cheeks as thousands of eyes peer up at me from the seats.

Applause slams around me. Excessively.

Without wasting time, I bend down, unlatching my ankle trackers. Carefully, I slip my muddied feet out and stand straight, distracting the audience from my contorted feet by mimicking a massive showgirl smile for the crowds, as if I don't spend every brutal day in the fields. As if I'm a talent girl, dazzling and worthy of applause. As the camera focuses on my starburst of golden freckles, drags its lens over my dirty-blond hair, it's clear that I'm a fielder—bathed once a week, always ankle deep in mud, cane stalks, and dirt. Tracked at almost all times.

My hair's tangled and unkempt, another sign that I'm not talent, who are allowed to comb regularly.

However, my bright-green eyes are young and sprightly enough, like a talent girl's. Talent girls are standouts in the Great Hunt, since very few of them will ever see this stage, and if you stand out, the snipers tend to save you for last.

From the stage, I can see everything on the outside of the bullring. There are four sectors of the military base. You don't want to be caught dead in any of them. The North Sector contains the living quarters of the highest-ranked military men, as well as polished buildings like the Command Centers, where the camp's crimes against humanity are organized, monitored, and sanctioned. The West Sector hosts lower-ranked military men and holds inhumane structures such as the Traeger Impound, used for public beatings; the execution chamber; and the Interrogation Department. The South Sector is where the rest of us live, work, and eat, in the lice-infested sleep barracks with no electricity or running water, subjected to the grueling labor fields and the ration stations.

But the East Sector with its sports complex roars with life, hosting tourists, resorts, and wildlife hunting grounds. As soon as you set foot onto the sports complex, you exist for tourists' entertainment.

Right now, outside of the sports complex, I know mobs of women gawk at our metal showers, shocked that so many laborers are packed in the unsanitary space all at once in the South Sector. It's Sunday, so they need to be quick—death week or not—to scrub the soil from themselves. Praying they'll be lucky enough that the water will be cold after a full week in the broiling sun.

Meanwhile, the Allied Force men allow their children to feed lettuce to the field-workers like they're animals. *Be careful! Hit them if they bite!* Girls are strutting around in the dresses we wear in the sleep barracks. Twirling and probably singing songs about dead men.

The wandering tourists want to see *nicer areas* like the concrete rinder platz, or cattle station—a platform in the camp square where roll calls are held for livestock. We stand there at three thirty sharp every morning, no matter how extreme the weather. Our blood smirches the ground, but it's cleaned routinely. Much more often than the metal showers, which are rusted, stained with urine, and gorged with the bodies packed inside. The nearest toilet in the South Sector is for talent only—the rest of us need to relieve ourselves in the minefields or showers.

Which makes the stench of the camp unbearable.

Last year, poor Elsko had his foot blown to smithereens when he risked the minefields by the island's shores for privacy. Now he stares anxiously at me and the rest of his competitors.

At the top platform, I glare down at my competition from the stage. Roughly seventy-five people will be inducted into the Great Hunt. The sergeant selects two sleep barracks for each Great Hunt season.

Right now, more than half of the field laborers in my barracks are glaring right back at me, ready to kill me for their own families. A schoolteacher in my barracks, Juneberry, taught me how to survive. She's the reason I can even speak Vikarian, the language of the Allied Force. I used to sneak into her sessions and pay her in stale grain. If it weren't for her, half of us would be lost at the barked Vikarian orders. But right now, her eyes are murder.

Juneberry could kill me dead.

Another man, Stanislav, was a doctor in his homeland. Now he's humiliated by the taunts of soldiers, but he never lets that stop him from cleaning our wounds beneath the slaughter men's noses. Dozens of fielders swarm to him, often paying him in gratitude, since he refuses real payment. Right now, his cold gaze is that of a killer's.

As if he could strangle me with his surgeon's hands.

Hazen Creed stands at the forefront. Boldest of them all.

In desperation for an intimidation tactic, I launch a self-absorbed smile on my face, right in front of them, copying Hazen Creed and his outrageously infuriating confidence. *Fear me. Hesitate to target me.* But Hazen smirks right back, dangerously perceptive, as if he knows I'm imitating him to survive, and he'll manipulate me for it.

But to my surprise, it *works*.

My brows lift as grown men in the audience roar at me, spit landing on my bandaged bare feet. Hefty fists pound brawny chests, the men too drunk to care if I'll live, only that I've agreed to fight.

"Remove your clothes and step onto the weight scale," the sergeant remarks as apprehension spreads through my shoulders. I nod. I step forward, removing the first layer of bandages.

My airway constricts as I scan the area. There are more people than I even realized. At least ten thousand blood sport fans are in attendance.

The forced-labor camp is located on Traeger Island, a military-occupied island on the coast of Former Makari-Africa. All the spectators sizzle in the poisonously hot equatorial sun as vendors pass out ice-cold beverages to attendees. Someone hollers, "Remove your clothes! Remove your clothes!"

The buzz of the fans instantly makes me feel trapped inside a beehive.

"State your age and full name."

I begin removing my bandage wraps. "Eighteen. Coa Wildflower Rangecroft—"

"I have a request!" a voice trills from the audience, and our heads spin. It's another girl's voice. "Over here!"

A gasp tears out of my lips.

The princess of the Makari-African Empire flashes on every screen. Real. In person.

Slowly . . . bewildered voices begin to rumble, and the sergeant looks away from me to zero in on the dignitary. The princess of a charred continent.

"Good morning!" she chirps into a microphone as if nothing's wrong.

As if none of her countries were annihilated. She behaves as if not one person was butchered. How can she sound excited? Thrilled, even?

I reckon she's shell shocked. In the last few decades, the Arctic has devastated the Makari-African Empire beyond recognition and left only a sparse quarter of its former population alive. It's not populated enough to be considered a country.

However, Makari-Africa is the Arctic's most treasured war prize.

In the Middle Ages, the world was filled to the brim with orún magic. Makari was rich with tribal warriors, deep-kungu oil (triple the value of crude oil), mountains of rare natural resources, spear soldiers that could burn villages, and makanza armies that could penetrate tanks and armored vehicles with their weapons. Now it's been rendered low and powerless in front of the world. However, Makari-Africa is the only continent on earth still capable of magic. Since the Middle Ages, only one bloodline now possesses magic—the Kōn lineage. This is the Kōn rain king's granddaughter.

There are six types of humans in this world: the fireborn, the rainborn, the huntborn, the sunborn, the darkborn, and the rest of the world without magic.

The fireborn are those like me, humans who create fire out of the air at the cost of their lungs and bones.

The rainborn are those who can heal themselves of cuts and fractures, splintered bones, and torn ligaments, at the price of shorter lives.

The huntborn are those who hear in greater detail than the birds, smell in sharper distinction than the hyenas, see farther than golden eagles, and sense danger faster than cat-sharks. However, it comes at the price of their rare births.

The sunborn are birthed in the sun, gifted with a closeness to the earth, the sky, and the spirits that often comes at the expense of their own heart. They feel the ache of the severed trees, the mourning cries of a dying snake, the shuddering tides of weary souls within the seas.

If the sunborns are born during the solar eclipse, they become darkborns capable of mind possession, mind reading, and manipulation of wild nature.

Ife is like the rest of the world, born without magic. It's evident by the Kōn rain markings on her cheek, which are a soft pink color instead of the rainborn light gray. The rain never gifted its color to her; instead it refused her as a descendant of rain, which turned her hair as pink as her markings when she was born.

I brace myself, knowing the Allied Force will torture her, as they do every laborer.

But she seems curious rather than afraid.

Don't show your face to them. Run. The Allied Force is notorious for public murders of political figures, luring them into ambushes with a false sense of safety. I suck in a breath. Petrified for her. *Run. Run. Run.*

But it's too late—the princess has revealed herself thoughtlessly. She waves avidly at onlookers. She's so tiny, shockingly small for a young woman, and my mouth drops.

A diamond tiara glints atop her little head.

As I realize how fragile her body is, my ears twitch. It's an involuntary reflex that happens whenever I can't believe my eyes. It's ludicrous that she's here to represent the tribal warrior empire of Makari. Particularly considering her family once dominated every inch of the continent.

"Interesting." The sergeant rubs his dry palms. "She's still oblivious."

The compound reeks of pungent sweat and dead wild game. The princess sticks out with dazzlingly bright diamond earrings in a private section. She's perky and chic, wearing a leafy dress of palm-tree leaves that exposes her lithe waist and thighs. Her heels are tropical leaves. Her butterfly eye-lashes are girlish—impractical.

"Vellvecht." *Attention.* The sergeant extends an arm in announcement. "Everyone stand—the ikä of the Allied Force: Ife Størmbane."

Ikä in Vikạrian means *princess*, although historically the Allied Force has never had royalty. In ancient Allied Force times, it was every man for himself. Every man for his family.

"Kisses!" Ife squeals.

Don't do this. I can't breathe. She's going to get us both shot. *Please, sit down!*

Ife's oblivious as she begins reading from a script they gave her. It's a crinkled parchment in her palms. She's too early, off cue and amateur.

But these executioners won't accept any excuse. *Don't shoot me.* My mind swirls, and I nearly vomit stomach acid. *I need to kill for my family. I made my decision.*

But Ife's achingly beautiful, a wildly gorgeous girl. She has rosy, pouty lips, flirtatious green eyes, a kitten nose, an intoxicating smile. Blush-pink hair. She's what little girls wish they will grow up to look like. She has a face that jus-tifies war from men.

Ife steals attention without trying; there's no chance she can stop this now that everyone's eyes are on her.

Men are arrested by her face. Her exotic, dark-brown skin

is rare in the pale, snowy Allied Force. Even Hazen Creed stops gazing at the rows of tourists to stare up at her.

Africans are basically extinct on earth, which makes Ife among the very last of her kind.

A valuable human souvenir.

"Welcome to the Great Hunt, everyone!" Ife reads her script excitedly. She slips a tuft of her pink hair behind her ear. "Thank you for inviting Ife—oh! *Me!* Thank you for inviting me to such a fun hunt!"

She holds her small brown hands over her heart. "It's an amazing honor to be here!"

She's about to be killed.

"Thank you all so much!" Ife claps. "Thank you most of all to my husband, Sniper General Maximus Størmbane!"

A young man of formidable height and dominant stature emerges behind her. If Hazen Creed is rugged and dangerous, this man in a clean uniform is the respectable version of him. His blond hair is more distinguished, his posture more disciplined. The Arctic girls scream over his classic handsome features, which are reminiscent of old films and even older preeminent money.

At the sight of him, fans explode. A full-blown havoc ensues at an earsplitting volume.

Their primal roar consumes my senses as the thousands of blood sport enthusiasts burst out of their chairs. Ballistic chants nearly blow out my eardrums as mounting shouts fill the worker camp. "Sniper General Størmbane!" Disbelief laps around the crowds. "Sniper General Størmbane is *here!*"

Screams electrify the camp.

Who is he? The terror inside of me won't allow me to focus. *I've heard of him. Who is he exactly?*

A flood of teenagers escapes the meat concession lines and

swarms for the edge of the silver compound tiers. Absolute pandemonium breaks loose as grown men leap over steel barricades, climb over the security ropes, fight past the blockade made by private soldiers. Fanfare blasts against my thudding chest.

"You don't know who this is?" Hazen asks me. "He's the future leader of the entire Allied Force and the future leader of the world."

Hazen points up at the high-set screens. "More important than anyone you will ever meet, besides the grand leader himself."

I can tell he's handing me information, and I keep note of each detail in my mind. As subtly as I can, I steal the opportunity to step slightly behind Hazen in case the riflemen at the perimeters still plan to shoot me for my earlier defiance. I don't put anything past them.

However, Hazen catches my movement, and with a haughty smile, he can't help himself. "Are you afraid?"

"Are you?" I say back, reprimanding myself for opening my mouth. I cover it with a fake wince. "My feet hurt a bit; I needed to move them around."

I make a show of hiding my bruised toes from him, hoping he'll make the assumption they're my greatest weakness. But he stares at them a second longer than necessary.

As the crowd begs Sniper General Størmbane to take the stage, he obliges. He leads Ife by the hand, guiding her, as if she might wander into traffic alone. There's a gentleness in her gaze that breaks my heart. She's barely tall enough to even reach his chest. *She needs to flee.*

He's around the same age as her, both of them older teenagers, and his dimples deepen. His trademark summer-blue eyes crinkle at the corners. Ife buries her nose in his arm happily.

I glance at Hazen to check his thoughts, but his eyes are still on my feet.

"Did you damage them in the fields?" Hazen asks, signaling he doesn't buy for a second that I am a talent girl. He's trying to figure me out, and the only thing he can probably tell so far is that I'm underfed and on the taller side.

I drag my good foot back. I can't exactly explain I didn't have access to emergency surgeries as a feral child in the wilderness and that they worsened and deteriorated; it doesn't fit the narrative. Back then, I had to become creative with treating my own injuries. Right now, I play deeper into the part of a humble, weak field girl. "The sugarcane harvest ruined them last year."

I sneak a look at him to see if he buys that answer, and his face is irritatingly amused, as if he didn't believe a single word. *Fine.*

I cut the act for now and instead try to decipher his status while I can. *Is Hazen Creed talent or a fielder? Who even is Hazen Creed?*

I've never seen him in the fields or at the beer halls; very few men are talent in the forced-labor camp. Their options are limited to mostly musicians and cage fighters, and neither last very long. By his knuckles, he could be a cage fighter, but he doesn't let on to either one as the screens shift back to Sniper General Maximus Størmbane.

Hazen applauds appropriately, but none of us laborers move an inch.

A film montage directs my attention to the wølven-starker. The Vikąrian word for *sniper.*

On-screen, Maximus Størmbane breaks the world swim record for the Subarctic Strait. Next, he scales a glacial summit with little equipment, Arctic permafrost thick at the glacier base. But it's his sniper record that makes my heart stop.

"The real kill count is sanitized for the public." Hazen maintains his gaze on the screen without flinching at the graphic murders of political leaders and government heads. "He's the finest sniper and sharpest military prodigy in the Arctic. The greatest in history."

Sweat drips down my spine.

I know that snipers are the closest thing the militarized Allied Force has to a religion, and right now, you'd think the carnage men were looking at a living miracle.

Trumpets violently blast over my head. Audiences are chanting at the tops of their lungs, visibly reaching to touch even an article of his dark uniform as Sniper General Størmbane escorts his wife to the platform's center. Right toward me.

He's here to let them kill me for entertainment.

I glance rapidly at Hazen.

Hazen mouths two words: *Stand aside.*

It's the third time he's helped me. I drag a gasping breath down my throat and step quickly away to make more room for Sniper General Størmbane, Ife, and Kømmand Sergeant Thorleiv Arcus, I situate myself next to Hazen.

A slaughter man still squints through his tactical rifle at me. I do my best to ignore him.

Inferior blood cannot last. Across the stadium, several screens declare the Størmbane maxims. *Blood and birthright.*

Despite the outright declarations of hatred, Ife does not seem afraid. *Why? What did the Allied Force tell her would happen? In front of everyone?*

As she treads closer, it's clear she is unaware of the world. It appears as if this is her very first time in public.

They're purging the earth, and the sergeant is right: she's oblivious. Fear leaks in my chest. *Run. Now, Ife.*

They are going to sacrifice you for tradition, then gloat over it.

"Respect the flag," Hazen warns me, and I stammer. I didn't even realize the Arctic flag banners had opened. Whenever the Allied Force flag unfurls, you must salute. I hurriedly put my left fist to my temple, but Hazen corrects me. "It's always your right fist."

I swallow, switching to my right and slamming my left down against my side.

On-screen, Sniper General Størmbane's aim is ungodly. Inhuman.

His cold accuracy instills terror in the rest of us. He's completely merciless.

His target-practice speed is horrific, and the sniper general does not miss. Not once. He punctures the center of the cranium, headshot after headshot.

I concentrate on Ife. As her leafy heels click onto the platform, you can tell she is just a dewy-eyed girl completely clueless of the genocide around her in the forced-labor camp, and I don't imagine the princess has been around a mass of people with access to her before.

She looks as if she hasn't been outside in years.

She clings to his arm, anxious at all the commotion and almost in tears. She attempts a brave face and grins sweetly, clearly utterly incapable of survival because anyone else would've run by now, even if escape is impossible.

"Chief Princess of Makari," the sergeant greets with his audience-friendly tone. But his eyes are set on Maximus Størmbane with admiration. "What quote would you like to share on behalf of these participators?"

"Be kind to everyone!"

Let her fend for herself. Don't try to save her, Coa. But I freeze.

Ife's soft hands grasp my fingertips as she stands next to me, intertwining our fingers in a tight knit. She snuggles my arm with both of hers. As if she always needs to touch someone in order to feel safe and loved. "I interrupted so that you can keep your bandages on. Are you mad at me?"

Oh no. She was trying to help me. Which only makes her incoming death worse.

My stubborn mouth can't help itself. "Run. While you can."

Ife blinks at me in response. As if not a single thought of self-preservation can exist in her pure head. Instead, she offers me a small fox grin as if she has an idea.

"You're tall and strong legged. What if we try a dance for your introduction instead?" She squeezes gently. "Does that help?"

"*Run,*" I warn, while her husband is still busy shaking hands with the sergeant, but she beams at me like we're friends.

"Oh! I've got it—we can summon the rain for the Hunt in the dance." She promises me it will be fun. "I dance all the time by myself; all you'll need to do is copy my hips. Only I've never summoned the rain before—"

"No. They will kill us."

"Kill us?" She gapes. "The cameras are for the movie. Did you read the script?"

"This is real."

She tilts her head, and I can tell she doesn't understand, but she nods like she gets it now. My blood pressure rises as the sergeant approaches. She waves at him.

"Oh!" Ife cheers. "I have such a fabulous idea! Can we all sing to the rain? We might get lucky, and it will rain good fortune on everyone."

"Not in the opening ceremony; the tradition is sacred," the sergeant declines carefully. He pretends to listen as she talks about how the rain is our friend and it will bring good luck to everyone.

After she's done, Ife nods obediently and kisses my cheek for good luck.

"The rain will bring something good. I can feel it."

I steam in fury. But Ife gazes at me quizzically, as if she can't imagine not getting a kiss back from me. Her eyes well up, as if she worked hard on meeting people for the first time and she might've messed up. She blinks back tears, gulping rapidly.

"I promise, the rain is our friend. Just trust me—it can heal everyone."

Her brain has the depth of a raindrop itself, even if she's the rain king's granddaughter, I've gathered.

Any *normal* country would slit the throat of a bull as a ceremonial sacrifice in honor of their military history. The Allied Force sends seventy-five people to their deaths.

As a war trophy.

Ife bites her roseate lips. Hard. And it hits me fiercely how utterly useless she is, which is exactly why the Allied Force chose her for marriage in the first place. She is a symbol to the entire world.

We are all overtaken and defeated. We never stood a chance against them.

CHAPTER 4

ELEVEN HOURS EARLIER

BEFORE DAWN

Murderous snow is packed against my rib cage. My blood is chilled down to the bone. I'm trapped in the path of an avalanche, my body freezing nearly to death—

I gasp. Awake.

Gripping my chest, I check my warm nightdress, my silk sheets. We're not in the Arctic anymore, and there's no distant siren of severe weather warnings or extreme hypothermia cautions.

Instead, there's an empty divot in the bed beside me, and the silk cloth still feels half-frozen from where Maximus Størmbane's ice-cold body slept next to mine. I couldn't stop shivering in his arms last night. Right now, across the bedroom, I can smell the metallic aroma of ammunition as his deft hands organize his lethal firearms.

He is an expert with each weapon.

Terrified, I keep my breaths even and quiet. *He's arranging his rifles. Again.*

Maximus uses the exercise to condition his mind. Every motion is muscle memory.

Every act is intentional. Every munition matters.

Meanwhile, war terrors barrage my mind at the sight of them, and the excruciating, traumatic memories threaten to resurface all at once.

Please, don't kill them. I'll give you my life, General.

Don't kill the children. Spare them. Please. Please.

My face suddenly explodes with pain, as if the gunpowder burns my senses. Memories crash together in my brain. *Don't shoot them. Please—*

Mercy. General, mercy.

I am going to kill Sniper General Maximus Størmbane.

I will kill him exactly like he killed my people, but I'm not naive. To everyone else, I'm his absurdly innocent, girlish wife, and no one suspects anything different.

I'm the closest person to Maximus, and it's my only advantage. It needs to be me who kills him.

Right now, this side of the world assumes teenage girls are incompetent. Brainless. Harmless. Obsessed with everything they desperately love. Men pride themselves on humiliating girls for daring to have passions of their own. Concerts are flooded with screaming girls, romance industries fueled by them, world premieres dominated by loyal teenage-girl fans with spending power.

And yet people behave as if girls aren't capable of anything clever or premeditated.

I am shameless about my premeditation. I know I should pretend to be meek and act embarrassed about my manipulative, calculated tendencies. But I am not going to lie to myself about my ambition. Every morning, I beg Maximus to use me. *Fill me up with your love. I need you desperately, Maximus. Use me, please. Use me all over. Everywhere. On the counter, against the staircase, inside the war room.*

It's an easy act, sounding so helpless and clingy. Maximus laps it up like milk. *I need you. Maximus, touch me. Can you feel how fast you're making my heart beat? Can you taste how breathless I am?*

Growing up, I understood early how the world works. At a young age, I learned people condemn girls who are ruthlessly driven and know how to seize their power. The same people who will criticize girls for using their own bodies will exploit those girls' bodies every chance they get. Because our bodies are meant for *them to use,* not for ourselves.

I noticed people never think twice about taking advantage of me—which is why I take advantage first. If you can convince others they are controlling you, you gain the control.

I murmur, "Your chest was freezing cold again. Are you all right?"

"Extreme-condition exposure preparation," Maximus responds. He's already making his way over. "Did I wake you, kitten?"

"Avalanche dreams. Can you cuddle me?" I whisper gently.

Maximus wraps his muscular arms around me, and I try not to flinch this time when he's as frozen as butcher's ice. "Drink läkøn. You'll sleep straight through the night."

Läkøn is an Arctic metallic beer—these Arctic men drink it like water. It's more barbaric than choking down icy køvma, the Arctic's extreme version of vodka. *Vodka builds men. Køvma builds soldiers.*

In their fatherland, there are the dark months,

unforgiving winter months. For six months, from Øtzken until Marzen—October until March—there is no sun, only a twenty-four-hour darkness known as polar night. The men are built in the dark, drinking metal to numb themselves to the severe temperatures as they hunt for prey. Despite their technological advancement, the men are fully prepared to survive on their own land and sustain their families; it is their definition of manhood.

Nimbly, I curl onto my silk pillows. "No—I'll sleep. Will you still attend my debut party?"

"I need to examine the stealth unit. The sergeant appears to have altered the West Sector, and I plan to observe every enforcer there." I can tell Maximus noticed right away that one of the sergeant's men slipped and called himself a slaughter man, which isn't a military rank in the Allied Force I've ever heard before. "After the examination, I will attend your debut."

"What if I ruin it?" I wince.

"You won't. Sleep, kitten. I'll keep an eye on you." Maximus kisses my forehead. I shiver.

———

Two hours later, as I sleep, a pianist composes ballads in the penthouse suite. The musicians' presence is a gift from Maximus to help me stay asleep as a selected harpist plucks beautiful chords. The elegantly dressed instrumentalists look as if they were ripped out of their beds and forced to groom themselves. The dry skin beneath their dark eyes is bruise blue, exhausted, as if they've been playing for strangers all night. I can't help but notice the welts on their cheekbones.

There are deep-red cuts on their chafed ankles, where

monitors blink green lights in the tranquil dark. Half-asleep, I squint, in case my eyes are tricking me.

Suddenly, an intercom turns on.

"Today is the Great Hunt. Are you awake?"

A hard voice blares into my ear. My hair designer from the Pacific Asiatic Islands will arrive at a godless hour soon. As if she's the grand military leader, she will force me out of bed, and for now, I turn over in my warm sheets and send a tired greeting to my pianist. I give a yawny hello to my harpist.

They seem surprised to be acknowledged in the room and treated as actual human beings, unsure of what to say. The composers in our mansions in Kilgrad are paid in the millions, and I imagine this is simply another easy check for the ones here. I need the morning to myself for my debut plans, so I make the paycheck even easier. "You can sleep in the guest suite and quit for the day."

"W–What?" My pianist freezes, as if I didn't speak properly. The bandage of his missing ear shifts; there's a mesh of dead skin underneath. "Porvet?" *Repeat?*

He has a thick Hallowell accent, but he still speaks shaky Vikarian, so I enunciate my words a bit clearer. "You can relax down the hall for the day. Your account will be paid."

Slowly, their shock turns to abject fear, as if I've given them a death sentence. If they were caught in bed, they'd be executed, you'd think, the way they both shrivel away from me. They act like I might hit them or call in the guards.

The harpists in the Allied Force wouldn't need a second offer to take a smoke break and remove their costumes for the day. But the harpist here strums even harder, nearly fracturing his splintered fingers at his frantic pace.

"What happened to your fingers?" I say conversationally, massaging sleep from my eyelids, realizing something might be wrong. The costumes are always detailed and realistic, fit for the theme of the hour, but it's his expression that concerns me. "What's your name?"

Without warning, my door swings open.

"Crowds are flying in," Kateri chirps, bizarrely bright and energized. "You need to stun them all!"

I mumble a few more words at my harpist, but his eyes plead for me to stop speaking to him, as if he can't risk speaking back. One of the night enforcers the sergeant sent with him stares at him as if he's already made a grave mistake.

I distract him with an order to open the massive curtains, even though it's still hours before dawn. There's a subtle shift in the enforcer's jaw at being given orders by a foreigner, but he delivers an obedient nod and treads to the window. The other night enforcers remain in place, scanning Kateri's retina. The harpist is forgotten.

The tension in his fingers decreases with a small breath of gratitude. "Enka." *Thank you.*

"Today will be a spectacular day!" Kateri exclaims at me as soon as she's fully allowed in.

Kateri is usually dry, sarcastic, and deadpan. She's seventeen and already disillusioned with the world, so I know she's acting this way just for me. She's even in the gray, shapeless Allied Force uniform they give to foreign women. A spike of urgency pierces her voice. "Did you get a full rest?"

Drowsy, I rise half an inch from my pillow and drag myself into another day in Allied Force territory. I inhale the thick air—dense, glacial, full of weathered metal. Maximus is gone already. His side of the bed is neat, cold, but a bouquet rests on the pillows.

I toss the bouquet on the floor and get up. *I need to kill Maximus Størmbane.*

If it weren't for Kateri, who doesn't know about my objective, I wouldn't eat, sleep, or get out of bed. Plotting to murder the Allied Force's favorite prodigy fills every crevice of my mind—but it's dangerous.

I am signing my own kill order.

I've craved death since I was a kid, fascinated with the idea of dying explosively for a cause. Kateri is different—she's the motherly type and feeds me when I'm too depressed to breathe or brush my teeth. She clothes me when I can't care for myself without war screams in every membrane. She's built to survive in subjugation and never retaliate.

Right now, she slides on top of my soft covers, brushing her thighs against mine through the silk sheets. The smoke from her cleansing sage prickles under my nose.

"Imphepho smoke—for good luck. And blessings."

Kateri tries to smudge the corners of my marital bed. She hopes for babies the way I pretend to, but I don't want a crying newborn, and I especially don't want *multiple* children. In the Arctic, women are expected to birth eight or ten soldiers for their country.

I'd rather bear crawl over barbed wire on my bare hands and knees before shoving out a baby.

"Are you excited?" Kateri asks, incinerating bitter-green leaves. "Be honest."

A plastic smile wraps my lips. "Of course!" I squeal like an airhead, discarding my silk night robe on the ground after dismissing the night enforcers and musicians for privacy. "The Arctic promised I could attend the full Hunt ritual. Wild!"

"What actually goes on during those . . ." Kateri seems to search for a tasteful word and settles on, "Rites of passage?" Her eyebrow rises as she glances at where the performers once were.

I can feel her curiosity as palpably as a touch or squeeze on my throat. *What will happen to these people?* The military does not broadcast the Great Hunt in its totality beyond the opening-ceremony weigh-ins and the final winner seven days later. Not many outside the military have ever *seen* a Great Hunt in full. They're kept secret—deep in the forced-labor camps.

That is the appeal for the tourists who fly in from all over the Allied Force. A chance to witness their soldiers' hardened masculinity in person.

Which is why I want to see what happens during their Hunts for myself. Knowing the frozen Arctic, it will be extreme and inhumane. *Do they even injure their musicians here?*

For some reason, I have the urge not to let the performers out of my sight for long.

A few men have assured me the Great Hunt is a fictional entertainment, as if they think I'm so fragile and soft I might collapse at the idea of real murder. They even gave me a script and informed me there would be cameras, as if it's a movie to thrill tourists while they're on vacation. But I have a dark suspicion now it's very real.

"Will those people all die?" Kateri asks finally.

"None of them should. It's a sport." I say it the way Kømmand Sergeant Thorleiv Vøhn Arcus reassured me.

I can't get his synthetic smile out of my head. There was sadism underneath; for a split second I could hear the dark pleasure in his voice at the mention of the Great Hunt.

What are they hunting? Large game or—people?

Kateri's slim hands clasp mine. "You'll do great. I swear, I'll have you looking so hot the whole audience will eat you up."

The world has rarely seen me—and I've rarely ever seen the world. I grew up in isolation, and I taught myself how to behave like an adult. It's instinct by now.

I learned by six that children can't survive war the way adults can. So, I decided my childhood was over—and my adulthood began.

But in isolation, I forgot what other people feel like. What *warm skin* feels like. Voices. Laughter.

Sometimes I went weeks, months, without seeing a human or feeling an embrace on my skin. My mother punished me with solitude, priming me for warfare. Some mornings, I thought I would die if I couldn't speak to someone someday.

By the time I was nine, the Allied Force had massacred eighty members of my extended family, aiming to exterminate the direct line. I was concealed even deeper for safety.

These same men now surround me. The Allied Force does not produce ordinary, compassionate men.

In this nation, military service begins at age six and ends at death. The Allied Force does not believe in retirement.

Six-year-old boys chosen to serve are removed from their homes and isolated for years in the mountains. Taught to kill animals and hunt for themselves, forced to be self-sufficient young boys.

It inducts them into early manhood.

After initiations, their savage physical training begins— the venge years. Intense exercises, endurance training, drills, and brutalization condition them into relentless, efficient soldiers.

Then their military career begins.

All of it is glorified by the public as "sacrifice" and "contribution to the empire." Yet the killer instinct instilled in these young men through torture and barbaric discipline has cost the world its countries.

Its civilians.

My family.

Right now, Kateri searches my face, and I betray nothing. There's no sign of hatred.

Our fingers weave together for good luck. Her warm fingers slip between mine. She's a real friend, a farm girl turned hair designer used for costume parties and island attractions.

Now, her fiery brown eyes are sharp, and her silken black hair is pinned back from her oval face, a signal that she is focused on her craft. She takes every detail seriously. I can't help but smile. She always looks inspiring when she's in her element.

"What if I forget my lines?"

Suddenly, Kateri kisses me, her lips melting against my soft cheek. "Tell yourself you are perfection. You won't forget." Sheets of silky dark hair drape over her bare, sunbrowned shoulder, which is wet with sweat. Hints of jasmine swirl around my nose. "The stars are aligned for you. Trust me."

I half tease, "Star reading is illegal."

Star reading is considered a "foreigner activity." All foreigner activity is punished.

Her poppy-red lips smirk. She's the kind of friend to break the laws to make you feel safe and read the stars and rain charts if it helps you.

My door slams open. Beauty expert Valeska Van Valken storms into the suite with a fleet of her own dressers. Our fingers rip apart before she can see them together.

"You!" My pulse spikes as her high heels bolt up the marble steps to my canopy bed. Her nails yank the silk curtains apart.

"Oh, good morning!" I lift my messy head. Innocent. "What's wrong?"

"*What's wrong?*" Valeska snaps back. "Did you . . ." She

pauses, as if she can't even fathom saying this. "Did you *refuse* an exclusive invitation to sit with actress Isla Moon for the Great Hunt?"

Isla Moon was invited to the Great Hunt? I swallow a groan. *They're letting in everyone.*

Isla is an immensely popular starlet in the Arctic at twenty-five years old. Tormentingly hot.

People always love young girls they can swallow easily and early. Fun, flirty girls who provide a break from the standard Allied Force women, who are dutiful, frigid, and intentionally cold.

Isla creates a fantasy. She garners obsessed fans—she makes you *feel* chosen while you watch her.

You feel like she's in bed with you, nestling beside you, affectionately caressing your spirits with soft understanding. You get excited for every scene she appears in, as if she's been waiting all day for you *personally* to watch her perform.

Isla Moon's cheeks are always flushed and pink. Her lips are voluptuous and famously cherry red. Her auburn hair is dazzlingly radiant. But it's her captivating blue eyes that rivet audiences.

When I first saw Isla in movie theaters, I loved her instantly. I couldn't pinpoint what made her lovable. Then it hit me: she made you feel wanted. It was like she was secretly madly in love with . . . *you.*

Except—the *real* Isla believes the wars never happened. She staunchly denies that her nation could possibly have eliminated billions of human lives with little to no consequences in her securely protected homeland. She believes the Arctic remained neutral when the world collapsed.

Meanwhile, millions more are at risk around the world.

Which is why I need to destroy the Allied Force.

Entirely.

I'm going to do it myself and seize the Makari-African Empire back. The world depends on it.

I will lay down my life for the world. Even if it kills me, and it will kill me.

Isla Moon would only be a distraction.

"Valeska, she's pregnant! Can't we leave her alone?" I groan again. "Please?"

"And miss out on her wave?" Valeska seethes. "Not a chance!"

Isla is milking this pregnancy for all it's worth, and the father is a mystery, which is scandalous for a husband-obsessed empire. Women here don't have babies out of wedlock; that is foreign behavior, and the fact that the media is letting her get away with it is creating a growing buzz.

Valeska's convinced that the Allied Force population might accept a foreigner next. Which would launch her career, if she's the first to succeed at it.

Compared to Arctic women, I view myself as lucky that Maximus is considered more modern than most husbands: he allowed me to keep a version of my first name. In Arctic tradition, the husband provides his wife with a new first name and replaces her middle and last name with his—it proves her commitment to him.

As a Makarian descendant of a chief, I didn't even have a surname before Maximus, just a title and my first name. Chief Princess Ìfẹ́.

Now, I'm Ife Maximus Barringẹr Størmbane. Every son's middle name is his father's first name. Maximus gave me back a part of my first name but gifted me his entire name, which made me feel suddenly under new ownership. "What's wrong with that?" Isla asked when I told her.

I joked, "Why not carve his insignia into my wrists instead?" I giggled. "That way, they can return me to him instantly, if I ever get lost."

Her eyes sparkled. "His initials emblazoned on you would be so romantic."

I moan now. "Valeska, Isla's probably drowning in new celebrities," I plead. "All of them are starving for her stardom."

"Exactly! That's the point!" Valeska snaps. She orders, "Bathe quickly."

Valeska has no idea the Great Hunt participators are about to be slaughtered or what that *feels* like. She makes millions a year, having become a highly sought-after vanity overnight. Vanities are hired to enforce compliance with Allied Force beauty standards: straight hair, thin lips, narrow nose, tall stature. But those aren't my attributes. I know my real strengths.

Early on, I realized my image of naive innocence is a secret turn-on. Especially for the older teenage boys of the Allied Force. A soft girl who exudes both purity *and* sensuality. An untouched, blooming girl who makes you feel warm and excited to be the first to explore her.

I pretend to wear my emotions on my sleeve. I care so much it's written all over my body. I'm always embarrassingly sincere. Genuinely heartfelt. Which stirs curiosity in the brutal Allied Force citizens against their will.

In the Allied Force, women need to be *sharp*, whip smart. Calculated partners who are both obedient and useful. Spouses who will force men to be masculine, who will remind them that the Allied Force is constantly at war and "weaker blood cannot last."

Allied Force women do not tolerate men using pain medications or expressing their trauma.

Shampoo is for girls. Ice cream is for children. I've heard it all.

Arctic women practice dignity and self-control. Police each other over skirt stains, torn pantyhose, and wrinkled dress hems. They dare not cry.

Women's ultimate triumphs are their marriages, even before their own children. That is, unless their children become more impressive than their husbands.

Meanwhile, I'm a fun time. An escape. I'm ditzy, excitable, and too attractive for my own good. Other young women might pretend to be demure about their attractiveness, but I am not, and I will never not leverage my assets. *Chase me. Play with me. Capture me.*

I've slid under the radar, easily dismissed as brainless. Now, I need to *stay* under the radar.

And I'll manipulate anyone in my way.

Lethal eyes glare darts at me, but I smile back.

"Women would *kill* for a single holograph with that huge of a star. And you're just tossing her away? Who do you think you are?"

"No one. I'm no one."

I smile wider.

CHAPTER 5

PRESENT DAY

LOCATION: THE TRAEGER ISLAND WAR CAMP

EAST SECTOR

Ife gives me a pinch for luck. "Everyone's distracted. If you're camera shy, we can step down." She grins affectionately.

Everyone *is* distracted with General Maximus Størmbane onstage, glistening as the sun blazes onto his uniform. The audience is glued to him; shoppers shade their eyes with their palms as the new Størmbane insignia pinned to their chests glint. It's as if no one else exists in his spotlight. I don't need another invitation to dismiss myself.

I wish Ife luck in return, thank her for her interruption, and tread down the steps, my heart pounding.

My eyes snap to the carnage men. But when the sergeant speaks, a dark premonition makes my scalp tingle. "Each hunting season, we select a political dignitary to be sacrificed for the Hunt. A living offering—for the svęgę."

Ife, run.

My fire itches uncontrollably to protect her, but I warn myself it will cost my life. Right now, the sharp tang of war-camp odors—sweating bodies, diseased skin, gunpowder—mingles with the perfumes of the elegant Arctic women who angle themselves toward the sniper general. Ife's clueless.

Even if I save her now, and I can't, later on down the line she'll get herself killed.

Outside, the brash teenagers haunt the soldiers' artillery stations, interested in the weaponry that has struck us all with horror for years. The young men carelessly flip through barrack-count papers, signing pages at random to leave their own marks behind over the names of laborers that signed for field supplies.

Without fail, these youths ruin lives each Great Hunt season, not knowing one illegible name could have someone accused of not returning an item properly and whipped for having a random name in their slot. The soldiers do not permit mistakes or misspellings; they're viewed as deception tactics. These Arctic tourists will get someone beaten tonight.

I draw in a sharp breath. *I need to escape. Completely.*

I make my final decision and focus on Maximus Størmbane and the events ahead. Calculating paths off this island.

Meanwhile, a kinetic anticipation thrums throughout the crowds, buzzing, giving me the feeling of being trapped in a beehive all over again. *Something is coming.*

A hot jolt of fear hits my spine. I choke out a small yell. "Ife—*run*—"

"Václav Vengerov." The sergeant announces the decision. "The vice president of Vraničar."

A smatter of quiet applause fills the packed sports complex, the onlookers visibly disappointed the African chief princess was not sacrificed. Not yet.

The applause dies down, but I freeze.

Beer cans are crushed, men belch, and the dense war camp reeks of masculine sweat and raw, hefty meat. So thick and heavy you can taste it in your mouth. Fans have been wildly entertained—until now. A random, foreign vice president has been called forward for execution.

As if it's nothing.

For a full second my mind cannot comprehend the obscenity.

"Vice President Vengerov, head to the section stage to accept glory," the sergeant commands him, as if this is a simple dinner invitation that cannot be refused.

A sizzle of electricity sparks in his comm earpiece, and he nods at a lieutenant, then announces: "Vengerov, take heart: you will not be alone. Please, stand as well for the next participators' induction—the Volkovs."

Alina Volkova stands in the rich section, a tall blond woman of maybe twenty-five, iron faced.

It takes me too long to notice—to realize—her twin brother is standing in the lines of selected laborers for the Great Hunt. Not Hazen Creed or Vice President Vengerov but a black-haired, six-foot man who has been beaten so severely, presumably by soldiers, that the bloodstain on his country's presidential uniform obscures the Vraničarian insignia. A gasp leaps out of my throat.

Of course. The Allied Force *dares* to put the presidential family of Vraničar in the savage Great Hunt. Humiliating a politician and murdering him live.

But the twin keeps a bold face, staring at his sister with his chin raised.

My gut gnaws, especially as I catch the tears hovering in his sister's eyes. I can't look; I can't watch this egregious abomination.

The burning fury and pure outrage that tint her reddened eyes are unmistakable. Her tears shimmer, almost overspilling—and I can't help but think of my own brothers. My little brother, Buckthorne, is just as stubborn as I am. He copies everything I do at eight years old. If I catch and skin a bird for extra dinner, he'll chase birds across the fields until he's sweaty, a bird in his fist for dinner.

As I look at the screen, Alina sends us a wave.

It's only intended for her brother, I'm sure, but she manages the salute wave, and very few in the crowd return it. Before the sergeant can introduce her—and mention the fact that she's about to witness her own vice president's death in the Great Hunt—soldiers approach her as if on cue. *No.*

No, no, no.

It's heinous. Yet Alina ascends the silver steps without a fight. With disgust, I realize they intend to include *her*—a world representative herself—in the Great Hunt. The dead president's daughter.

The Great Hunt this year includes both Hallowell and Vraničar. Each Hunt season, I'm used to seeing fielders, canteen workers, and suppliers head to the feared East Sector Stadium, but these are more world-famous politicians than ever before. It feels as sickening as it always has.

My stomach is plummeting in dread.

Last summer, Head General Barringer Størmbane murdered President Emil Volkov and his oldest sons. The soldiers made us witness the broadcast before curfew.

The head general is the father of Sniper General Maximus

Størmbane and the leader of the whole Allied Force. He's committed more genocide than any man in history.

Every morning and noon, we're forced to watch inferiority tapes about how worthless we are. How useless our lives are. The head general is rarely shown, but he is always known.

On the day he did appear on-screen, I stopped breathing when President Volkov was shot to death.

The soldiers mocked his lifeless body afterward. They spit on the Slavic victims shipped into the island for labor.

Hazen Creed gazes at me. His perceptive expression makes me feel exposed in his eyes, as if I'm naked myself, and he can read every thought in my mind this time. "You're welcome for all the assistance. My pleasure."

"Thank you kindly." My voice is sarcastic.

Hazen Creed delivers an overconfident smile. Cocksure of himself, even as he notices I couldn't keep up the fake meek-girl act for long. It ain't my nature. "Your pants are dry, Rangecroft. I expected you to urinate in front of the slaughter men's rifles."

"Nah. Dry as dust."

"We'll see if that changes."

"Death threats don't unnerve me. Hope you know that."

"You seem resilient for an American." Hazen smirks. "I like that."

"I'm not an American—I'm from Hallowell."

"Same difference, if you could forgive me. Americans are just Hallowell citizens with more money."

I grate my molars together, and I don't waste time bickering with him. I take advantage of his willingness to talk. "Why are they tormenting the presidential family again after they shot almost all of them last year?"

"It's tradition." Hazen's features darken, as if he doesn't want to see it for his own entertainment. But there's no real weakness or boyhood inside him, as if he killed them dead years ago. Hazen stares straight ahead.

Be grateful. Be grateful they didn't kill you. I tell myself I'm lucky to even be alive—the soldiers could've shot me dead. I could be hanging from the rafters. But I still feel like a coward for not speaking up against what's dead wrong and for leaving a young woman like Ife up there with wolves.

I can't protect my kin if I'm dead in the dirt.

I need to kill these two politician twins, and to be coldly honest, untrained diplomats are better to face than experienced soldiers, I figure. *Maybe I got a chance after all.*

Only in the Allied Force could you feel actual *gratitude* for being given a chance to fight to live. *Thankful* to battle to the death over hideouts in which you can escape trained snipers concealed throughout a deep jungle. There will be two bulletproof shelters allotted. It's expected that seventy-five people will kill over those metal boxes.

Nothing is too drastic for the Allied Force.

Hazen gazes down at me, at my atrophied body, and I realize he's sizing me up. Until he smiles, kind again. "You've got good bones and height—that should help you."

Ife said the same thing. "Mostly just tall."

"Tall helps." His charming smile doesn't expose whether he's being compassionate or belittling, but it doesn't matter either way.

"It will help." I'd cut his throat for breakfast, but he doesn't need to know that.

I refocus on the stage.

Slavic women and men choke down cries of anguish. I know, deep in my painful chest, why the Volkovs are special.

My first guardian, Whitelaw, taught us bits and pieces about world history before the collapse. He said the Vraničar Empire unanimously *chose* to keep electing the honest, hardworking Volkovs as presidents year after year. Electing by genuine democracy.

These are specialized, highly educated people. The twins famously grew up with wealth and status, prepared for world politics and diplomacy, not survival competitions.

How to run countries fairly. Not snake through minefields.

How to restore fractured communities. Not crack jawbones.

You don't kill people who know how to run the world better, fairer, than everyone else. Vraničar was applauded for its ethical elections, its poverty reduction.

The three principles of Vraničar were integrity, truth, and equality.

The poor were a higher priority than the rich, their needs more urgent. That's unheard of these days.

Now, they're sent to die here.

Alina nods, the unspoken leader of their people. She refuses to beg or sob. I feel admiration.

The stark sunlight hits Alina Volkova's iron-willed face. Her thick brown eyebrows and mountain-blue eyes are set.

She's as blond as a sunflower. Fiery.

The Vraničarian girls in my barracks told us how Alina fed the hungry during the man-made famine the Allied Force inflicted on her people. Soldiers removed food from residential homes, burned agricultural fields to the ground, polluted the soil, and slaughtered farmers who knew the land. It was a scheduled starvation, and it felt more personal than prior wars.

The Allied Force restricted movement. Banned citizens

from escaping; blockaded the airports, train stations, highways; shut down the naval transit systems; enforced curfew.

Citizens endured harsh checkpoints on the roads, and Allied Force soldiers had absolute power.

No one departed; no rations were allowed. One by one children dropped dead, flies surrounding their bodies; millions died within weeks.

Elsko sobbed about how Alina had opened her own estate to the unsheltered, no matter how haggard they appeared, when the bombings first happened. She refused to abandon them to sequester herself in safety. Elsko saw grainy images of Alina sleeping outside her own home with a rifle to protect those packed inside, earning the nickname the Rifled Woman.

Elsko knew then that it was only a matter of time until Vraničar was destroyed. One woman could not defend them all.

Now Alina says, "I accept." She removes the presidential pin that symbolizes her family and untangles the pearl necklaces from her gold hair.

"Welcome to the Great Hunt, Alina Volkova. Let glory lead you."

As the vice president and the cabinet are slowly herded onto the silver platform, they straighten their posture and salute her, but she's focused.

Her eyes glare at the sergeant.

She undoes the intricate maiden braid of her fine hair. She winds it into fishtail braids instead, removes her pearl earrings, and tosses them at the feet of the sergeant. Audiences lean in close, hungry to watch her strip.

Right now, there is no fanfare, no trumpets, no war drums, no applause—it's as silent as stone in the East Sector.

Teenagers sit down, abandoning the artillery stations, sneaking in to find seats among the quieted adults who stare ahead at Alina Volkova.

Suddenly, her twin barrels past the other captives, as if breaking out of a shocked trance.

"You swore she wouldn't be hunted—you gave your word," he spits furiously at a carnage man, his words vibrating with absolute fury, hurled with rancor. "I paid you everything I had."

The carnage man responds, "She chose to die with you all."

"She will *not* die. My people will not die. Watch your words." The twin's eyes are pure malice. "These soldiers are aiming at her *despite* the agreement that she would never be inducted. You need to order them to stand down."

He's right; three soldiers aim for her head.

As if hoping for a historic headshot.

I can only imagine what happened when the twins were taken. If they had a chance to converse before saying their goodbyes, it'd make sense for them to decide that Alina would stay to lead their people and the other would join the Hunt.

But the Allied Force will never squander an opportunity to humiliate its political rivals.

The twin sets his hard jaw, growling as if he could kill this carnage man with his bare hands. He fumes, "Order them to stand down right now."

The carnage man remains in place.

"Fine. We will survive, and when we do, I will kill you."

But the carnage man smiles. "Valor's luck to you."

Seventy-three people will be dead. I glance at Hazen Creed, then at the brawny Slavic men, their hard thighs thick as tree trunks, then at several Hallowell men, as muscled from war as bison. Poor Elsko looks as helpless as I am.

He doesn't have his glasses anymore—and he looks like he might cry again. His glasses were blown up by the mines. He and I bonded over having one good foot and one dragging foot, the pains of nerve damage, and the relief of leaning against one another on the march home from the fields. But right now, Elsko avoids looking in my eyes, so I avert my gaze too and stare at my good foot. *Fight like hell for me, okay? Fight like hell.*

Don't quit on me for seven days, and we're safe.

In my head, I also send Elsko's surviving foot good luck. *Treat him well. Don't quit on him either.*

The sound of mud-crusted boots on a smooth surface takes my attention.

"All of you will pay in blood." The twin shoots a death glare at the sergeant's face, which would be considered a threat in any other situation, but the black-haired twin doesn't care. "Especially *you*, Kømmand Sergeant Arcus."

"May glory be on your side."

The twin shoves past him, storming across the platform to his sister. He barrels past the slaughter men, and none of them halt him. The sergeant has raised his hand. The tears in my eyes would spill now if I were the one staring at one of my brothers, Hucket and Buckthorne.

"Alina." He cups her rosy cheek in his palm.

"Mikoš," Alina whispers back. Her pink lips kiss his scarred hand, a farewell and a murmur of love in one gesture. "You know I will fight."

"Use your teeth." He chuckles, somber. My eyes sting with tears.

To steel my nerves, I bite my inner cheek until my mouth floods with the coppery taste of blood.

Yet Alina succeeds in not only composing herself faster

than me but ironing her face to an inexpungible conviction. There's no doubt in my mind that she believes they'll win the Great Hunt.

That they will kill all of us.

Hazen and I glance at each other. Without meaning to, we step closer to each other. We're both willing to kill in return; Hazen's face declares it all.

Nothing unites adversaries faster than a common enemy.

For Buckthorne and Hucket—I'd kill them. I'd kill them all.

Hazen gazes down at me, his intimidating expression even more impenetrable. The eye contact is suffocating again, reminding me briefly I saw him naked before I even knew his name, but we subtly exchange nods. His warm hand brushes across my fingertips. "Allies?"

He smirks as if we should be galvanized. Two pampered diplomats will be easy kills.

But I don't smirk back. "We'll see, Creed."

The sergeant speaks. "Vice President Vengerov, prepare for sacrifice." The solemn vice president of Vraničar steps forward on the silver platform for his dismal fate.

As he's shot through with bullets and his blood enters the bronze basin, the crowd explodes with delight. The Great Hunt officially begins tomorrow at noon.

A few surviving Vraničarian cabinet members blink back tears of despondence and hopelessness.

Without warning, Mikoš makes a gesture that must mean something grotesque in the Allied Force. The complex goes from boisterous and roaring to dead silent. Chatter stops; not even the balmy breeze moves. The entire forced-labor camp ceases its movement.

I suck in a breath.

Alina, if she's smart, will publicly reprimand him. Whatever he just did, she needs to save them both, fast. But her fingers move—signing a slash at her own abdomen.

I gaze at Hazen. "What's she doing?"

His golden facial features darken in the oppressive atmosphere. "In the polar expansion, hunting units would bring along adult members of their villages who were considered useless or undesirable, kill them, and leave their bodies out to attract packs of predators. They could continue hunting long distances, across glaciers, and bring back enough animal meat for people to survive the winter. She reminded the Allied Force of one of its coldest historical moments."

My eyes spin toward the adult section, and not one visitor smiles. Not one.

The amusement has drained from their faces.

It'll be a miracle if the Volkovs survive this, especially with a target on their backs—they just brought up dead Arctic citizens to a crowd of Arctic citizens. You do not insult the dead in their culture, and even the lowest Arctic citizen is considered superior to foreigners, yet the Volkovs mocked their vile history.

My gut sinks to my feet for them. They chose death. Together.

As the weigh-ins resume and the grueling process of stripping the participators of their dignity and clothes begins again, Ife performs one act of bravery that stirs the agitated crowds but tremendously relieves every woman on stage: she asks that the women not strip—because the rain says so.

If the rain says not to, it's good enough for her, which makes it good enough for the sniper general. The Volkovs have angered the sergeant so deeply his attention is no longer on the act of stripping; it's on the act of murder.

As I step back into my tan shorts, I recognize his slaughterous fury from the execution hours, and I know I only have one chance to escape.

For the second time in my life.

CHAPTER 6

I only trust one person in the entire world. He is currently aiming a butcher knife at my throat. Ready to kill me dead.

Get ready, Coa.

The other strays will kill me too, if they find out I'm plotting to run away from the commune. They'll skin me themselves, like a wild hog caught in the mud ruts. Especially my older sister Rawley, who's watching us now. But I focus on my older brother, Hucket.

His face is constricted, deep in concentration. He has a soft, natural blush, all over his face and arms. He is a decent lure for suburban folks coming to our shows. They like his sunbaked brown skin and messy brown hair. But he still can't afford to miss his target tonight, since his knife throw will be the show's main attraction. Hucket will be electrocuted if he fails, Caner warned. It's our new legal guardian's most savage threat yet.

A hot sun warms the dense swamp. We're surrounded by

tangled forests of cypress trees and a labyrinth of slow-moving waterways. Lazy streams snake through the knee-deep swamp like it's a viper pit. Cautiously, Hucket grinds his teeth. Bitterns nip at the larger birds, warring over the summer's scattering of bowfins and bullheads.

It's familiar, only a few miles from the beach wilderness where we raised ourselves. We live in the town of Blue Moon, where some of the only options are becoming a waitress at the Stateside Diner or being the proud owner of a local Piggly Wiggly. It's decent work to be a mechanic at Rittman's Tire Shop, or a schoolteacher even, but I don't think I'm fit for polite society. I've never fit in with domesticated folks much.

"Ready yet?" I ask Hucket.

"Hush."

"I'm liable to fall dead asleep."

"*Hush.* You'll lose your head otherwise."

Ospreys flap their wings against the overgrown vegetation of the wetlands. Cattails, watercress, and freshwater mussels are intermixed with white-tailed deer and chattering squirrels. The aromas of musky milkweeds, animal scat, and decayed carcasses waft from the thick water.

The Blue Moon wetlands are on the outskirts of Hallowell, a country in the North Atlantic Ocean situated right between Britain and North America. A mountainous nation, Hallowell's filled with wetlands, swamps, and bayous roaring with life, including alligators, catfish, snappers, crocodiles, and crayfish. Folks never go hungry here—so long as they're willing to work for it, they'll catch a nice meal.

Everyone's close knit round these parts and tighter than blood.

But Rawley is watching with narrowed eyes, preparing

to strike my trachea if Hucket misses.

Hucket's not my preferred practice partner—he hesitates with girls—but Rawley might actually kill me.

Rawley's heart is only half-moral, exactly like mine, which is dangerous.

Except if you find yourself alone in the wetlands with Rawley staring hard at you, she's contemplating ten ways to gut you and sell what's in your pockets for profit, and the rest of her mind's working on the eleventh way in case anything goes awry.

Rawley's storm-green eyes are intense. She wears her dark hair in blunt waves, frayed everywhere. She's still feral in several ways, but she's verbal now. She can speak in full sentences on her own, and sometimes I get jealous that she doesn't even stutter like me.

By nature, Rawley always prepares for the worst. She's ruthlessly ambitious, relentlessly hardworking. Similar to me, and we ought to be best friends, like actual sisters even. Only we loathe each other.

We tried to murder each other no less than fifteen times when we were younger. We've only tried twice now that we're a little older.

But Rawley would commit any savage act to dominate the strays and prove herself toughest.

Hucket's the safest option for me right now, but he always stalls. Hucket's issue is that his heart is almost *fully* moral. He gets beaten at home by Caner often, cornered, and it makes him sensitive. Afraid of his own shadow sometimes. He has a gentle face that makes you want to hug him.

I might have to kill Caner and skip town, if he *really* fixes to electrocute Hucket. I won't stand for it.

My peanut butter sandwich is packed, and a fresh bottle

of ox milk will last me a quarter of the trip to America. I don't mind starving the rest of the way. I heard they have swamps there too. I can take care of myself.

No one will kill my brother. Even if we ain't related by blood, we all were orphaned by the war in this wilderness between the beach and the swamp. That makes us as good as blood in my eyes.

"Aim for my scalp," I direct Hucket, calm. I move my dirty-blond hair out of my eyes before fixing his own knotted hair. Ready. "Audiences will love that."

I grin lopsided, for his sake, but I try not to think of what's ahead. I've wrapped my bare feet in bandages; I couldn't find my shoes, but I've spent most of my life without them. When our first legal guardian, Whitelaw, raised us, he raised us feral. Wild. It brought audiences in droves.

People don't live like that anymore. It's an oddity to see wilderness kids, feral strays parentless from the wars. Chewing coyote bones in our teeth. Snipped fox ears on our heads. Otter skin wrapped around our waists to give us tails just like all the other animals. Hares and mutts were our siblings, since we didn't know better. We were certain that we were kin with any small game in the wetlands, all of us infected often with diseases and festering wounds. We buried our dead and moved on, eating what we caught and wrestling each other in the mud.

Whitelaw had us put on shows to earn our keep. It helped that I had a special talent to show off: I breathe lightning. I'm one of the few humans in the world still capable of magic; only one out of eight hundred million people born outside of the Kōn village live past infancy with magic in their blood.

It's said that magic was given to humans by a meteor—a similar phenomenon to the asteroid that collided with the earth thirty-three years ago and destabilized the planet. Throughout the past century, a series of impact events called the Antøx Asteroids have set the world on fire, upsetting the tides, triggering devastating natural disasters, destroying the world's economies and livelihoods. However, none of them were as bad as the largest, which hit thirty-three years ago.

The mass extinction that followed it was almost as devastating as that caused by the six-mile-wide asteroid that once eliminated three-quarters of the vegetation and animal life on earth, including the dinosaurs.

Every country was left vulnerable. Except one.

Whitelaw told us about the world before we were born—how dire it was, how in need of aid. But instead of deciding to salvage the world, an Arctic nation called the Allied Force seized it for itself.

Back then, magic would've been a critical support. Whitelaw said magic like that only exists now in the deepest, most concealed parts of Africa. He promised to take us one day, but now he's dead. The state gave us over to Mr. Creighton Tytheridge, a violent disciplinarian.

I named him Caner for a reason. I will never use his real name.

Everything changed when Caner arrived in the nearest town and found our beach wilderness. He set strict rules in place. *Young ladies* wear itchy cotton cloth called dresses. *Young men* wear trim wool attire called tweed suits. And you'd better not get even a scrap of seaweed from the shores on your hem, or he'll cane you so hard with a hickory rod that you'll wish you were dead.

Rawley was caned once all over her back. She couldn't move for a week.

When he was alive, Whitelaw never raised his hefty palm

against us. His warm belly was always filled with loving, boisterous laughter. He had a hearty temperament, always kind and understanding.

Whitelaw never hurt us, even when we dragged mud inside the nice, polished homes of private audiences. Even when we ate on the scrubbed floors, like penned kits, once we had our own mansion. We were not housebroken yet, still unused to having dinner tables, mattresses of our own, or plenty of money from live shows.

Suburban people paid to bring their pristine children to see how much more indigent other children were.

Even now, we prefer to sleep bundled together beneath blankets woven out of dandelions, cuddled under the stars, like always. We've built a tight, desperate connection between ourselves—I called us bear cubs growing up, 'cause I truly believed we were. Whitelaw called it *separation anxiety*.

I didn't know what that meant, but Mr. Whitelaw Rangecroft had gone to university and studied to be a philosopher of psychiatry, so I figured he knew. His gold spectacles seemed intelligent enough.

Whenever Whitelaw tried to take one of us into the main town to the grocer, the butcher, or the tailor, we'd all break out into hives or get drenched in cold sweat, like bucks frozen in a predator's stare. Blood would drain out of our faces as we struggled with the sudden change.

Then chaos would erupt. We'd cry our eyes out, screaming, clawing him, and he'd have to load all of us back into his truck.

Meanwhile Caner weaponizes our "separation anxiety." He'll force one of us into the nearest clean town or city, all by ourselves, to be "educated" for weeks at a school. No matter how much we wail, bite him, or tear at his suits, he'll rip us apart from each other. Even if we knife his tires or smash his expensive windows, begging for our littermate back.

By now, I'm desensitized. It's happened so often—strays gone for stretches at a time—I tell myself I don't mind much whenever they vanish for a week or a month. But my nails are always bitten to the quick, and my tailbone-length hair comes out in clumps in the bathwater.

Whitelaw, back when he was alive, theorized it was because we had what he called *psychological enmeshment* with each other, which he said inhibited independent development. We were emotionally reactive to one another—if one stray was in emotional crisis, we'd all be in emotional crisis. We instinctively felt each other's emotions, thoughts, fears; it almost made no sense to use words. It was an extreme closeness to each other without boundaries, and it concerned Whitelaw.

We couldn't function without each other; we missed each other like a stolen heartbeat, impatiently waited like excited pups at the beach for the others to return to the commune safe. Hungry to be a complete unit again.

If one of us died, it helped to know at least where they were buried. At rest.

But whenever a stray is temporarily banished, my mind won't let go of them. I'll wonder if they're eating enough, if the tidy suburban children are treating them humanely or reducing them to a circus act. Even Rawley.

My absurd mind will fret over her too. I'll hyperventilate so hard I'll be in distress, worried about if the searing summer heat's making her skin flare up with hives and if she packed enough brewed peppermint or aloe vera leaves.

Caner only lets us live freely, without rules, when spectators pay to watch.

Random families, typically. Single men. Schools. I've

eaten fire at birthday parties; I've struck glass bottles at break-neck speeds for weddings, and I mostly split lightning for applause, no matter how dangerous it is.

But if we're not paid by spectators to behave freely, then Caner orders us to wear hard leather shoes whenever we leave the mansion, to wear presentable uniforms at all times, and to clean ourselves after every meal. With soap and linen washcloths. It's unnatural.

My whole body despises it.

Caner forbade us to stitch together reed grass for shorts or wear wheat hats padded with coyote fur for warmth—we must wear parka jackets with metal zippers, and pleated dresses with spruce fittings in acceptable hues. Stockings. Scratchy hosiery. Matching sleepwear.

No belching at our meals. No urinating in the shrubs. Hucket was caned for that several times until he learned better.

Most of us had phlegm-yellow or missing teeth, swollen and poppy-red gums, and blackened tongues. Caner brought in the county dentist to pull the rotted teeth out and had us brushing our teeth after each meal.

The older strays love Caner. I can see why. He keeps them healthy, doesn't act like they're freakish. A few of them re-member their parents from the war, and I reckon he reminds them of those parents.

I've never had parents, at least none that I can remember, and I never wanted any. I can't imagine someone giving me rules from the instant I was born, dictating every aspect of my life like an autocrat, and I pity everyone who has to be raised that way—especially in the clean-cut suburbs and re-stored metropolises.

Without Caner, there'd be no reason to leave, but life

without Caner doesn't exist anymore. Now, I want to live alone in the backcountry, with acres of my own to live exactly as I want. Especially if I need to stop him. Permanently.

Last week, a hare was caught in a mousetrap. It was hurt real bad. My little sister Rabbit would've nursed it back to life. She loves rabbits and hares so much the name stuck. But I slit its throat. I knew it was dead either way. I figured ending its pain was best for it. I've always been that way—now I figure taking a man's life to spare the rest of my kin pain ought to involve the same type of determination and willpower.

For a new location, I've considered the cities, but I don't like them much. The noise. The self-importance. I'll admit I like their aircrafts—British planes fly over our nation all the time. During severe hurricanes and floods, the British government sends relief supplies and the Americans send funds.

In return, Hallowell agreed to be annexed into Britain and America's North Transatlantic Empire. We're now British American citizens.

I contemplated a real education, only I don't like learning much either. When Whitelaw found me at six years old, I was nonverbal and feisty. I kept biting and hollering instead of using words. He said had I been any older, formal education would've been nearly impossible. Even years later I could barely spell at all, even my own name, but he said my vocabulary and speech were impressive given my history.

Now that I'm twelve, I still read at a kindergarten level. I can't figure out written words any good, but once they're spoken, I learn quickly. Faster than others in my situation.

Sometimes I like the storybooks the schoolteacher, Ms. Satem, reads. I've improved by miles.

But I never liked the way it felt to be in a crowded classroom with girls that judge you just 'cause you grew up without shelter. Boys that spit at you for living in the wild. It made me as furious as a ram when I was young.

Now, carefully, I examine Hucket again. I check to see if he's ready as a cloud of blackflies lands on my nose.

"Riptides will be in by the time you hurl it at me," I taunt and half smile.

"Distract him then." Rawley smirks, clearly praying he'll cut me wide. She'd win our unspoken rivalry. But real slow, her brows knit at my impatient tapping foot. "You got somewhere to be? You're never in a rush. Lazy as lard."

"No rush." I avert my gaze. "And I ain't lazy. Mind your business."

Now her brows lift with interest. "Seems like I oughta mind your business." She folds her arms. "What's going on? You already in deep trouble or fixing to make it?"

"Fixing to make it," Hucket teases, despite the fact that he ain't pitched nothing yet.

"Fixing to *eat*, soon as Hucket grows himself any pluck," I say back, and I glower at him to shut it.

Except Rawley can always see right through me, and now her eyes are slit. Even though I keep my mouth shut good, she catches every thought between my ears. I realize I despise being enmeshed with anyone.

I blow a sharp exhale of smoke through my nostrils.

"Bull girl's nose is smoking." Rawley grins. "Means she's nervous."

Concentrate on the plan, Coa. I ignore the "bull girl" insult. I'll likely make it halfway down the Blue Moon town road before my feet are blistering and bleeding. I plan to walk the full thirty miles to the nearest bus station, out in Severs County, and take the electric bus from there. I've saved enough money, buried the rest of my hefty savings here for the others, in case of emergency.

Figure I won't need currency in the American wilderness.

Everyone says that Blue Moon is like Florida if it had more wilderness beaches and wetlands.

A crumpled map wilts in my pocket, and there's a spot marked that's five hundred miles away. The ferry to America departs tomorrow. I'll need to walk the last fifteen miles to the Florida wilderness on my own, tread on welted, blood-soaked toes. But once I protect Hucket, I won't care for the pain. Hucket will be safe.

An egret shrieks above, then swoops into the swamp waters like a swan. It's already preparing to hunt well into the dusk near the shallow water for its prey.

I clench my jaw. "Crap in the rut or get out already, Hucket."

Even though he's an older teenager and should have more guts in him, he's been whipped so much that he's as gun shy as a schoolboy. His golden-brown curls stick all over his sweaty ears.

Hucket squints in the hard sunlight and cleans the knife with the tip of his shirt. "I'm trying. You can't afford to be on an operation table on my account."

Of course he's thinking about me. "I reckon I could have open-heart *surgery* in the time you're taking."

Even though Hucket's not ready yet, sometimes you need to shove him off the cliff. His body will figure out how to land. If only he knew that about himself, he'd be more ready to defend himself.

Her mouth wicked, Rawley instructs, "Aim for Coa's temple—wind's northbound." She's lying right through her jagged teeth with a sly smile. But Hucket's frown tautens.

"Keep your advice." His dark eyes deepen; he's finally

prepared, I hope. "Both of you."

"Suit yourself. It's her face."

Sprouts of saw grass and ferns wrap around the hum of insects and rising croaks of awakening amphibians. As Hucket works up his nerve, his golden-freckled face pinches, and he lets loose the butcher knife. At last, the throw is precise.

It cuts a hair above my scalp.

A pinch of emotion climbs up my throat. Hucket was the first stray I ever met in the wilderness. We were the ones who gave each other our names.

I was nonverbal. I'd never heard language except from passing travelers, distant caravans, a few vagabonds, and sparse hikers.

Hucket was verbal, and he outlived his parents by the time he was seven or eight. But he'd witnessed so much trauma he could only hiccup. His hiccups sounded like *huck . . . et . . . huck . . . et.* So whenever I was searching for him, I'd mimic his sound. "Hucket. Hucket."

He learned fast to answer to my callings and even made bird sounds of his own that sounded too humanlike to be the birds. Knowing owls and ducks were my favorite, he'd call out, "Coo-a."

Coa. Once my ears caught his voice, I'd dart through the bald cypress and tamarack to reach him. Eventually, we instinctively learned to stick together. My name's been Coa ever since. I wouldn't change it for the world.

But Hucket is ready to live life without me. And now I'll have to live life without him.

CHAPTER 7

"You won't be electrocuted—so long as you don't let the audience get in your head," I assure Hucket.

We carve our way back to the mansion through the saw grass, the wild growth so high it reaches my chest, even though I'm tall for my age. Only Rawley and Hucket are taller than me.

Rawley can't help herself. "Hucket, you'll be even safer if you give 'em enough time to deliver breech calves before you hurl the knife."

Hucket lowers his voice. "Real hilarious, since you ain't the one he'll be preparing to electrocute to death."

Hucket's sensitivity is heightened, as if he's cornered all over again. Hucket always takes a beating for the young ones, and it's made him afraid of adults. Petrified of punishment. But none of this is fair.

A heavy silence spreads in the air.

I break in. Rage boils in my chest. "Caner tries to kill you, I'll strike him dead. You know I will." Hucket understands that.

But he points out, under his breath, "You ain't ever killed somebody."

"I'll resolve that real fast, believe me." Cold fury rises inside me. "He won't kill you."

But Hucket scratches behind his ear, like a newborn whelp that doesn't know what to do. He mumbles, "Half of everyone loves him."

"Is terrified of him," I correct. "It ain't the same."

"*Isn't* the same," Rawley corrects, if only to be a pain. But deep down, I know she's just as disturbed as we are at the thought of a stray electrocuted by Caner. One of us gone in such a brutal way.

Rawley's ma went in a dark way too. Her ma was mentally unwell, incoherent most days, and we always found the woman gnawing on spoiled carcasses. Before we knew it was a slur to call her brainsick, we didn't know why Rawley was so defensive and protective of her—as if Rawley were the parent. But when her ma passed, real slow, I saw a mean spite grow in Rawley. As if the world robbed her of the only thing she loved, and she'd never forgive it for that.

Since then, I can tell Rawley has built an inner wall, and she will never let it down for anyone again.

I started calling her my sister in my head so she could still have some family left. Only I never told her that 'cause I figure she doesn't want me as a sister. She just wants her ma back.

Sometimes, I still catch Rawley looking over her shoulder as if for glimpses of her ma. She's still used to keeping her in sight.

Right now, Rawley cuts through the overgrowth with a blade she crafted when she was eight. It's still solid and still sturdy. Of course it is—it's Rawley made. She can make near anything.

"Hucket's got a point." Rawley says it like she's thought about it endless times. "Several strays took a liking to that piece of crud, and for what it's worth, they're real fond of the ritzy suburb life out in Severs County. I once heard Buckthorne ask Creighton if he could call him Pa, like he was his actual daddy or something."

"'Cause," I start, grappling with how to say it, sensing already they won't grasp the truth, "like Whitelaw said, trauma bonded them to him. Caner traumatizing them forced attachment to him in some backward way, if that makes a dollar."

Rawley shakes her head. "It doesn't make a dollar. You're both short a few cents."

I don't know how to confess that I felt that way about Whitelaw sometimes. It was Whitelaw's idea to keep us feral and tour us around the restored suburban areas, exposed like exotic beasts, laughed at, and fawned over. Petted by strangers like domesticated animals.

But Whitelaw also tucked us into bed each night. He read us imaginative, creative stories. Expanded our worlds—we would've never left the swamp. Heck, we didn't even know it was called a swamp, that there was an actual name for it, or that there was anywhere much beyond it.

Whitelaw brewed us chicken broth whenever we caught winter fever, cooled us down in scorching summers with ice baths. He taught us the words *morals* and *ethics* and how ethics is the practice of your moral principles.

Whitelaw never jabbed us. Never caned us.

Yet Whitelaw also taught us very few people on earth are truly moral *and* ethical. Even him.

"Whitelaw's dead," Rawley says, hard, as if she can read my thoughts. "Dead. Better for it." Her storm-green eyes find me. "Creighton ought to be dead too. But the little ones love him, so leave him alone. It broke 'em when Whitelaw died."

No one breaks her cubs' hearts. Not even Rawley can find it in herself to shatter their precious feelings.

But Whitelaw didn't simply *die*. Caner murdered Whitelaw, all to gain total control over us. I'm sure of it; only I just can't prove it.

That's part of why I need to leave. I need time to figure out when and where he did it. I already know the why.

But in Hallowell, the punishment for murder is death. It's known as the death-for-death law. So if I ever kill Caner for what he's done—or what he will do—I'll be executed myself.

Unless I run.

But suddenly, Rawley's palm lands on my shoulder. For a rare moment, she pauses the rivalry between us. "Whitelaw used us—he didn't care 'bout us like you think he did."

"Sure. You'd know all about that in a parent, right?" I snap. Sick to death of her.

But Rawley recoils, visibly wounded, as if I struck her in the face. She cuts her gaze away. "My mother cared about me."

"She didn't. You know she didn't." Rawley's ma didn't even know who Rawley was, but no matter how vicious Rawley can be, I can't ever say that. None of us can. But I could tell her ma didn't know her—the woman didn't even know her own name. Her mind was devastated by the destructive war.

"She was ill—she couldn't care much. Her heart cared," Rawley stammers, waiting for me to agree with her. To assure her that her mother loved her deep inside. But I remove her palm and trudge on. She always hits after Whitelaw. I'm past tired of it.

Rawley snarls at my back, "Don't speak on my mother, *Coa Rangecroft*. Not ever."

"Sure thing—" I start to mutter, but she snatches me and squeezes my wrist behind my back.

"Not ever." She glares. "Just because you were born alone in this world—"

"I don't *care* that I was born alone. *You* care 'bout being alone 'cause you're weak."

"And you'll die alone in the world too," Rawley snarls. "Do you hear me? Not one parent even *wanted* you. You never had a mother. Never had a father."

"Perfect!" I bark.

Hucket breaks it up. "Enough. All of us are together for a reason. *We stayed* together for a reason—let's act like it."

I half nod. But I can tell Hucket's on Rawley's side with this. Her ma was her real flesh and blood. Whitelaw was just a man who discovered us in the wild. They'll never see him as my real pa.

At last, the mansion comes into view. Pitch pines bunch around driftwood shelters we made when we were younger, back when we were on our own.

We used to sleep in those beach shanties, nestled inside for heat in volatile winters. Out back were a few acres of fields we worked under the harsh sun, before going splashing into the ocean to cool off, crashing into the salty waves. Memories fill me now of entangling ourselves in moss, swinging on leafy weeping willow branches, or wrestling in mud pits. Laughter. Tears. Hiding up in the buttonwood trees whenever we were in deep trouble.

None of us had it in us to tear all this down. I hook my finger around Rawley's, mumbling, "Your ma cared about you. I was dead wrong for saying otherwise." Shame heats my cheeks. "I'm sorry."

Rawley shoulders me. "You know I won't let you die alone, Wildflower. We die together."

"Always."

Rawley whispers, "And Wildflower? If I were a parent, you'd be decent. I'd keep you." She elbows me and I snort.

"You wouldn't be able to get rid of me."

We stride toward the enormous, lavish mansion. It's a white, three-tiered structure—it always looks like an ivory wedding cake to me. The green clematis vines and English ivies wind around the columns and antique windows. Elegant.

Caner's private study is attached on the left, and our quarters are on the right. Multiple outdoor living spaces sprawl across the hedged property—a spacious patio, a sun-warmed deck, and a gourmet outer kitchen.

I tense. But Caner's truck isn't here.

I announce as soon as I get inside, "Hucket made the knife throw."

"He did?" my older sister Evelie asks. She's chopping garlic cloves at the sterling stove. She's the oldest.

She's beautiful, pale, and willowy.

Evelie Vérra wears her chocolate-brown hair in light-blue ribbons, almost always. Sometimes they're navy-blue ribbons if she's feeling dangerous. But she's prim and proper—the opposite of dangerous.

A few city folk treat her like she's fragile or difficult to gaze at, 'cause half her face is burnt. But to me, her scars are what makes her even more breathtaking.

Evelie has fight in her. She tried to save her parents when their home was burned by explosives during the war with the Allied Force. Takes guts.

Evelie smiles now. "Hucket—that's amazing. You'll do great tonight." But Hucket tramps into his thick-paneled room without a word, pensive.

I shrug and pretend like it doesn't matter. "He won't be electrocuted tonight, long as he doesn't let the audience get in his head." But it's gnawing at my brain to even think about Caner electrocuting one of us.

Baby Rabbit balances herself on the tables. She climbs over everything now that she can walk. Little Buckthorne naps with the hounds. Evelie spreads out the garden turnips. "I have a plan. We leave tonight."

My heart stops.

Rawley drops the net of largemouth bass she caught.

Evelie always wanted to be a normal teenager. She hated losing her cushy suburban life, when she traveled to Paris and spent summers in Florence with her parents. Now she's stuck having to take care of strays instead. I reckon it's why she's put up with Caner for as long as she has. Her perfect childhood was stolen by those bombs.

But her chosen life now will not be stolen by Caner.

"You found my maps?" I ask, tentative.

I see another of my crumpled maps, my escape plan, on the kitchen counter. Enmeshment, separation anxiety, over-attachment, or whatever anyone wants to call it—this wetland is all I've ever known. It's my first safe place—my only safe place so far—and it's hard to swallow the overwhelming emotion being propelled up my gut.

"You'd really leave with me?" I ask.

Evelie declares, "No one will fend for themselves here on my watch. We all leave together."

Rawley's cynical. "Won't Caner track us down?"

Evelie slams down the knife into the turnip neck. "If he does, he'll be sorry he did."

CHAPTER 8

"You need a K-Ration for this." The carnage man declines my ration card without even looking. My tired eyes blink rapidly. *Stay awake, Coa.* I squint at the slate signs above his head.

RATION STATION 41:

THEFT PUNISHABLE BY BULLET.

FOOD IS A PRIVILEGE.

NO SLEEP ON FRIDAYS WITHOUT K-CARD.

CAMP REMINDER:

NO OUTSIDER IS PERMITTED TO LAY ONE FINGER

ON ARCTIC SKIN—WE WILL KILL EVERY FOREIGNER IN SIGHT.

Next door to the ration stations is the greasy Butchery, filled with fresh real meat for the sergeant and his men. It reeks of cigarettes and beer, a secret hangout for the carnage men, who thicken themselves on authentic beef after hours while the rest of us digest watery oats mixed with animal slop that we share with the butcher's hogs and steer. On Saturday, they feed us corn and scratch grains *after* the chickens are full. On weeknights, they hand us the lesser chicken feed made of barley, rye, and wheat middlings.

But Friday is on everyone's mind. In the Traeger labor camp, no one is permitted to sleep on Fridays when the tourists arrive, unless they have K-Rations. Field-workers can buy themselves two hours of sleep in the barracks.

It's one of the only benefits of not being talent. Talent must work whenever the soldiers beckon them—K-Rations or not.

I check the ration card again, squinting harder in the vicious sunlight.

R-Ration.

Crap. The letter's smeared with sweat and soil, resembling a slanted *K*. But it's an R-Ration card.

Still, I can hardly bring myself to stay on my aching feet. I'd collapse into the dry bushes and sleep there if the soldiers wouldn't shoot me.

I would risk it if it were next week already.

The Great Hunt season starts next week. Soon, this area will be flooded with sightseers and tourists, and therefore slaughter men will be on their most polite behavior, complete with pristine uniforms, plastic smiles for guests, and courteous gestures.

They'll open doors like bellmen and salute the younger kids in the ration lines. If a worker is dead asleep on the ground, they let vacationers snap a smiling holo with them. Won't even disturb 'em.

But you'd better hope *real hard* the carnage men don't memorize your face for later. They rarely forget.

Right now, the carnage man spits on my brown sack dress. I recoil.

"K-Ration line only. Move along."

I smudge his spit off me and pivot away from the sleep barracks. Even though every exhausted bone wills me to stay, beleaguer him until he relents and I can just shut my lids for even thirty seconds, I keep moving.

Mentally, I prepare myself to travel back through the fields to reach the West Sector, where a soldier distributes ration cards one privilege at a time. Three miles away. All the way back *here*, in the South Sector of the camp, is where you use the cards for food, rest, or better supplies that make your cleaning shifts easier.

For example, if you have a C-Ration card, you can use a mop for an hour instead of scrubbing the canteen's metal floors with the standard toothbrush. You're done more quickly and won't have to traipse all the way across the forced-labor camp in the boiling humidity for another toothbrush once the bristles wear down.

This week, a deadly heat wave has the entire camp sweating, even the austere slaughter men. We're getting harsh sunburns so malignant our skin bleeds and blood vessels burst in our bodies. Our nausea is so thick most of us are lightheaded.

Mothers are grieving, helpless to save their dying little ones. Stanislav, the doctor, barely sleeps now, even when it's not Friday; he's always sprinting between barracks and silently delivering crucial medicines and calming herbs for the little ones. He's the one keeping the children alive.

I can't imagine the forced-labor camp without him.

Right now, Stanislav stands in line, his work uniform soaked with sweat. His neck is lobster red with sun exposure. "Coa. Chew these as you walk—they'll keep you awake."

Stanislav knows everyone's name by now. We're all his patients.

"Don't use all of them at once." He smuggles small coffee beans into my palm and smiles.

"Thank you so much." My heart lifts a little. "But I can't. The elderly laborers will need them for tonight."

The slaughter men love to oversee the raids of laborers caught sleeping, shoving people onto the ground, ripping them out of the beds, and smashing their teeth with fists for moving too slow.

Stanislav examines the purpled bags beneath my eyes, saddened. "The British might still rescue us."

No. They won't. They haven't come in the two years I've been here—they never will. I'm so bone tired that if I don't shut my eyes, I'll collapse. I only nod.

Laborers attempt to cool down shirtless whenever the carnage men aren't watching. Everyone avoids the bronze barracks during the day, even for cleaning hours, as they turn into thermal traps of agony.

But I can't stay on my feet much longer. I'd rather burn.

Out of the corner of my eye, I see that Evelie has reached the front of the line and is digging in her pocket. "My sister can have mine," she says, sliding her K-Ration onto the rickety table. "It's double stamped for five hours. We'll split it."

The carnage man snatches the card. "Five hours? How was it approved for five hours?" He squints his eyes against the heavy sun, checking the card for forgery. But it contains the official Traeger seal and comes back clean as he swipes it in the scanner. "Two hours each. That's it."

He doesn't return it to her, even though she still has an hour left. Evelie almost never uses her ration cards for herself, saving them for Rabbit and Buckthorne so they can have extra helpings at supper in the canteen, larger crop sacks for the harvest, or a wheelbarrow to carry the sacks.

My cheeks flush with hatred. I whip back to the front of the line before I can stop myself.

"Return her card. She's earned it—" The words jet out of my mouth, but I don't back down as his sharp eyes burn into me.

"What the hell did you say?" he demands. He rises from his seat.

Stanislav carefully moves me behind him. "I think she meant that you forgot to return her ration—"

The carnage man grunts. "I didn't *forget*. These rations are a mercy given to you. None of you deserve them—you live and eat as animals. You will die as animals." He sinks back down into his seat, in the needed shade, since it's too hot to beat me for my words.

"*You piece of*—" I start, but Evelie's words take the wind out of my lungs.

"You're right. Our apologies." She speaks in her suburban voice, the one she used in affluent neighborhoods and charity banquets whenever we had rich clients. The voice she originally had before she gained a different accent, orphaned as a preteen in a wetland commune with a pack of children to care for. "We appreciate your generosity."

He dismisses her, but the rancor is unmistakable. His nationalist hatred is so acrid you can taste it, all because we weren't born in the Arctic.

I shove my blond hair behind my ears, trying not to tug it all out. Stanislav gives me a pity pat on the shoulder. I thank him before barging into the barrack.

Evelie tidies up the bottom bed, ignoring me as I holler about that carnage brute. Part of me wants her to yell at me for endangering us, and the other part is disgusted with her for her subhuman acceptance. "We ain't inferior to them!"

But she pats the threadbare pillow for me to lie down. She reminds me how tired I am. "Sleep, Wildflower."

Evelie curls her thin body round mine, like an otter mama with her whelp, and it's not until several minutes later that I realize she's put her body on the outside. Nearest the aisle, in case the carnage man comes raging back in. Evelie physically shields me from him, even in her sleep.

Tears sting my eyelids, and I whisper out an apology, words choked. But Evelie doesn't treat me like I'm uncontrollable, feral. She presses her lips to my ear. "When did you build this camp?"

"I didn't," I quaver.

"Were you the one who forced innocent people into it?" she asks.

"No."

"Then don't apologize for someone else's cruelty. It's not your burden to bear."

CHAPTER 9

IFE STØRMBANE

TWO HOURS BEFORE WEIGH-IN CEREMONY

"Head General Størmbane demands to meet you. There's been a change of plans before the ceremony," Valeska announces, anxious. Cold fear wraps around my throat. "Right now, Chief Princess."

The sole leader of the entire Allied Force is here? He's visiting the Great Hunt islands?

"He's directly inside Ironhaven Hall," Valeska warns. *Don't do or say anything senseless. She'll target you for life for tanking her rise to the top.* "Stand straight! The second I can, I will replace you with a sharper woman. There's a twenty-year career on the line."

She snaps at my guards, "Escort her to breakfast."

My palms become slick with sweat and my heart thumps painfully in my chest as I'm led to the breakfast cage. Any men's mess hall in the Allied Force is called a cage, and knowing Allied Force men, I think the name is appropriate.

Some men here eat like they still catch and kill their meals with their bare hands. You have to beg them to use serviettes and bribe them to wash their hands.

Crimson dots on the resort hall ceilings inform me I'm being watched closely. Valence Security Megacorporation: finest in tracking. I undo my floral gold pins, my pink hair spilling down to my dark-brown waist, and the cameras whir even closer.

Part of me refuses to even breathe until the camera lights are gone, but my pulse always accelerates whenever I'm around Head General Størmbane. I can almost taste my heartbeat right now.

Head General Størmbane visits only a few times a month. But unlike my morning team, he's not a frivolous assistant.

He can identify a liar, a traitor, or an assassin in seconds. The head general has executed people at the international banquet dinners and continued eating afterward like nothing happened, wiping his bloodied steak knife clean with a tablecloth.

Inhumane is too soft a word for him. He's torn civilizations off the earth. He's the reason two-thirds of the world population is gone. His family is the reason over half of the earth is pulverized and currently being rebuilt by the Arctic.

Our eyes meet as I walk forward. He's a mountain-size man with an authoritative demeanor. As I approach, one of his severe slate-green eyes glares down at me, the other obscured beneath a weathered eye patch. His rough scars spread over his surviving eye, completing the intimidating image.

Some men would get rid of deep scars, but not Allied Force men. To them, scars build character, and modern male beauty standards mean nothing. I swallow.

Head General's salt-and-pepper hair is cut short and close. It's marked with a thick scar where a serrated blade cut open his scalp from above his hairline to his rugged cheek. In the Arctic, millions of fans believe he's deadly handsome, the best-looking national leader the world has ever seen.

His killer's gaze is on me now, his expression furious.

He's never pleased with my behavior. But Head General doesn't speak yet. Pretending to be unaware of his sentiments, I smile sweetly. His calloused hand swallows mine. "Victory to the Allied Force, my ikä."

"Victory to the Allied Force, Head General Størmbane!" I chirp. "Good morning!"

Metal automatic doors peel open and display a luxurious sunbathed reception spread out ahead. The hard scent of køvma fills the atmosphere, as well as the aromas of exotic meals: rare rhinoceros confit, near-extinct Arctic hunter eagle with blood-oil sauce vierge, and crusted python. Courtesy of the Rainsford Resort Megacorporation, which produces all things to do with tourism and hospitality.

The resort itself is a pure-white arch that towers over the mountains, which contain five million acres of big-game hunting. Most billionaires and trillionaires possess our own opulent resorts, pampered with mountain sanctuaries complete with helipads to avoid too much human interference.

While it looks like the ultimate tropical destination outwardly, boasting hand-cleaned powder-white sands and a cerulean ocean, the resort overlooks distant labor fields, weary bronze barracks, and multiple signs that read PUNISHMENT SECTORS.

There's a fleet of top-rate kitchen staff and on-hand concierge services, and aerialists are flown in for entertainment, but the island always reeks of burnt flesh and charred bones, as if this place is the site of a mass cremation.

Maximus stands from the head of the table, opposite from

his father's designated end. Maximus takes me in first, like I'm a breath of fresh air after a strenuous swim.

Famous explorer Maximus Størmbane has rabid fans drooling outside already. Blood is smeared on his jaw and streaked across his riding outfit. It's not decoration, like other Hunt costumes mocking tragic deaths from past years' films. He's back from a violent sport. The corner of his mouth is bruised as he melts his lips over mine. "Good morning, kitten."

"Morning, Maximus." I gaze up at him softly.

"How did you sleep?"

"Not a wink. Too excited."

"Even sleepless, you look like a dream."

His dark-blond hair, slick with sweat, drips perspiration right onto my cheeks, and his suntanned skin looks flushed from adrenaline. But his overall body temperature is still as frozen as the Støn Mountains.

I shudder involuntarily.

Maximus doesn't have to be forcibly bathed and dressed to be ready for the Great Hunt. Fans would devour him right here in this natural state. Helpmaids burned my scalp this morning as they straightened every curl; Valeska detested the style Kateri had chosen and ordered it redone. The rest of my body was waxed bare, my fingernails stripped of acrylics. The Great Hunt is about *tradition* and *history*; none of the modern nonsense was allowed.

Maximus only needs a quick shower, a tuxedo, and an expensive watch. His classically styled blond hair doesn't have to be harshly manipulated. He's already their ideal paragon of Arctic masculinity dressed in the attire of his famous rifle club.

His dark equestrian short-sleeve shirt is expensive and makes his skin tone seem healthier, his arms and chest nicely defined. His professional riding trousers are well fitted, and his riding boots are overpolished and only slightly bloodied. He's the epitome of an Allied Force male.

Envy seethes inside of me, but I'm gathered up in his embrace, hemmed in by his scent of cologne, prized horses, and sweat. "Your debut party will be extraordinary, kitten." Maximus kisses my forehead. "Victory to the Allied Force."

"Thank you, Maximus." My throat dries. "Victory to the Allied Force."

When I first met Maximus, I thought he'd be menacing, especially given his height, reputation, and muscle-bound body, but he was more good natured and approachable than I expected. But I never forget what he's capable of.

What his military history has achieved.

What his family has done.

His ancestors eliminated empires, but his father, Head General, is on track to outpace them all. He's already decimated three continents. None of the other autocrats ended this many lives this quickly.

The nation boasts, *Head General was born to end nations.* Maximus, soon, will be expected to finish the national objective and bring about the Victory Year: the year every nation will have fallen to the Allied Force. Each foreigner exterminated.

Victory Year parties are being prepared right now. Citizens greet each other with early pride. *Happy Victory Year. Victory to the Allied Force.*

Raw emotions boil up my throat, but I pummel them down, neglecting the breakfast spreads. I don't eat or drink anything from animals, not even a drop of goat milk. Instead, I turn to Maximus's younger brother. Thorsten smiles brightly.

"Victory, Thorsten."

Thorsten's a little boy so tiny that the giant onyx chairs and tables swallow him up, but he kicks his legs with four-year-old excitement. Thorsten's finally missing his front teeth and grins at me in secret.

At night, Thorsten crawls into bed with me and Maximus. He's a heat-seeking missile, breathing all over our faces. He always carries armfuls of vintage dinosaur comics and no less than three space photos. Paper is a rare sight in our time. But Maximus and I prefer to limit his use of simulated reality. He adores seeing our exotic garden animals and lets them bite him, hoping he'll gain superpowers. *Can I become rainborn, Faefae?*

Thorsten's at the age where he desperately hopes he'll recover his hearing, since the war obliterated it when he was an infant. He's endlessly curious about what everyone sounds like. The cadence of their voices, the volume of their laughter, what laughter even sounds like. But *especially* how movies and action scores sound. He can feel the heavy, brassy vibrations, but he can't pick up any noises.

It's pure silence.

Above all, he loves being deaf. It's his own superpower. But being a kid, of course, he wants even *more* superpowers.

Right now, he hugs me around the waist, quickly, before his father can catch it. I slip him some Makarian vulus. We grin at each other.

"Faefae. Victory to the Allied Force."

The explosion that stole Thorsten's hearing also damaged his eyes, causing scars on his retinas and making lipreading hard for him, but Head General has never allowed him to get surgical treatment. Every young man must overcome adversity on his own.

It's primarily Maximus and me who raise Thorsten—Head General is at his home twenty days per year. We use Vikąrian Sign Language with Thorsten and include him in almost every conversation when he's around. Maximus became fluent in the language.

Thorsten's face lights up whenever Maximus is around. Maximus acts like a father to Thorsten, cooks for him when he's sick, ensures he drinks enough echev when he has a fever, patches his wounds from slipping on ice, secretly teaches him swear words, and tucks him into bed and thrills him with wild space adventures that Thorsten soaks up with fascination. Maximus is his favorite person. Maximus performs enthusiastically with huge facial expressions and spares him none of the dramatics. Warm gestures the head general has never attempted.

Thorsten firmly believes Maximus is the coolest hero ever. His posters are all over the Kilrød—which is the Vikąrian word for the Arctic region.

But now I catch sight of Maximus's middle brother. Late. Vørian Størmbane strides in with his Allied Youth League uniform on, a silver-and-black insignia branded on his attire. A glare on his face.

"Vørian. Victory to the Allied Force." My throat almost closes.

Vørian is the spitting image of Head General. If Head General Størmbane had icier green eyes and shockingly silver-blond hair, Vørian would be his mirror into the past. Vørian has the same bold, square jaw and prominent chin. He's vicious and aims to take Maximus's place as the Executioner.

Maximus had his warm mother to raise him for years, an affectionate and kindhearted woman, but she didn't survive.

Vørian, four years younger, was instead raised almost entirely by the military, as ordered by Head General. He was seized immediately after their mother died. His generational hatred and military violence are in his veins, the same caustic blood as Head General.

They even share the same maxim: *Vikąrek ivør.* Allied only.

Neither would know true allyship, beyond the Allied Force, if it strangled them. Vørian is the appointed captain of his Allied Youth League unit. Elected last year.

All they do is recite supremacist speeches, attend nationalist rallies, and nearly kill each other in hypermasculine, gruesome sports. Many are depraved members of several rifle clubs. That is, when they're not recruiting other purebreds, eager to enlist more youths as zealous militarists.

From Vørian, I learned the difference between purebred and pure blood. Vørian considers it a personal insult to be only called pure blooded.

He's not solely *pure blooded.* He doesn't *only* have perfect, 100 percent Vikąrian blood. If pure-blooded citizens aren't fully indoctrinated and bred into understanding their superiority and duty as purebreds—then all they will be in life is wasted good, pure blood.

And no good blood should be wasted.

In his view, Maximus is wasted blood. Maximus believes the Allied Force is the greatest nation on earth, but Maximus does not believe in its citizens' genetic supremacy. There's no evidence to suggest it. Their military expertise led them to their domination.

Maximus rarely bothers to attend executions anymore, but Vørian orders them. He refuses to miss them.

Last month, a public execution held in Warholm was

paused due to a severe flood warning, threats of lethal hailstorms, and freezing temperatures. Vørian insisted on carrying out the execution himself. He's more trained, more strategic, than his peers, which *also* makes him more dangerous—since he's the most connected and powerful.

He slaughtered that man with animalistic rage.

Vørian was made captain after that. His ambition is dark—glowering in Maximus's shadow. Maximus smiles at Vørian. "Victory."

"Victory to the Allied Force." Vørian frowns.

Vørian's fourteen, already two frustrating years older than Maximus was when Maximus killed Makari's leader, yet Vørian has nothing to show for his own glory. He's never smelled the Vraničarian mountains he now owns, the snowy woodlands from Atka, or even the lush spirit banks that once lined the now-destroyed ancestral bone temples in Makari. Vørian never bothers learning anything about the foreign cultures other than our vulnerabilities, frustrated he can't decimate half the world himself yet.

More than that, he's fanatical over entire volumes of unspoken rules.

There are several that I've had to learn. Such as the fact that it's unacceptable for me to call any Arctic person *compatriot*. It's considered disrespectful from a foreign-born. Most citizens won't stand for it, even though millions address each other as *Arctic brothers, komrades, vatørs,* and *compatriots*. In the military, Maximus may address lower-ranking soldiers as compatriots to display friendliness and show he means no harm if he appears unannounced. But they cannot respond in kind to him.

I didn't know at first, until Maximus and I packed to visit Warholm to attend Head General Størmbane's semiannual national-unification speech. I sensed that under no circumstances could I address Head General as anything other than Viker (*father of my spouse*), Vikęm (*father*), or, best of all, Head General Størmbane.

I clap. "Everyone, it's my debut party today!" I giggle, my sundress glinting in the light of the chandelier. I press my hands together. "I wanted more glitter, but I'm so happy!"

"Will there be real fights?" Thorsten grins, signing *explosives*.

"Plenty," Maximus promises.

"Wise selection." Head General Størmbane takes his seat. His scarred eye seizes me. "You designated a remarkable location for the Great Hunt. A Makari-African island with hexes and deadly spirits. Exactly as you described."

"I am thrilled to pay homage to the islands of Makari!" I beam.

They have no idea what's about to happen. Kaipo—the sun king—lives on the island. Before the bone king died, there were four chief king brothers born to a fireborn mother— the bone king the oldest, the hunt king the second born, the rain king the third born, the sun king the youngest. All chief kings are humans who are massively supereminent in magic. Each set of chief kings' capacity for orún is unsurpassable— until they die, and the new kings are born.

When he died, the Kōn ancestral bones chose the next bone king. The hunt artifacts will choose the next huntborn king. The rain will choose the next rainborn king. The sun will choose the next sunborn king, or the solar eclipse will choose a darkborn king.

This place is not like Traeger Island, which was uninhabited before the Allied Force claimed and renamed it. Kaipo is an untamable power—protective of his islands.

All the soldiers will be met with his fury: Madness. Delirium. Mind possession.

Which is why I selected the island. It's my first silent sabotage of the Allied Force.

I will send the Arctic snipers to their deaths—right under the Størmbanes' noses.

CHAPTER 10

COA RANGECROFT

NIGHT AFTER THE WEIGH-IN CEREMONY

Any sniper like Maximus Størmbane will kill us all. I need to take action and escape the island with my siblings.

I will hold a soldier hostage if I must. Right now, the night air is dead.

Silent.

Even the Slaughterhouse is bare. The Butchery is the only building that houses actual meat. The Slaughterhouse is where the slaughter men live, as the Carnagehouse is where the carnage men live. This darkened, barbed-wired area's advantageous for them, located deep in the live-stock South Sector, far out of sight of the West Sector, where the professional soldiers and military enforcers reside.

The slaughter men's depravity is unrestricted in our area. Kømmand Sergeant Arcus allows them full control to maximize our suffering. Meanwhile, they live near us in glorious, impressive structures. Celebrating our deaths with fresh cigarettes, beers, and dancers. The luxury is jarring so close to the inhumanity.

Near the burial fields, my barrack is once again forgotten. Emptied. The canteen dinner will be dismal meals of potatoes and watery broth, but my competitors need as much weight as possible. For one hour, they can eat as much as they please. All the laborers are filling themselves, except me.

Distantly, nationalist speeches are blaring over the Carnagehouse. Laborer children are shrieking, used for target practice by laughing teenagers with stones.

Deep in the burial fields, beyond the gruesome odor of rotting bodies and incinerators, there's only one place in the forced-labor camp that's not floodlit by massive watchtowers. An unspoken dead zone where young foreigners lose more than their lives and the carnage men can commit obscenities out of sight. Their boots drenched in blood.

However, Sniper General Maximus Størmbane's arrival has triggered a dramatic avalanche of attention. All the carnage men are hungry to catch sight of him and have abandoned the dead zone.

Except one.

I track him soundlessly. Soon, I realize he's not even a carnage man. He's a far cry from a slaughter man too, merely a rich teenage tourist in a paramilitary uniform he bought at the ration stations for outrageous prices. I'm disappointed—but determined. *He'll have to do.*

He's pillaging the desolate sleep barracks nearest the burial fields for souvenirs within minutes. He dressed himself up real fancy in military regalia that clinks and clanks with his every movement. Announcing his every motion. A clueless mistake that feeds me courage.

He's shorter than me—I have maybe four or five inches

on him. He's wiry, with natural teenage muscle and a healthy lifestyle, it appears, but pampered. Untrained, wearing ill-fitting boots.

He tromps around the stacked beds. As I crouch on a bunk bed six feet above him, I quiet my breath.

This physical attack is crucial. I need to secure an escape route for my siblings, and he needs to give it to me. He arrived here somehow, and he might've noticed something critical, or at least useful.

I only have minutes until soldiers realize there's too many of them crowded around the sniper general for all of them to meet him, and a few might lash out in the dead zone in fury.

Some of them are also distracted by Ife Størmbane, who excites the soldiers. She's illegal. Exotic. As the selected laborers were led out of the East Sector, the carnage men thirsted for her, brashly jawing about wanting to taste her magic for themselves.

The military rumor is that drinking the blood of her family can make you live forever. Your progeny will be immortal soldiers.

The carnage men are never the smartest. They believe anything that sounds impressive. But their distraction helps me—for now. I'm running rapidly out of time. *The slaughter men will be back soon. They know better.*

The tourist coughs.

Checking over his shoulder, he sifts through the women's socks, inhales depraved lungfuls of their dresses.

Winged insects crawl lazily through the heavy, humid night air. Unaware of what's about to happen.

I grit my teeth. *Now!*

"What—" He gasps as I thrust a bedsheet over his head, suffocating him. I launch the full weight of my lunging body onto his back, and he crashes hard, face first, into the dirt floors. The impact should be violent enough to crack his rib cage.

But to my horror, the padding of the fake uniform and the false medals break his fall. His fist is quicker than I anticipate—ramming into my jaw and rattling my teeth.

"Foreigner!" he calls, momentarily blinded, and despite the danger of attacking an Allied Force citizen, punishable by execution, I almost laugh. His cries blend with those of the women shrieking for their hunted children. He's as helpless as we are for once.

"Cry more," I snarl, tying the bedsheet tighter to plunge him into the dark. We wrestle.

The carnage men always warn that laborers are not permitted eye contact with any Arctic citizen. We're not allowed to even *breathe* within eleven inches of their pure bodies. There's a stark sign: *No outsider is permitted to lay one finger on Arctic skin. We will kill every foreigner in sight.*

Well, I've always been crap at following rules. I choke him with the bedsheet, letting him flail beneath me like a crayfish. "Done fighting yet?"

Even with the new bruise to my jawbone, I yank harder, almost asphyxiating him.

Now, he thrashes like a gator in a net. Finally, I snatch his small gun. Press it against his spine.

"Hands behind your back."

I'm not senseless. I'm not going to kill him. I'm using a scrap of fabric to avoid leaving fingerprints, but sweat dampens my palms and makes it hard to grip the pistol.

Every young man over the age of sixteen is encouraged to purchase a firearm.

My heartbeat is a primal drum. "Hands behind your back, I said."

He's not listening. Struggling beneath me. I've been subjugated for four years by these Allied Force men—I know their voices by heart, and I mimic the tone of their commands.

"Lie still."

"Release me. Now."

A metallic click. His ears perk with fear.

I disengaged the safety so he knows I'm not here to chat. "Lie still on the floor. Hands behind your back—"

"Don't pretend you're Allied Force." His frantic voice fights to sound as if he's the one in control. As if he's not the one with a gun cocked right behind his vertebrae. "You're not Allied Force. That's not a military accent. I can tell you're faking it."

I didn't realize there was a military accent in the Allied Force. But it's not my concern. My sweat is my concern. Loosening my hold.

This needs to be quick, before this escalates into a fight and I leave my DNA on the floor.

He repeats, "You're not Arctic." His panic is turbulent, but he grinds his teeth harder. "Don't you dare pretend you're an enforcer. Who are you?"

I know he's goading me, demanding answers, so he can identify me afterward. So I fall into his open trap. I switch to a high North Hallowell accent, polished and proper, like that of people I worked with in the fields before the last Great Hunt unceremoniously eliminated the last of them.

I direct, "Be silent. Stay down."

"Hallowell trash. I knew it," he spits. He strains to reach his waist. "I could smell your—"

I boot him in the back of the head. "Stay. Down. Don't move. I won't repeat that again."

He's defiant. His fingertips flex outward, grasping for

something on his waist. Bending, I search him for weapons, and sure enough, there's a blade.

Several stolen sugarcane-cutting blades. Too many of them.

What do I do? Do I tie him up before I throw all of them out of his reach? My mind sprints wildly. Locked in the dilemma. There are two actions to consider, because if I attempt to restrain him and he's more physically fit than I expected, he could overpower me during the struggle, and I'd miss my chance to seize his knives. But if I remove all his weapons first, then restrain him, what if he manages to snatch one? He'll slit my—

Abruptly, he whips his head backward, smashing it into my nose. Blood spurts out. Profusely.

My DNA is everywhere.

Coa. Think! He knows my plot to harm him without being identified later is now compromised.

No. It's complicated. Not ruined. He has skin, clothes, and hair; all of it can be cleaned of traces of your DNA. All of it. I need to knock him unconscious—

My boot slams down on him. "Not so fast."

Aiming, I squint, lowering his pistol to point squarely at the throbbing jugular vein in his throat. He swallows a gasp. "Don't shoot me."

Obviously, he thought his head thrust would damage me critically. Stun me at least. But I've been through hell. He's got to hit me a lot harder than that. "You didn't even crack my nose."

He pants. Out of breath. "If you kill me—your whole barrack is dead. Forget just your family," he roars, realizing I must be a laborer. There's a note of terror in his voice. "Any field workmates you have, any friends you've made—"

"Don't got any friends." I shrug—he can't see it.

"They're all dead. Every child. Every mother."

"Want me to weep about it?" I kick him back down onto the ground, earning a cry of pain as his cracked ribs slam into the dirt. "Cross your ankles."

But he knows that struck a chord. Children. Mothers. My voice shook, and I regret it. I loathe it.

I loathe him.

And it's mutual. His voice is as vicious as a chainsaw. "You'd better not shoot me, you ingloriöt." *Inglorious foreigner.* "I will break out of this and hunt you down."

But he's still visionless. Head confined in bedsheets.

That's my only advantage now. The gun is practically useless if I can't kill him.

So I tie his ankles together with another bedsheet, careful not to drop any of my spilling, gushing blood onto the fabric. Belatedly, tingles of increasing pain spike up my nose. *He struck me more savagely than I thought.* But I smirk, hiding my horror. "Don't worry your small head about finding me later. I will kill you now. Your brain will decorate the walls."

"No. My brain won't," he spits, knowing I would've killed him by now if that were my intention.

Still, I give him a dark laugh, fighting down panic. "We haven't had our own decorations yet. You'll be the first."

I relocate the pistol to his injured rib cage, finally thinking of a new plan.

He gasps for air. "Wait—wait. Listen. I am not military affiliated; I am only a patriot. You need someone *military affiliated.* Do you understand that?"

His voice is guttural. Desperate.

"The Allied Force military did this to you, laborer. Not me."

I know he's wasting time, hoping someone will break in as he rambles. We both know that if I fire this weapon, the report will be audible over the screams, and the slaughter men will come. A gunshot is too distinct. We both know that.

He fidgets as I take his knives, his stolen, soundless, sugarcane-cutting knives. The slaughter men won't hear a knife, and human skin's much thinner than the hefty sugarcane I've been laboriously cutting through for four and a half years straight.

Fifty-four months. 1,642 days.

I'd gut and clean him like a hog with even the smallest knife. If I went with my sharpest knife, it'd be even faster, since I've spent months trapping, skinning, and cleaning vipers from the fields to eat.

Finally, I press the knife to his ear, drawing his blood. Silencing him. Heavy sweat from both of us gathers on the handle. My nose is a faucet. He finally puts his forearms together behind his back, and I tie him up real tight there.

I pin his ankles to his wrists for good measure, hog-tying him.

"See? Was that hard?" I snap. "Where are the badges held?"

Birds chat. Insects chitter. No words yet.

I try again. "Which—"

A small chuckle. It grows in his throat.

"You need full Arctic blood," he cries out, laughing.

"That's not your concern."

His laughter's deep and full, almost diabolical. "No. I mean to access anything. The doors. The badges. The ships. You have to pass fifteen soldier-blocked checkpoints to even *board* the tourist ship. There's also a helicraft that lands you on the ship. It costs one million vikęs per ticket," he continues, ignoring the swell of my breaths. The rising frightened gasps. He's finally nonchalant. "The military performs extensive research on every passenger. I could close my eyes and approach any soldier and he could tell me my eye color, my piss color, what height I was at six years old. All of it is stored in his wristchip."

"His what?"

"Wrist insertion—" He snorts. "I forget you primitive savages are at least a hundred years behind us. Never mind."

Anger cracks through me. "*We're* the savages—yet your folks are the mass killers, destroyers, pillagers—"

"Only *half the country* is affiliated with the military, ingloriöt. Not everyone is in the military; you need to be chosen. You think the greatest military on earth accepts every single man who enlists? Only the finest are inducted."

He behaves as if half the population of a whole nation being associated with the military is normal. To him it is.

I do the math. During the mandatory propaganda tapes, each morning, the Allied Force glorifies the disturbing fact that their military contains 350 million soldiers. This boy said *affiliated with the military*. So that's not even *exclusively* soldiers. That means associates, personnel, and family members could be *more* than 350 million—if each of the soldiers has at least one affiliation. That means 700 million people could be *half* of their population. Which means their complete population might be over one billion.

Maybe more.

I snarl in vexation. "Continents are *dead* because of the Allied Force. *Barbarian*."

"Are you going to weep about it?" he snaps back, snidely using my own words.

I stop wasting precious minutes. I don't have much time. "Give me four methods to leave this labor camp through the

East Sector or the West Sector then. Alive. Only then will I reconsider the next step."

"What's the next step? Homicide anyway?" He scoffs.

"Castration." My voice is cold.

"You wretched ingloriöt! Your lineage will—"

I stomp his head into the ground. Not to kill him but to knock him out. It dawns on me, with an icy sense of discovery, he's telling the truth. My breath heaving, I steady myself against the bunks. Dizzied.

Lightheaded.

My chest lurches. My nasal cartilage stings, one nostril inflating with blood and damaged tissue. Revelations bombard me where I stand on unbalanced feet.

These soldiers know every last thing about the laborers. Including me.

They know me down to my blood type, height, and weight, and they broadcast that information to the audience so the *onlookers* can gain familiarity. My current escape plot disintegrates. I'm going to have to run another way.

More than ever, I'm grateful that none of my stray siblings and me are actually blood related. Even if they test each of our blood samples against each other, it will conclude that we aren't related. So even if they order every member of my family put to death and check each laborer, only I will die for this.

I stare at my blood splattered on the ground, leaking into his hair, drenching his brown collar. I need to clean all of this. Now.

I drag him into a corner, unconscious, and retighten the restraints with new bedsheets. Firm.

Cautiously, I sprint into the burial fields, not halting to vomit by the crematory, not pausing to rest as I suffocate on the smell of the incinerated, fighting through bleary eyes as it hits me harder that there's no possible escape.

You don't cry, Coa. You fight. You think.

Only a few people have escaped this island successfully. As far as we know. I catch my breath only when the floodlights are near. I need to gather myself and collect my thoughts.

Think, Coa. Think!

I sprint to wash myself in the laborer basins and clear my mind. It's a five-minute run. I approach the fish-market cabin and go inside even though it's closed for the day.

Sailfish and barracuda hang on the walls, angelfish cover the wood tables, and snappers are scattered along the saltwater-damp floorboards. Syringes for cloning the island fish are neatly stacked by Hammer, a heavyset fisherman outfitted in bloodied rubber boots, a tight apron, and a hard expression. His handlebar mustache is thick and black, blacker than his dark eyes and deep-brown skin. His voice is gruff. "Trouble?"

I lie quick. "No, sir."

"Good. What do you need?" Hammer's not the kind to ask many questions anymore. He lost his thumb for that. Twice.

"The basin, sir."

He nods toward the back.

Oddly for a fish market, there's no fish grub, hooks, or reels. Not even rudimentary spears. None of that is needed for the scientifically duplicated fish. But the cabin reeks of algae and briny water all the same. Only talent are allowed to eat fish—and they are not even provided actual fish.

Hammer's voice follows me. "Holler if you're in trouble. You hear me?"

"Yes, sir." Emotion catches in my throat. I focus on the

dark-walnut wood panels of the basin room. "Thank you kindly."

"Best of luck out there. In the jungle, stick to the roots and fish. That'll last you."

"Course," I murmur, scrubbing the discolored skin quickly. Blood and beatings are common in the forced-labor camp, so he barely glances twice at my injuries. "May the British save you, Hammer."

Wet footsteps. "You believe the British are coming? You never seemed the type to swallow that nonsense."

I keep my back turned, spilling out the truth. "No, sir. They abandoned us. I pray they're all dead."

"Smart girl. Stay sharp. Come back."

Come back. That's the deepest expression of love you can utter in the South Sector. My eyes nearly water. All I can manage is a nod. *Come back to us. Get back alive.*

Curfew isn't for another sixty minutes, and before I leave out the back door, I give myself five extra seconds to check for any lingering blood. But my quaking knees can't remember how to move.

By the time I dart forward again, it's too late.

As soon as I leave Hammer's fish market, an Arctic man snatches my arm.

CHAPTER 11

Hazen Creed.

"The execution needed work." Hazen is smirking already, and I can hear it in his infuriatingly confident voice. His waves of blond hair are princely, even in the dark. Right now, he follows me to the Dredges, where the manure of cattle, hogs, and bulls is kept, despite my best efforts to ward him off with the stench. "Are you escaping?"

"I have no idea what you're talking about." I load a wheelbarrow with droppings, hoping the abominable sight and overwhelming musk will repulse him. I grew up with hens, foxes, cattle. Animal scat never bothered me much.

"There's no plausible escape—"

The edges of the wheelbarrow are aged, speckled with rust. I force myself not to look at it as I scrape a handful of rust into my palm. "Of course."

"A conclusion—"

I shove rust in his eyes, but he quickly pins me to the ground. He has more dexterity than the paramilitary teenager.

Hazen's eyes are closed, as if he anticipated the attack. When he opens them again, his green eyes are not reddened and teared with watery lacrimal response. His hands are larger than I expected on my body. He could split my head on the rocky path and end this in one blow.

Worse, he could squeeze the air out of my throat and prevent me from screaming. A slow death.

If he found me, how soon could the enforcers find me?

I thrash beneath him, as wild as an angry bison.

Hazen grunts. "And what was that for?"

"Arctic men kill," I seethe. "*I kill first.*"

Hazen wraps an even more confident smile around his voice. "If I was going to kill you, you'd be right next to him."

"Next to who?"

Hazen produces something from a bag, and the squelch of damp fabric lands next to my ear.

A blood-soaked uniform.

My lungs are robbed of oxygen. "You killed him?"

"Amateur mistake to keep the witness alive. Consider yourself in my debt, Rangecroft." Hazen lowers himself, pressing his knee into the base of my spine. The heat of his breath bristles against my ear. "By the way, the next time you're hesitating about either tying a man down or rendering him weaponless—don't waste that time."

Shock still slams my body. "You killed him?"

"It wasn't difficult. Prepare for the island."

He took his life. I scramble. "Which should I have done first?"

Hazen turns me over onto my back, then peels off his shirt to wipe the rust residue from below his eyes. "Depends. Are we allies?"

He killed even before the Great Hunt began. Who knows how many allies, enemies, and counterplans he's made?

I wasn't born yesterday.

"Not a chance—" I start, but as the shock subsides, I suddenly realize my hands are bound and my knife has been stolen. I struggle against the restraints. *He tied me up?*

I thrash, kicking like a bantam chicken, wondering which he did first: steal my weapon or tether my wrists.

Was it one fluid moment? Is that all it took?

Hazen leaves me to free myself. But I'm a survivor. I hoist myself upward, dazed, woozy on my feet with how hard he took me down. Slowly, I regain my balance. Then, not wasting another second, I use the jagged barrow screw to free my hands, then my ankles.

I inspect what Hazen used to bind me.

It's the paramilitary uniform of the Arctic teenager.

Stained with blood.

CHAPTER 12

I bury the paramilitary uniform in the more distant burial fields. My damaged nose throbs with splintering pain, still leaking despite my best efforts. I swipe hot blood from it—

A hand lands on my arm. *Hazen.*

"Stay away from—" I snarl.

Bright whiskey-brown eyes stare at me. Surprised.

"A Great Hunt participator!" an Allied Force citizen—not Hazen Creed—shouts. "A Great Hunt participator! No way—"

His hand slaps over his mouth. His huge eyes are in disbelief as he takes in my wispy dirty-blond hair. He grasps my arm again. "A participator! Are you Coa—"

My knee drives into his stomach before his boisterous voice can reach anyone else. By now Maximus Størmbane could've retired to his residence with his wife, and the slaughter men could have returned to the Slaughterhouse.

I grind my teeth. I'm 120 pounds and underfed, but the teenager likely didn't expect his gut to be rammed. As he doubles over, fear stops my blood.

You attacked another Arctic citizen. Already. My eyes dart around, searching for any soldiers. *You wretched ingloriöt.*

I've already knocked out an Allied Force citizen. Then Hazen killed him. Then I *kneed* this one in the abdomen. It doesn't seem real.

My mind doesn't process it. I can't imagine how much trouble I'm in. *Before* the Great Hunt even begins. *Wildflower. Stay calm. Get out of here now.*

Come back. I cannot stay on Traeger Island. We cannot stay.

Boyish groans shoot through the boiling-hot night air, and the teen's thick eyebrows knot beneath messy beige hair that falls in his whiskey-brown eyes. I already know other fans will notice him, even though he's not in a paramilitary uniform; he's a pretty face by their standards, his lips soft and pink. Which puts me at risk. *A lover could be searching for him. An admirer.*

Someone hoping to win a husband.

Right now, he's drooling with pain, so I drag him up behind the massive manure mounds, swallowing my nerves to apologize, make a deal, something. *Keep your strays alive.*

"Sorry, did I scare you?" he asks.

"No. Are you all right?"

He grunts. "My friend bought merchandise. They own a few replicas of the field uniform. You're a blond. For a split second, I thought you were my friend—"

I blend in. Good.

That's the only benefit of tourists on the island. Fake makeup. Fake costumes. Everywhere.

Even though my bloodied nose will give me away, in the nighttime, it might be hard to tell. I could play it off as costume blood.

"A real-life Hallowell citizen! *Sick.*" He touches my hair. His fingers dig deep into my tailbone-length tresses. He studies a lock of my filthy hair, now reeking with cattle scat.

"Do millions of you really dye your hair to mimic ours, like they say?"

Dye our hair? "No. I was born blond. Not everyone wants to copy you." *Even to avoid murder.*

His boyishly charming dimples deepen, and his skin pinkens all the way to his ears. Like he can't believe it. "Real foreign hair then. Killvę." *Spectacular.*

"I'll sell you ten inches of my foreign hair, authentic Hallowell, if—"

"I know everything about Hallowell!" he boasts fanatically. Obscenely loud. A spray of golden-brown freckles is splashed across his nose. Grinning as if he can't believe he gets to gush about this, he blurts, "Literally everything!"

"Keep your voice down."

"Cowboys, milkshakes, crayfish, just ask me. Seriously—ask me anything," he challenges. Proud of himself. "I know all about your famous western movies. All of your sports champions. Especially Clift Rutter. One of my favorite country boxers of all time."

I need to get away from him. "Look, do you want an autograph?"

"Can you tattoo me? Write *Glory before fear.*" The teenager towers over me as I crouch. I'm ready to punch in his trachea and run. But I control myself.

His harmless face and soft fingers are blatant markers of higher class. His boyhood is all over him. Hazen's masculinity and manhood killed any sign of his own boyhood. This young man is as friendly as a golden retriever. *But is he rich? Did he win a free ticket here? How do the ticket systems work? Could he buy my way out of here as a bribe to the carnage men?*

More than half of the tourists brought their best attire, but there are still poorer vacationers compared to the wealthy class of the Arctic. A few look as if they dragged their clothes out of bargain bins. Yet even they made it here somehow.

He could've won a free ticket.

He speaks too loud for a hunting season like this. He'll get us seen and make me a target. Especially now, as he pats himself all over dramatically, drawing further attention. "Wait! Sïvęt! I must've left my tatt ink on the ship."

"Where can you find tatt ink nearby then?" I ask, hoping it will send him on a wild-goose chase.

"The East Sector has tatt ink at the resorts. My family owns the closest luxury resorts, right next to the Størm-banes—"

Owns luxury resorts? Plural? He's from a hotel-baron lineage? But something greater sticks out to me.

Right next to the Størmbanes? Ife almost got me killed earlier, and I can't let her endanger me twice. It's too dangerous to even risk running into her again.

"I can't stay." I trudge on. "I need to report to the barracks."

"But you're headed that way." He thumbs right at the burial fields and dead zone. The bone-chillingly grim atmosphere makes me shiver. As if even the Slaughterhouse and Carnagehouse themselves are warning me about what these soldiers will do to me.

I narrow my eyes. "The Great Hunt begins at noon. I need *rest*."

His face crumples, as if he's watching a once-in-a-lifetime chance slip through his fingers. "Can I snap a holograph at least? Escort you halfway?"

"No. You can't tell anyone you saw me either."

"Swear on my life, I won't tell a soul. On all my honor."

My eyes harden. The Allied Force is without honor. All of 'em. He could scream to his friends or anyone else nearby the second he walks away. I'd be senseless to leave him by himself.

Already, I feel a bullet in my back.

"Come on. Move fast."

"Bray, by the way. Bray Rainsford." Bray reaches for my hand, and alarm rises inside of me. It could be a trick. But Bray smiles. Sincere light-brown eyes gaze back at me. Earnest. "I'm a massive fan of the Great Hunt—"

"Let's move."

Bray Rainsford. The boy who's going to get me killed.

CHAPTER 13

IFE STØRMBANE

NIGHT AFTER THE WEIGH-IN CEREMONY

I throw up on the walls of the beer hall. Valeska glares at me with animosity, but I can't hold down my dinner. I saw the bodies of runaway laborers who attempted escape, desperate not to set foot on the hazardous island. A riot broke out an hour ago at the dilapidated laborer canteens.

It happened right in front of us during our night tours. The sergeant cut our guided tour short to extinguish the riot, sending in the enforcers as laborers rebelled. Plates crashed against the uniforms of the enforcers, their dark gear splashed with broth; pots from the kitchens went flying over heads, the laborers shouting commands to surround the enforcers. To steal their fully automatic handguns.

A few fled for the nearest wired gates.

"There are always men that run." Valeska glowers, as if it's common sense. "Not all men can handle pressure. Don't cry over them; pull yourself together."

Human beings. I saw *human beings* get killed right in front of me. Mikoš Volkov led a revolt.

Captives fought back and took up arms all at once—all over the canteens. It was chaos. Slavic citizens refused to hide like prey on the island. Hallowell field-workers didn't want to be part of a mass killing, contributors to murders, accomplices in the killing of their own people. They're human beings. Now, they've been hoisted like banners in the demolished canteens, riddled with bullet holes—

I quake.

Soldiers anticipated the revolt—but that was the point. Mikoš did not aim for the enforcers. He targeted tourists.

While the enforcers were laying siege to the worn-down canteens, the workers returning from the fields attacked tourists, beating them viciously with wooden barrels, kicking them into the dirt, violently slashing at their skin and clothes. They used anything they had, and I'm certain their tools would've been even more damaging, had they been able to smuggle materials out of the detectors I saw on the tour.

Mikoš Volkov was more darkly intelligent than they estimated.

Now, he's a symbol of defiance. A slain martyr. As armored vehicles moved us to the secured beer halls, I heard Alina's cry of anguish as she grieved over his perforated body—

My knees almost give. I'm still shaken from the massacre. It won't even be *publicized.* No other nations are likely to find out about the island atrocities. It will be blotted from history. No record left of it.

The last international empires left on earth—the North Transatlantic Empire and Alvorada—have no idea what's coming once the war comes. None of the tourists even *died.*

But Vørian wanted to see the revolters dead. Replaced with new victims sent to the island.

He wanted to shoot down Mikoš Volkov himself.

Another splatter of vomit splashes out of me and hits my pedicure. I kick off my heels.

"We're on a strict schedule." Valeska's own stilettos click in the gilded privacy section of the beer hall. "What are you doing? *Are you barefoot?*"

"Give me a minute—"

"Put those heels back on at once!" she hisses over her slender shoulder, horror alive in her gray eyes. She's openly terrified someone will see me with puke and blood on my floral dinner dress and from now on that disarray will define her career and clients. "We can't be here longer than a minute. Half a minute. *Put it back on.*"

"I need a *second.*" Tears fill my eyes.

Public executions are not supposed to happen. I slam my hands over my ears. Gunshots still ricochet in my head—

Maximus unbuttons his tuxedo jacket and shirt, taking them off as I numbly rub at my eyes—as if I can erase the images. He removes my dinner dress, then covers my body with his crisp button-up shirt. Warmth floods my skin from the fabric. An amused smile appears on his lips. "There, that can be a style, can't it?"

My brows knit, not registering. "What?"

"Women wear men's shirts as fashion now. It looks good on you," he compliments with a warm voice.

I realize he's being kind, talking me through it. His thumb swipes blood residue from my bottom lip.

"No one in the crowd saw you vomit; everyone was transfixed by the fights. You're safe." Maximus buttons his shirt up my trembling body. He moves my hair aside, pinning it behind my ear. "Here, half-buttoned will look intentional. You can wear it better than I did." He winks.

I ran for the escaped men, as if I could stop the bullets with my bare hands. Blood spattered all over my—

"T-Thank you, Maximus," I say, shuddering. His expensive shirt swallows my body, given Maximus's height compared to mine, and it grazes my lower shins. His sleeves flood over my small hands, so I have to fold them several times to free my wrists. I fix my tiara. "Thank y-you sincerely."

"Don't mention it." He runs his hand over an Aphelion Megacorporation vending machine, which dispenses a fresh cup of ginger tea. An advertisement pops up: *Become a savage! Live like the islanders!* Aphelion is the official drink sponsor of the Great Hunt.

Hatred boils my skin.

I'm grateful Maximus went after me. I don't know what my fist would've done to Vørian's face. What problems that would've started—I have breakfast with the Størmbanes again tomorrow. I need to focus.

Maximus pushes his calloused hand through my silk-pressed pink hair, bringing the tea to my lips. Steam pools under my nose.

"You tripped, didn't you?"

He's telling me what to say. Giving me an excuse.

I nod, grateful. "I'm steady on my feet now." I gulp the tea. "Sorry I embarrassed you."

Maximus chuckles. His warm blue eyes crinkle at the corners, as if he's entertained by the idea. "You can't embarrass me." Maximus checks the time on his wristchip, which scans in front of his dilated pupil. He's charming and unaffected. "I've seen grown men cower at the sight of blood.

You didn't even faint." Maximus looks down at me. "My little princess is resilient."

I can't protest that I'm not little; my line of sight is below his chest, especially without heels. So I look up at his expressive eyes. "It won't happen again," I promise.

"I'm right here, beside you, even if it does. It's hunting season, but it's not war." Maximus kisses my forehead. Valeska chokes but recovers herself quickly. "Victory to the Allied Force."

"Victory."

Maximus pulls me against his solid abdomen, and his cologne fills my senses as I sink into his arms. As if everything has calmed.

But even if it's not war, it's a *live* hunting season, a hunt with real people and real families. Real death. There's blood on my hands; *I* will condemn those innocent people to Kaipo Island.

I chose that location in hopes it would kill all the snipers, but my choice has also sentenced almost a hundred other people to death.

Stomach acid gurgles up my throat. Painfully, I swallow it back down.

Except, to Maximus, the island is somewhere to enjoy tradition and spend time with me. For years, Maximus worked over a hundred military hours per week, and now he's assigned to the propaganda campaign—adventurism and exploration world records. It's designed to showcase him as something other than an extraordinary soldier and military general, to make him appear more relatable to the masses.

As if they could ever match his historical accomplishments.

That has always been the issue with Maximus Størmbane—he's immeasurably inspiring but never relatable. He isn't within realistic reach.

He's a prodigy.

Beyond that, I *asked* for this Great Hunt location. I can't vomit at the first sight of blood in front of everyone now. I need to be exactly as excellent as Maximus.

Against my will, though, a tiny cry climbs up my throat.

What's wrong with me? Tears come again, and Maximus dries them from my cheeks, swiping the remaining blood off my lip.

He's explored Arctic summits, body-filled canyons, and life-threatening thousand-meter drops; none of it fazes him.

"Drink some water and lie down for a few minutes. You'll feel better."

If that's not an Allied Force man, I don't know what is. Just a little blood. Just a little death. Nothing to cry over.

Drink a chilled beer later if it's still bothering you.

Makarian warriors consider crying a sign of strength and humanity. Allied Force soldiers are required to damage their tear glands with specialized chemicals the soldiers inject into their own eyes to ensure they never cry.

The raw chemical burn is said to be one of the most agonizing pains ever created.

It is an excruciating test of resolve and masculinity. The destruction of their tear glands is incomplete, allowing their eyes to be lubricated as necessary, and the soldiers' vision fully recovers, but the chemical substance permanently infiltrates their systems and prevents their glands from producing tears of emotion.

The men can't cry with human tears, even if they want to.

If a man is on a hunting trip and gashes his hand, he's expected to pour køvma over the wound, wrap it tightly, and keep hunting.

A year back, Thorsten knocked out a tooth on a bear

hunt; Maximus had him gargle cold køvma to keep out infection. They hunted all day, sun on their cheeks, and fished until Thorsten had buckets full of his favorite salmon shark.

More than that, Maximus doesn't *care* about those foreign men. They would've died anyway. The execution of runaways is an expected part of the tradition, as Valeska said. Maximus gazes at me as if I don't understand that.

"Thank you, Maximus. Sorry. I can't thank you enough." I bury my face deep in his chest.

"Don't worry about it." Maximus presses his mouth to my delicate hair.

I sent my own ex-fiancé to die, and Maximus is not fazed by it. Maximus did not blink once when Hazen Creed was condemned to the jungle, even though they've known each other since before they were young recruits. Maximus had the same look in his stoic eyes when he removed Hazen's ring from my finger and slid on his own.

"Are you feeling better?" Maximus asks now as I softly untangle myself from him.

"Much better. You're always so good to me." My eyes sweep down, as if I'm overwhelmed by my love for him. "You're my universe. I truly can't thank you enough."

"I can think of several ways to thank me." Maximus kisses my neck. My throat. As if we're alone, his eyes flick up at an electric banner advertising Euphoría—a pleasure megacorporation. "But that can be later." He gives a roguish smirk.

Valeska can barely swallow her audible shock.

"Take her through a private entrance," Maximus commands my guards. "Keep the bodies out of sight. I don't want any hysteria around it."

CHAPTER 14

NIGHT AFTER THE WEIGH-IN CEREMONY

"I *love* your history," Bray gushes. He slows me down, putting me in danger. We strut past the South Sector dance halls as if we're friends, nearing the sector border. "Hallowell boasts the best seafood."

Hazardously, I carve my way through the minefields of the island outskirts on the South Sector. It's a longer route to the East Sector, but it's safer than cutting directly through the official South-East Sector border and its checkpoints. The minefields are deathtraps even soldiers avoid due to the fact the explosives obliterate the bodies of anyone on foot. Elsko would've lost more than his left foot if he'd been on these minefields instead of the ones by the shore. These mines are meant to keep South Sector livestock away from the ritzy tourists in the East Sector.

Right now, watchtowers are glutted with tourists on their guided vacation tours. The floodlights are timed, and one floodlight illuminates a patch a meter to my right. In twenty minutes, it will cover my exact location.

We need to outrun the timer, but without blowing ourselves to pieces.

Bray mentioned a tourist ship. That could be our escape
route—but I need to view it first to be sure.

I've snaked through these dirt minefields for four years.
It's a regular shortcut for me since I've never minded the idea
of being blown to smithereens—I figure it beats the grueling life in the forced-labor camp. At the end of the workday,
at seven at night, we're expected to hike seven miles all the
way to the North Sector to turn in our work stamps. I cut
through the East Sector instead, praying most days for an
explosive.

But right now, I can't risk death. Except double murder
is far more likely than setting off a mine, since Bray Rainsford can't shut his mouth. He's louder than ever.

I remind him, "Copy my *tracks*."

"I am—"

"One wrong step—you'll blow us both to hell," I warn
him under my breath, but Bray's hardly paying real attention.

Bray rambles, "Denim jackets and blue jeans—free
market, antitrust measures—the Allied Force could learn *so
much* from westerners."

This boy even *smells* like the Allied Force. That overex-
pensive, belligerently important cologne they always wear.
I used to think it was their natural scent, but it's a signature
of their elitism somehow caught in a bottle.

Bray offers me a genuine grin. "I collect Coca-Cola bottles, by the way. *Real* Coca-Cola."

He grins wider. Lopsided. As if stealing American bottles should impress me.

Bray climbs through low-barbed thickets after me.
"Cowboy hats are my favorite." His freckled face brightens.

"Gunslingers, outlaws, Marlboros. It's sick." He smiles, his dimples deepening.

I warm inside a little. Imagining his lungs filled with deadly smoke.

Suddenly, fanfare blares. Drunken tourists, tipsy girls, and thunderously rowdy carnage men spill out of the distant beer hall on our right.

My blood runs cold.

"Welcome to my debut celebration!" Ife calls out. She's inside, gleaming, as glitzy as a showgirl. She dances on a raised sphere, encouraging a stream of tourists to enter. "I love parties!"

She's surrounded by security guards, and there are more enforcers than I've ever seen in my life. She's blowing kisses to the crowds. She doesn't care or doesn't know that every foreigner on this island will be murdered.

Including me, right now, because I'm moving so *slow.* Bray's expensive sweater flaps in the howling wind. He stands completely still and gazes across the mined grounds. "Wanna go inside?"

I fake a grin. "Of course. Later." *Eleven minutes. Only eleven minutes left.*

I'm counting every minute in my head until the floodlights flare this area.

The shipping ports are in the East Sector beside the Restricted Port. I've seen laborers carry packages and containers straight from the eastern shoreline. But I've always been curious about the superyachts.

"You should rub shoulders before the Great Hunt. Everyone who's anyone parties at the Reintęk Beer Hall." He elbows me like we're best friends. "*You're* anyone now, Coa Rangecroft. Your stardom will be wild. Think of stratospheric fame."

Bray grins like he's proud of me. His eyes glimmer. "Fame?"

Seconds drain by before it hits me. Does he actually believe it's a voluntary show? That we enter this competitive and violent contest for money? Like professional staged wrestling?

Clearly he, like some other fans, hasn't even researched the billions of bodies and inhumane stories from the Allied Force's atrocities. Brutal mutilations, human experiments, mass gassings, and graves. Minefields. The entire opening ceremony of the Great Hunt was a tribute to Belgium's history of stripping Africans naked for human zoos, caging the naked men, women, and children, and having visitors feed them like animals. Belgium killed over fifteen million Africans in the Congo alone, brutally amputating the limbs of children and families as punishment for not harvesting impossible amounts of rubber for the Belgians.

That is why we harvest sugarcane and rubber on Traeger Island.

The Allied Force shows us foreign history during the mandatory broadcasts, allowing us to piece together the fact that it is deliberately repeating history.

However, to the tourists who are simply on vacation, the entire Great Hunt looks staged. Even Ife was clueless. *The cameras are for the movie. Want to read my script?*

Part of me wants to ask how many Allied Force citizens there are—but I don't want to risk him becoming suspicious.

Bray drags me back to earth. "She's out of this world." He stares up at Ife on the platform for a second longer than necessary, and I have to pull him forward. But it dawns on me.

"You like her?"

Bray's ears turn so crimson I almost think he's having an allergic reaction.

"She's *breathtaking*." He shoves his hands in his pockets as he watches her swirl, her island wrap skirt spinning, her hips swaying. Mesmerizing everyone around her. Her flirty mouth quirks. Her bandeau top is made of attractive flora. A bowa flower is pinned at her ear. Her allure's indescribable.

The walls drip with condensation inside, and bodies bash against each other, the music blaring as loud as air-raid sirens. Beer smoke hits you right in the nose. For once, I'm grateful my nose is clotted with blood. I can't stand the toxic, fiery aroma of läkøn.

Barrels of foamy, amber beer blockade the noisy, eager crowds of vacationers. I imagine the excessive body heat spreading as young men wrestle each other in the dirt road outside, teenage girls giggling at the rigid men attempting to dance. You wouldn't even believe this is the Allied Force audience after hours, thousands of miles from their fatherland.

When the young tourists are out of sight of the staunch traditionalists, they always find it safe to kiss each other feverishly against the beer hall's wooden exterior. Their arms and legs get tangled around each other as they smash themselves together and clutch each other's clothes.

Right now, I ensure we stay well out of their view. As far as they're concerned, I'm turning in my last work stamp.

Bray bites his pink upper lip. "She's radiant." *That's useful.*

He's my way out of here. Once I check for myself that he is as rich as he claims, he might be able to bribe the carnage men for tickets for me and my siblings. *Ife Størmbane—*

"Ife's generous," I say, minding my footsteps. "She loves equally generous friends. Did you see us onstage together?"

"Holding hands?"

"Yeah, we're good friends. She interrupted my weigh-in

to personally wish me luck," I add. But he's not listening; he's enslaved by her beauty on the elevated sphere. Bray studies her as she dances, lovesick over her slender waist, her rose-bud lips, her doe eyes.

"She's so innocent it kills me. She's my dream wife."

"She's already married. Aim for—"

"Anything can happen." Bray smiles at me with impossible hope. His light-brown eyes dance with mischief. "Stars align when you least expect."

"What about Sniper General Størmbane?"

"Maximus Størmbane can get engaged dozens of times. He was previously engaged before his marriage; he famously changed his mind with Marsa Reicher, who almost any man in the Kilrød would kill over. The ikä deserves someone who'd love her for the rest of their life. Devote all of their attention to her."

"*You?*" I laugh, then bite it back. *Shut up. Shut up.* "Makes sense. She could choose you . . . off the island."

"She only needs to meet me again." Bray's agile body hops over a visible mine track and leans under a barbed-wire gate. "She probably doesn't even remember, but we met on the rooftop of my family's resort when she first arrived in the Allied Force. We slow danced in the snow."

I hardly listen. We're finally entering the West Sector. I feel my lungs swell with hope. My nose is still harshly bruised, and my back aches, but it all feels worth it now.

"Coa, I'm passionate about the ikä. I'll always protect her."

He's as serious as a heart surgery. His palm flexes, helping me down and through the barbed wire.

"I've analyzed every blood sport imaginable. Combat, enemy approaches, stealth. Survival tactics and terrain navigation. Which is also why, believe me, I know all the huge winners when I see them." He winks at me.

"You're right, she's breathtaking and radiant." I haul myself under the next barbed gate. My cheek is sliced open. "Isn't she?"

It clicks. These men don't really *see* exotic women often in their fatherland, so they're obsessed with her. She's the most popular face in the Allied Force right now. Rare. Illicit.

By Isla Moon's next movie, they will be obsessed with her instead. As always.

Women are trophies to be conquered and displayed.

Bray Rainsford doesn't know anything about Ife, not concretely, and at the same time, he must realize he just confessed his adoration out loud, and that makes him laugh. But I *need* his money. I pretend he's the funniest person I've ever met. "I can get you a private meeting with her if . . ."

His brow rises curiously. "If . . ."

Humid island air wafts around me. *Ask him to bribe the carnage men. Ask him now, Coa!*

It claws my throat. My ears burn with nerves as I prepare to ask him to break the rules for a foreigner.

A whistle slices through the air. It's a sniper's bullet.

CHAPTER 15

"Get on the ground!" a voice thunders from behind. Pairs of metal boots punch the dirt. Invisible enforcers now become visible, having tracked us down with silent boots. Entirely soundless. Until now.

They stayed back far enough that we didn't notice their presence.

Now, I see their footprints. Fear combusts inside of me. *No, no, no, no, no.*

A whistle screams through the air. A sniper's bullet tears past my wrist.

I sprint for safety. A wild race for cover. Any cover. Shots crack around us, and the wind I feel as they pass tells me they're too close. Making my heart hammer in my chest. *Run faster. Run!*

On this side of the gates, the ships and seacrafts are in sight. The superyachts are swollen with tourists.

"Move! Move!" I shout back to Bray as he jumps over the wires. He trips and grasps at his chest. Gasping. Bleeding from the bullets.

I eye the treacherous ocean. I'll swim through it, if I need to. My heart suddenly feels defiantly heavy, sinking in my chest. Bray collapses to his knees. I'm faster than him, but I realize I can't abandon him to die. *No more running, Coa. There's no escape. Not this time. End them.*

Take them all with you.

I pivot, ready to send bolts of lightning into the necks of the carnage men. But instead there's a throng of slaughter men. Dozens of them. Bray gasps. I freeze. *They knew we'd try to escape. They knew.* Wicked grins now stretch across their twisting faces.

You were handpicked.

They drew me right out into the open.

If they want me dead, they'll do it. I realize now these aren't bullets grazing our skin; they're metal tranquilizing darts. The slaughter men are hunting. They're permitted to select their own prey—for their own sick enjoyment and thrill.

They knew I'd attempt to escape—

"Found another Hallowell runaway. Told you they'd bite."

One of them unloads a rifle from his shoulder and aims between my eyes. Another tranquilizing dart punctures my throat. An explosive crack.

"Darts iv my ches?" I hear fear shoot through Bray's voice behind me. His speech slurs. "Why? Wha—"

Slit!

His thin sleeves rip open. The slaughter men are done warning us to surrender.

"Come forward." It's an order.

I do not.

"We will not kill you." The head enforcer is an expert, dictatorial, but reliably disciplined. As he emerges from the slaughter men, I recognize him as one of the conformists to the protocol.

The enforcers would only be here if a person of high value were in the proximity. *Did Ife Størmbane follow me? Where is she?*

The thunderous sound of dozens of metal boots hitting hard dirt fills my pounding ears. *No. No. No.* I run back to grab Bray, the boy who can save my siblings.

Bray Rainsford is my only chance left.

Raw, vulgar lightning tears out of my palm, but Bray shoves me behind him. Protecting me with his body. My back slams into the earth. That boar head ruins my offensive strike as he attempts to shield me. A slaughter man releases a throaty laugh down at us as two huge, useless barbed-wire fences explode behind him from my lightning. It would've killed him.

"A fireborn like the sergeant said. You actually proved yourself interesting."

The leading soldier shoves past him to leer at me. His face is alive with hatred. The name tag on his chest reads *Vørian Størmbane*.

His boot slams me down. Hard.

A bloody rasp escapes me this time.

My brows lower. I refuse to beg. I refuse to allow any sound out of my lips. But my eyes widen in horror as his lips curl upward. Every pale feature looks sadistic.

"Don't steal all the fun, Initiate Størmbane." Two slaughter men approach him. "It's the custom here to share your targets."

"Her head is mine." A bullet almost hits my head, whizzing over my scalp. I expect hot blood to splash over my eyelids in case it grazes my skin. But Vørian's smirk disappears as the head enforcer speaks.

"Don't kill them. Kømmand Sergeant Arcus can examine the fireborn. The other one looks as if he's Allied Force."

But Vørian reaches for the holster attached behind his back and switches weapons. A monsoon of darts attacks our skin. Aiming to kill us.

CHAPTER 16

The Interrogation Department is painfully dark. Which is psychologically manipulative.

There's not even a dim light, and it's grungy, filthy. The soldiers do not operate by visible light; their headgear allows them to see.

We enter the lurid building at the ground floor and are then forced to descend four floors and instructed to wait. I expected to be taken out and shot in the rubber fields, a brutal punishment for attempted escape.

Valence Security Megacorp cameras record our every breath. The red dots of their surveillance are the only source of light. My brain is thick and drowsy, my mouth dry from the tranquilizers, my throat like sandpaper. Even the water they give us tastes like static.

Bray groans.

Kømmand Sergeant Arcus comes to greet us, apologizing for the violent storm of tranquilizer darts. But the darts were only partially full, showing he intended for Vørian Størmbane to have his dark enjoyment blitzing them at us rather than shoot one potent dart. *Scum.*

Their advanced medicine removes all visible traces of the darts, and the metal darts themselves didn't knock me unconscious, but I can't move. I can barely think. My mouth hangs open.

A hazy cloud of mosquitoes gnaws at my nape. There's an indistinct wet spot beneath my bare feet. I've been stripped of shoes to disorient me.

The concrete reeks of urine, human feces, and indistinguishable stenches I can't recognize. But I do know there are twenty levels deeper underground that are more unspeakable than this.

"You are diabolical." I hear Bray's heated voice to my left. His wild hair is even more disorderly, his puppy face contorted with fury.

He's lucky most of the soldiers weren't even aiming for him.

Bray could save himself, but he thunders up to Kømmand Sergeant Arcus himself. Whiskey-brown eyes like a hurricane. He stabs his finger at the sergeant's chest. "You are beyond evil. Not to mention *unethical*—it was my fault she was off location, and you didn't even ask questions. You just tranquilized us!"

"Your family has been notified. Our apologies to the Rainsfords." Arcus's smile is plastic. Tamed for the wealthy tourist.

"Apologize? Did you *hear* what I said? You tranquilized *human beings, your own contestant*—"

Kømmand Sergeant Arcus responds, "Were you warned not to interfere in the Great Hunt?"

"It's a blood sport!" Another jab. "This is *real life*. You shot us with real tranquilizers—"

"Touch me again, before your family arrives, and—"

"I don't *care*," Bray yells. His freckles explode with fury and redness. "Shut up and listen." Bray steps closer, challenging the sergeant's authority in front of his subordinates. A heartbreaking mistake. "Your men—"

"My men would put you in the Great Hunt, if it were up to me." Anger flashes in Kømmand Sergeant Arcus's eyes. Bray has no idea this coldly savage man is capable of brutal mass homicide.

"Trust me, I'd love that," Bray dares.

A volatile silence. It terrorizes the air. They glare each other down.

"Bill the Rainsford Resort without limit and remove his details from the West Sector information bank." Without a second of hesitation, Kømmand Sergeant Arcus steps past him and exits the room.

"Tell them you didn't mean it. Run now and plead with them to forgive you and to forget this ever happened," I try to tell Bray, but my words are slurred by my drowsy mouth. By the time he catches the fear in my eyes, it's too late.

Once his details are removed, the sergeant can discard him into the ocean when his men are finished with him, and not even the tracking devices will be able to locate his dead body.

CHAPTER 17

NIGHT AFTER THE WEIGH-IN CEREMONY

Sobs choke my throat as soon as I'm in my suite. Panic swells, and I order everyone out. *Dead bodies. Dead bodies.* My lipstick smears Maximus's shirt. I scrape my makeup off entirely. I shove my palms between my thighs to keep them from—

"Reinforcements have arrived." Kateri breaks into my suite with snacks, fresh tissues, and an obscene mountain of ice cream. With extra blankets.

Kateri's nose, lips, and cheeks are swollen and red. She's the kind of friend that doesn't just let you grieve alone but cries with you. It reminds me of nights in the Arctic when the expressways and hypertrains were frozen over with snow, rails iced thick, the territory dangerous and dark. I'd insist she stay the night. We'd cuddle up, watch a movie, and fall asleep in a heap of blankets.

But then she'd scream awake, sweating from dreams of the Imperial Hokori Military naval ships—the ones that destroyed her island, the soldiers that invaded—and I'd pull her under the covers and let her sob against my shaking shoulder. *You're a survivor, Kit. They harmed you; they didn't destroy you.*

You're not damaged. You're whole. You're whole.

My voice wobbles now. "I'm not crying—"

"No, don't even fake it." Kateri sits me up, undoing the intricate hairstyle Valeska will kill her for ruining.

Kit brings a pile of silk pillows, a chilled rag, and some calming hibiscus oils. "My entire island was wiped out. I witnessed—I witnessed my mother, my aunts, people that raised me, every friend I knew—" Tearst gather in her sweet brown eyes. "Forget them. No pretending today."

Ōheo was her homeland. One of the eastern Asiatic islands full of predominantly women and girls, a matriarchy, where Kateri's grandmother was born. It was famous for its healing mud, doulas, and earth potions. Its mud water helped not only the fertility of plants but their growth—their largest export was flora. More than 16 percent of the world's supply.

After one of the larger asteroids hit, and after the Allied Force defeated Former Asia, some of the people who had managed to flee in time formed Ōheo. Ōheo joined the refugee empire of Alvorada. But it was not spared.

The Imperial Hokori Military Empire, which had owned the majority of Former Asia, was now a collection of struggling colonies, a defeated empire. The Hokori military did not approve of Ōheo seeking additional international alliances. It meant the Hokori military would lose a portion of Ōheo's exports in agriculture and electronics.

Therefore, the Imperial Hokori Empire threatened to no longer send military aid and economic support to Ōheo, despite how necessary it was for protection and infrastructure.

Ōheo ignored the threat, and its queen not only signed

diplomatic alliances with Alvorada but increased shipments in order to export sufficiently to Alvorada.

The next month, it was pillaged by the IHM. In the horrific aftermath, thousands of the found bodies had to be burned out of respect, including Kateri's mother.

The rebel Kòng Zhì Empire now owns the entirety of the territory after it managed to overtake the Imperial Hokori Empire. The Ōheo boats that managed to escape desperately tried to reach Alvorada. However, they were intercepted by the Allied Force.

That is how Kateri arrived in the Kilrød.

"I'm so sorry," I say.

"I'm fine. My sister saved our lives when she won the Hunt." Kateri goes silent for a moment. "She won before the rest of us were even taken to an island. She never spoke again after."

Neither of us could imagine what she witnessed—until now. Her sister Kāten hasn't spoken a word to this day.

Kateri scoffs. "Her snotty little mooncalves don't remember a thing."

Kateri loves them and refuses to let me help her pay for her bundle of siblings, nieces, nephews, and orphaned children. She'd never accept Allied Force money. Never.

I'd die first.

Kateri only works here now because select Ōheo survivors are forced to serve their own obliterators.

People travel to the rebuilt Ōheo for luxury vacations. Snazzy tropical attractions. Meanwhile, islanders work long nights in the Arctic in exchange for food, clothes, and accommodations.

She wipes her nose. "So yeah, let's do something. Eat something, stuff our faces, and cry it out. We'll get through this."

This is a catastrophic loss, and I feel it so deep inside that I can't get rid of it. "I sent—I sent—" *I sent people to die out there.* I know the only way to save billions of people is to grieve, move on, and strategize, but I can't fathom it. I can't confess to Kateri what I've now done.

All those men will never get to see their children. Those women—

Kateri grabs a bowl, scoops out some melting ice cream, plumps it into the bowl in heaps, and sticks two spoons in it.

"It's soupy," I mumble.

"Rich-people problems." Kateri laughs through her tears. "And that's why I stole fudge. It's the only ice cream we both can agree on, and it's still good liquid, solid, cold, or hot."

"Forget ice cream. I wanna punch something." I get up.

Kateri leans over, slides a metal bat out of her supply bag, and sets out some clay figures badly painted to look like soldiers. She's the worst artist in the world. "Thought you might need a venting outlet. That's why I'm late. Took forever to paint these."

"Head General?" I scoop up the middle one. Its left eye is gouged out.

"Does it look like him?" She grins craftily. "Huh. Didn't notice."

"You didn't have to show up, Kit." I hug her close. "Thank you."

Kateri blows my bangs out of my face and laces our fingers. "Real friends always show up."

CHAPTER 18

COA RANGECROFT

AN HOUR BEFORE THE GREAT HUNT

The Great Hunt starts in sixty minutes. I need to report to the Trenches soon.

The carnage men slapped a book on each barrack table and offered everyone two choices: examine the book of African island plants and animals translated to English—or enjoy a warm final meal in the canteens.

Everyone else chose a fine canteen breakfast. A mockery, but a hearty meal of promised pork knuckle, blood sausage, and boiled potatoes.

I memorize as many pages as I can, inspecting every photo and exploring every word in the glossary.

Suddenly, a sound on my right makes me jump.

Hazen Creed has entered the slum barracks, and he sends me a conspiratorial smile. "Sleep well?" His sea-green eyes search mine for any sign of tears.

"Like a baby." I avoid stretching my bruised spine, windpipe, and chest.

Hazen's cautious. "Are you hiding another pack of rust?"

"You'd be sightless by now if I was." I tuck the book out of his view under a bunk, and I unwrap a package of bitter enhanced beef. It's six hundred calories packed with extra protein, part of my hidden emergency stash acquired over four years. I bite through it now. "Are you prepared?"

All I need is to win the Great Hunt and get to one of the secured hideouts. Even if it kills Hazen.

"I feel alive." Hazen admits it breezily. As if unconcerned with the knowledge that he's going to be taken through the Trenches to be hunted in twenty minutes. "I plan to make Arctic history." Hazen simply smirks.

As if he knows something I don't. Of course, he's keeping his information close to the vest, which is intelligent, but it signals to me he has an advantage I don't know about.

Still. I owe him something.

"Thank you for taking care of that . . . tourist. I appreciate it. Profoundly."

I've cheated death too many times as it is. Now I'm heartbroken from footage of Mikoš Volkov's murder.

It's all over the military base.

"What tourist?" Hazen winks, his natural charm abundant. "As far as I'm concerned, this is the first time we've met since the weigh-ins."

"Perfect." My heart lifts a little. In the ramshackle canteens, I know groups are forming; alliances are already happening. This could be my first win, and I figure we ought to be allies like Hazen offered.

I'm in no position to refuse anyone at this point.

Right now, Hazen and I don't pretend that we won't take advantage of each other. We both will use each other like our lives depend on it, which is why I'm glad neither of us has to say it.

I try to calculate everything myself. "There's seventy-five victims, only fifteen snipers. Right?" I fight not to sound frantic for a plan, gnawing through a pack of thickened beef strips. "We outnumber 'em."

"Do you know what snipers are?" Hazen's brow rises.

"Of course," I respond. "They're sharpshooters."

He sounds slightly amused. "*Sharpshooters* is what women and kids call them." It's as if it reminds him of what I am—only a woman. "Foreign politicians use the term *sharpshooter* as a gentler word to not scare civilians. The Arctic reality is grislier."

"Military men, trained soldiers, whichever," I insist, "*we* outnumber *them*. Right?"

The official snipers will be presented in the Great Hunt soon. They'll know my face; examine every ounce of baby fat in my body, every vulnerability in my movements, every hesitant pattern in my steps; and take note of my shriveled feet. I can't take them on without a plan. After years bent over sugarcane, I'm not the fastest runner, and I need to be prepared.

Hazen splashes his jaw with water from the rusted sink. "You think we outnumber them?"

"Don't we? Seventy-five against fifteen provides *us* the upper hand—"

"Quick question—do you know what a magazine is?" He cuts me off before I can respond. His eyes are hard. "Cartridge duplicates? Ammunition? Boresights? Have you seen a TEV2 distance rifle clear a killing field? Heard a high-capacity magazine with extended artillery modifications wipe out a mass of bodies during a military execution?"

I stop eating. "Killing field?"

He shuts his sea-green eyes, as if the question tells him everything he needs to know. "Right. American."

"No," I grit. "Hallowell."

"Same difference." Hazen points his chin at the guards stationed outside the barracks. "You don't even know what a cartridge duplicate is. Count how many guards there are."

I lift my chin and show off my ability to count. "Seven . . . eight . . . nine—"

"By the time you took a breath and started, if an Allied Force sniper lurked nearby, all of them would already have been vaporized."

"*Vaporized?*" I gape. Shock zips through my spine.

"At his slowest. Whatever you *think* you know about Allied Force technology, you understand nothing." Hazen provides brief examples. I remember the tourist that said, *I forget you primitive savages are at least a hundred years behind us.* "The Allied Force has antinuclear weapons capable of turning nuclear missiles into mere oxygen—American nuclear weapons mean absolutely nothing. Bullets are outdated by a hundred years—half of your people don't even know the difference between a bullet and a cartridge. But thankfully, this is a vintage island, which means antique firearms."

Hazen exhales.

"These men want the glory of hunting foreign enemies down themselves with rifle relics. Which is why the Great Hunt is an *old* tradition."

I get it—it's why it takes place in an old-fashioned forced-labor camp.

Hazen spreads creamy white shaving cream over his facial hair. It smells like cologne. "This is how the Hunt will operate, *if we're lucky.* Most likely, a sniper will want to make a spectacle for the audience, give young males and recruits something to copy. Kids will grow up wanting to be *that* sniper, not us. They only want our remnants." He lays it out. "The typical sniper will spare half of his future casualties in the first nights, then spend the rest of the days in his own style picking the rest off. At no point will he ever need further ammunition."

They have enough bullets for all of us, hundreds of times over.

I mutter, defeated, "They could plot to kill us all at once at the shoreline if they want." My throat squeezes so tight it hurts. I fight not to cry. But the defeat of that escape attempt broke my spirit. *I will fail everyone. Evelie. Hucket. Rawley. Buckthorne. Rabbit.*

I gather myself.

"Alliances are everything," Hazen replies. He scrapes his straight razor across his masculine, hairy jaw until it's clean shaven. "But we can't all kiss and hold hands with each other either. Some of us need to die." His sharp eyes scan the remaining victims devouring the feast in the nearest canteen. A curl of his golden hair falls in front of his hardened eyes. "Blacktail bucks are the youngest snipers, the most eager to prove themselves to our countrymen."

Hazen's eyes slide down my shivery body.

"They're going to come after you first."

"A woman." I set aside my meat strips.

As soon as I put them down, Hazen helps himself to my beef pack without asking, stealing a healthy bite where my saliva lingers. "Precisely. Experienced snipers will always get first selections—brawny, formidable men. By the time there's any leftovers, the blacktails will want to make a vivid, historic spectacle of their own for fans to gawk at." He chews.

"If there are any large laborers left, they might prove difficult for any inexperienced marksmen and could overpower them, smearing a permanent stain on their family name. Blacktails will save them for last, when they're more sure of themselves. Often the fifth day. But the weak die first—"

"I'm not weak."

"You are weak—in their eyes. But I heard you shot lightning at the enforcers."

He knows. The acidity of the beef spreads like a toxin over my tongue.

"Rumors. Lies. A distant dry lightning struck last night."

"Your nostrils smoked during the weigh-ins."

"You hallucinated. There was no smoke."

"Apoye éyeń emā—tutum ékèni," Hazen says in a language that sounds Makarian to me, as if I'm supposed to respond back in the same dialect or even understand what he said.

"I'm not Kōn."

"My mistake." He rinses his tense jaw. But he's subtly made it clear—*that* is why he singled me out, why he risked his life to take the stage to prevent my death. He sensed my advantage and capacity as a fireborn. Whether I admit it to him or not, it's clear he's convinced.

Hazen moves on. "Do the words *extractors, coverts, blood-saws,* or *triggers* mean anything to you?" He assesses my eyes.

"What are bloodsaws?"

"Beasts on the island that will drain you of every ounce of blood. Corpses are unrecognizable after."

I reach for the book. "You mean *afeni?*"

"*Bloodsaws* is what we call them. The only defense—"

"Is to mask your scent with their slime. They'll believe you're one of them," I supply swiftly. Eager to prove myself.

"Extractors must be another type of Makarian beast. I can figure them out—"

"Extractors aren't beasts. Not in that regard. Extractors are snipers that will venture out to retrieve fallen or injured snipers." He explains the next set. "Coverts are snipers that will never leave their hideouts and will still-hunt. Be prepared. Still-hunts aren't banned this season—they are *rampantly* encouraged after that Volkov revolt," he warns.

"Still-hunt?"

"Noiselessly stalking your prey—or stealth killing."

"Understood."

Stealth killing. I save that in my mind for later. Maybe I can ambush a sniper.

But Hazen disabuses me of that idea. "Covert snipers are stealth snipers that camouflage themselves and wait motionlessly for you to enter their scope, and then shoot. They will keep the skinning traditions alive—they will skin you like exotic game. *That* is what we are to them. Their exotic targets. Wild game. You cannot outmaneuver them."

A chunk of beef sticks in my throat.

Hazen gnaws through more of my protein beef, washing it down with my bottle of water.

"Extractors will move all over the terrain, and your eye is never sharper than theirs. Your aim is never more precise. Your cause is never greater than their own."

"Because they are the avengers of fallen snipers." I nearly vomit. "On a mission."

"Exactly. Extractors devoutly believe in *brotherhood* with fellow snipers." Hazen grinds his teeth. "They are the die-hard snipers."

The worst kind then. The ones who won't quit, bleeding to death or not.

I just need to avoid them at all costs. But . . . "How many types of snipers are there?"

"Varies. The main ones are coverts, extractors, blacktails, poachers, and trappers."

"Poachers are snipers that will poach us," I say, catching on. But Hazen shakes his head, irritated, like I'm not indoctrinated well enough in Allied Force culture for this threat ahead.

Hazen Creed dries his damp jaw. "Poachers are snipers that *poach* other snipers' prey. The most hated snipers. Instead of one predator on a target, there will be two in competition to kill you." He continues, "Trapper snipers are snare experts, specialized in rigged deadfalls and trip wires."

"Trip wires?"

"Traps with signature flairs. Unique inventions designed for iconic kills. You trigger one—"

"You're dead."

"Worse."

Emotion stabs my chest. "None of this is possible to survive."

The Great Hunt can't—

The bronze barrack doors slide open, and it's the sergeant—what did Hazen call him? *Arken. The butcher.*

Hazen delivers a brutal reminder. "Welcome to the Allied Force. Nothing is ever fair, only earned. Glory before fear."

It hits me. Hazen Creed knows *all* of this for a reason. He's ex-military.

It's in his posture, his stance, how he expertly pinned and tied me. Even the precise way he shaved. His skill with a blade. His mysterious connection to the Hunt—he's military affiliated.

CHAPTER 19

IFE STØRMBANE

ONE HOUR BEFORE THE GREAT HUNT

I sit for another breakfast with Vørian and Thorsten. Trying to keep my vomit in my stomach. Trying.

I squirm. As if we're each under interrogation, tension rises as Head General Størmbane enters the breakfast cage. "Everyone, stand."

Without Maximus here, the three of us stand in anxiety. Thorsten salutes the leader of the Arctic, but he's immediately ignored.

Victory, Thorsten signs, but Head General strides right past him.

"Executions of the surviving rebels are tonight." Head General trains his marred eye on me. He's heard of my meltdown. His calloused hands are the size of bear paws as he reaches for his steak knife. "I trust you will each have decorum. I will hear of nothing else."

"Yes, Vikęm."

"Yes, Viker."

"Vørian, you will not order executions without explicit authorization. Escapees are for soldiers to hunt down themselves—this is Kømmand Sergeant Arcus's island. He should never inform me otherwise. Understood?"

"Yes, Vikęm."

"Ikä. You will control your emotions in public. I will not tolerate any other behavior."

"Yes, Viker." I nod, staring at my feet. "I apologize. It will never happen again."

"To ensure that it doesn't, you will commit your first set of bear killings. You will meet with Maximus as soon as we return to the Kilrød."

I freeze. A killing set will alter the core of who I am, but I quickly nod.

"Yes. Of course." I don't even drink animal milk, let alone taste their flesh, but there is absolutely no other response to his brutal command than absolute agreement. Even if the command is to hunt big game in a ritual where I'm expected to eat the bear's raw heart right there in the field.

We're permitted to sit.

As the tension subsides, Vørian spits, "I need to be seated *closer* on the island. I'm tired of being cased behind VIP glass like a mud hound." He tears a lynx foot with his canines. "Vraničar is finally in a Hunt, and the balconies are too far."

"We're in the perfect center," Maximus responds, entering the cage and saluting the rest of us. His famous rifle club uniform is fresh. "Victory to the Allied Force."

Head General responds, "Victory, Maximus Barringęr."

As always, Head General Barringęr Størmbane acknowledges his favorite son. His perfect successor. To the extent that he will at times refer to him as Maximus Barringęr to show pride. As if Maximus is Barringęr himself.

"Center?" Vørian grimaces, voice deepened. "I need to see them ripping each other's dirty throats out up close. Hot blood on my skin, like on a real hunt." His brand-new trophies of polar bears, dark-spotted anacondas, and panthers glint behind him.

Maximus kisses my fingers. His lips are warm. "Ife chose an advantageous viewing location." His resolute voice leaves no room for protest. That's Maximus's special ability. When he smiles, it's disarming. You forget he shut down your idea permanently. "You'll love it when you see it, Vørian."

"You'll see tons of blood," I promise tensely.

"Yes, on a *screen*." Vørian rolls his ice-green eyes. He jams his thumbs between his molars. "I wanted it in my *teeth*. There's no point otherwise—the war ended before I could even see anything."

That triggers me. I feel the uncontrollable urge to snatch him and describe *exactly* what war with the Allied Force is like—*really* like—to show him the reality of what he worships. But all he demands is executions. There's no empathy left in him. "Can I be honest? Your breathing was my priority, Vørian. We love you very much, and we only want what's best for you."

Vørian snarls, "Medics are filthy liars. My oxygen rates met regulation."

Medics don't lie. Välliance, the giant megacorporation of health, nutrition, fitness, and hospitals, boasts the best medics in the world.

I've seen Vørian heaving for breath, gasping for his life, determined to beat Maximus's institute sprinting record at all costs. Horrifically, one morning, his institute found him collapsed. Vørian refused medical attention, glowering at Maximus's gold statue gleaming across the track. A paean to his undefeated record.

For Maximus, unbeatable athleticism comes easily. He's just one of those born exceptional.

Vørian narrows his eyes. "Maximus forced Kømmand Sergeant Arcus to deny me access to the Reintęk Beer Hall on Traeger Island. Vikęm, when can I enter?"

Vørian fully believes adult beer halls are where all the best hunts happen. The kills too grisly to show wider audiences, the violence more intense than at nationalist fitness clubs. Vørian refuses to believe people just fight, drink, feel each other up, and dance terribly for *fun*. These military men haven't been around women in months, some of them years. Decades. They forget how to behave. Hungry to release their carnal instincts.

Men around Vørian don't dance or sing. Most have already destroyed a majority of their tear glands by the age of twelve. It's unfathomable to any of them to indulge in feminine activities.

But once these men see nonmilitary men with women on their arms, kisses on their cheeks, they attempt to dance. A mating ritual that Vørian can't comprehend.

"I'm ready." Vørian lifts his chin as if it ages him ten years. "I want to attend."

"You're too young, Vørian," Maximus dismisses. "Drunk adults are not for children—"

"Good. I'm not a child." Vørian meets his eye.

"Of course, shooter." Maximus smiles, chuckles. "But if you have to ask for permission, you're still underage."

"Your 'wife' barely looks older than me."

I freeze. None of them know the truth—I am the bone king's youngest granddaughter. Not the rain king's oldest granddaughter. I turned sixteen recently.

Vørian leans forward. "I'm a year from becoming a

military adult, if you forgot. I'll rip through a match with you. Now." Vørian stands.

He means a killing set, in which men compete shot for shot in extreme big-game hunting against scientifically enhanced apex predators.

Vørian holds Maximus's eyes. "Bet I'll bring down a red-fanged bear. You can even set it to a bite force of three thousand psi. Max speed of sixty-five miles per hour. No ammunition."

"Long range? You don't have better aim." Maximus smiles softly at Vørian, as if he's being adorable. "At your age, I could hunt two mountain hypertigers faster than you could lace those nice boots, Trigger."

"Don't need better aim. First kill wins." Vørian's mouth actually forms a rare smile. "You don't even hunt anymore."

Suddenly, he scowls at his own words, glowering at me in muted rage. Vørian acts like I changed Maximus's nature since *I* don't eat meat, and I've seen enough kills. But Maximus stopped eating meat near me to respect my diet, and Vørian acts like I defiled his whole bloodline.

Altered Maximus's brain chemistry.

To Vørian, real men never convert for other people. Meanwhile, Maximus still eats *pounds* of meat per day, more than most men, but Vørian wouldn't understand normal consideration.

"We can hunt now and still be on time for the Great Hunt," Vørian offers. There's almost hope in his eyes, hope that his older brother will spend time with him. Even if Vørian can't stand to admit it, he misses living with Maximus. During Vørian's military training, he lives on Mount Ivkør—*Mount Thrasher*—where all military initiates live until graduation.

Head General Størmbane lives in the most militarized city in the world—Warholm. That is where Vørian's forced to live when he's not on Mount Ivkør.

Maximus, Thorsten, and I moved out of Warholm. We live in Kilgrad, where lush green pastures are more abundant and summer temperatures reach thirty-two degrees Fahrenheit, which is considered tropical in the north polar region.

Vørian's eyes shine with admiration whenever Maximus attends his hunting sports or takes Vørian and Thorsten on his expeditions.

Maximus never misses a birthday and personally cooks their favorite meals. He remembers every drink and recipe of their mother's and replicates them for his brothers. I cook for them the most, but it's special when Maximus prepares their meal.

Each year, Maximus is the first one there at Vørian's award ceremonies, smiling with pride at him.

Maximus has a way of making you feel how much you're loved.

But Maximus rises now. "Some other time, Vørian. Ife and I have international diplomats arriving soon. Besides, hunting animals isn't half as impressive we think it is." He kisses my temple.

Vørian's eyes fill with animosity.

"Are you being serious?"

"Deadly serious. Tonight is an important opportunity to examine the multinational guests—"

Vørian snaps forward. His fists tight. Nose pinched.

"Those ingloriöts aren't coming under our roof. You should've never invited them." Vørian's ice-green eyes become colder than his silver-blond hair. "Executing them is the only way to ensure the future of the Allied Force—"

Maximus reprimands him. "Watch your language, Vørian."

Vørian's fist slams against the table. Clattering the silverware, shaking the plates.

"Maximus—did you suddenly forget what contributions to history *you* made? How many are dead from *your sacrifice* to our country?" Vørian seethes. "Did you forget *no nation* helped the Allied Force when we nearly went extinct? Name one continent that provided aid. You can't. All these weak, lazy slęv—"

Slęvks? I gasp.

"Vørian, watch yourself." Maximus's jaw becomes florid with blood. "You are in my wife's presence. You will not disrespect foreigners in front of her."

"*I* am in your *wife's* presence? She's in *mine*."

"Stand down."

But Vørian stands and launches into one of his birthright tirades. It's an unholy experience to witness; I can't even gaze directly at him for long. It's as if he's possessed by hatred. Uncontrollable fury that makes him spit and froth at the mouth.

"You could *never* do what Father did, and what I will do in the future," Vørian tells Maximus. He glares at me for a blazing second, then looks accusingly back at his brother. "How can *you* lead us to the Victory Year? You're too deep inside diplomatic trash to *obliterate*—"

"Stand down. Final warning."

Vørian's eyes are monstrous.

"I will plunge the earth into darkness, soaking it in their blood. I will steep their crops with their lineages' blood and drain every last empire left of filthy foreign life. Suffering will infect their lungs, and they will plead on their knees to our grand soldiers, but I will *drench*—"

"Enough," Head General Størmbane interrupts this time. "Stand down, Vørian. You were given a direct order from a superior."

Maximus warns his brother, "Do not ever disregard my orders again; I will suspend you from the youth league in Warholm. Every last rifle club in the Kilrød. Do you understand?"

Vørian grunts. "Understood."

But I catch Barringer's eyes examining Vørian, considering his potential. Someone who vowed to never get married. Someone who swore to never corrupt his destiny with distraction. A boy who was shipped away to the North Leopold Institute well before his counterparts, where war criminals raised him.

Right now, Head General is gazing at someone in his bloodline who will, at last, commit any atrocity to keep the Allied Force in power. Head General has had eleven sons—only three are left.

Out of all eleven, the only one he's ever regarded with reverence is Maximus. His equal.

Vørian is a son that is far less impressive than Maximus, but he has twice as much passion for his homeland.

He is willing to kill millions of people. A necessary commitment in Head General's view.

But passion alone can't lead a nation. Maximus performs his duty better than any son with heart. Any man with devotion. Maximus is extraordinary—knife sharp. Efficient.

Like his forefathers, Head General Størmbane could've let himself be addressed as High Kømmander Størmbane. Instead, Barringer understood the value of symbolism. Of his being seen as the everyman.

The man who represents every Arctic man.

Head General Størmbane is the dominant man every man *thinks* he is.

However, Maximus is unmatchable. The superior Arctic man.

The overly accomplished Allied Force man every man aspires to *become*.

Yet Vørian Størmbane is the new generation. The brutal Arctic inheritor.

He will complete their global objective. He will bring the Victory Year and inherit the earth. The final end of the North Transatlantic Empire, the rest of Makari, and Alvorada, to secure permanent victory for the Allied Force. My pulse pounds in my throat.

I see the totalitarian this boy's rapidly becoming. The war criminal militarist.

Even more painful, Maximus claims Vørian used to be sweet, kind, like Thorsten. Vørian blushed at girls from Former Asia; he was infatuated with their beautiful, distinct features. Before he was raised by the military and indoctrinated.

Then he changed.

He swore to kill every last foreigner left alive.

CHAPTER 20

FIFTEEN MINUTES BEFORE

THE GREAT HUNT DEPARTURE

We're escorted to the Trenches. My blood freezes.

I've walked through the Trenches myself before—they're a deep, charred set of dirt troughs for victims to march through as onlookers gaze down at us. Acrid odors clog your lungs; it suffocates you with the bodies of past victims' families.

If I don't survive the Great Hunt, my five siblings will be buried here.

Above us, callous snipers wear the blood of the slain Mikoš Volkov. His blood is splattered across their faces and eyes, smeared down their uniforms. They dump his lifeless body into the trough.

"Don't show fear," Hazen Creed warns me. He strides over the bullet-filled body. "They sense it."

The revolts stopped nothing. The inevitable is coming in five minutes.

Maybe it wasn't supposed to stop anything. Maybe it was meant to be a symbol.

Symbol or not, laborers are forced to cheer for snipers and hail them with rice upon their arrival to the Trenches. Each grain will be handpicked off the dirt afterward and sent to the canteens for the laborers' dinner.

Right now, proud spectators fill the fields, and a few spit on the marching participators.

Hazen runs a hand through his tousled blond waves. He's calm and prepared. *What does he have planned? How rigged is the Great Hunt?*

A sudden shriek rips through the air. It steals away my thoughts.

Someone slashes through the laborers and splashy vacationers, and he vaults straight down to me. I'm almost too slow to react. The hairs on my skin rise.

The head sniper snorts his sour breath down at my face.

"Where's your lightning strike the enforcers claimed?"

I don't risk a response in front of my competitors.

A bull-necked man was chosen this year as the head sniper—a seasoned marksman. He stands with scarred cheekbones, thick features, dark hair—and his ammunition is already packed in the bandolier strapped across his bison-like body.

My eyes land on his tactical gear—spattered the most heavily with Mikoš Volkov's blood.

His breath's lethal.

Suddenly, he grasps me, demanding an answer. Violently, he sinks his heavy fingers into my skin until it hurts. If I didn't want to save my fire, even the knowledge of it, I'd scorch his face. Show him *exactly* where my lightning is.

He thrusts a hefty stack of vintage vikęs in my free hand.

"Here's your bet winnings if you survive the first night. If there's smoke inside of you—I suggest you use it."

His smirk is sickening, as if I'm an easy pelt. The sniper loyalists above us love his bulky look. Eager teenagers wear paramilitary uniforms bought at the ration stations in support, bandoliers like his clipped across their own chests.

Meanwhile, this man gazes down at my new uniform. My cold black utility shirt, dark-green camouflage trousers, calf-length black terrain boots. It all feels alien on my body.

Above us, the young men practically salivate over his cruelty.

But I clench my jaw so hard my teeth could shatter. *No response. No response. No response.*

He doesn't deserve a word. He's wildly popular, apparently, but the fanfare isn't as heartfelt as when they roared for Maximus Størmbane or Hazen Creed, and it visibly bothers him. He cuts glances up at the vacationers and across the massive crowds. Eyes them all.

Dominant dark-brown eyes glower down at me, suddenly, as if I'm the reason this cold-blooded continent prefers better-looking men and more marketable participators. He behaves as if I'm insulting him by denying him a response or sufficient fear. I'm sure it's an offense too great for him to bear from a woman in public, much less a half-starved, 120-pound girl, but he laughs it off. A bitter, snapped-off chuckle.

"She's afraid." His eyes glint with hostility.

Real slow, Hazen shoulders past me.

"Afraid of you? Didn't think that was possible." He steps in, flashing a smile with his dazzlingly bright white teeth. *He's risking increasing his visibility—what is he doing?* "Kaiser Arcus. Always good to see you visit your brother, Kømmand Sergeant Arcus, but I must confess, I didn't recognize you outside of your father's shadow." He forcibly shakes Kaiser's hand. "You're much smaller than I remember him being."

Kaiser snarls, as if without the cameras, he'd strangle Hazen for that. "Are you trying to be funny, son? My father is—"

"Was. Your father is dead, or I would've greeted him in the Great Hunt instead of you." Hazen's six-foot-two frame is fearsome. Evenly matched with Kaiser's height. "If I remember correctly, Killian Arcus died of natural causes . . . Strangulation is very natural these days, I hear."

He's dead? Killian Arcus was the man every field-worker feared. The apprehensive dread and whispers were inescapable whenever it was Great Hunt season. His name sank abject fear into everyone. Once you went into the Hunt with him—you never returned.

Not unless he wanted to keep a witness or two alive to inform the rest of the laborers of their impending extinction. He was seventy, which is extremely rare for the Allied Force, visibly healthy, still sharp sighted. *He's gone?*

What will that mean for us—a higher survival rate? Will I last past the first night now?

A ferocious punch of color coats Kaiser's veined neck, and his dark eyes narrow. Slaughterous. "Watch what you're implying, boy. My father"—he spits on Hazen's polished boots, a phlegm of bitter yellow—"is a legend, alive or dead. He would've never stood near a traitor like you."

"And yet, here you are a foot away from me, Kaiser. Are you, then, the least impressive Arcus with your father and brother?" A flash of violence sparks in Hazen's gaze.

Kaiser grunts. "You're a low excuse for a man, traitor trash that was woman raised. Bred and reared by a wench. No one will mourn you when the time comes." Kaiser turns to the jammed audience over our heads. "He is filth that colluded with the foreigners to degrade our patriots!"

A Great Hunt is meant to be an act of humiliating terrorism *against* the foreigners only. A sacred tradition after every targeted country's dismal defeat.

But a silence stretches, a few coughs rattle, and some iced drinks tinkle. It's resoundingly quiet. The dirt-packed Trench walls don't even carry his thunderous voice. The outrage Kaiser expected is missing, and it's clear these vacationers prefer a more violent entertainment.

The silence is so overwhelming I almost laugh.

"Arcus, I apologize if I offended in any way." Hazen steps farther forward, his voice facetiously earnest. His face is almost obscenely good looking in comparison to Kaiser's. A lock of gorgeous dark-blond hair curls against his brow. "We all know how deeply proud your father would be that you couldn't think of anything original to contribute to Arctic history other than to steal his fame by inserting yourself in *his* Great Hunt. But think of it this way—you'll never need to introduce yourself, because your father did all the grunt work. His everlasting gift to his son, who couldn't even wait for him to retire." His smirk darkens. *I know what you did to him.*

"Don't you dare speak another accusation to me." Kaiser cuts the distance between them until they're almost nose to nose. "You will be annihilated. You will be obliterated from the earth. You will become waste for the cretins of the island. I'm warning you."

He fumes.

Kømmand Sergeant Arcus, standing nearby, smirks now. As if conspiring with Hazen Creed.

It clicks together.

The sergeant is using Hazen, and *that* is why Hazen was included in the Hunt.

But what does Hazen get in return? Why did they slander *Hazen* as a traitor?

Hazen wraps amusement around his face. "I'm dying of thirst for this death combat then." He refuses to back down. "I don't fear a man who killed his father."

Now, the crowd is riled, uproarious, riveted: Hazen's declared his accusation—out loud. The men's voices are nearly drowned out by the cacophony of explosive chaos. Kaiser's eyes are slit.

"The Hunt is going to begin in sixty seconds. When it starts, I'm coming for you first, miscreant. I won't miss."

"Don't miss. You'll humiliate yourself twice." Hazen smirks wider.

Kaiser's voice is a low threat, too hushed for the onlookers to pick up, but I hear everything. His voice is full of loathing, eyes full of caustic venom. "I will never be humiliated by a traitor. You threw away your military future for my useless, feeble sister, and it will cost you both."

"We'll see which one of us dies out there." Hazen leans toward him in return and whispers in his ear. "Are you prepared to meet the monster my mother created? I won't need to run from any of her brothers."

"There's nothing to meet."

"Famous last words."

A chant for Hazen Creed swells already, wildly, instead of the Arcus name.

The soldiers' boots squelch over the mud as they lean over the Trenches to gaze down at Hazen. I stand taller in preparation. *Thirty seconds.*

Kømmand Sergeant Arcus nods at Hazen, as if they both

understand Kaiser's fuse, exactly how to manipulate his emotions and distract him.

Meanwhile, Kaiser growls something menacing too low under his breath for me to catch. But Hazen responds, "I look forward to it. You'll reunite with your father soon enough."

"My father should've killed you as a newborn welp. The very second my ingrate sister birthed you."

"Yet here I am. Ready to kill you instead."

It would be undisciplined for Kaiser Arcus to kill him here and now. He must reserve it for the Hunt. At this rate, it's going to be the most anticipated Great Hunt event the labor camp's ever seen, and the crowd doesn't even know that Hazen is being sent into the Great Hunt to kill his uncle.

But as Hazen locks gazes with a fragile woman in the crowds, everything becomes clear. He betrayed his stoic, rugged manhood—his entire military future—over a woman.

PART TWO:
THE MANHUNT

CHAPTER 21

Rowboats carry us toward the island. Murderous tropical downpours burst from the skies—like primal warfare.

Ferocious rain pounds against our skin.

Ear-shattering prehistoric screeches detonate from all directions. Antagonistic spirits circle the rowboats with disgust. Sulfur soaks into our boots.

Ancient seawater clambers onboard. My strategy is to stick to Hazen Creed like wax. *I am going to win the Great Hunt. I am going to win.*

The roughly fifty barrack laborers that revolted—and were executed mercilessly—are now replaced as easily as exchanging cloth in the Arctic. Grief swells in my chest—some of the barrack girls *slept* next to me, washed their weathered hair behind me in the metal showers. Several of them chose execution instead of the terror of the Great Hunt.

Girls with no mothers left. No children. No other family. All alone.

Never give up. Right now, my teeth grate together. I

need an ally I can kill if I must—and now more than ever, I won't choose my own barrack mates. I need an ally I can manipulate.

Use as a human shield.

Hazen nods at me from across the hazardous waters. Focused.

He's almost guaranteed to be safe for the first night. The highly anticipated climax will be him against Kaiser. It would be anticlimactic to kill Hazen in the beginning, but silver hovercraft drone cameras still track Hazen, circling him now like vultures, warring with the exotic birds that send themselves, *intentionally*, into the hovercrafts' engines to annihilate themselves. *What in the hell?*

I've never seen that before. I duck from shrapnel when the engines explode. Fragments of electronic parts land everywhere.

I can feel the island breathe. Hiss. Seethe. *You are not welcome. Turn back.*

Despite the birds' attacks, the remaining cameras still glide over Hazen. He's the participator with the highest entertainment value. He'll make it to the sixth day with Kømmand Sergeant Arcus's instructions. Maybe the seventh.

Kømmand Sergeant Arcus *has* to have given him instructions, special advantages, warnings about locations. Anything.

Problem is, right now, a drowning rain drenches our clothes, blisters down our limbs. Hazen's on the other side of the cracked, splintered set of rowboats they chained us to. He's six boats away on my right. *Who picked this island?*

I've seen Great Hunt survivors return, shell shocked, speechless, but they ain't *never* mentioned flesh-eating waters, ritualistic beasts.

This is entirely new, unknown territory.

I search Hazen's face. He's inscrutable. Likely thinking of how to kill his own uncle, Kaiser. But I'm choked with fear.

There are four victims on each boat. Nineteen rowboats are chained together, which makes about seventy-five competitors by my frantic count. Hazen's the only ally I've made.

I stay alert.

But without hesitation, a destructive flock of self-sacrificing island birds launches itself into the auxiliary drones. *Again.* A final threat.

However, more silver drones loom on the horizon. The Allied Force is determined to record the Great Hunt for the tourists sitting in the canteens and harassing laborers in the barracks. They always set up screens to watch.

The prehistoric island snarls, warning us not to enter. That it's weaponized.

Once it becomes clear the intruders will not heed its warnings, the horrors begin.

Deadly birds dive from the sky.

A victim writhes, convulsing, and I almost shriek as an army of sharp-beaked creatures bombards him and the others, helpless in their rowboat. Birds of prey drive themselves out of the grim sky to devour them all. Skin, polished boots, belts—everything.

"Hell! What the hell!" I leap back, wishing I could leap out of the accursed rowboat. But we're all chained.

Then—the screams grow louder.

CHAPTER 22

My vocal cords strain as I shriek.

Another rowboat is brutally invaded by electric eels. Laborers gurgle for help as the rowboats sink so rapidly that not even our cries of shock can outpace their quick submergence into rimy waters. Gone in a blink.

Only a spatter of bubbles is left of them on the roiling sea. Now, mass panic explodes.

Desperate, I thrash against my chains, fighting for my life. Hollering! But it's useless. Our steel chains are bolted inescapably into our scratched rowboats. *Please. Please. Those people are gone. Gone.*

But we still ceaselessly sail forward into pure-white mist. Exposed.

Wrathful vapors of milky tropical fog snatch our shirts, rip at our pants, tear at our boots. As if trying to wrench us back from the island themselves. Violently furious that we dare encroach on its living land. Its primordial seas that existed before humanity.

Mosquitoes lash at our shins, shred at our jaws, our eyes.

Right now, an insidious, cold feeling washes down my body. *We are not leaving this island alive.*

It becomes clear. None of us are leaving alive.

Even darker, I have a sense that we're being watched. Not just by cameras. It feels like *thousands* of invisible pairs of dilated eyes. All of them blink at once. Then disperse. An involuntary shiver sprints down my sweaty spine.

We enter a wall of unbreathable heat.

The rowboats are motorized at the bottoms. Electric chains hum around our wrists. *"One hundred ninety seconds,"* a set of crackled speakers announces above our heads. Hover drones hide in the palm trees, fleeing the birds.

"Locate shelter. Snipers will begin shooting in one hundred eighty seconds. Locate shelter."

What? Rapid water sloshes at our boots, waves lapping greedily to get inside. Voracious for flesh.

Brightly scaled fish leap to get away from the desolate, remote island. Exotic creatures attack over our heads. Squawking and shrieking for us to flee back. Away from the island.

As if pitying us for what the island will do.

CHAPTER 23

IFE STØRMBANE

"Are you *attempting* to ruin every last aspect of my career?" Valeska demands as she barges into my suite. "My most prominent client cannot *shirk* mandatory appearances."

I gasp. Speechless.

A group of tourist men chased me down, demanding squeezes, kisses, holographs, and autographs, and it's *my* fault?

"None of them were going to abduct you. You're married to a Størmbane," Valeska snaps. "You *lure* these men with your tiny dresses, flirtatious smiles, kittenish dances, then get scared when weak men approach."

These were *not* weak men. These were men attempting to imitate Maximus Størmbane. They demand his life. His military career. His status.

His woman.

Entitled to his entire being. A parasocial obsession.

In the homeland, Allied Force men *despise* me. Their

hateful glares are inescapable. Their grunts of disdain are vitriolic. Each time I enter a room, their disgust at foreigners is blatant. Their unfathomable hatred is unmistakable.

I never thought I'd prefer their cold hatred. There, at least I know where I stand with the men.

But now I stammer. Smear away my tears. "But aren't Arctic men always disciplined? They can't control themselves?"

"*Military men* are disciplined. That is why military service is necessary." Valeska glowers. "This is exactly why men shouldn't be permitted to abstain from military training. Without duty and structure, of course cheap exotic thrills captivate them. Their mind is unrestricted. But *you as a woman*—"

My main guard, as always, interrupts her.

Pacer Vanmark.

"Let's end this. A woman is not responsible for the actions of men. Men are not accountable for the behavior of women. Her fame is not her fault. A small dress is not an invitation. These men were already dealt with by the sniper general himself. Are we good to leave?"

Pacer Vanmark's an elite operative of the Allied Force, ever adding to his myriad list of duties. He's the only guard I trust.

"Are you better now?" he asks me, specifically.

I nod.

"Crowds always upset you. Are you *certain* you're well?"

"My debut celebration was perfect." I leave out the aftermath: vomiting, crying, hyperventilating. "Crowds don't panic me anymore."

My skin's still raw from gripping myself, petrified of so many real faces. All at once in front of me. *Get it together, Ife.*

Pacer's own skin is suntanned today, a healthy tone,

making his blue eyes stand out more. Even Pacer's dark-blond hair is bronzer, golden strands of it falling in his good-looking face, which is perfect for ritzy tourists. His jaw is broad, and he's smiling with his sharp mouth.

"Mistress Van Valken should apologize. She canceled nap time." Pacer winks. He's handsome in an all-black polished uniform; it must be for the Hunt.

I roll my eyes and hurl a pillow at him, forgetting momentarily we're not alone. Safe.

He catches it and tosses it aside.

"I feel terrible, Pacer." I pout. "The only difference between you and a real vacationer is your uniform. You must be so jealous that our vacation is your work hours."

Pacer smirks. "At least I don't need a professional nursemaid." I hate that my heart feels lighter, but I can't help it. He makes things *bearable* around here, even when he's teasing me. Pacer leans toward me now.

Somehow, his voice always sounds conspiratorial, as if he's secretly on your side. He grips both sides of my mattress and comes close. Nose to nose.

I inhale his minty breath.

"Very strange, my ikä," he muses as he pretends to examine my sleep marks. "You survived a riot, not being buried under mountains of silk and pillows. Are pigs flying outside? Should I harpoon them down for everyone's safety?"

My lips open. It takes everything in me not to claw his eyes out.

"The pigs miss you sorely," I reply instead, composed. "Millions of them whine furiously to get their king back."

"The birdbrained pink flamingos outside are *far* more infuriated—they're utterly beside themselves without their empress." *Flamingo brains are smaller than their eyeballs.* Pacer knows he wins this round since I can't curse at him in front of Valeska Van Valken, but in a truce, he presses my fingertips against his lips and bows. "The birds themselves will have to kill me to take you. You're too important to me." His blue eyes gaze at me.

My debut means everything to him. Its success is his career promotion, and his career promotion is *my* increased ability to infiltrate.

It's what makes us perfect friends, if only he knew.

"We have a huge day for once." I beam when Valeska's eyes are on us again and our private bubble evaporates.

"More important than attendance?" she snaps.

"Her next appearance will be lauded, Mistress Van Valken. I'll make sure of it," Pacer assures her, hand over heart. His blue eyes smile in earnest. "My ikä, I prepared a script for you myself that you'll read to the visitors for your next speech. Safety first." For a second, I don't feel alone.

"It's . . . not too hard with your past?" I ask. I need to know. His indigenous tribal empire went extinct when he was fifteen, and the Allied Force commemorated their victory with a Sveren. The word, which means *reverence*, refers to an event in which the Allied Force asks foreigners to kill their own people on the Allied Force's behalf; in return, the foreigners and their families may live and serve under the Allied Force.

Native tribes of the Arctic Circle lived in impenetrable cavern communities deep within mountain ranges and glaciers or beneath sea level in order to escape the Allied Force. Their spiritualism and connection to their ancestors were vital, and their culture had perfected hunting for survival, so they didn't need supermarkets or congested cities. However, the Allied Force wanted to ensure *all* of the native tribes had been eradicated.

Not one native was allowed to live in hiding.

Pacer's tribe, the Huškut, included the top seekers, trackers, and hunters of the indigenous Atkan Empire. Therefore, they were used to eliminate the last survivors.

Pacer had three younger brothers to care for, and he killed to protect them.

I don't blame him for it. I can still see its scars on him: the colorful, lively Atkan Empire is now gone.

Before, I couldn't fathom why the Allied Force committed any of this when it also experienced total devastation. Near extinction.

The average lifespan in the Allied Force is only fifty-five. Its continent is full of heavy metals, such as lead, mercury, and, most lethal of all, vatrium.

Vatrium is effectively indestructible, several dozen times as durable as tungsten. But it permeates Arctic waters and glaciers, their gear and firearms, just as mercury and lead are inconceivably high in their diets, leading to various metal poisonings.

A decline in brain function is the first sign of vatrium poisoning.

Heart, liver, and kidney failure are the next significant signs.

Aggression, acts of violence, uncontrollable rages, and memory loss are typically the last set of signs of severe vatrium poisoning; by then it's too late.

Eventually, the victims die of it.

Meanwhile, in Makari, the Kōn villagers' average life span used to be 215 years old. Our cells often grow rapidly *younger* due to volcanic orún airs, keeping us youthful for decades. The Kōn kings lived over 350 years.

Historically, we've outlived every other ethnicity on

earth. Invulnerable to vatrium, lead, mercury, and most other heavy metals.

However, we were not discovered for millennia. A hidden tribe.

Meanwhile, the Allied Force was nearly exterminated due to the extreme, frozen conditions. Few crops could survive. Villages starved with only meager frozen fish and nearly impenetrable glacial oceans that hardly yielded enough meat for dozens to survive on, let alone thousands. It took weeks for strong men to break the thick surface. It was never enough.

The wilderness was rife with deadly predators. Not to mention the temperatures in the mountains, which plummeted as low as negative one hundred degrees Fahrenheit, were too frigid for the human body to endure during long expeditions in search of meat. Hundreds of hunters dared to venture in—only a few would return.

Now, it is the most powerful region on earth. This happened not by accident or pure luck but by brute force. Once the Allied Force discovered its natural ability for war, the neighboring regions were raided and pillaged. Foreign men were softer, pampered by warmer temperatures and abundant livestock. Arctic men were inured to barbarism.

They outlasted the weaker men in every war.

Arctic warfare became increasingly necessary to forcibly seize the nearby nations. As the Allied Force gained expertise in warfare, it became second nature and an innate skill in its military. However, grisly winters in the Allied Force lasted nearly year round. Populations kept dwindling to near extinction as soon as deep winter came.

Therefore, specialized forces became essential. Snipers were the preferred method by which to destabilize foreign governments, assassinate political figures, and murder military leaders. Snipers could end an entire foreign regime without a full-scale army—only select men at long distance to kill government officials and disrupt elections. Incite chaos. Generate collapse.

Amid the instability, the large-scale Arctic military would invade and seize control. Soldiers plundered the country's natural resources and forced the terrorized masses into hard labor, then eliminated the population and kept its raw materials. Once the Allied Force defeated the weakened nation, its military finally departed. Nation by nation.

Skull by skull.

The Arctic used the natural resources of defeated countries as their own to feed their hungry, grow their young into adulthood, and protect their territory from foreigners. It created further isolation—and oblivious Arctic citizens looked to the military as if they were saviors.

The military fed them, warmed them, clothed them. Soldiers provided housing *and* kept the homes safe. Above and beyond their duty.

Increasingly, victories were celebrated, and everyone leaped into action to do their part. It was the beginning of the end for the rest of the world, but no one knew it at the time.

It took me months to gather this information—stolen history books, classified military records, forbidden confession tapes. Maximus had access to a gold mine. But I had to be careful in our home.

I studied ferociously. I learned how, in the Engineering Era, Arctic inventions multiplied, scholars prospered, and engineers pioneered advanced technology.

At long last, the Allied Force gained the ability to turn its mountains' subzero landscapes into beneficial resources. This transformed the continent into a leading world power.

But citizens never again wanted to endure the piercing, freezing climates. They were finally wealthy enough to immigrate to lush landscapes such as Germany, Switzerland, and Norway. Which meant thousands abandoned the homeland in droves—and the Allied Force's population was once again depleted.

British and Norwegian citizens were seen as sophisticated, eloquent. Citizens soon began giving their children Anglo-Saxon and Nordic names. Germanic surnames arose, as Germany and Scandinavia were viewed as more social and friendly, as well as breathtaking in their gorgeous highlands, hearty woodlands, and snowy mountains.

But these changes diluted their own Allied Force culture.

How could the fatherland's leader tie the nation together? Unite its countrymen?

The nation needed depth and profound meaning to bind its citizens together and keep them within the region.

Thus, the promotion of ideas like *birthright*, *national superiority*, and *perfect blood* to rally the homeland began. This was the beginning of war becoming genocide, but few predicted it at the time.

The Allied Force had committed genocide in the past for its survival.

Its actions were out of necessity—that was its claim then.

However, now the Allied Force was no longer struggling to survive, and still the genocide continued.

The Nationalist Era started as military propaganda intended to retain and increase population numbers. Marriage was deemed vital—critical even—since the military finally discovered men and women who lived together for prolonged periods of time could produce as many as eight or ten children.

No. Ten *soldiers*.

Soldiers had previously lived in military bases and barracks their entire lives. From age six to retirement. Many of them would never meet a woman, even if they lived long enough to retire from the military. But now, both men and women were incentivized by a promise of future land ownership—if they produced soldiers.

Many were enchanted by the idea of someone to experience life with. They were curious about the opposite sex. But more people were interested in the idea that their *birthright* was not some random plot of land in the Arctic—but the entire world. That their own blood was far superior to any other in human existence.

A phenomenon exploded across the nation.

I don't think the Allied Force *expected* an unprecedented historic movement. An unstoppable sensation that made even the lowest class become educated on their blood superiority. Their maxim became *Soil, blood, and birthright.*

Students were taught only full-blooded Allied Force citizens could withstand the northernmost Arctic temperatures: it was how they'd successfully overcome the Extinction Era. Children believed that Arctic technology was unmatched and was the reason corporations, metropolises, and advanced cosmopolises had progressed into total affluence. Meanwhile, better employment opportunities arose, infrastructure improved, and new holidays were introduced to promote happiness and unity. All of it was strategic.

Community oriented.

A people who thought as one. Believed as one.

The civilians praised their military for being willing to massacre all other nations and rebuild the world in their image. All for *Arctic citizens.*

These are the people I'm up against. A younger Pacer never had a chance; he had no leverage.

I still remember how he told me that during the military raids, his mother kept him and his brothers safe for barely a night before the chaos bled into her brain and she threw them into the tundra wilderness, screaming the soldiers were going to kill them all. But I've never seen determination as raw as it was on his face even years later.

Pacer fought grown men, his skull was fractured, and his thumbs were lost to frostbite.

But he was authorized to serve under the Allied Force.

"Which Svęren was it?" He smiles now. "I don't remember. It's been forever."

But I know his stories. Pacer tells me them at night, beneath a cloak of stars and when the universe is quiet. When it feels like we're the only people in the world, I cling to his stories, the vibrant traditional fabrics of his people, learning every gritty detail about the Allied Force. They changed his name to Pacer Vanmark—he's not even allowed to disclose to me what his real name was. As if it didn't exist.

Kateri can't divulge her full original name either. They named her Ekaterina.

Ekaterina was close to her original name, as both names included the letters of her nickname, Kateri.

Right now, I glean from Pacer all I can about my biggest threat, yet I can't escape the tragedy in his eyes. It's still deep and alive.

His mother was his world. He knew she was only pretending to lose her sanity so they would leave her behind, and she wouldn't slow them down.

I deeply respect Pacer as a friend, not only because he's useful as my head guard but because he and I understand what it means to lose family. To lose everything. But he's loyal to the Allied Force, intensely dedicated.

I can't explain it, but Pacer always follows orders and never refuses. He passes for them so naturally—born blond with pool-blue eyes. He's so fluent in Vikarian you'd think he was born in the Kilrød.

Pacer is diligent in everything; he even carved time out to learn my habits and understand how I feel among all these strangers. A real friend to me. He's made every effort to make my transition smooth, as much an outsider as Kateri and I are.

But Valeska waves away our conversation now with a flick of her hand. "You're eighteen. Women your age dream of babies, popularity, and social climbing," she snaps. "Straighten yourself." *Or else.*

I am straightened. I am driven. I crave revenge for half a globe, and I will sign my own death warrant if I must.

Now that I'm married into the Allied Force, my access is perfect, and the Allied Force doesn't suspect anything. I will be their destruction. I will end the Allied Force.

Permanently.

CHAPTER 24

DAY ONE, NOON

Another rowboat is lost. Already.

And by *lost*, I mean completely evaporated. A hostile, cotton-white rain vapor scoured their bodies. Dissolved their whole rowboat. Their shrieks filled the air until the excruciating end.

Now, wails of women pleading for help penetrate the air. The cries are powerless to end the Great Hunt, but nonetheless they surround us in multitudes: "Please!"

The screams are mimicked by island spirits. Mocking us. *"Please! Please!"*

We're trapped.

An uncontrollable panic rises. Hysteria breaks out among the remaining laborers. After a second, a desolate feeling sinks over us—as if we all know it's the end. The Great Hunt will not be canceled. This island will not be placated. It will devour us all.

One by one.

Gnarled, ancient kungu trees emit a heavy, repugnant stench. An acidic rancor spores into the muggy air as they attempt to repel us from their territory. I breathe. Breathe.

I need to make a strategy. Fast. As soon as we reach the island.

It dawns on me that the soldiers must be suffering too. Equally as unfamiliar and vulnerable; the African textbook contained very little compared to the staggeringly dangerous reality.

Africa is the polar opposite of their natural climate. They will need to be on their guard and learn the depth of this island in real time with us all.

It might buy us a day. Maybe two. Before they enact their military creed, which is *Tøx rein—Adapt and seize.*

Ahead, a dense, storm-gray steam covers the head of the thick island. Whispers, shouts, and trickles of inhuman laughing voices lick my ears. I bite down abject terror.

But the island is not my greatest immediate fear. The island might be reasoned with after a decent sacrifice, if the African textbook is correct. But these snipers will stop at nothing for their hard-earned glory.

"In one hundred twenty seconds, find shelter. Sniping will commence." A calm, automated voice slices my thoughts. *"Repeat: In one hundred nineteen seconds, find shelter. Sniping will commence."*

Something catches my attention. An overstretched grin.

Across from me, the contestants replacing those who revolted are menacing. Bizarre. Some of these people are smiling gleefully, as if they're serial killers finally given the chance to kill at their own pace, will, and unstoppable pleasure.

I've heard rumors of the Traeger Impound. How the

prisoners of war are forever changed. Psychologically damaged beyond recognition.

One of them gloats, grinning wider at me. The Traeger Impound insignia carved into his neck. He gives me a dirty wink.

Meaty fingers grasp my hand without warning. *How did he loosen his chains?*

His greasy hand smothers mine, and he flashes his rotten yellow teeth at me. I tear my eyes permanently from Hazen as he disappears into the island steam.

"Coa Wildflower Rangecroft, good to meet you!" The Traeger Impound prisoner's beady little eyes glimmer, as if there's a thrilling secret I don't know about. "My instincts tell me to be patient, calm, *composed*. But I can't—"

"Can't what?" My glare snaps at him.

A mosquito nips my cheek. "I can't stay still near easy prey!" He laughs hysterically, as if he's hilarious. Spit and phlegm spray out of his mouth and dribble down his scruffy chin, but because his wrists are chained in front of him, he can't do much to wipe it.

He slackened his chains, somehow, but they're still on. "Do you get it?"

Wild eyed, he appears even more animalistic, with a poisonous frog's face. He is from Hallowell, deep in the south, I can tell.

"Got it." I'm barely paying attention to him; instead I fix my eyes on a slobbering, weeping man next to me. I need to stay sharp. He's howling frantically in his chains. *But his fists are ready.*

He's going to start killing soon. It's Elsko.

Knowing him, he'll use his tears to trick the others. I don't blame him since he got his foot blown off. If he can't out-brawn 'em, he'll outsmart 'em. Elsko's smarter than half of us—and he'll attack. Viciously.

Suddenly, the barbarian squeezes me again. His thumb crushes my knee. Beady eyes drink me in. "Captivating island. Very tasty-looking creatures."

My knee jerks, but it can't boot him backward. My ankles are chained, being eaten alive by gnats that crawl into the rickety boat. "Chimpanzee tongues. Salamander tails. Have you tried it?"

A flood of heavy, sunless black clouds lurks ahead. Ready to swallow us alive. My heart beats inside my throat.

The barbarian seems too titillated to be a threat yet, as if he's playing with his food, but I don't need to be fast; I only need to be faster than *Elsko*. As horrible as it is, it's true, and by the way he still skirts any eye contact with me, he'd do the same. He knows how agonizing my damaged feet can get.

But then the barbarian squeaks.

"Clever idea! Very clever girls here." He flicks his eyes at me and Czarina, a rich girl from my barracks. Czarina glares at me.

Czarina and Rawley got bad blood, which means Czarina and I got bad blood.

Rawley thinks she's uppity. Czarina thinks Rawley's low class. Crass.

Her eyes are knifelike. *Stay back.*

"Did you hear me? I called you clever," he repeats. "Say thank you. It's very rude to ignore a compliment."

"We ain't ask for it," I cut.

I avoid looking at Czarina, 'cause I don't want to count her as an opponent or ally. Not until I need to. Above all, I don't underestimate her for a second.

She's survived this long for a reason.

"Don't be rude!" he suddenly roars, lunging toward me and tugged back by the chains. Czarina laughs.

My brow rises. She throws her head back in wild laughter, watching his blood simmer beneath his pale, flaky skin. Wet, bloodshot eyes.

"What are you giggling at, girl?"

Livid rage covers his blistered skin. His chest expands and constricts with disbelief.

"Massive man body—fragile man inside," she spits in her Vraničarian accent. "We do not fear you."

The barbarian points his chains right at Czarina. Eagerly. "You will—see. Watch."

Czarina chuckles. "I see *now*. Frail man. Hungry for attention." My lip can't help but twitch in amusement. I admire her guts. She laughs harder, but soon, she can't stop laughing, as if she's at the brink of her sanity and someone yanked the last nerve. Her dark hair spills loose, mouth wide, tears streaming.

"I'll kill you!" he screams. A choleric bolt of fury leaps out of his mouth.

"Do it," Czarina dares. Prepared.

Only now do I see the three-inch nail in her waistband. She must've stolen it from the canteen tables during the final feast.

It makes my eyes widen. If his neck lurches any closer to us—she'll have a good shot to stick him.

His glare's murderous.

I follow her lead and giggle, forcing out a titter of laughter like the Arctic girls at the ration shops and boutiques. The posh Arctic girls that are always huddled together, linked arm in arm. "He's so cute. Look at him—he really reckons he can hurt us."

He's right. She *is* clever. *Come closer, frog man.*

His eyes dart between us. "I'll cut your throat! I'll kill you both!"

Thick tension squeezes hard around my throat. But Czarina's almost doubled over with laughter.

After a few breaths, Czarina and I look at each other, and we nod. *Stick him. Then get out of here.*

Ahead, there's vegetation everywhere, it seems, once you get past the meters of sand. We can disappear into the sand dunes covered with emun bushes.

A bloated sky shatters and pours even more gray torrential rain onto us. Lashes of rain rebuke us for refusing to listen, like we have any control over being here. Nature brutalizes our limbs and necks. Snapping against our wrists.

A vise grip yanks me out of my thoughts, and I realize I'm clutching myself as the countdown approaches its end on the scratchy speakers. They're so blaring, so loud, I almost can't hear anything else.

"In ninety-eight seconds, find shelter. Sniping will commence," a polite voice informs us. *"Repeat: In ninety-five seconds, find shelter. Sniping will commence."*

Murky waters are bristling with filthy, noxious yellow plumes of fog and mist. They choke my mouth. My throat goes dry.

My eyes try to find Hazen, and I curse this yellow fog *and* myself for only securing one certain ally. But as he glides into view, he's surrounded by hefty men himself. It'll be a miracle if he can slip past them without losing a neck or a limb.

Czarina is my best option right now.

Water spirits trickle against my hot ears, and my teeth clench. A new urge nearly overwhelms me, a hunger for blood rising out of nowhere. Urgent. *I'd win if I scorch this entire boat with flames.* We'd be the fourth rowboat eliminated—but I'm invulnerable to my own fire on the outside. Smoke fumes from my nostrils.

Kill them and win. A voice now inside my head lures me to destruction. *Do it for Rabbit, Buckthorne, Hucket, Evelie. Rawley.*

I'm not dense.

The water spirits only want to swallow more dead bodies, to pull victims underwater. They don't care if I live.

My safest option is to not get distracted, not get shot, and *sprint* to safety. Sprint through chaos, bullets, panthers, gorillas, snakes, anything that might be waiting for us on that island.

But the barbarian's eyes gleam with savagery.

"Seconds. Only seconds before we can *really* have a blast." His eyes devour our shoulders, knees, feet. He rocks himself back and forth. "They never let me have fun in the impound."

A sudden rage consumes him.

"You'll regret laughing at me. Do you hear me? *Regret it!*"

He swings for Czarina. Czarina swings back at him.

It shocks him. I reckon he didn't expect a slender girl to do that. But she didn't reveal her weapon. Not yet.

He smashes his restraints, attempting to break 'em. But the electricity jolts him onto the rowboat, writhing, wrenching, until he stops resisting.

"Seconds," he huffs to himself. "Sixty-five seconds."

Foreboding clouds gather above our heads—plunging us into darkness. Growls of heavy thunder rack my nerves.

It takes him roughly ten seconds to recover.

Soon, he's giddy, barely able to contain himself again. His tiny eyes dart between us, as if he doesn't know who to go after first.

"Fifty seconds."

I squeeze Czarina's knee, for comfort or because she's familiar, I don't know. *Don't fear. Don't fear. Don't fear.*

I tell her, "We can do this."

I don't rightly believe that. But I choke down my own apprehension, straining at my chains, desperate to rip them off. I don't care if there are Africanized bees, fire-breathing lynxes, invisible chest-beating apes; I'm getting on that island.

Anything to get out of this mist.

Czarina folds her slim fingers over mine. "Your sister has fast fingers. In the sugarcane fields."

That's as close to a compliment as you'll get from girls like Czarina or Rawley. Girls with pride.

When we first arrived, Czarina was one of the first laborers to bring me out of my shock and my grief. It's the forced-labor camp's tradition for field-workers to try to soothe newcomers with stew, something hearty to steady them into this new, harsh reality.

If the newcomers are lucky, a few workers might even help them meet their quotas.

It feels like a lifetime ago now. Rawley didn't appreciate yielding more sugarcane than everyone else and yet still sleeping on the bottom bunk, where the rickety top bunk could collapse on her at any time. But Czarina was equally stubborn, insisting she'd been there longer, earning her the seniority of top bunk. They locked horns like rams nonstop.

The compromise was to share the bed.

If Rawley beat her to the barracks first and took up more sheets, Czarina would steal both of their pillows. If Czarina purposefully stood several minutes too long in the bathing stall, using up the hot water in their section, Rawley would steal Czarina's ration cards. For weeks, we thought one of them was liable to wake up tossed outside in the dirt, if not become as close as family.

But they were two willful, ambitious girls. Never did see eye to eye.

Right now, I put their past behind us as Czarina warns me, "Stay sharp. Your family still needs you."

I don't think I've ever seen Czarina with any living family members. It's always best to never ask or assume, to let the refugee disclose if they've got any family left.

"Thank you," my voice rasps, my throat chafed by the pungent fog, "for what you did. The turkey soup."

Czarina's eyes snap to me. "Don't think I won't still kill you, if I need to." Her raspy voice rakes the fetid air. She whispers, "But if we stay out of each other's way—I want to try that Hallowell pastry your sister won't shut up about."

"You'll get the best slice of apple pie," I promise. "Flaky and warm."

"I'll bake you a soft cut of smokvara. Tastiest dessert in the world." She squeezes my fingers. "Vraničar survived in my heart. I'd share it with you."

I couldn't point out Vraničar on a map—but I know Czarina's a mixture of different heritages. Czarina mentioned the Romani genocide of her ancestors—how the brutalities committed against Romani people have been overlooked in history too often. Vraničar soon became their home. Her mother gave her a Vraničarian name to honor their generosity. Now her home is gone.

Czarina's prickly, but she allows herself a second of vulnerability. ". . . May you live, even if you die."

It's an old Vraničarian prayer. I've heard seamstresses whisper it to those whose barracks were selected for the Hunt.

The barrack girls murmur it to the chosen girls awaiting their fate in the Trenches.

It reflects the belief that you can live after death. I like the saying fine.

But I smirk despite myself. "We won't die."

"My ancestors survived several ethnic cleansings." Czarina tries a smile on for herself. "We'll see if I am as blessed."

"You are—we are."

"You're not scared of me, sweetpeas?" the barbarian asks, scratching his brow. "Are you ignoring me?"

"Not ignoring you." Czarina gives a lopsided smile. "I will sacrifice you to the sea."

He's silent. She gave as much edge to her voice as she could.

He only grins wider.

"*Twenty seconds.*"

Czarina wraps her pinkie around mine to get my attention. I don't know why, but it's a last-minute comfort. "Be steady," she whispers. "Run. I'll be right behind you."

She's a quick study. She's always been swift to catch on to everything in the sugarcane fields. When it will rain, when the fields will be burned, when the next bed counts will occur.

"*Twenty seconds.*"

I brace myself. *Adapt and seize.*

CHAPTER 25

"Twenty seconds. Secure shelter," an automated voice warns.
"In seventeen seconds, sniping will commence. Secure shelter."

Suddenly—the air goes still.

The atmosphere becomes swollen with sweaty humidity.

Deadly silent.

Dangerously, the barbarian is glaring at Czarina. She glances at me: *Get ready.*

"Fifteen seconds."

Ahead of us, primordial, unnaturally huge, primitive green kukbak trees populate the sandbank and crowd over each other. Palm trees shove out of the earth like fingernails and scrape the sky, which is rumbling in outrage.

Distant howler monkeys bellow. At least, I think they're howlers.

The primal sound of their piercing screeches is unbearable.

I grimace.

"Scared?" the barbarian asks, then offers, "I can eliminate you first."

Czarina cuts a castrating glare at him.

Another retributive thunderbolt bashes the seas. So loud

it makes my muscles clench before I realize the sound is the island itself.

The barbarian man grins like he won a billion vikęs. "This is the best part. Watch." He copies the drones. "*Ten seconds.*"

Finally, the scratched floorboards of the rowboats swing open like shark jaws to reveal prized silver weaponry—axes, spears, swords, machetes—which are then lifted to the surface. Compulsively, we all lunge for them.

Yanked back by the chains.

The snipers are already concealed in their positions, I'm sure. They're simply waiting for our cracked, dented rowboats to slam the shore. They're going to open fire on us. No matter what the island warns.

"*Five seconds.*"

My heart bangs against my ribs as I watch him ready himself for attack. *Check your surroundings. Be prepared.* Where can I run? Right? Left?

In both directions are prolific growths of overgrown palm trees, gnarled kapok trees, and knotted balsa trees that will plunge us into a creepy velvet darkness. Dozens of colorful exotic birds of various species circle the skies like vultures—screaming in unison: "*Leave! Leave! Leave!*"

Vines slither over us like snakes and mangled branches clamber onto the splintered rowboats. Right over our feet. They taste our boots, coil over our shins, grip our hips. Before an electric shock spurs them away.

It appears there's no direction I can run where the sand dunes skirting the island won't slow me down like piles of deep, soiled snow.

There! I spot a hideout I can run to.

But it's right near the shore. It's a trap.

Everyone seems to sight it simultaneously. Now, the Great Hunt begins.

"*One. Glory to the Hunt.*"

Hot sunlight scorches the back of my neck. Sun peeks through the bulky fog. The chains snap off us.

"*Zero time remaining. You may begin hunting.*"

The barbarian lunges for Czarina—earning a three-inch nail in his eye. Tissue and blood fly everywhere. And the barbarian howls.

I shove him overboard, with all the strength in me. Savagely, I attempt to sink him into the waters with a spear. I aim for his back—but I miss and shove it into his shoulder.

"Come on! Come on!" Czarina grasps me. Before I can try again, she pulls me off the boat, but I turn back.

I'm swift. I steal a sword and stab it right through the barbarian's rib cage, not risking the chance he'll recover and come find us.

Czarina stashes as many small knives as she can. Once Elsko collects as many weapons as he can, I launch him overboard. He's always been crap at swimming.

Even before his foot injury, he was a shaky swimmer, but the water is safer for him right now than the bullets. He can't run faster than the bullets that are coming, and knowing him, he'd try.

That is the only favor I give him.

Now, we're both off—thrashing hard and fast through the perilous waters until we reach the shore. Already, the gunfire is a wall of noise.

Bullets whiz past us, terrorizing and menacing, their cracks earsplitting. Screams, cries, and pleas explode around us as sprinters breach the soaked shorelines. Several laborers are instantly shot and killed.

Noxious gunpowder spreads everywhere.

My eyes stream from smoke, and my throat's on fire from the gritty air. My heart palpitates wildly.

Raw adrenaline and fire are volatile in my lungs, but I don't stop. I can't stop running for my life. I can't let go of Czarina's hand.

We nearly reach the hideout before skidding to a halt.

Men tackle each other to the ground, pulverizing cheekbones with grit and rocks, throttling each other with vines, snatching ankles—anything to drag each other away from the open metal hideout. Swords, spears, and hatchets dive over my scalp.

I can't even see right.

Women are ripping through ligaments, biting into flesh, brawling and clawing over each other in the clamor for the hideout shelter as well, warring for their families. But blood splatters onto my boots as a woman's shot in the knee right in front of me. She's as good as dead. I know that.

You can't get far with a blown knee. *I know that. I know.* And yet . . .

I whip around, letting go of Czarina's fingers, losing her in the chaos.

The injured woman can't sprint anymore and slams into the ground. I help her up, and she snatches me like a lifeline, grasping my hair, shirt, trousers. "Please!"

A bullet tears past my wrist. There's something wrong with these snipers. It's as if they're completely sightless due to the jungle mist—they'll shoot everyone and end the Great Hunt in one day.

Not even half a week.

The tourists would've come all this way for nothing, which is exactly why the Great Hunt provides a rank in the first place. It's not only an estimation of how long they believe someone can hide from them but also their method of savoring the most interesting kills for the audiences.

Shelter. Shelter. We need shelter. She scratches my eyelid. "Please!"

"I'm helping you! Stop scratching!" I yell.

But guilt clambers up my throat. *How much can I even help? She's as heavy as me.* I sling her over my shoulder and race forward. I run straight into the snarling undergrowth. I prepare to follow Czarina.

A flock of birds scatter, and snowy oror monkeys drop their nuts and fruits, bolting high into the trees as snakes are torn open with bullets.

It's a barrage of bullets and blistering gunpowder that renders us senseless. Whatever aerosolized tear gas they're using attacks my eyes and lacerates my skin, scrapes my insides out.

They're gassing us. Don't breathe it in. Don't breathe.

It's like the Hallowell war all over again. But I don't slow down, don't stop to catch my breath where the air's cleaner; I sprint deep into the leaf-covered valley's brambles for Czarina.

But the woman cries, "Hide me!"

I will. But it's difficult—she can't possibly be concealed enough. I lift her over my shoulder. Searching for deeper cover. Viperous vines reject my presence, slitting my ankles.

Sweating, the woman's growing heavier on my back. It's muggy, airlessly hot, and the sand's even mushier than it appears, my boots sinking in up to my calves.

There's no time to look for Czarina. But my instinct insists I glance over my shoulder.

Hazen's right there. He has two men on him.

He strikes his machete at their heads, only so the assailants raise their arms to block his attack, leaving their stomachs vulnerable. He slashes straight through their abdomen, slicing their necks afterward. He's chillingly fast, even with his face cut so deep the bone is exposed. Drenched in blood.

Out of nowhere, a sniper trudges onto the dunes—over six feet tall. Lanky. Uncertain.

His eyes bulging with fear.

Wait—that's not a sniper.

It's a Great Hunt fan. His bloodied blacktail uniform is mutilated, mangled on his body. His rived boots stumble as he drags the detached limbs of what must've been his companions, judging by the torn paramilitary uniforms that match his own. The island left nothing else of them.

More fans boldly, brashly enter the fray.

You can tell they're fans because none of them are wearing the standard-issue sniper uniforms, only the paramilitary attire they could purchase, which is an ignorant mistake.

Another Great Hunt fan dressed as a blacktail sniper roars, blatantly trying to show off for the drone cameras, sprinting with his battle-axes in his grip. He runs full speed toward a Vraničarian woman.

I blink through burning eyes. It takes a second for me to realize he's heading toward Czarina. A war cry in his throat.

His arms raised.

His boots spray sand everywhere with each thunderous stomp. Tripping. Stumbling.

Czarina is attempting to enter the hideout. Waiting for an opening in the crowd of laborers. As if she senses that if she doesn't get in now, she might never get a chance.

"Open the steel door!" people beg. "They're shooting

at us! You need to open the door!" Fists pound on metal. "Open!"

Whoever's locked inside won't listen. They're safe for a week.

If they can survive without food or water and with whatever injuries they've already sustained, they're not leaving. But the rest of us are in danger.

Czarina's in danger.

Blood is hammering in my ears. My body roars with panic.

In shock, I realize I'm sprinting toward her—despite the bullets spraying everywhere. Tear gas spreads. The blistering pain leaks into my eyes, throat. The air sears my lungs.

As I rush forward, a fresh pack of Allied Force fans breaks into the mayhem.

One of them grips Czarina, and she's desperate to escape.

A pitchy whirring sound whips above our heads. A silver hovercraft from the Arctic military itself unleashes spears, maces, machetes, and axes in front of the fans. *Don't say we didn't help you.* But it's no act of generosity.

The military is hoping for an epic moment to share with the tourists. To prove Allied Force superiority—that any civilian is physically capable of dominating any foreign enemy.

Drone cameras monitor the scene.

But I glance around rapidly. There are handfuls of rabid fans. *How do we get past them? What will it take to get Czarina out of that fan's grasp in time?*

There's no shelter immediately visible, nothing but sand, a rock-studded beach shore, and a deeply hateful, vine-heavy jungle. But even if we burrow ourselves deep in the gritty sand, it wouldn't take much for a sniper to find us on foot. That is, if the amateurs don't get us first.

But Czarina screams, and I don't think—I act.

I don't mean to do it—this isn't some bid for glory—but I have a dark feeling it will make me a target.

My bloodied fingers grasp a bundle of silver spears. I focus. My tongue burns one of the metal tips into a fiery weapon of savagery.

My eyes land on Czarina. *Now.*

I launch the weapon into the fan's throat—I don't miss. It's more firepower than I'm used to—as if the island's pure orún overcharged the blast. It flies right through his trachea and—unexpectedly—also straight into the beating heart of the fan behind him. Two competitors with one spear.

Czarina wildly flees into the bush. But not before she motions at me to run.

For my life.

Stunned, a dozen Great Hunt fans gape at me in horror. Before they sprint for weapons to kill me.

CHAPTER 26

IFE STØRMBANE

DAY ONE, NOON

I lock myself in my bedroom suite. The footage of the Great Hunt has been broadcast all over Traeger Island. *Bodies. Bodies. I sent all those people—*

"What's wrong? Wet the bed?"

I spin and see a Makarian intruder sneering back at me, his face twisted with laughter. *Impossible. It's my older brother. How is he here? On Allied Force territory?*

"Ayi! What did they do to your *face*?" He eyes my girlish, glittery makeup from across the room. His eyes trace my pink eyeliner, my now-signature butterfly eyelashes—and his laughter roars.

I glare. *How did he get here?* Some of Zaire's golden-brown curls come free of his messy topknot, and his light-brown skin is bright, bringing out his pale-green eyes under curtains of long lashes. A pretty boy to all the village girls—but an arrogant pain to me. I haven't seen him in three years for a reason.

My cheeks burn with fury that spreads like wildfire. I leap out of bed, right in his face.

"They'll kill you! Get out!" I demand. I think of Head General Størmbane still down the corridor in Ironhaven Hall. Victims already hang from the rafters like flags. *I'm in the middle of exacting vengeance against the Allied Force.* Zaire will be next, breaking in like this. But there's no resort, fortress, or bastion my thieving brother can't sneak into. He even crawled through the sewage, by the reeking stench of him. "Are you *trying* to get killed?"

"Killed?" Zaire echoes. As if Head General Størmbane isn't only a thousand feet away.

His firm body slouches against the wall. His shoulder dirties the expensive oil painting of Maximus's great-great-grandfather. The originator of the "perfect blood" doctrine. The ideology that it is impossible for the Størmbane blood to be contaminated, stained, or desecrated, since it is perfection itself.

"Is execution how they greet incomers in the Allied Force?"

"Yes, carnage. They'll *kill* you for trespassing. Worse—"

"What's worse than execution?"

But we both know.

"Don't answer that." He shrugs. "To them, I'm just a lowly performer." Zaire pouts with his soft pink lips.

He spins irreverently, displaying his stolen exhibition uniform.

There's probably a poor human-exhibition victim gagged and tied somewhere right now, only hired for a few weeks for the Great Hunt to give rich tourists the *full experience.*

But Zaire fears no man in his way.

Thief. Zaire smirks. *Dirty thief.*

I don't want his death on my hands. His blood.

Our parents will never forgive me, and Mamà already hates me.

"You need to leave!" I order, storming up close to his face, hissing this time through my teeth. "Now."

I think of all the loneliness I just felt, the unbearable ache of losing my people, missing my family, sending innocents to die, and it *all* evaporates. If the Allied Force senses any sign of deceit, Zaire will get us *both* executed, and I'm not dying until I save the rest of Makari.

Or take the Allied Force down with me.

"Go now, while you *can*."

"Is that any way to welcome your big brother, bed wetter?" He messes up my jeweled hair, dodging a slap to his cheekbone. He grins.

I bow exaggeratedly and use the traditional pronunciation of his name. "Chief Prince Zàirẹ, would you prefer being assassinated indoors or publicly?"

"Publicly. And could you bow lower? I miss remembering you were born years after me." He's lucky this dress is too delicately crafted for me to *really* force him out, limbs and all. Zaire gazes down at me, and I'm irritated that my tiara quits at the middle of his neck. He's average height, but I'm still shorter than him. I was the one malnourished the longest, isolated for years without consistent access to sunlight—all of it stunted my height.

Mamà never wanted to remind the village of what I was. A descendant without magic.

Zaire eyes my new dress, likely noting how costly it might be. I can practically see him doing the trade calculations in his eyes. His insult barely hides itself. "Gorgeous dress."

"Shut up." I stab his chest with my finger. "Or would you like to have your blood splashed over the hem like

Vice President Vengerov? Because that's exactly what will happen—"

"You won't let them kill me." Zaire yawns, dismissive, lazy like a lion. Airy with his dismissal as he tours my luxurious vintage penthouse suite like he owns it. His grime-covered boots scrape thick mud across the imported marble. The rest of Zaire's brown-blond hair tumbles loose as he frees it from its bun.

Zaire whistles, taking the opulent decor in. He has musty grass stains on his knees, grease on his elbows, grimy sleeves rolled up, and gutter sludge with a stomach-turning stench on his knuckles. But Zaire sneaked in through the sea and sewage for a reason.

He always has a reason. Determined.

Pacer appears inside the room, waiting for my word to kill Zaire. He entered soundlessly by passing through the solid wall, a magical ability that comes from a rare trait of his Atkan heritage. Now, he lifts his palm up to signify *kill* and cuts down to mean *release*.

I cut my hand down. "He's fine! He's just leaving."

Zaire's lucky Pacer didn't kill him immediately.

We almost look alike, but Zaire boasts high cheekbones and a slender, more angular and chiseled face. By now, he's nineteen, and it breaks my heart how much I missed in three years. He's skinnier now, and it pains me that he appears almost emaciated, his cheeks hollow.

He must be starving—raw hunger must've crazed his brain enough for him to dare to do something this dangerous—but he's right. I won't let them kill him.

I'll think of something; I always do.

"How's my crafty little sister?" Zaire reads my mind.

"How are Mamà and Babà?" I finally spit out, asking after our parents. I look away.

"Alive, disappointed," he says in a strained way, and I know it's more than that. My mother's doubtless infuriated with me. I ran away from home on my thirteenth birthday to live in the Arctic, surrendering our empire to our own killers. A traitor to our whole empire.

I never forget how much my people revile me.

But what else is new? Mamà has despised me since I was born. I didn't even have the decency to die at birth. She tried to murder me out of embarrassment.

Her pride is as tall as her elegant body.

The direct line nearly *always* bears children with orún.

Only my grandfather comforted me with stories of heroic descendants without orún—and he always reminded us that the chief bone king, the sun king, the rain king, and the hunt king—all of them had a mother who was an extraordinary warrior with features very similar to mine.

But I've never been extraordinary; I've always had to *earn* my triumph. I've always had to sink my canines deep into the flesh of my enemies for any victory.

I was born in warfare. I am war.

Of course, Zaire is perfect looking with his lionlike caramel hair and bold green eyes. He is not only a beautiful boy to our mother but someone with healing orún like herself.

While my mother loved him deeply, she warned me that my wild beauty would be my only selling point. I would need to be wise.

She detests that she never succeeded in killing me. I can feel threat, danger, already.

She's coming. One day.

But I can't expose the truth to her—how I planned this infiltration, desperate for revenge against the Allied Force for killing Makarians—so I clear my throat.

"Father is still rallying the western regions?" I ask.

He nods.

"Pacer could've killed you." I raise my chin. A show of authority. "You could've been—"

"Shot dead by the Atkan? Ayi." Zaire shudders slightly, chilled. "His bullet tore through my throat; he caught me instantly."

Zaire rubs his neck. But he has healing abilities, so he's already fine. "I managed to get a word out. He knew I wasn't lying when I said I was your brother and I'm not here to hurt you."

I could've told him that. Pacer can do more than pass through objects and walls; he can tell if someone is lying. It's why Pacer is valuable to the Allied Force top military personnel.

"So, bed wetter, you exploit acrobats from your home country to amuse the Allied Force tourists?" Zaire scowls acerbically. "What's that about?"

"It's for optics." It's all I can say. A dangerous situation can be made fatal by words alone. I learned that lesson.

The night Maximus killed my grandfather.

CHAPTER 27

I settle into my private penthouse botanical alcove, letting Zaire sit on the hidden end. We're surrounded by wild, herbaceous plants and rows of pellums flown in for the occasion. I scrape forward in my veranda seat.

Zaire and I last saw each other over forty months ago, so I sneak stolen glances at him now. The Aphelion bot pours us iced refreshments. Zaire always teased me about my delicate nose and full lips. Now my nose has become iconic and my plush lips are envied. Women are even injecting their lips, inflating them to look like mine. Girls rip out their ribs to copy my waist. *I have influence.* "I—"

"So you married that man?" Zaire asks derisively in our made-up language.

All my hairs rise.

"Leave it, Zaire."

"Do you know who he is?" he snaps back. Hostile.

Zaire was there when Maximus killed our grandfather. I was eight, and Zaire personally held me back so I wouldn't get myself shot next. I clawed Zaire's arms, screamed at the top of my lungs, cursed him, kicked his kneecaps in, but he never let me go. Never let me get killed.

Maximus snapped a bullet through my sweet, elderly grandfather's skull. The bone king of Makari.

Higher than the sun king. Higher than the rain king.

The highest king in legend.

According to legend, the original sun king established Africa and ignited an empire. But the eightieth bone king, my grandfather, *united* Makari and made it prosper.

Makari revolutionized its economy with its own vast natural resources. Crude oil, gold, diamonds, lithium, cobalt, uranium, solar energy.

Warmhearted but warlike, Kōnkon—*Grandfather*—turned Makari into the empire-continent it is now.

Was.

A sniper's shot; that was all it took after my grandfather surrendered himself for his grandchildren. He'd removed his formidable katákà, a shielded crown, and his impenetrable dashiki. *Spare the children, please. Mercy, General.* Brain matter splattered everywhere, and Maximus was hailed immediately: The King Killer. The Killer Sniper.

Zaire was eleven years old.

The Allied Force had besieged our compound in the night, smoking us out, smothering us with fire and explosives, dragging Kōnkon in front of us, in front of the world, and letting Maximus—a dictator's son—kill him.

As a war prize.

I knew then we needed to fight smarter, not fiercer, in order to live.

That night, I lay by my grandfather's cooling body for hours. My cheek throbbed on his missing heartbeat. They didn't even let him keep his eyes but decapitated him according to their tradition. At eight and a half years old, I soaked in his blood, gripping what was left of him. Sobbing. His gold kòagbe rings were splattered with his blood, and no one moved to salvage them.

I felt his pained soul depart from his heart.

Something in me changed. I can't explain it. I didn't just want revenge; I wanted *decimation*. Even at the cost of my own death.

The night air was thick with flames and gritty smoke, and I saw Maximus. I instantly recognized his Roman-red Arctic-bear insignia on his tactical gear. His maxim is *Şebę nøll*: "The bear is not saddened." Arctic bears do not cry for their kills. It's a matter of victory, glory, hunger.

Maximus gazed at me, looking back into my teary eyes, and his blue eyes were so indifferent. So bored he didn't bother to hide it. You'd think he was at a senatorial conference. Maximus eyed my grandfather again, watching his brain tissue trickle from his skull, and then married me seven years later. Smiling right in my face.

But back then, Zaire's fierce hand kept me still. Like whenever Mamà attempted to kill me, he always made sure I survived. No matter what it cost him.

"I know who he is. Leave it alone." I can't *believe* I can still understand and speak our foolish made-up languages. "Ikai is okay?"

My parents have a family of leopards. All of them are swift and acute. Ikai is my favorite, the cleverest. I always felt like an ordinary girl in the valleys, sleeping under the hot sun with our lazy leopards. I didn't know a world outside existed. Before everything changed.

"Fine. Anyway, I can't believe you actually made it this far, bed wetter. Good for you." Zaire tips a gold lager up to his lips, flicking his gaze around, stopping at the curtains. Zaire knows they're worth millions, stolen from Vraničar, displayed right in the faces of the diplomats.

Bed wetter. My lips curl back in response. I'm no longer the scared eight-year-old girl I once was, peeing on the reed cot for months straight because I was petrified the Allied Force would kill me in my sleep.

"I could have you executed for calling me that," I say casually, holding up my chin just to exhibit how much I've aged. In case he missed it. "I could have you sent to Kegęr for that."

"The Execution Range?" Zaire refills his refreshment. "Now, we both know I'm too handsome for hard labor."

"The Allied Force has executed for less."

Zaire throws his curls back in booming laughter.

"Execute these hideous heels first! Then we'll talk," he howls, snatching my leafy heels. "You'd better kill those tacky outfits of yours next."

"Get off!" I almost giggle, punching him hard. I *hate* these restrictive heels they keep forcing me into. "Everything else I wear is scandalous to them. Even *this.*"

"*Obviously.* They are frozen in their caveman thinking and barbaric methods." Zaire helps himself to another pitcher. "Bed wetter, if I designed you, you'd appear effortless, cool. Think: claws, horns, puma teeth. More royal than you appear on-screen."

"Wait . . ." I tease. "Are you envious?"

Zaire smirks and turns to inspect my intricately perfumed serviettes. "Nice designs, how much?" He dangles my monogrammed silk napkins. "What are the going rates for kept wives these days?"

"Kept wives?"

"Don't tell me you scrub these marble floors by hand? You're not in charge of housekeepers and gardeners. You're merely a decoration, as gorgeous as these curtains. Everything provided and paid for by the Allied Force."

"You *are* jealous."

"Deeply jealous." Zaire snorts. "Insulted, actually, that they didn't ask me instead to marry some general. I'm prettier than you and a huge fan of hideous shoes, tacky patterns, and ridiculous hairstyles—"

"You know *what*—"

"Oh, I would've married any general they asked. Although maybe not the King Killer himself—"

"Shut—!"

I hear the doors jolt open as someone enters the vintage penthouse suite—it must be a Størmbane, as only they have access. By the sound of it, ten soldiers accompany them, and my stomach plummets to the floor. There's a commotion of enforcers as their barely contained excitement mounts. *Is Head General Størmbane here? Did he overhear Zaire?*

Did Pacer inform Vørian of a foreign intruder?

Metal boots forge ahead, nearing my private floor, rounding the corner to the bedroom. The shouts and cheers are cut off abruptly, meaning the Størmbane has dismissed the enforcers for the evening, and by the sound of his boot steps, he is headed in this direction.

I gaze at Zaire in terror. It's too late to hide him in my room.

Too late to escape.

CHAPTER 28

COA RANGECROFT

DAY ONE, AFTERNOON

An axe slices over my ear. Nearly cutting my skin.

Another metal hatchet whistles past my sweaty cheek.

"Hand me another one!" someone orders behind me.

I don't care that I'm injured. I don't care how much bodily damage the killing field caused. How many bullets and arrows have grazed my ankles and shins, split open my belt leather. I do not stop running.

Not for anything.

"Kill that ingloriöt! Get me a spear!"

I dive into the deep jungle, sprinting between its yanyan bushes and the carnivorous shrubs that pounce on humans like hyenas to feast on our flesh. Waves of heat and fetid air fill our noses, and my chest is soaked with perspiration.

I tear through vines and winged Venus flytraps. Pump my arms harder.

"She killed Ivsën and Helker!"

The oddest part is—I didn't even *mean* to generate that

much fire. The island orún came alive within me, and I couldn't control it. Besides, if these had been *actual* blacktails, my attack wouldn't have worked. Blacktail snipers would have arranged themselves in formation instead of blundering around like rabid animals. Hazen warned me about the snipers' coordination an hour before we left, but he didn't warn me about Great Hunt superfans sneaking into the humid jungle.

Real blacktails, I reckon, would have spread themselves out and watched out for one another. Kept eyes on all targets. Not all gone in at once. But these eager fans can barely run through the tangled trees.

I've quickly learned to keep my footsteps lighter, faster, to escape the vines that try to snatch me. Swerve and twist *with* the jungle, instead of fighting against it.

A gasp punctures my throat. Ahead, I spot bright-blond hair. Alina Volkova.

Alina struggles to carry two elders—an aged gray-haired man and woman with wounded scalps and mauled uniforms. They must be heavy, like the woman I had to leave behind as the fans pursued me or else risk both of us dying, but Alina refuses to abandon them. Refuses.

Gritting her teeth, she shoves one boot in front of the other. She's alert, darting her sharp eyes back and forth, as if wary of predators.

Mountain-blue eyes glare at me to stay back, catching me instantly as I race her way. Her glower orders me to find somewhere *else* to sprint. But a horrifying realization has already hit me—she's the more famous target. World famous.

And I know what Rawley would say. These aren't *our* elders. Not *our* kinfolk.

Not our problem.

Selfishly, I could benefit if the fans spot Alina, as they might become glory hungry. If I'm faster than her, it might be enough to divert them entirely from my path.

They can reclaim the dignity they lost as they were mauled by the island and by laborers.

Except, as much as it frustrates me, I'm not soulless. Neither is Rawley.

At heart, I can't sacrifice others for my own skin, and Rawley wouldn't either if it really came down to it. Even though I viscerally want to live, my boots pivot east, away from the flytraps.

Alina bolts for a covered area to hide the elders, but it's too late.

"Alina Volkova!" someone yells behind me.

"You're lying."

"I swear! Right there!" A girl's voice.

Alina gives me a cold glare, probably thinking, *I am going to kill you for this*.

But the Great Hunt fan who appears to be in charge thunders in rage, "I don't care if it's Kaiser Arcus himself— she just speared Ivsën through his windpipe. I'm killing her."

Now, I have no choice. As if a murderous cobra were after me, I need to outrun everyone in sight. Alina must feel it, too, increasing her speed to widen the dozens of yards between us.

But Alina stops real sudden. Abruptly. Hovering.

I spot the trip wire almost too late, and both of us dive out of the way, into the yanyans. But the elderly woman tumbles over the wire.

The trapper snipers already set their traps. They're making quick work of the island.

Gasping, I attempt to dart away, but the scope of the snare

is wider than we noticed, and several nets yank us breathlessly into the air. Suspend us.

All of us.

But not before a hot spray of thick blood slaps my face as the elderly woman is speared by a harpoon. The elderly man feebly attempts to help her, but her eyes are gone.

And he's killed right after. A triggered axe slashes open his neck.

Don't move. No one move.

My eyes squeeze shut as I prepare for instant death, but what happens next is worse. The fans trigger the second wire as they approach, loading brass arrows into a crossbow. There's five of them—and now they're netted in the air right next to us. Their weapons dropped.

But no explosions or extra knives are unleashed. Not yet.

Which means a trapper sniper will spot us. And he'll be on the way to kill us himself.

I squirm, struggling to tear through the nets. But they're made to resist most weapons Hunt participators could get their hands on. Not even a serrated knife could carve through this.

"You're dead! Dead—do you hear me?" the leader roars at me. His lead-gray eyes threatening.

"Vane!" a girl screams in pain. "My arm—Vane!"

One of the nets has ferociously mangled her arm until it's almost detached from her body. She pleads, "Get me down! Somebody!"

"Give me a knife!" Vane orders. "Now!"

Their weapons are trampled beneath the growling crowd of panthers that prowl out of the yanyans. Awakened by the shrieking girl. The predators' pupils are whitened by spirits.

"Shut up, Kïva!" another fan hisses. "You're attracting them."

"My arm!" Kïva wails hopelessly. "I don't care! They can't even climb!"

"Who told you panthers *can't climb?*" Vane hisses, searching his dark blacktails uniform for anything, ripping out pockets, testing smoke rounds that won't detonate. "Are these vrëneks fake?"

"Kïva didn't want to be caught with *actual* weapons," someone snarls. "Snipers will deliver us the real supplies. Relax."

"Relax?" Vane seethes. "These animals can run at *fifty miles per hour.* They can bound eighteen feet to kill their prey in a tree. And Helker is dead."

There's a lethal silence.

"A sniper will be here soon—what can we do?"

"Fine," Vane spits. "And when he gets here, tell him that one's mine." His eyes are alive with unfathomable hatred. Staring right at me.

"Wait! I have a knife!" someone declares, to my horror.

Thankfully, their aim is atrocious. As they attempt to toss it to Vane, who opens his palm, demanding to have it so he can cut himself down and kill me, it instead bounds at least three feet *over* the nets.

Vane fumes. "What useless pansy taught you how to hurl a knife, Hett?"

I scamper higher inside the knotted net, knowing a deadly trapper is already on the path, likely pausing the construction of his next snare to see if this one has caught anything.

My orún has a price, as all magic does. Whitelaw warned it will cost me my lungs over the decades. Just as the lungs of heavy smokers succumb to disease, my lungs will be poisoned by the fumes of my excruciatingly hot fire.

My lightning bolts are at a deadly temperature the earth rarely sees, and my flames even more so. Whitelaw's always cautioned me of it.

But Whitelaw is not here.

Bloodthirsty panthers are already ascending the trees with breathtaking agility. Clawing through thick kapok bark without any effort. Stalking over the branches—nearing us.

Even the fans staple their lips shut. Wide eyed.

I rush.

I need to engineer this exactly right.

Now.

I belt a thrust of flames from my tongue. To my amazement, the net melts, sizzles, then tires of itself, until there's a hole large enough for me to drop ten feet to the ground. But I clench my fists. Clutching the safer net areas. Gazing at Alina.

You don't have time, my mind warns. But I feel largely responsible for her two open-eyed elders lifeless on the ground.

Twice in one day, I don't think—I act.

I swing myself with enough momentum to grasp her rope, twined with some mix of metals, and I lick it ablaze. Alina leaps out of the net.

She stamps out the flames mauling her clothes before they can burn her. She shoots me a violent glare.

"Sorry. I'm sorry," I breathe, lungs spent. "Sorry I got 'em killed." As I tumble to the ground, I attempt to remind her, "None of this is our fault."

I only did what I had to for my siblings.

A voice pleads.

"My arm! Please!" Kïva shrieks in pain. Vane gives in.

"Volkova." His voice is a command. "If you don't leave us for dead—I'll put in a word to the snipers for you." He snaps when she begins to tread away from him, "It's valuable—you know it is."

She halts.

"Vow it," she says. To my shock.

"I vow," Vane swears. "Now, *you* vow not to leave us for dead."

"I vow not to leave you for dead," Alina says politically, and it floors me that she'd even trust them. Any of them.

But slowly, she heads over to their pile of weapons. Hefty crossbows, war hammers, knives, brass arrows. Stealing from them, right in front of their faces.

Reverently, she shuts the eyes of the murdered elders. "May you live, even after you die."

She shuts her own eyes for only half a second.

Her satiny blond hair's still the exact hue of wild sunflowers. Braided into a laced crown out of the way of her face. She speaks.

"I won't leave you for dead—since I don't plan to leave any of you alive at all."

She loads the gilded crossbow and, one by one, shoots them in the skull.

The last one, Vane—blaring choleric curses, *completely apoplectic*, watching all of his friends slumping over dead—is shot in the gut. An agonizingly slow kill that will last longer.

Alina stands. The leader of her people.

She commands him, "Tell the sniper I killed you for Vraničar. For my mother. My father. My brothers."

Without hesitation, she turns to the whirring, humming hovercraft cameras and harpoons them all before glaring at me.

"If you ever think of setting foot in my path again, I won't care that you're young or a war refugee. I will kill you the same way I did all of them." A threat.

I'm too stunned to even speak. I nod.

She pins the crossbow under her arm. "Snipers can't know which way you went now. Move."

Plunging into the valley, Alina Volkova disappears.

CHAPTER 29

IFE STØRMBANE

DAY ONE, AFTERNOON

Is Head General Størmbane coming? I can handle anyone else.

I've memorized each Størmbane's gait. Listening hard, I discover it's Maximus who's coming. Head General's footsteps are direct and hard. Authoritative. He commands a room before he enters it.

Maximus has a distinct military confidence to his steps. But there's an underlying experienced stealth, a seasoned sniper. His march is designed to announce him for the other person's sake, not his own. My heart gallops.

Zaire is an intruder. He will be treated as a threat.

Maximus will annihilate him. I need to think quickly.

I shove Zaire and dash for the metal double doors of the main bedroom. I slam them shut as fast as possible. "Sprint over there!"

Zaire bounds over the vintage trestle like an actual acrobat, powered by overwhelming adrenaline. He lands lightly on scuffed boots, tracking swamp water all over my plush

Vikąrian rugs. The ones Maximus's *grandmother* gifted us for our wedding, and I groan.

But still Zaire treks farther down my suite, before going onto his seaweed-stained knee. He swings his hands devoutly together in false servility to me as my heart pounds in my throat. *Think. Think.* Maximus must hear all the noise. The doors open.

"Ife, the diplomats are settled. Are you feeling—?" His words sever completely and he doesn't finish his sentence, because his sharp, below-zero-blue eyes catch Zaire now.

I toss a burst of glitter in the air, stolen from my makeup vanity, as if Maximus popped in on a surprise ritual for the sky and rain. As if I haven't been caught with an unsanctioned intruder.

"Maximus!" I smother his face with kisses. "*Amazing news! The rain promised to bless us all—*"

"Who is this man?"

Maximus's prominent jaw locks in rage. Beyond the windows, tar-black clouds broil in the skies, hissing with rapid lightning and seething rain. But the weather still doesn't match Maximus's unmitigated fury.

"Maximus, bunny. The rain is our friend and—"

"Who is he?" Maximus repeats. His eyes are slaughterous as he demands his security unit. "Establish a perimeter and check his body. Take my wife to safety on the main floor."

Soldiers surround the bedroom, eleven of them restricting exits as my voice is drowned out.

Shockingly, it never occurred to me until now how much more *dominant* Maximus would be than Zaire. As Zaire stands and Maximus's imposing frame towers over him, my husband has six inches of brutal height over Zaire. Maximus's shoulders are broader, his chest more muscular. *They're half a foot apart.*

The stark contrast only emphasizes how frail Zaire has become, with his shrunken cheekbones and thin body. He's not a challenge.

Maximus could kill him bare handed.

Maximus vowed to kill all threats to his family, never to allow history to repeat. Eight of his older brothers are dead. His mother was killed. Maliciously.

By an intruder.

Without warning, a guard slams Zaire onto the ground, jamming his face into marble so violently his neck audibly cracks. Blood spurts out of his nose.

"Stop! What are you doing?" I cry. "Get off him! Stop it!"

I tear forward, but Maximus restrains my waist. As they search Zaire for weapons, pockets tear, buttons shred, nylon rips. I can't see any of it as the auxiliary military bursts into the room, metal boots stamping on rugs and marble. I writhe against Maximus's arm, but he holds firm. "Head down with the main guards. The entire area will be locked down."

"Locked down for what!" I plead.

"There's been a military breach. His weapons—"

Tears spring to my eyes. "What weapons? I invited him!"

"You invited an unknown intruder upstairs?"

"An *acrobat*—to praise the rain! The raindrops will shower us all soon!" I rasp. "We're preparing a blessing offering with ritual knives."

I pull free.

"Watch. Show him!"

But Zaire is trapped. Blood oozes from his scalp. It leaks into his tawny, leonine hair and onto the marble floor. A sight I can never erase, even though I squeeze my eyes shut. Frantic. "Maximus, he's a guest! He's our guest!"

"Secure Thorsten in the third annex," Maximus commands a lieutenant, who snaps his regulation boots together and salutes him.

Another soldier informs him, "The intruder has no seal. Not to even enter the island—"

Zaire spits, "I'm a last-minute rain performer. Weren't you expecting a rain praiser on the island?"

My brother's voice is deadly cold. Suffused with hatred.

He glares at Maximus from the ground. Maximus glowers back at him with muted, primal aggression. As if he could rend his flesh. As if he's remembering every man that killed his older brothers. I squeak out a squeal.

"A rain dancer!" I beam. "Look! I wanted him to display a shí'a'kì for the diplomats—thrill them with *actual* rain-calling Makarian traditions. They'll love it, honestly."

Despite hearing Zaire choke, I grit my teeth and bathe Maximus's face with lovesick kisses, wrapping my arms around him, as if I can't possibly tame myself.

I plead, "The rainstorms love us, and we must honor the skies."

An hour ago, Pacer informed me there was a military breach. Missing uniforms. Vanishing fans. A dead soldier. Rumblings of terrorism. *They can't associate that with Zaire. There's no way he has anything to do with it.*

Now, I speak so fast I almost spit words.

"Aren't you excited? The rain clouds will be ecstatic!" I gaze up at Maximus through my soft lashes and toss another burst of glitter. "A shí'a'kì has *never* been seen by outsiders." I watch Maximus's eyebrows knot, see the grind of his severe jawline as he takes in Zaire's coarse, smeared skin. Then Zaire's knives scattered on the ground by the guards. "Aren't you going to greet him, Maximus?"

"Ife." Maximus sets a physical barrier, himself, between me and Zaire. "Are you all right?"

His intense eyes evaluate me hard, as if I'm suffering from gullibility. I've seen mercenaries examine their targets with less intensity than Maximus examines me. But I blink, clueless.

"Bunny bear, of course. The skies will favor everyone; I can feel it."

"How did he get in?"

"He's highly recommended," I promise, avoiding his question. "The sky itself chose him. The sky is our protector; it speaks to the rainfall."

Maximus's eyes narrow. My throat dries.

"What's wrong?" I blink.

"Why is this man in our suite?" He levels a hard gaze at the knives. "Not in the atrium rehearsal quarters or in the main arena?"

"We had to gather the blessings in *private*. Otherwise, someone might try to steal the rain's blessings and anger it."

Wrong answer. Maximus nods to be polite but then turns to address his sergeant. "Rɛv vren icer."

Get me an ice bucket.

There are dozens of extreme Allied Force methods of interrogation that involve a single bucket of ice and little else. No electrocution needed.

Raw panic stings my lungs. *Get this under control.*

"Ask Pacer," I insist. "This has nothing to do with the breaches. He'll confirm it."

But Maximus fumes in dark rage at Pacer as he officially emerges. "Vanmark, come here."

My skin sweats with fear as Pacer steps forward. *Lie, lie, lie to him. Please, for once, lie.*

Pacer dutifully salutes. Calm. "Sniper General Størmbane."

"Did you authorize him?" Maximus's hard eyes scrutinize Zaire's wet boots. Soles clogged with sewage and soiled seagrass, destroying the expensive floor polish. "What purpose does he have coming to the Allied Force territory?"

"He was vetted and has no ill intentions," Pacer assures him. "He is a rain praiser, as he says."

"A *trained* rain performer," Zaire grits out, underneath a heavy enforcer kneeling on his spine. He expires a spittle of bile. "It's the highest honor to serve the rain and the regal Kōn family." Zaire's eyes glare in despisement at Maximus. "She has a surprise for the world."

Maximus's features darken. "My wife?"

"Yes. A world announcement."

Maximus directs his soldiers, so low I almost miss it: "Svẹgẹ en re."

Dispose of him.

"Maximus, stop!"

The room goes silent.

I realized I screamed, and my echoes bounce off the imported Carrara walls, ringing back to us. Tears brush my eyes, and I fake a sob. "I invited him. For a reason." *Think. Faster. World announcement.*

I squeeze my eyes shut and blurt out a lie that might alter my life forever: "I had a vision . . . that our sons would mean a rebirth of your family. I wanted to surprise you and celebrate afterward."

I dig my canines into my cheek.

"The rain promised to bless us for our children."

Maximus has never said it, but I can sense he wants sons to restore his damaged family, recover everyone he's lost. Keep their memories alive. It's why he altered his reproductive system to produce only future sons.

All his close friends are dead. He has more murdered cousins than living. The earliest military years of his life were his brothers' funerals. He was trained to be undefeated. Precise. Perfect.

In the Allied Force, at six years old, children are inducted into the military and taken to live in the mountains. Proctors examine the children and have them fight to the death in bear caves. Only those who survive the cave matches continue to the Arctic glaciers on Mount Ivkør, where they endure two bloodless winters until they turn eight. Forced to rely on each other and bond as brothers. The process forges self-sufficient youths strengthened against adversity—built in brutal conditions.

The purpose is to end their childhood. Each boy enters the bear cave three times. In the Arctic glaciers, the proctors never inform them of the hour, day, week, or month. It's deliberate isolation; their komrades become their world: how they eat, how they live, how they survive. Dependent on each other—yet ferociously self-sustaining.

Then, at nine, expert military training begins. In the wilderness, year after year, until they are deemed men.

Then the unspeakable ritual of increasingly barbaric challenges begins, the relentless, grueling induction to manhood known as Mengę. *First survival.*

After Mengę, there's the rebirth known as Först. *First manhood.*

I still can't speak about what occurs in Först. I can't even repeat it without my eyes watering. My guts wrench every time.

The Allied Force mass-produces *child soldiers.* Killer children. Maximus endured his military training through dedication; he understood his national duty. His nation depended on his sacrifices. His nation became his cause. He bore the pain for it.

Killed for his brothers.

But when he returned home, eight years later, all of his older brothers were gone. He'd forgotten about his own family. He'd failed to protect their lives with his own.

He won't make the same mistake twice.

"Yes," Zaire exhales, nearly drained of air. "A surprise birth celebration."

But Zaire glares at me as if I'm the most dangerous fool alive. *What have you done?*

Right now, Maximus gazes between me and Zaire. His piercing blue eyes darken with concentration, analyzing everything in their path. My pulse accelerates.

My naturally doe-like green eyes are wholesome, warm, loving. Zaire's green eyes are mischievous, cunning, sly. I can tell Maximus has figured out we're related—his mind only questions *how* Zaire is related to me.

But I realize Maximus can also sense Zaire is here for a reason, likely to take me from him and separate our family. Maximus would kill him before that ever happened.

"Maybe keep him with the exhibition rainfall drums?" I ask, almost hysterical. "Amaze the diplomats another time?"

That will give me time to think. The conclusion of the Great Hunt can't be more horrific than the start. It can't.

Maximus's mouth opens, so I steal my chance. "Give him a chance to shock the crowds. Live. We can announce our family." Zaire's lips snarl.

Zaire has too much pride to be *entertainment* for the Arctic masses. Particularly with finicky raindrums, since the corner of his lip is already scarred from the time his prized raindrum burst and cracked his jaw open.

It's what gave him his permanently crooked smile.

But I need to think on my feet. The Allied Force military will brutalize Zaire for breaking their protocol. Every inch of the Allied Force is an airtight regime—even on foreign territory.

Zaire needs to stay low enough for the military to forget this, but it will not. The Arctic does not forget. The Arctic does not forgive.

I chirp, "*Aww!* Now the rainbirds will fly off!" I pout. I almost sob with gratitude when the heavy enforcer relents on his vertebrae.

The tension finally breaks. *Zaire can't belong to them. The military will kill him.* I squeeze myself so I don't gasp out loud for air. *I need to get him out of here.*

Maximus orders one of his guards to speak to the exhibition conductor about the rain-calling spectacle. My heart rockets against my ribs. *Release him, release him, Maximus Størmbane.*

CHAPTER 30

Zaire darts a venomous glare at me as he's finally escorted out. His nose bandaged and cleaned. His eyes are urging me to escape. *You need to flee, Ife. Run.*

"Thank you so much! Make sure those raindrops don't wet your bed!" I shout, desperate to make him laugh.

Zaire hurls up a finger, and Maximus almost notices it.

Maximus takes a seat, and the enforcers depart. The remaining fury emanates from me, making it impossible to look at him. I can't *believe* what I let out of my mouth. I'd rather eat hot asphalt than become bloated with babies. I have to get myself out of this.

Assassinate Maximus before it ever comes to that.

I need space. Somewhere to think. But Maximus's never furious with me for long, as if it's against his nature to hold a grudge against his own family. He's lived enough to understand how insufficient memories become when they're all you have left of someone. It renders most fights pointless.

But I'm ballistic inside. Explosive with rage.

Still, before I can step into the bath to splash ice-cold water on my heated face, rugged hands grasp my waist, pulling me into his massive frame. Maximus maneuvers me onto the edge of the tub. "Visitors are dead on the island. Everyone needs to take precautions."

"He was only a dancer," I say, soft. "Not a security breach."

"He was a breach." Maximus's voice remains patient. "Several military breaches have occurred during this Hunt alone. Everyone needs approved identification for entry. It does not matter if we're not in the homeland. Intruders turn deadly, unmarked strangers, men—"

"A surprise dancer was going to thank the rains for me. The rain has rejected me all my life." I pout, but I pretend to surrender and slouch my shoulders. "Sorry. I didn't mean to cause any trouble—"

He kisses my bare shoulder. "I know. You didn't cause trouble." His jaw sets; I can hear it in his voice. His mind is revisiting every decision, every movement, that occurred. What he might've missed.

"Blud vør," I whisper, even softer. *You are my blood.* "You're my everything. Thank you."

My gentle fingertips caress his cheek. Distracting his mind.

Maximus sets his eyes on my hands. "Everything's new for you on the outside, isn't it?"

"All the time. Why?"

Maximus vows, "I'll examine how to simplify the regulations so you understand."

I bury my face in his neck, inhaling a hint of his expensive cologne. "Thank you. You're so kind, Maximus. How are the ambassadors?"

Maximus chuckles. "Corrupt as ever."

"How do they make you feel?" I always ask about Maximus's feelings, as though they're more important than my own. The most important in the world.

Maximus loves being cared for. He won't say it directly, but he enjoys having someone devote their entire life to him. I cook nearly every meal for him, preparing for hours, and treat him to massages and deep baths. Lovingly. I create a warm and supportive space for him and Thorsten, listening to their thoughts and dreams. Making rich, savory homemade meals and encouraging their ideas of new traditions for our small family.

But even if he met a thousand diplomats, it's the same response. Maximus has no feelings for foreigners, and at times, his complete desensitization is almost as frightening as other men's absolute hatred. He bears no hatred.

It's not even neutrality he feels; it's full detachment.

"I'm fine. How's my princess?" Maximus asks. He bites into the exposed skin of my shoulder, and his arm drifts around my waist. He kisses the petals in my hair before his lips find my nape and trail down my spine and into my dress. "Is she happy?"

"Happy to be alone with you, *finally*. I brought you a gift."

"Show me," he whispers, pulling me onto his lap. I feel all of his heat.

Maximus gazes at me like I'm the only person in the universe, like no one else exists. His expression's bare with me. The most potent emotion he's capable of. He regards me as if I'm his personal miracle, created for him as an escape.

I lie about asinine stuff all the time—how much I miss him, *need* him—in front of his friends, guards, family. It's an easy throwaway. They're just words. But Maximus's smitten with my silly behavior. Deeply.

He melts every time.

My gift is always the same—a shower of warm kisses.

Maximus kisses my palms in return. "I love the gifts. I missed you more than life."

We live together. How is it possible to *miss me*? I don't know. But for Makari, I slip my arms around his neck. I peer through my sweet lashes up at him. "Missed you more." I nuzzle my nose against his. "I always miss you more."

Maximus drinks in my gaze, and I press my flushed cheek against his and hiccup. Suddenly, a tear almost wets his ironed tuxedo shirt. A dramatic sob explodes out of me.

"What's wrong?" Maximus sits up on the white marble bath.

I hiccup. "N-Nothing."

"Tell me, Ife." He smooths my hair back and moves my bangs out of my eyes so he can study them. "Just say it."

"No, it's *embarrassing*."

"Tell me. I'll take care of it."

"No, I just . . ." I bury my face in his tuxedo shirt. "I miss you even when you're right next to me," I murmur pathetically. I interlace our fingers. "I know it makes no sense. But you leave on military expeditions every month. Sometimes for days. And it makes me feel helpless, like I can't be without you even a second, and I-I don't . . . I don't ever want to, Maximus. I can't bear being without you anymore."

Mirrored feelings. Whenever Maximus admits a feeling, even missing me, I copy that feeling to make it feel shared.

But silence swells in the room. Not even the automatic steamy bath runs anymore.

His lips flatten. "Ife."

Ugh, I said too much! I bite my cheek, bracing for the worst. *He caught on!* I messed up twice already—

"I'll always come back to you." Summit-blue eyes stare down into my own. He squeezes my fingers. "It's only a matter of when, not if. Never forget that."

Maximus melds his fingers hard with mine.

"Thank you, Maximus."

"I feel alive only with you lately, Ife," he admits against my lips as we breathe each other's air. Our foreheads warm each other. "You give me purpose."

My lips spread as I hear him. *Purpose. Responsibility.* Most Arctic soldiers return from war to their cold wives and strange children who barely recognize them. Only their hounds love them unconditionally—a solitary existence. Maximus savors our warm family. He understands the loss of it.

"You're my favorite person, Ife. I knew when I first kissed you, how nurturing you were, how gentle, I wanted to feel that feeling for the rest of my life. Eternity is short in comparison to how long I want to be with you."

"I love you, Maximus. More than anything in the world." I lean myself against him, closing my eyes, feeling our hearts beat hard against each other. "But why me?"

I know if Maximus hears himself say why he loves me, it will only reinforce his own belief more deeply. I'm his lover when we're alone; his healer; his confidant; his best friend; his carnal release. "Why am I this special to you? I could've been anyone."

"No, you couldn't have. You are a perfect example of what a person should be." Maximus chuckles. "You put others before yourself. You treat Thorsten and Vørian as if they were your own family. You carry inexhaustible good-will and natural kindness. You make me a better human being, and seeing you helps me regain a sense of my . . . humanity."

"Really?" I murmur sweetly, as if he's never said it before. "No other woman has done that for you before?"

"Allied Force women have always helped me become a better man. You make me better as a human." He removes his metal cuff links. "At times, I am so desensitized I forget I am even human. Does that make sense?"

I gaze in adoration. "I am that helpful?"

He kisses my ear. "Always."

I return his kiss with fervor. "Without you, I wouldn't have broken out of my timid, isolated life. You saved me. Thank you for letting me run away to you."

His warm blue eyes crinkle as they smile down at me. "I would retrieve you a million times over. The world deserves a pure heart. Pure art." Maximus gazes at me in devotion. "You are art everlasting."

Breath leaves my lungs. "Maximus . . ."

Electricity sizzles up my spine. Maximus Størmbane looks different right now, and I can't breathe. He's handsome like daybreak. Dreamy like fresh sunlight. The atmosphere feels magnetic and seductive.

Art outlasts life, Maximus always tells me. In reality, Maximus loves the *idea* of me, the art of me. That's actual power I hold, a power that I need to maintain—at all costs.

A person is imperfect. But an *idea* of a person can feel like perfection.

That's what *actually* sets me apart from any woman he's ever met. I'm his *idea* of humanity. What it might look like.

I am his tangible hope that he still has his humanity. Maximus abandoned it over the years, but with me—he has the potential to restore it. To repay his inestimable debt to humankind. To feel like he's a human being, not some callous killer.

A man capable of redemption.

I've learned when you inspire someone's belief that they're more than they actually are—you hold true power.

"You are too perfect, Maximus." I kiss him, gently.

Maximus meets my eyes completely. "Life feels like perfection, refreshed, with you. Instead of decimating, I'm *creating* for the first time with you. It'll be our family, something meaningful, and entirely ours. Aire res." Meaning nothing is above that. "I plan to make your visions come true."

"You're poetic." I gaze up at him with pure affection.

"For you." Maximus drives me to his lips.

Since his Arctic expedition, we've hardly had a moment alone together. We're no longer watched now. At all.

His hungry hand already grips my sweaty sundress, dragging the first layer of fabric up. I can feel the heavy exertion from Maximus to not be too rough, his teeth caged with effort, his free hand nearly denting the metal edge of the bath.

His starvation reminds me of our breathless, possessive, torrid nights pressing each other against the doors, biting into each other's skin so no one could overhear us, suppressing our sounds. Barely careful enough to lock the doors properly. When neither of us was engaged anymore, we were required by society to wait politely before he pursued me, except Maximus didn't bother to wait, and I couldn't wait, keen to keep alliances with the Allied Force.

"I want you," he always breathed against my cheek. "Be my wife."

We were hormonal teenagers back then, making out whenever we could; it didn't matter where. If it was sacred, restricted, or random, we barely paid attention. We didn't even know the depth of what it meant to be husband and wife; it sounded adventurous to our ears.

I didn't pretend to be innocent with myself—I knew what he wanted, and I also knew what I wanted. An even exchange.

Maximus made every excuse to visit me in the foreign

embassy, and I happily behaved as if we had very important matters to deliberate in private.

"I need you so badly it's killing me," he'd whisper. "Live with me."

After I made him chase long enough, I pretended I needed a week to make my mind up. My belongings were already packed—I never fully unpacked them—and I thought to myself: *This was too easy.* Only later did I learn the truth of the Allied Force—Maximus would change my name and I would be expected to birth ten sons for him. That was only the start.

Now, my swollen lips part, warmth spreading across my cheeks from the sensation of his clean-shaven jaw finding my neck. I make a small sound as he kisses my throat.

Tightly, I squeeze my eyes shut. *Don't throw up, don't throw up, don't throw up on him.*

Don't feel anything.

Hormones flood my bloodstream, a familiar toxin, as I inhale his natural pheromones mingling with my own, my perfume mixing with his distinctive cologne. Intertwining. I taste his skin, tongue on tongue, and lips on lips. We're pressed so tightly against each other the friction becomes unbearable.

Water fills the bath rapidly.

I kiss him, urgently, impatiently, a million fibers of electricity racing over my belly. My traitorous brain demands more of him. Everywhere.

We've always tried to be polite and decently behaved, like conventional husbands and wives in society. But we're uncontrollably greedy for each other. We've always been rabid for each other, stealing territory on each other's skin, claiming it for our own, and right now, wild lust brings us back to our past.

The diplomats need more time to process their crisis and catch their breath. They deserve their last moments to themselves. Therefore I pretend I don't care there are diplomats waiting for us downstairs. That I don't care that the enforcers are standing by to open the doors for us to enter while we're busy with each other.

Fabrics are ripped and discarded, stockings torn and abandoned; his palms are sticky between my thighs, and all my sense escapes. My knees press together at the movement of his skilled hands. Heat gathers between my water-slick thighs. My hands gather his shirt into knots in response.

My floral strings float on the water.

My teeth nip his ear without softness. Maximus doesn't make me feel nauseous now. It's not just his words. He *feels* different. Hotter. Steamier.

Contain yourself. All my first romantic experiences have been with him. *Use your head, Ife.* But for a split second, I wonder if the emotional attachment I fake with him is real, if I'm attached to him. If I'm clinging to him now out of guilt for sending humans to die. If I'm distracting myself to assuage the pain to the point where I believe he's all I deserve now as a war criminal myself. Stomach acid spurts up my throat, choking me. I cough. *You're not attached. Don't be an airhead.*

Extreme conditions. Traumatizing experiences. Psychological impacts. All can create emotional bonds. You are not bonded—you are too intelligent for that.

I know better. Even now, I know psychological responses don't care if you're clever and sharp—you can't control it sometimes, so I convince myself it's completely natural to have desires and lust; it's part of being human. There is nothing filthy or dirty about girls having thirst. Hormones are completely normal, I tell myself.

Besides, I rationalize, Maximus's fingers aren't freezing cold, like they are a quarter of the time. His body feels like the Iceberg of Tacitus some nights. But right now . . . right now, his hands are dangerously warm. Dangerously expert. His scent, his aura, is driving me out of my mind. That thirst becomes aching, irresistible, and we start to miss each other's mouths, kissing anywhere we can.

He swallows every breath of mine down his throat. *You are art everlasting.*

We make direct eye contact, and all my thoughts scatter. "Please."

"As you command." Maximus smirks against my throat, his experienced hand moving under my sundress. Hiking the skirt up my waist. My hips rise.

The doors slam open, and we fly apart. Head General Størmbane barges in with a flood of enforcers. The crunch of their boots sends fear up my spine. I gasp, tearing farther away from Maximus.

Before they can reach the bath, I adjust my sopping-wet dress. Maximus stands in front of me.

Head General's coarse shadow stretches across the marble.

"Head General!" Blazing heat scampers up my face. "Victory to the Allied Force, Head General!"

"Victory. Are you not attending the island celebrations, Maximus Barringer?"

Barringer stares at our flushed faces, mussed hair, bitten lips. My drenched clothes. His eyes narrow. But he doesn't speak.

He removes his leather gloves instead. My eyes widen. Head General is out of uniform and casually dressed, for him at least. A fitted black shirt emphasizes his sturdy build, and dark-green hunting trousers stop in tall, polished black boots.

But blood splatters his gloves and the toes of his boots. *He killed someone . . . but who?*

I gasp. The world tilts toward oblivion. But as if reading my mind, Pacer shakes his head as he salutes. *Not Zaire.* Head General glances at Maximus, as if he has serious information.

My cue to leave, and I beam. "Sensational opening! It's hard to catch my breath, right, Maximus?"

Maximus chuckles. "It is always hard to catch your breath, Ife."

Barringer glances at me for barely a second. "You enjoy the Hunts, Ikä?"

"Oh, I love them! They're thrilling. All this excites me."

"She buzzed in my ear all night." Maximus smiles.

"Maximus, *stop.*" I swat him playfully. But I did ask him a million questions. Strategizing about how the victims I sent to Kaipo's jungle will survive, and it *is* making me breathless with fear.

How could I have surrendered into escapism? Even if all is lost for those innocents, I need to figure out how to decimate the entire Allied Force.

How to utilize Kaipo Island to rupture the entire Allied Force military there.

Maximus and Barringer depart for the war room, finally discussing things I'm actually interested in. But the solid automatic doors shut behind them, and the walls are too thick; I can't hear anything.

Still, I know what they're talking about. Stolen uniforms. Missing fans. Dead fans.

Dead snipers.

Which is why, beforehand, I shoved three bone readers in the archaic balcony eaves in the war room and slipped one more in the blush-pink peons. Places they'd never notice. And if they're noticed, they're just bone king heirlooms. Passable as decorations.

But the bone king used bone readers to record war meetings. The meetings will reappear as visions when I sleep. His presages were never by accident.

But my ears are open as well; I'm always listening and researching.

Waiting to end the Allied Force.

By magic or by force.

CHAPTER 31

DAY ONE, EVENING

I gasp.

I skid to a halt on my trek for somewhere safe to sit and take inventory of my wounds. My endorphins are still high octane, and it takes me a minute to realize what I ran into.

Who I ran into.

Stanislav—the doctor—spears down a man right in front of me. I reckon the doctor's already been through hell—his uniform's torn to shreds, and he has four tourniquets, almost one on each limb. Two on his right leg.

Gunshot wounds.

I'm shocked to even *see* him. Everyone should be fanned out on the island, keeping their heads low and praying they don't run into each other. It's how you survive.

But he's delirious, murmuring to himself, fist gripped around another short silver spear. My heart rate accelerates. If I make one sound from these usha bushes, he'll spot me and end me. A cry is pulled out of his throat.

"Needle . . . Stat . . . Patient . . ." he cries out. In grief, he discards the spear and attempts to rip the last of his tattered uniform to stanch the blood blooming from the man's chest. As if underneath it all he will always be a doctor. "Forgive me . . . I didn't mean . . ."

He's broken. Ruined. A far sight from the warm older man who sneaked coffee beans into my palms two years ago. It would be a mercy to end him now, but I can't.

Still, my heart thumps with danger. Soon, his loud sobs will attract enemies.

I need this area. It's *perfectly* concealed. If there were a hidden sniper, by now he would've shot us both. *I need this area.*

Both of us are ragged and bloodied. As Stanislav howls, I need to flee. But sure enough, Stanislav hears my footsteps in the thicket, and without hesitation, the half spear is right back in his grasp. Yanked out of the chest of his victim.

A shout is trapped in my throat. "Wait!"

I lift my hands in truce. For a heart-stopping moment, I expect to break through to him. "It's me—Coa Rangecroft."

But it's useless. Stanislav charges forward, growling and foaming at the mouth, as I sprint for cover. Due to his gunshot wounds, I outrun him, and I'm deep in the jungle before I hear a sniper locate his growling and shouting.

Soon, a fury of gunshots ends his war cry.

And I realize his spear went through my wrist.

———

I stagger, nearly collapsing from pain. My incisors crack from the pressure of my jaw gritting through the agony. *He speared me.*

Damp, humid air is thick on my mouth. Wings flutter. Exotic birds call. The heavy jungle breathes in a chorus of vibrant, dark greens at night. It's sleepy with comfort, as if placated by the amount of blood sacrifices it's enjoyed. For the first day, at least.

Across from me, spotted monkeys pull their young close for midnight.

Drowsy, I sit on a charred stump. I don't even know what could char this stump, but I need rest. Voices rise all over. Distant screams, cries of anguish.

People maim each other.

I cradle my head in my hands.

The jarring terror of the Great Hunt has rendered me traumatized. My wrist is mangled, my hand limp, useless, and discolored, despite my best efforts to mirror the tourniquets Stanislav made for himself. But I don't know much about tourniquets or their purpose to begin with.

Hopeless, I can only wait for the inevitable. The likelihood that this might be the last time I have my hand attached.

My chest heaves with exhaustion, before I hear a clumsy set of footsteps.

It's a Great Hunt fan.

I back away, clearing sleep from my tired eyes with my bloody arm.

Bray Rainsford.

I gasp. "How are you here?"

"I bribed a brown-gear enforcer like everyone else." Bray's breathless with concern. He doesn't even know enforcers wear black and slaughter men wear dark green; the man he bribed must've been a carnage man, since they wear brown. "Are you okay?"

Tears of anguish are crusted in my eyes. I can't feel my

left wrist any longer, and I don't know if that's worse than if it were screaming with excruciating pain. Even in the amateur sling I made for myself—it's disastrously damaged. Numbed.

Sleep is senseless, and if Bray can find me . . . *the snipers can.* I get up to keep moving.

"I saw the gunfire at the resort. Everything's hyperrealistic." Bray offers, oblivious, "If you want, I can make that splint look professional."

"Didn't use a splint."

"*No splint?*" Bray reaches, but the thought of his upsetting the wound almost makes me scream like an animal.

My body lumbers forward instead—still dazed from killing two Allied Force citizens. Still numb from hearing Stanislav's final moments.

My bare hands are still smeared with blood. But they don't even feel like *my* hands. No matter how long I stare at my own palms, my mind can't even process it.

One of my hands doesn't even have *sensation.*

"We'll need survivalist techniques. All the best televised survivalists, explorers, and extreme adventurers craft a detailed strategy—"

I snap, "How did you even find me?"

He's atrociously clean. Even had time to shower.

"The enforcer had a camera drone that locked on all seventy-five participators." It was that easy for him. "There's forty now."

We're almost down to half? They killed almost half of us already?

Ignoring my own rage, I keep trudging through the pestiferous underbrush.

Tauntingly, images of a smirking Vørian Størmbane

eager to shoot at us burn through my eyelids. I'm trapped here. With no escape.

The best I can hope for is to spread out like everyone else and keep my nose out of trouble.

"Five tools of survival—everything we need to start with," Bray starts. He lists off our necessities. "Cover elements to protect us from hostile nature. Ignition materials to stay warm at night when the jungle's temperature changes—"

My eyes widen. How does he know the weather shifts on this island? Who told him that?

"Did you bring a copy of the textbook?"

"What textbook?"

According to the African textbook, temperatures will plunge, violently, and in the unnatural breeze, I feel it starting. As spiteful as this landscape is, we might be battered by hail one night and swimming in mudslides the next. It's possible with orún this powerful, which *wasn't* mentioned in the text. I doubt the Allied Force knew about it prior.

Which is why I need to find a good spot and keep inside of it.

Hopefully, the hexed island will kill the snipers before they can kill the rest of us.

Bray lists from memory, "Containers of water to sustain us through brutal heat and long distances. Not to mention food and sources of sustenance, which is why cutting tools—"

He stares at my purpling wrist. "You *sure* you don't need a splint for that?"

"Sure as sunrise."

Bray glances around for a place to rest. His eyes scan over a seemingly endless swamp broken only by nesting crocodiles ahead.

He rambles, "So wild. I used to visit the safaris and

artificial wildlife centers on summer breaks. We studied the Makari-African Empire nonstop in our institute. Eighteen years of Makarian knowledge right here." He taps his head of unruly light-brown hair. Grins. "And yet I've always dreamed of Kaipo Island."

Now this place has a name. Kaipo Island.

"Kaipo is the sun king, associated with spirits, hallucinations, mind possession."

Hallucinations? Mind possession? Stanislav seemed possessed when he looked at me, but I reckon it was mostly his struggle to survive in conditions designed to turn him from man to beast.

"Bet you all studied." Hazen knows more than he should about Makari. Its mythologies. Its practices. He even *speaks* a Makarian language.

I suspect the Allied Force always learns their enemies better than their enemies know themselves. Adapt and seize. I reckon they truly pride themselves on deliberately creating whole generations of experts on foreign cultures in order to eradicate them.

The Allied Force citizens are taught no one aided them during their centuries of famine.

But Whitelaw said the globe remembers anyone who set foot in the Kilrød was enslaved. Put to work to search for resources and food until they died.

Right now, Bray's limber fingers use one of his utility knives to cut orún-thick swamp vines. He drains them into a canister that beeps. "Here. Medication."

I gape at him. *How?*

He shrugs like Evelie does when she's concocted a medical salve all on her own. Humble yet proud. "Baruru always have medicinal properties. These devices remove toxins—so even the most poisonous baruru vines are safe." He gently lifts my bloodstained knee, the fabric of my trousers torn, and spreads his thumb across it. Applying the medication to my skin gingerly.

Light handed. Respectful.

Slow, though, and I take it to spread on myself. Hesitant.

He cautions, "Baruru *are* magic based. Fair warning." He tastes some. "Truthfully, outside of simulated reality, I've never used Makarian herbs . . . mushrooms . . . flora . . . Goodness." My wound all but evaporates. "Glories—!"

I slam my hand over his mouth before he can excitedly alert snipers or competitors to our location.

"It works," he says, muffled. "Do you *feel* that?"

I feel it immensely. Even I'm taken aback by the way he just harnessed healing orún magic. I reckon it wouldn't work anywhere else but Kaipo Island—the sun king's ancestral island.

My larger wounds are trickier—the process takes longer. But I'm so grateful for the potion that my eyes nearly water.

Mostly asleep, the jungle tangibly respires with scuttling insects, stinging mosquitoes, moist air. Bray mixes them all as he heals my body and indulges in the herbs' taste.

A spirit screams.

I can never get used to it, but their screeches are always inhuman, far too high pitched to be one of the competitors, and at least that gives me a little comfort.

Until I realize I could be screaming next.

Flurries of slippery leaves and rain-soaked flakes of dirt whip across our faces as the mighty kapok trees shake them loose for the night.

Raptors search for easy prey, forcing half maimed rabbits into meerkat holes. Lemurs blink at us—unreadable. As if there are no souls left in them.

An unsettling feeling swells around me. As if something is about to happen.

Bray's oblivious. He smears some of the healing paste onto a scrape on his elbow, then catches one of the hares for dinner. Babbles on. "Only a hundred and fifty hours left."

"A night and six days." I try to speak around the emotion squeezing my throat. I want to ask after my siblings so badly it hurts. *Are they executing entire families already? Those of us who died today?* But I know he won't have that information, so I ask instead, "Do you know what happens to Great Hunt winners?"

"Wildest movie productions ever." Bray smiles like I should be proud footage of me might be paraded through the Allied Force.

I'm not surprised at his exhilaration. But something else makes me stop cold.

The temperature of the air around me drops to freezing. It claws my throat. I see a dead body rotting in the dirt.

The elderly woman Alina Volkova tried to save. Drenched in blood.

A vision. *She's already dead.* No—no. I shake my head—but my brain seems to tilt.

She's a hallucination from the baruru. Bray just intoxicated us by accident. As much as I try to grip reality—I completely lose it to total delirium.

Leaving us easy targets on the ground.

CHAPTER 32

IFE STØRMBANE

DAY TWO, NOON

Psychological warfare begins.

The soldiers barely feed the laborers or give them water—but apparently every noon, sharp, all laborers are forced to gather in the rinder platz for propaganda broadcasts. To learn about the glory of the Allied Force.

To remind them of their inferiority.

The Allied Force's infinite superiority.

The rinder platz resembles an outdoor livestock pit, with scrubbed-clean concrete floors, weathered walls, and screens above the metal barriers.

Valeska and I watch the laborers kneel on bare concrete. "All hail the grandest continent on earth—the Allied Force. All kneel before the perfect honor of the Vikąrian flag. A nation born to cleanse the world of inferior blood. To purge the world of foreign cretins."

They repeat the doctrines. Tourists watch from behind the barriers.

"Foreign blood will not last. All countries will fall to the Allied Force. Hail the rise of the New Kilrød. Praise the perfect blood of the Arctic. Celebrate the dignity of the Allied Force military—"

A wail.

My breath catches.

A dehydrated baby squalls for water, squirming in his terrified mother's arms. It's at least a hundred ten degrees out and senselessly hot for anyone to be outside without cover, let alone kneel on bare concrete. The enforcers flood the area. The mother's swift, wrenching out a wet cloth and squeezing it into the child's thirsty, seeking mouth. But it's too late—

Apparently, they are not permitted to move during the footage. Unless it's to salute or kneel.

Punishable by death.

"Wait!" the mother cries. "Please! He'll stop!"

Her Vraničarian accent thickens, punctured by broken Vikạrian pleas. "Mercy! Please, he's only a week!"

I shout from behind the crowds, "He won't cry! One more chance—*don't shoot!*" I clutch Kømmand Sergeant Arcus's glove. "By Størmbane Command, I order you to halt them, please!"

Two rifle shots.

Painful.

Permanent.

I anticipate a blotch of blood on the barriers. But as I pry my eyelids open, I see they were warning shots. Kømmand Sergeant Arcus sends me a manufactured smile. "As you command."

Valeska gasps in shock. Repulsed. "Sir, she was born outside of civilization. Excuse her." She adds quickly, "She does not represent the high quality of my work."

A foreign-born commanding an Allied Force *military officer.* Insolent. Preposterous. The Størmbane Command is reserved for military-ranked Størmbanes.

For example, Maximus may use a Størmbane Command to countermand orders from a far-older general of higher rank. Vørian Størmbane would not be permitted to use a Størmbane Command since he is an initiate, not a graduate.

But Kømmand Sergeant Arcus honors the command, and I get the sense he would've perversely enjoyed witnessing the murders.

The broadcast continues, "The Allied Force Department of War thanks all visitors for their contributions to the top specialized subdepartments: The War Department of Advanced Technology. The War Institute of Education and Research. The War Bureau of Financial Security and Treasury."

The Allied Force recording gloats about how well spent the tourists' taxpayer vikęs are. It reads out nearly each and every public sector of the government funded by the Allied Force citizens.

"The War Division of Agriculture and Commerce. The War Administration of Megacorporations. The War Association of Reproduction and Family."

Women birth future soldiers on-screen. The Allied Force depicts the births without hesitation.

"Every Allied Force child born outside of the military is rendered to the Allied Force Department of War. It will be their duty to serve their country. Their pride to gain glory for the Allied Force. All citizens come together to improve the nation."

All of it is systematic.

The Allied Force does not even need 350 million soldiers. The whole country functions as a military itself. But I feel the heat of the onlookers' gazes on the back of my neck as my face is distributed across the broadcast.

"Therefore, we invite you all to create a soldier today."

CHAPTER 33

"Has Sniper General Størmbane enjoyed the events?" Kømmand Sergeant Arcus plasters that synthetic, sickening grin on his face. But his muscles are visibly corded beneath his uniform—as if he's not used to not holding complete authority over a victim. As if the roles should be reversed between us.

Meanwhile, as we exit the rinder platz, female laborers scream for their children, torn apart by soldiers demanding more laborers to replace the dead field-workers.

"He's only six! Kier!" a mother cries out.

Kømmand Sergeant Arcus's jagged mouth has the smile of a sawshark. A man of savagery. Straining to hide his true barbaric nature. His eyes return to me, and he appears civilized. Welcoming.

My bones turn to water. Thorleiv Vøhn Arcus is beyond heinous.

"The sniper general extensively evaluated my men," he mentions with an insidious tone. He compresses his dark gloves behind his back. "Please inform him that all my men will now meet regulation."

The sergeant's men called themselves *slaughter men*. The

abject fear on the pianist's and harpist's battered faces is imprinted in my memory. Whatever Maximus uncovered, he was disturbed enough to threaten to shut down Traeger Island. I take advantage. "Oh, perfect! To celebrate, do you mind if Maximus and I keep your musicians in the resort?"

"The musicians?"

The musicians will be safer within the resort, where the enforcers are stationed.

Anxious, I speak fast. "All of them, if you can have them all moved into the Rainsford Resort."

We're alone and I'm trapped with him as Kømmand Sergeant Arcus opens the East Sector gates for me and repeats himself. "The sniper general. Has he enjoyed the events?"

"He loves them!" I add, "I'll make sure he sends along his regards."

"Excellent." Kømmand Sergeant Arcus nods, releasing a tense breath. "Keep the musicians."

He discards them as if they are materials, not men and women.

He carries himself even taller now, providing a blood-soaked tour of the forced-labor grounds. First, the Traeger Impound—the detention center for new arrivals at the war camp. It's next to the Interrogation Department, which is a metal structure I've rarely seen any laborer leave alive.

Usually, they leave within an indistinct body blanket.

Suddenly, Head General approaches me—as soon as I step inside the Interrogation Department. Kømmand Sergeant Arcus and I both freeze.

"At ease."

My temperature rises. "Victory."

"Victory. Kømmand Sergeant Arcus, close the department for the chief princess. Five minutes."

Kømmand Sergeant Arcus exhales. Disciplined, his boots strike together as he exits. "Victory to the Allied Force, Head General."

"Victory." Head General turns to me, his eyes militant. "Many in the Allied Force have been singing your praises."

He's lying, testing my gullibility and whether I'll have the presence of mind to pretend to believe him. It's something Maximus would never do. My mind jams, almost too shocked to keep up as I force myself to settle my frayed nerve endings in front of him.

The reek of dead bodies is inescapable. There are moans of victims being dragged out by their arms. Cries of newborns held as bait in front of weeping parents.

Head General Størmbane doesn't normally bother with casual talk. He typically kills first. Especially if he already suspects a traitor near him, a snake. *No one is above execution.*

All of my intestines coil into knots. "Singing my praises? That's so kind, Papa."

Too thick. Too thick.

His eyes turn icier than usual. *I know you recruited an aerialist spy,* his eyes seem to say. *I know about the listening devices.*

I shake that fear from my mind. But even Valeska Van Valken watches me from across the dingy building. Closely. *Why is she here before I am?*

Head General's lips touch the tips of my fingers. His famous killer good looks are captured by a flood of holographers. He dismisses them with his gloved hand after the department is closed, obstructing all light from entering the dim building. "My ikä, Makari has borrowed from so many cultures to inspire its names. Please, remind me, what does your name mean?"

I flick my eyes up. Absurdly sweet. "Ìfẹ́ means *love.*"

"Exactly. Love." He tries my name on his tongue. "*E-feh.* Sounds close to *evrę*?" *Betray.*

Our height difference is staggering. Head General is six feet seven inches, brawny like a butcher, so I step back to even it out. I read his face. It's olive toned, inexpressive; nothing gives his thoughts away. With a square jaw and deep scars across his rough skin, he looks like a bulky Huntsman with a war strategist's mind—and a tyrant's ability to control. A dangerous combination.

I examine him quickly. He possesses one clear green eye, peppered silver hair, a prominent chin, and a chilly, unsmiling mouth. I even study the material of the patch over his absent left eye. But I really see nothing that gives away his *thoughts.*

I swallow. "Yes. Um, it is close."

"Love and hope go hand in hand in your culture. You have over a dozen words for hope. A hundred for love. Neither of which spared your homeland from the Allied Force."

"Yes."

"Useless, empty ideals. Are they not then?" Head General frowns, then scratches his clean-shaven, scarred jaw. He reaches toward one of the decorative torches on the tables where tourists can sit and dine as they watch people being tortured. He lights a cigar. I can't breathe.

He brings it to his angular mouth.

"Love, raw hope, they deceive, drug, and mutilate the truth. They're falsely hailed as . . . exhilarators." His tone tightens. "Galvanizers. But perhaps they also can mend things, before further death is absolutely necessary."

Before further death is absolutely necessary.

We're not talking about the same thing anymore. He's talking about what we're *not* discussing: my plans. I stir, suddenly aware of the sweat pooling at my nape, my damp palm swiping at it. My eyes shoot to exits.

They're all blocked. Barricaded by a fleet of enforcers. *No.*

He motions in several grizzled enforcers. Three times the size of me. *No. No. No.*

I turn my voice up, sweeter and flightier. "Ayi! I know all about hope. Maximus gifts me so much *hope* for our future. Our *babies*, oh, babies! Did he inform you? About my announcement?"

Barringer glances at me.

I whisper as if it's a secret.

"I envisioned our sons, and Maximus is beyond excited. He's over the moon and wants fourteen of them." I list them on my fingertips. "Thorsten, Jäeger, Holter, Wulfgar, Sladę, Barringer." I list more on my shaky fingers, begging them to still. Trying to swallow. "Ridge. Vørian. You know, Maximus promised for our fifteenth, he'd reverse his operation so I can birth a girl. I have her name already prepared, of course. Semper paratus."

The silence is lethal.

I quickly fill it in. "Her name will be Ėré Størmbane. Ėré— daughter of love. You're going to be a grandfather soon."

I notice his imperceptible glance at my waist. There's the smallest twist in his lips, but it disappears, just as easily as I can. Mothers aren't needed to raise a child.

Not in the Allied Force.

"My ikä, have I ever told you about my own father?" He releases a current of dark smoke. Answering before I can respond. "My father was the high kømmandęr before he relaxed and became a farmer in his late years. He wanted to grow essentials instead of razing everything, but he knew the value of hope." He looks at me.

"To sustain his generous farm feeding the nearby towns, he slaughtered boars every morning. He fed our humble towns. Much like you, my younger brother despised the killings of innocent animals—relating to their helplessness."

Another beat of silence.

He knows. He knows exactly why I don't eat animals. Barringer learned me without saying a word, but there's something else.

He despised the killing of innocent animals—relating to their helplessness. Animals. He means Makarians. Head General knows I secretly despise the killing of us—knowing the Allied Force kills foreigners the same way it kills animals, with the same techniques, gather and kill—so I've avoided eating animals. My heart breaks for them. I grit my teeth now.

"Do you know what my father did?"

My tone is full of fear. "No."

"He made my brother execute every boar, bare handed. Every day. He never counted them to check, but my father was never to be disobeyed. Eight boars needed to see death per morning. My brother loved animals, men, women, and his friends—in that order. What did my brother do?" He stares at me.

"Defy him?" I whisper. Raspy with terror.

He nods. "One summer, he only killed six per day. Then four. Hoping they would live, perhaps expecting they would escape. Except the nearby wolves noticed where the spared boars were hidden and raided the entire area. Over twenty women died."

"I'm so sorry the wolves killed the women." I grip my chest. "That destroys my heart to hear."

Silence.

"Your father killed them?"

I can't breathe.

"No. I killed them. And the animals. And his friends."

He doesn't flinch at his words.

"Do you know what a killing field is?"

My mind stops. Head General turns to me, an imposing figure of muscular brutality, and a horrific final quiet swallows us. His large hands are locked behind his back. Hands that have killed millions. Indifferently.

High Kømmandęr Størmbane's oldest surviving son. His sharp ice-green eye seizes me.

"My father fed the military base. Raised a nation of men. How often did my brother sabotage the Allied Force after that?" Head General asks. "Who did his older brother become?"

Cold ambition burns in his eye. Focused entirely on me.

He's the same dictator who eliminated the Meridian Empire, scrubbed it from history, then eviscerated the second-largest empire by patience and brutal strategy alone.

And Head General gazes at me directly now. I bite my cheek to keep from gulping in apprehension. I invited his attention. My intestines weaken.

"Treason against the wrong man can end an era of peace," Head General says in perfect South Makarian. "He will not be a man at all."

It's a South Makarian phrase. Certain men stop being men when challenged, turning inhuman. They do not forgive infiltrators in their camp.

Don't grow a mind too bold for yourself, Ife. Don't say anything heedless.

Cold boots step toward me. His dark psyche has a sinister, glacial chill, sending pressure down my spine. I swallow. Thickly.

"Hundreds of your precious animals are still alive at my

discretion. However, all my sons and I do is hunt animals—and our vision is clear, even in the dark. Are you aware of this?"

"Yes, Head General."

"And you love them? These animals?"

"Yes, Head General."

"And my sons?"

"With all my heart."

"Excellent, my ikä." He kisses my fingertips again. "Indulge yourself. Savor my provisions exactly as I provide them for you. And your life will be as sweet as your pure look. Stray from your parameters, and it won't be men like my brother who find you." His words steal the oxygen out of my throat. "You are my family now, my stunning little daughter, and I want you to be strictly as I dictate. Is this fair?"

His warning. For now.

"Yes." *Don't say anything reckless. Don't*—"But—but didn't you love your brother?" I blurt out thoughtlessly, words slipping out before I can catch them.

Kømmand Sergeant Arcus stalks in our direction, the five minutes eclipsed. Barringer nods at him, releasing my fingertips.

"Beyond reason. I cared for him beyond reason. I killed hope, not him." He gazes back at me.

He might as well have done both; he's too sharp not to know that.

Still, it was effective; his brother helped him take over the earth. Eastern General Sladę Størmbane controls an entire region of the Kilrød.

It would mean nothing to Head General to kill me. Maximus's last shred of humanity.

"I understand." My voice is too fragile. I hate the pathetic sound.

Head General kisses my temple. His scent of hardened glacial ice, pine smoke, and military gear fills my senses. Vatrium. "Remember, you can't bite into something poisonous and expect survival; that's not its nature. We welcome you into our family—and our empire—without reservation."

His whole empire is a toxin. He designed it that way.

"Thank you, Viker," my voice squeaks out. "Victory to the Allied Force!"

Barringer passes through the fleet of Kømmand Sergeant Arcus's men without a retreating glance. I realize anyone not native to the Allied Force is an animal to him—available for killing. No, wait.

He killed his own women—Arctic men see *themselves* as the deadliest animals alive. They'd eat each other alive if it came to it.

That is why every man wants an army of his own bloodline: when the world is theirs, the real competitions begin.

My heart thrashes in my rib cage.

CHAPTER 34

C O A   R A N G E C R O F T

DAY THREE, AFTERNOON

"Where are we going?" Bray slumps over a blazing-hot trunk covered by acidic fire ants on the third day of the hunt. Aged, snarled vines hiss at him, but like me, he's too fevered from the baruru to care. Our skin ravaged. Our clothes soiled and lacerated.

Our wills to live shredded. Whittled down to nearly nothing.

His recovery from his hallucinations is grueling and dark. Baruru toxins drain me of the will to live.

All day yesterday, Bray was stumbling through the jungle with delirium, a cowboy chasing after outlaws that didn't exist.

My trachea aches. It's a miracle we haven't been found as we greedily sip rainwater from drenched leaves. A typhoon is coming.

I can smell it, sure as sunrise. I realize I have to flee to the mountains. But then it hits me anew—*everyone* will be fleeing to elevation, to the acrid mountains.

This vindictive island could wipe us all out with a catastrophic landslide.

"We're finding Hazen Creed," I repeat to Bray for the millionth time. "He knows the most about the Great Hunt."

I explain the plan, explicitly, even though I know Bray's going to forget it in a literal second. As he wobbles to his knees, he collapses over me. "*Where* are we going?"

As soon as he's unconscious, I conceal him deep in the tangled jungle floor, instead of taking him with me. He's too heavy to carry on my back, so keeping him out of sight will have to do.

I squint. I can see glimpses of storm clouds on the darkening horizon. We're almost out of time to search for nourishment and water in decent sunlight.

"Creed . . ." I moan breathlessly into the moist air. "Hazen Creed."

I don't realize Hazen's already located *me*, even when blissfully cool air reaches my skin. I don't question it. I'm too overheated and sweaty to care about the bizarre sensation of slurping on my back. Slurping.

With a jolt, I bolt from the ground and find a bloodsucking pefê slug on my shoulder. A shriek of disgust rises up my throat, but a hand slams over my mouth. "Don't move."

Ocean. Earth.

Hazen Creed's signature scent is unmistakable, despite the heavier addition of blood. He holds me against him.

He plunges a knife into the creature. Discards it.

But for almost another minute, he keeps holding me in place. That's when I hear it. A thundering rush of competitors hunting down Hazen Creed. Thrusting their machetes through the gnarled vines.

He smirks against my ear. "How good are you at combat?"

"Depends on the size."

As the hunting competitors begin to come into sight, I see these men are huge. I try not to show fear, but there's no way I'm entering their path of destruction. I don't have to wonder if Hazen might've done something to infuriate them; they're cursing at each other. A thick-armed man hollers, "You let him kill two of us!"

"*Let him?* He nearly slaughtered me himself."

The largest huffs. Blood dribbling down where his ear should be. "Which way did he escape?"

"Leave him. Parley, he baited us into the snares, then attacked the survivors. He's Allied Force—"

"He's *Allied Force*?" Parley swallows. "You're sure?"

The heavy-built man nods. "Bet my life on it. His Vraničarian accent is fake. I assumed he was one of the Slavs—till he killed 'em dead." The three of them are the size of massive boulders. What weapons could Hazen have *possibly* used to take out several of them?

I snatch Hazen and pull him against me behind a twenty-foot kapok tree, whispering, "Let the snipers handle them. Look at their *size*."

Hazen gazes down at me. As if half of his face wasn't mutilated by them. "We need to eliminate the strongest—in three days, it will be too late."

What's happening in three days? What does he mean by that? *Kaiser Arcus will kill me by then, that's what.* Kaiser will be on the hunt for us. Crap. I gather my sparse items off the matted jungle ground. I need to conceal myself while I can. I escaped death four times already.

Stanislav died in the one perfect spot that I found. All I would have had to do there was forage for food and avoid the trip wires. There has to be another place we can hide.

But Hazen is determined—full of pride and arrogance. The drones themselves are tracking him since he's prime entertainment, except Hazen is locked on annihilating the entire island himself. I realize it's not pride—it's calculation.

He calculated every aspect. Himself.

Which makes him a deadly partner.

Even to me.

"What are you planning?" I ask him, but he ignores that question and decides to attack the incoming competitors.

"On my count." Hazen does not understand fear itself. Ready for more warfare. But as soon as his back's turned, I take off sprinting.

"Parley! Look!" I hear the smallest of them shout, charging after me himself. Hazen has already lunged from the jungle cover behind me, plunging his machete up to the hilt into the largest one's abdomen as he dodges the hard thrust of the thick-armed man. Hazen's nearly clobbered on his skull.

Parley hesitates, caught between attempting to save his allies and saving himself. He glances at me, likely realizing that he can pick me clean of any weapons, food, or water, then escape Hazen.

As Hazen's boot slams into the solar plexus of his opponent, he earns a violent punch to his cheekbone from another attacker. He still does not stop. He's a man of the wild, maneuvering the ancient vines to his advantage, throttling the man as he entangles him, suffocating him—

"Argh!" Parley swings his wooden rod at my head. He misses my scalp but lands his next fierce blow on my spine, knocking the air out of my chest as I crash into the ground.

Instantly winded, dazed, I gasp in pain.

Adrenalized, his eyes are blown wide. He misses my skull

again by barely an inch, no good at aiming for a head blow, then kicks my gut. Blood jolts between my teeth.

But I take advantage, biting into his ankle. Tearing flesh out.

He cries out, unprepared for the strike of lightning I plunge through his heart.

It's not enough to kill him, since I don't want to waste my energy, but it's plenty to leave him scrambling on his hands and feet. Almost convulsing. "What the hell are you!"

I spit out skin and tissue. Wiping my mouth. "Watch behind you."

He turns, and Hazen's machete splatters his head over the wild grass.

Half of Hazen's right eye is missing now.

Not the sea-green iris, but the corner of his eyelid is ripped out. As if reading my expression, he storms right up to me. "You ran away like a coward, *Rangecroft.*"

He seethes the last word like a curse.

I grip his shirt. "Your nation almost killed me, *Creed.*"

My voice is a hoarse whisper, and my spine still smarts from the rod.

"I don't control the Allied Force military, partner," Hazen hisses hotly, his breath on my lips. "You think I *want* to be here?" His eyes fix on me. "You think I enjoy spending my days being hunted with foreigners?"

Hazen speaks over my silence.

"Your body has Makarian orún—somehow. I could tell the minute you stood onstage. Smoke curled around your nostrils. You wasted your lightning on almost killing that man."

I snap, "Don't lecture me when I watched you massacre people. Don't think I don't know what you're capable of."

"You aren't a saint yourself." Hazen stares at the glob of ankle flesh in the wild grass. He follows me, ducking through the underbrush. But suddenly, the earth trembles. "Don't move."

His next word silences me completely.

"Banza."

The serpent.

A loud slithering sound fills the still air. Even fire-breathing lemurs won't risk certain death. They scuttle up the kapok trees. Banza is a Makarian serpent that can kill you in a single glance—from Bray I've learned Kaipo's protective of his islands.

Banza is rumored to be the size of a freight train. Long enough to cover almost a quarter of the island itself. But enshrouded completely in twigs, vines, shrubs, rotten vegetation, aged soil. You could step across it and easily mistake it for part of the deep, wet jungle.

Bray claimed Banza has totally lost its hearing over the centuries, and winged creatures have gouged most of its massive eyes out, but its gaze is still lethal.

Bleary eyed myself, I blink rapidly to clear out the last of the dizziness from Parley's kick to my gut, only to find the remains of two bush-covered still-hunters.

Dead snipers?

Banza reached them first. Which means extractors will be on the way to retrieve the bodies. We need to move. *Now.*

Panic rises in me, and I try to sprint, but Hazen wrangles me beneath the abrasive, pungent poko bushes. "Are you out of your mind? *Do not move. Not one inch.*"

My head spins.

"Where's Bray?" My panicked eyes search for Bray's unconscious body, now missing from where I concealed him in the wild jungle. I rip apart the rotting vegetation, heavy rain clattering off leaves, stalks of bamboo, but no one else is here. "I left him right *here.*"

"Who?" Hazen asks.

"The Great Hunt fan I was with," I respond.

"Over there. Good thing you have him," Hazen whispers, low. "You'll need to practice your first real kill."

"Kill him?" I bluster. "Why?"

"Because the snipers will kill *you*. Biting ankles is pathetic. You're better than that; you need more practice fighting to kill. While you can."

"I've already—" I swallow down a small tug in my throat. *I've already killed two people.*

"Don't tell me you think the snipers will be as easy as those Hallowell men?"

I manage a nod. "I'll practice. But not Bray." This whole island is grieving—and that's the point of the island. The unbearable heat, the blatant eeriness, the volatile wildlife that is bewitched and aggressive. This island is where Kaipo grieves—in private. He mourns his brother here.

I get the sense Hazen's Arctic-calibrated body prefers low temperatures. His golden skin is profusely sweating, and he's visibly uncomfortable in the heat. Kaipo Island is an aberrant location to him. An unwanted location. The dislike is mutual, but Kaipo might not wait a week for him and the Arctic men to leave.

"We'll need to prepare, then find shelter—" Hazen starts, but a rumble silences him as Banza inhales our scent. But my desperation to find shelter before the severe cyclonic storm becomes unbearable.

"What did you manage to gather?" I whisper.

Hazen opens his makeshift sack and produces jackseed, wild turkey, reef fish, *and* chimpanzee cutlets. There are even more self-constructed supplies in the bottom.

He even made time to handcraft a thicker machete.

"What meals did you catch?" Hazen asks.

But I shake my head. "Nothing yet."

"What were you doing this entire time?" Hazen demands, and I want to punch his jaw. *Surviving. Poisoned. Anesthetized.* But I spot Bray. Since he's unused to orún coursing through his veins, unlike me, he's just now rousing out of his hallucinatory state, drenched in sweat and nauseated. He's going to move—

"We need to stop him," I warn.

"Smite him, then."

"What?" My head whips toward Hazen.

He gazes at me. "You need to practice your lightning strike. *While you still can, remember?*" There's no hesitation. "We need to distract Banza. If I hurl my machete at the tourist, I'll need to retrieve it from his body. If you incinerate—"

"We ain't incinerating—" I shake my head clear. "*I* ain't incinerating anyone."

Why do Hazen's words feel like he's inside my mind? How powerful is the orún that we're inhaling? Is it blending our minds together?

His sweat's heavy, thick, and I can tell as much as he conceals it, the orún serpent unsettles him. I feel it in my bone marrow.

Magic is the opposite of Arctic technology.

"I'm going to retrieve Bray," I say, untangling myself from Hazen's arms and tight grip.

"Don't be senseless. Why would you risk your life—"

"He has information on his wristchip," I inform him, "knowledge he bribed a carnage man for. It might be used to locate the snipers. We can track where they *exactly*—"

Hazen moves me out of the way. Faster than I expect. "Let me get him then." *You might fail and endanger us.* "Stay here. Don't move."

"Sure thing, komrade." *I know about you too.* Hazen halts when he realizes I've figured him out. "You're ex-military."

His mouth tightens, but he doesn't respond. "Stay here."

I roll my eyes, but I realize I can be *sharper.* I can steal his food and bolt.

I can be safe on this island. Alone. He foraged enough for two people to live on for days.

Meanwhile, Hazen moves at a rapid pace. Almost like he belongs in the dense jungle. Barely hampered by his injuries. Like Bray, he must have known which vegetation contained healing properties, but unlike Bray, he had been trained by the military to cut them with greater precision. He likely didn't let any more drops than necessary touch his wounds.

He didn't poison himself by accident. But he definitely used Makarian orún.

Meanwhile, even though I'm achy and exhausted, I *am* considerably healed. The baruru's soothing brew in my blood sends a tidal wave of relief that laps over me.

But Hazen freezes.

Even I freeze—feeling Banza's gaze. Ominous. Direct.

Simultaneously, we shut our eyes. Our panting breaths sync for the first time. Matched in dark fear.

A poor howler monkey attempts to leap toward its mother in the distance. It's caught in the wet jaws of a boa constrictor with such a voracious snap that a mafura tree creaks in trepidation. The wind cuts in half.

It takes nearly a minute for Hazen to move again. He puts a hand over Bray's lips, stifling the sound of shock since the teenage boy didn't see Hazen coming from behind. Hazen whispers something in his ear.

Bray nods. Afraid.

I steal Hazen's smallest catches. I wrap them in a palm leaf and tuck it into my pocket carefully.

"You saved my skin," Bray whispers to Hazen in thanks when they clamber over to safety on the ground a meter ahead of me. Hazen smiles grandly at him—as if he didn't just plan to kill him as target practice before he discovered Bray was useful.

"Of course. Anything for a compatriot."

"Can you pass me your wristchip for a second?" I ask Bray, rather delicately in my opinion, but they both stare at me as if I've grown two noses on my face.

"Um, I'd sort of have to detach my entire *wrist* to remove it. It requires a scalpel, anesthetics, surgeons—a whole operation."

"Oh." Now I understand why Hazen didn't just seize the chip from Bray as soon as he got close—it's an embedded identification chip that's wired into the person's nervous system and tissues. I reckon it's only functional if the person's alive, the way they make it seem.

I crouch deeper into the growling but harmless poko bushes. "Can you check where the snipers are?"

"Of course! I can't wait to meet them—"

Hazen snatches Bray. "Don't alert them. They'll kill us."

Bray blinks at him. "*Kill* you? Doesn't your contract include film breaks? Cast interactions?" He squints at the airless, oppressively hot sky and searches for drones. "The cameras aren't watching."

I break it to him. "This isn't a movie."

"But the dead props—I saw, like, dozens of killed extras at the shore of the set. Hyperrealistic and everything," Bray gloats, as if he figured out how they managed to make it appear viscerally real. "I grabbed a bunch of souvenirs and snapped sick holos."

I grimace. It's sick for a different reason.

When Bray presses his wrist, a hologram displays the carnage. My eyes water. I'm reminded of what I've contributed.

I claimed two of those bodies on his recording, and the woman shot through her knee at the beginning of the foray is now dead, almost headless from bullets.

But Hazen is calm. "Private education?" he asks, as if Bray's answer is about to explain everything.

"This isn't the Extinction Era. Not *everyone* needs to be in the military," Bray replies defensively. He's astute enough to already have figured out Hazen is ex-military but not astute enough to realize when to stop talking. "These—"

"Murdered." Hazen doesn't hold back. "Every single one of those people in these holographs is dead. Killed victims."

My head spins to the right. I've never heard Hazen call any of the foreigners *victims* before. As if he didn't see us as victims— but as outsiders. Laborers either dead or soon to be dead.

Until he was hunted with us.

Hazen Creed seems to have not considered us living, breathing humans with heartache, unbearable love, raw emotion.

But now he can feel Kaipo's grief at night. Like we all can. Sharing Kaipo's pain.

As the mental fog clears, I still realize none of the Allied Force citizens are redeemable.

All of them need to be eradicated.

Whether I survive with these people or not, I only need 'em for the week.

I dust my hands. Rise to my steadier feet. Mind cleared. "Let's move, before the serpents reach us."

CHAPTER 36

IFE STØRMBANE

"This announcement is *absolutely special* to our hearts," I practice, glancing over my shoulder at Maximus, who nods in encouragement, sending me a supportive smile. "And I would love to share it with you all."

I need to save Zaire. I need to regain Head General's trust. Fast.

All I have to do is announce we're preparing our home for a baby. Who cares if it ever comes when Head General's warning still shoots through my bloodstream? *Anything can be poisonous, my ikä.*

Stay oblivious. Stay naive.

Hot rain drizzles on our noses. A humid gray sky stretches over our heads as darkened rain clouds close in, carpeting the eager crowds with drizzle.

As I stand near the microphone, a sea of Arctic faces turns to me. Thousands of bodies. My heart slams like a jackhammer, threatening to break free from my chest.

My breaths grow rapid and shallow. But I swallow.

I stumble over my words, and the world spins uncontrollably. *Don't pay attention to their faces; faces make it too real. Close your eyes—they're not real if you close your eyes. You're alone again.* Against my will, I force my eyes open. "Welcome—hello—good—"

"Vraničar!" a man bellows down below in the parade arena, raising his calloused palm, earning wild roars. As if it's part of the show.

"Vraničar, we can never die!" he declares in a heavy, thick eastern Vraničarian accent. "But the end of the Allied Force has come tonight!"

I gasp.

The private seating area falls silent, and my ears feel like they're on fire. I glance at Maximus. He's rapt, leaning forward. Listening intently. The crowd collectively appears confused, delayed, in shock; even the enforcers stop talking among themselves. Rain dancers choke on disbelief as fanfare stops and trumpets pause. However, Kømmand Sergeant Arcus pierces the man with a bloodless death stare as we all gaze at him.

Head on.

Slowly, Head General Størmbane stands.

We wonder if we heard the inciter wrong. At least I do. The canteen rafters are lined with the heads of revolters; there's no way this man signed his own death warrant. It's easy to mishear people in the strong breeze. The high wall between us is sixteen feet thick—it even separates the closest exclusive seats and the grimy parade floors of the bullring—but I heard the words as clear as day. I struggle not to beam in pride. Thorsten glances up at me, confused.

But I'm riveted.

If your plan is to win favor from the field-workers, you just earned it. I'm furious with myself that I didn't think of it first. Paying a field-worker to alleviate—

"And you!" the man growls directly at me. His eyes incendiary.

My ears perk and I bend forward, lured toward what he has to say.

"We'll kill you, you spineless woman. Kunem ti se životom. We will all make your faithless blood run from scalp to feet! These are your last days!" His voice is rancorous with rage; his eyes are livid. "I am Dragan Blažević, and I vow it on my ancestors. Not even Kōn lineage will grant you safety, *traitor.* I will end you!"

A high whistle from the crowd. A few people cheer on his speech as though it is still a rain performance.

Zaire, who's packed in the stands with the ceremony stallions, and I exchange looks. His green eyes are blown wide in terror. It sinks in that it's for *my sake*, that three empires fully hate me.

Maximus steps forward. The audience waits for his response with bated breath.

He orders the man's death.

I stammer, "Max—Maximus, wait."

This will only increase the hatred, and the man only gave threats; he can't actually end the Allied Force tonight.

High-ranked enforcers flank me suddenly, armored in their stealth gear, and escort me back to the private seats despite my protest. Armed men block my view by standing bicep to bicep, ballistic shields towering in front of them, and not even a slice of sunlight peeks in. My world goes completely dark.

Like the sun is gone. Rain batters their tactical shields.

Dragan Blažević ferociously continues his speech, but the

Allied Force enforcers are already making their way down to the stands, marching through the crowd, their metal boots clanking, intent on reaching him. *No, no, let him finish! Let his people hear this!*

This isn't about me. If it were about me, I'd burst into theatrical tears and milk the moment. But this could revitalize the spirits of the field-workers and laborers—they need to be emboldened. I hardly have the power to save myself, let alone an island of laborers. I need to study how I can organize help to rescue them. Until then, they're all vulnerable and at risk without a leader daring enough to challenge their crisis. *How can I replicate his words? What will bolster the masses?* Even if Dragan's hatred *is* aimed at me, the subjugated field-workers need this strength. To see him, hear him, *feel him.*

By any means necessary.

There may come a day when forced laborers can revolt and escape the island.

"Pacer!" I yell desperately. I can't breathe, as if an unseen hand is squeezing my lungs. Adrenaline escalates wildly inside me. A frantic chaos of blood and fear. My seat's so closely protected I have to smash my legs up to my soft chest in the tiny bit of room I have. I wrap my trembling arms around my knees. "Pacer!"

"I have you," Pacer assures from behind me. His voice remains serious, calm. "I always have you."

Hearing him allows my closed throat to loosen its grip an inch. I force my legs down, to show confidence. Praying for Dragan to receive a slow death at least so he can valorously fight till the end and die a martyr, rather than being abruptly ended by some old-fashioned gunshot to the chest.

However, the Vraničarian presidential cabinet in attendance submits the order for death by sword. A loud proclamation that few argue against. It will be quick and effective, a blade straight through the jugular, fast enough to not hurt, but still respecting the Allied Force by killing him. Then the bullring recreations will continue.

Keeping the peace.

"Whip him to death. Don't listen to them," Maximus orders. His butcher-like voice is as indurate as the northern mountains as he commands the guards. "Three hundred electric lashes. If he runs, hunt him to the ends of the earth."

Three hundred?

Thirty electrified whippings is a punishment reserved only for the vilest perpetrators, but *three hundred* lashes is unheard of. In the Extinction Era, foreigners were treated like bulls and whipped fifty times after an offense.

The point was to instill fear in the onlookers and force the victim to submit. The victim would likely never forget the whipping for as long as they lived, but they *lived*.

Panicking, I try to reach Maximus, before he makes the mistake of his life by allowing this in modern times, especially in front of foreigners. But he can't hear me amid the cheers, shouts, and hollers; it all happens too fast.

The Allied anthem thunders. It sounds like a death march, and trumpets explode in my ears. As if on cue with my thoughts, the execution anthem, "Dreg Sęvkę," booms.

The title means *Send them to the gods.*

The ancient Allied Force did not judge or speculate about where anyone would go after death. They killed and sent them straight to whatever gods the outsiders believed in to deliberate over it.

As if even the foreign gods were beneath the Arctic people.

I squeeze my eyes shut, trying not to imagine thick, brawny Allied Force enforcers taking bullwhips from the guards. Trying not to visualize them storming over to Dragan Blažević, their maroon capes gathering arena sand. I try not to sense the sheer amount of visceral pain this man will feel in seconds.

All Allied Force punishment bullwhips are electrified. Always.

Three hundred? It's supposed to be thirty. Thirty.

Even that's unbearable. An electric whip?

It's impossible not to jump when the first bullwhip lands. So loud the birds scatter, screaming and squawking. The high violins of the death march are terrifyingly sharp, and the horns blare fear. Stern rain barrages our skin.

Dragan has been captured and is held up by four enforcers, a rope at each limb. By the second lash, he doesn't even give a grunt, holding his own. The electrical, sizzling *zwhick!* is terrorizing. I shove my fingers into my ears.

With the fifth lash, another savage whip joins in. Another. Another. Another. Brutal, fast, the impacts sound excruciating with their bloody *zwhick! zwhick! zwhick! zwhick! zwhick!*

Blood splatters across the gazers as the lashes echo. More enforcers snatch whips, hitting harder, and finally, Dragan grunts.

"Fourteen!"

"Fifteen!"

A live counter races, frantically trying to keep up. Beeping.

"Sixteen!"

Sixteen lashes, and his grunts turn to pained cries that almost match the high *zwhick!* of the thrashes as the hefty men flay him alive. His throat dries out by the twentieth. He almost full-on screams on the twenty-fifth lash, made deliberately nasty by one soldier aiming for his neck, and I jump. Nearly out of my skin. I can't see him myself without the massive screens, but on the monitors, his eyes scream like he wants it to stop, *needs* it to stop, almost like he's willing to apologize—but his voice refuses.

"Maximus!" I scream. "Maximus, stop this!"

I stand on my seat to look over the guards. My fingers slip, the guards' protective gear too polished, bodies too tall, clustered together. Finally, two horrific minutes later, I see Dragan for myself. It's just for a split second, before Pacer wraps his arm around my waist and pulls me down, but Dragan no longer looks like a person. He's a heap of raw flesh.

CHAPTER 37

My throat catches the moment I see Dragan, and I feel the irresistible urge to stop his torture.

I try to shove through the enforcers, but *these* stealth enforcers choose to be made of carbon steel. I turn, gazing up at Pacer, seeing his eyes sprint from side to side. He's alert for any assassination attempts, and my breath becomes short. The world closes in as I beg to be let out so I can see Maximus and talk him down.

Maximus doesn't want any verbal threats against the Allied Force? Fine, but don't prove to the world your pride is so fragile you'd kill over it. It hasn't even been two hundred lashes yet.

And Dragan will have a hundred more after that. It's barbaric.

By the two hundredth lash, I'm shrieking, tears tracking down my face, hands clawing over my ears. It's my fault; it's all my fault.

But Mamà's sharp voice cuts in my head. *Stop your crying. Force his death to mean something.*

Dragan will die for his people, the pride of Vraničar.

Killing the Allied Force with words.

I stop crying and remember his last excruciating hollers, his last wails, grunts, and weakened cries minutes ago. It took forty strikes for him to go unconscious; I'll launch forty strikes against the Allied Force.

I strategize: if I can gain full control of Maximus, I can get to Head General Størmbane, neutralizing them both. I consistently have access to Maximus, and Barringer's sons are everything to him. When Head General's gone, many will swarm to fill his seat of power, but they can almost be guaranteed to get corruptively greedy and sabotage each other. They don't have his mental fortitude, his visionary strategies, or his admired lineage. There are too many empires still left to fight them; they will fail.

"Ugh, no skin!" One of the onlookers grimaces after the execution is over. I overhear them as I am escorted back to the Størmbanes and high officials.

"What did he even look like again?" Vørian asks, his ice-green eyes gleaming with malice. "What colors was he wearing? Tell me. It's all blood now."

Kømmand Sergeant Arcus snorts. "Ivory rain cape, I think. It's all too crimson to tell now."

Vørian mutters, "I would've rather him pitted one against all of them. It would've been more entertaining than—"

I wish I could rip aside my guards. *The man died!* I want to scream. *And you're worried about entertainment? For what? You were in diapers during the war!*

Even though the body is confirmed dead, chaotic whips terrorize for several more minutes. A raging cacophony of bullwhips pulverizing at once. By the three hundredth lash, only the bones and scraps of various tissue remain. Black matter scattered everywhere.

Maximus resumes the bullring's recreations, his chest heaving. His breaths bludgeon out hard and fast.

Thorsten gapes in horror.

It feels like centuries, but the stealth enforcers finally part from me—in trained unison—only at *Maximus's* request. He finally sits. Exhaling harder.

For an hour afterward, Maximus is still fuming. He doesn't even look at me. His breath is vulgar now.

You. You caused this, I wait for his furious eyes to finally accuse. *This hatred aimed at us—at me—is your fault.*

"Maximus—"

"Are you all right?" He leans over and dries my watery tears. His stark eyes try to be soft; they're not.

I shove his hand away.

"You're safe, I swear it." Maximus palms my wet nose, wiping it clean, trying to search my eyes. "He's dead. He'll never hurt you. Never." Just hearing his own words renews his murderous rage. "I'd decimate anyone who dared. No one stands against my family. No one alive or dead."

Enforcers cover us in front, and I'm grateful, because my mouth hangs open like I'm feral. I feel feral. Frozen in shock, I can only stare at his sanguinary face. His knuckles are locked and bleached of color from how tight his fists are gripped.

His mouth is tense, his skin inflamed.

I gasp, peer into his steaming eyes, and witness his wrath in the flesh. Bellicosity braises the core of his smithsonite-blue eyes; it distorts his prominent features.

My mind clicks it together. Maximus didn't order the execution and cut down Dragan's life barbarously because he threatened and insulted the Allied Force.

It was because he spoke about me.

CHAPTER 38

COA RANGECROFT

DAY FOUR, MORNING

"He's messing with me, right?" Bray whispers, a few footfalls behind Hazen. As if Hazen can't hear him. "Getting inside my head? He's lying about the carnage scene of the Great Hunt?"

Hazen severs thick, raveled vines with a machete. Clearing our path away from snipers. Focused.

Bray gulps back tears. "Those people at the shores? Wrestlers, televised survivalists, blood sport athletes, it's all faked. You know? Virtual media—"

"I'm not any of that."

"Because you're a cast member—"

"No." I rip my eyes off him before I can see his wide, damp eyes well up with intense emotion, raw disbelief, heavy regret.

I feel him enter into a heartbreaking distress. It's like I can feel the frantic speed of Bray's heartbeat. It pounds strongly throughout my chest. As if it's my own.

'Cause I've seen it on dozens of war refugees.

But I can't stand the sight of his tears. 'Cause how can he take a *vacation* to a labor camp and then be the one allowed to break down and cry? He still has a warm bed to go home to—a lavish resort. A life.

My life's gone. I can't slobber in tears and allow myself to break down.

For four years, I've been numbed to constant grief. In the forced-labor camps, it's something you become used to, and something you can never get used to at the same time.

I've cried so much these past years, I'm 'bout drier than a sun flare. Yet, for some reason, this uncontrollable aching . . . it makes me feel human.

It reminds me that I used to be someone. A Hallowell girl who waded through the wetlands. *Someone.*

Even a small touch of humanity feels significant. A luxury.

I haven't felt it in so long; I don't want it to go away.

Involuntarily, I tread closer to Bray than to Hazen. Greedily wanting more of his feelings near me. As much as I can get so I can remember what it feels like . . . what innocence felt like.

But I can't help myself. "Seriously. You didn't know what your nation does when it decimates other countries?"

I sound like Hazen when he's insensitive, but I don't care.

With his mop of brown hair a mess, Bray blinks. "Snowboarding is my life. Winter sports are everything, and when I'm not in the snow resorts, I'm catching up on my classes on foreign nations." Bray wipes his weeping face with his arm. "That, or I'm watching gore movies with my friends, or playing virtual reality games. But it's just that—fake gore, you know? My parents are good people, and they shielded—" His eyes shine with agony. "The Antøx Asteroids caused the damage of the earth. But I never grasped the extent. The cost."

Hazen gazes at him. As if he's silently sick to death of Bray's ingratitude. As if Hazen and other good men bled for him as they secured the Allied Force's survival for the next generation. Yet Bray is spitting the sacrifice, the brutalities of war, right in his face. But Hazen says nothing about it.

I don't mention that there's no such thing as a good Allied Force person, not even Bray's parents.

Bray pleads, "Can we return to the shore? Just so I can see for myself if it's real?"

"Not if it won't stop your bawling," Hazen snaps. I balk. Heated.

"He needs to see this Hunt is real—" *Those laborers mattered.*

"What can he change by complaining about it?" Hazen scolds. "If he wants to sit and cry his eyes out, by the time they dry, he'll still be in the Great Hunt. But be assured, I *will* return to the shore—for weapons. We'll pick those dead bodies clean of their weaponry, because in case you forgot, Kaiser Arcus wants our heads."

I shove my boot into the dirt. Even if part of me knows he's right—there ain't no time to wallow—it still doesn't pacify my hatred of him. Particularly if he's stealing from the dead. "Real cold of you, komrade."

"Welcome to the Arctic. Compatriot." He drags a hand through his golden waves. "Seize any advantage you can."

"Typical." I snort.

Hazen warns, "The area's a kill zone. Advanced weapons. Demolition. Indirect fire. There will be a kill team." His eyes darken. "These snipers won't take mercy on us for being underdefended. We *need* to search for additional defenses."

I seal my mouth shut.

Hazen cautions, "The kill zone will be crawling with poachers. Right now, hidden covert snipers are biding their time to skin you alive. Extractors will be retrieving dead snipers, treading all over the island. Trip wires from trappers will be set in heavy terrains that victims will most likely flee to for *safety*. Be careful of triggers and keep your head on straight."

My intestines knot.

Hazen does not relent. "Keep alert for anything unnatural—malformed bushes, disturbed trees, reflective ground, unnaturally cleared earth. If the jungle ground's flat and smooth—it's by design."

Hazen forewarns us to forget the dead. They're gone.

"We can't bring them back."

Bray practically gasps at the contempt, infuriated that Hazen snapped at his grief for dead victims, not even allowing us to mourn their demise. "You're military. How are *you* not racked with guilt?"

"Guilt and sorrow are two different emotions," Hazen responds. The sun hits his sea-green eyes, turning them a lighter seafoam tone. I watch him struggle not to roll his eyes, like we're missing the meaning of all this.

I snarl. "As a soldier, you made your choice. No one forced you."

Hazen severs vines with his machete. "My entire family is military—"

"I would've run," I seethe. "Before I killed innocent folks."

"That is why you and I are not the same. I don't run."

"Yet you're *ex*-military, branded a traitor." My rage magnifies. "Seems like you should've run while you had the chance."

Hazen halts. "You're speaking without any context. That is one of the most dangerous actions to commit," he says. "And I never said I didn't feel deep guilt. I regret my contribution."

But he feels no sorrow.

Bray exclaims, "If you truly regret your participation, then what do you have against us displaying our emotion?"

"It's repulsive—useless to the living and thoughtless to the dead," Hazen replies without mincing words. As if men shouldn't waste time crying when it could be spent finding a solution. "Not to mention I can't tolerate the feeble sound of it. I don't respect the pansy sight of it." His jaw clenches. A muscle pounds against his suntanned skin. As if the idea deeply enrages him.

"Fine. I'm a pansy," Bray fumes, right in his face. "But at least I didn't contribute to mass murder."

"Didn't you?" Hazen rips apart another vine. "Even if you didn't know of the genocides, it doesn't spare the lives of everyone killed. Your family likely funded it."

"They would *never.*"

"What do you think everyone's taxes fund? *Military genocides.*"

Reddened eyes dagger Hazen. "I fully *hate* you," Bray whispers.

Hazen responds, "Hate doesn't bother me. You can get anything done with hate—utilize it. Now, focus on retrieving the weapons."

CHAPTER 39

"No one taught you to be a good person?" Bray asks Hazen, despite having declared his hatred not even an hour ago. He won't let it rest at only that. "Not one person in your family is kindhearted? Thoughtful?"

Hazen's family is cold blooded. I know part of his family history: his uncle is the sergeant, his other uncle is the head sniper of the Great Hunt, and his grandfather was the head sniper of the Great Hunt before him.

I was right. Hazen's ex-military. It's in his posture, his gaze, his movement, his way of speaking to hide it. *That's* what makes him intimidating. He's a trained soldier.

He's the kind of person who could easily smile in my face and slash my throat later. And he'd have the experience to do it. Not to mention he's charming enough to hide his intentions. Beyond that, Hazen knows more about orún magic than he lets on, and he speaks a Makarian language. Perfectly.

The Allied Force studied Makarians to better kill them all. But that was before his time, yet he still had the dedication to learn it.

Now Hazen polishes off his machete.

We have an imaginary barbed-wire fence between us. If we're going to depend on each other for the week, one of us needs to climb it. After that I can leave them for dead.

My life depends the most on it as the foreigner, so I speak first.

"I was born in autumn." I don't rightly know *when* I was born, exactly. But Whitelaw estimated it must've been months after the annexation war began. I was one of the abandoned infants without a birth certificate or any known family.

But now I expose my entire life story, as far as I know it, to Hazen and Bray—since my kin's life depends on it just as much as my own. Everything from being feral to being a show attraction in Severs County. Practically everything.

Practically.

Bray climbs the barbed-wire fence after me. A single son born to excessively wealthy, nurturing parents nowhere near the military, as his father despised it. Bray is a sports fan who has close, fiercely loving friends. They drink beers on Fridays. Snowboard recklessly on Saturdays. Cram for exams on Sundays. Host rowdy parties on Monday nights. Then repeat once it's Friday.

Now, we wait for Hazen. The jungle breathes on us for another minute before Bray forces himself to ask, "What about your family, Hazen?"

"Nothing to report."

"Fine. Coward." Bray retreats. "Pretend you came from nowhere for all I care. Hide in a corner like the other military men who pretend they were born without feelings."

"I do not hide."

"You're concealing—"

"It's inconsequential. But I'll pacify you." Hazen takes in

a sharp breath of air. We're running out of time, but neither of us trusts him, and he must sense it. "My birth father mentally brutalized my mother so severely she fled to Kilstad. She means everything to me." His intense eyes meet ours.

Silence consumes me, and I listen. Intently.

"I fight for my mother and little brother." Hazen returns to carving through the noxious undergrowth of the pathless jungle. He keeps us moving. "My mother didn't put shoes on her feet; she threw me in a bundle of blankets, pretended I was a batch of winter donations, and escaped. It took years for her to trust anyone. After school, I headed straight to the public hypertrain, departed at a different stop each day, and came straight home. She'd burst into tears if I was a minute late. Thinking he'd stolen me. I would be an animal if my birth father raised me."

Hazen keeps his eyes locked on us. To ensure we know this isn't a game for him. This is not a chance he's willing to risk losing.

"My mother met a new man after four years. My adoptive father, who worked at the Kilstad Census, where each citizen's wristchip is routinely checked for authentic Allied Force heritage. You can't purchase groceries, attend movies, order necessities, enter buildings, buy homes, rent apartments, or use school items without a working wristchip. Mine broke at school once, and she had to take me to the census. She fell for him instantly. He was warm with me, kind, and considerate to her. She'd never experienced it before. Her brothers reviled her weakness, and her father tolerated her enough to send money here and there as long as she kept her existence silent."

Right in my heart, I sense the story is going somewhere dark. I brace for it.

His presence turns into something too cold and familiar to look at, so I examine my boots. "My adoptive father was light blond, pale, except he was half-foreign—I never knew. Born in a neighboring country similar to Switzerland or Sweden; he never mentioned. He hid it through paying for donated blood from hospitals and approving himself at the census. He taught me how to ride a bike, swim, climb, catch, and he educated me on the fact that there's strength in emotion. That being *charming* wins you more advantages than absolute fear and authority. That being patient, good hearted, and loving would earn respect." Hazen lifts his index finger. "That every human matters, no matter where they were born."

I wince. "Did he get caught?"

Hazen's voice grinds through his teeth. "The census did a random triple check on its own employees—and he never came home. Terrified, my mother phoned the nearest soldier station, and her own brother, Kaiser, sent her location to my birth father." Hazen's expression sets into a dark glare. "My birth father almost drowned my younger brother the minute he saw him."

Hazen recounts how savagely his father dragged the boy to the house's massive pool. Held him under with thick fists. How much strength it took to remove his father from the boy's lifeless body. It almost took too long to resuscitate the young boy.

"I'm so sorry." I almost tell him about Caner. Almost.

I can't. I'm not ready to talk about it yet. He's in the past—and I plan on keeping it that way.

But losing *Whitelaw* almost killed me. Worse than having to live under Caner, and I can't gather up the pluck to speak about Whitelaw much either, at least not without crying, so I don't try.

The hot, humid air weighs us down as rain falls. The rutilant jungle exhales.

My heart never got over Whitelaw's death. He showed me what it might've been like to have a father, the way I saw in movies. Only mostly I didn't know I wanted it. I never really *cared* to know about my actual parents. I figured if they didn't want me, I didn't want them either. Especially once I had Whitelaw.

Rawley didn't understand him, is all. Whitelaw Rangecroft came from an affluent family, but he had to forge a name for himself. We helped him do that, and in return, he helped educate us. It was an even exchange.

I reckon young children ain't supposed to live in complete wilderness. Not all our lives, like we would've without him.

Rawley only saw him as a pathetic exploiter who cared primarily about what *we* could accomplish for *him*. But she forgets, before him, Evelie had to wrangle us all on her own. We were dying of diseases and infections. She had no real adult help. Evelie taught us numbers, letters, and words, but Whitelaw taught us how to *read*. Speak clear with full sentences. I wouldn't even know half the complex words I know if he'd left us in the wild. If he hadn't tried as hard.

Without him, I'd say *ain't* all the time instead of saying it only sometimes. I'd never bother to pronounce full words—unless I feel like it—and I already don't always bother.

Whitelaw raised us. He wasn't perfect, made plenty of mistakes, but he said from the start: *I'm not ethical or moral, but I will try to be as kind as I can.* He stayed. More than I can say for the adults who didn't want me.

Deep down, I know the pain Hazen feels. When you lose someone you loved, it's like part of you died with them.

"I'm sorry. Truly."

I assumed *everyone* in the Allied Force benefited entirely from the Allied Force's generous offerings to its citizens. Safe homes. Secured income. Frequent meals. Free vacations. But there's a dire price if you're not *precisely* like them. Blond hair and blue eyes aren't enough. Tall stature and a stoic mentality are not enough. The North Pole is theirs; the world is theirs.

Even Norwegians were killed, even though their towns were some of the closest to the North Pole.

The Arctic Circle isn't enough for them—the Allied Force is superior to all other nations in their eyes.

Their nation is the greatest on earth; anything else is an obscenity to them.

Hazen finishes his point. "The military reverted my mother's official name back to my birth father's name of War-grave, and the station has held my brother captive ever since." Now, it makes sense why he's here, why he was branded a national traitor. "My mother's mind broke almost instantly. I know she'll die without my younger brother, her last con-nection with my adoptive father, and out of her love for our small family, I joined the Great Hunt."

Hazen's gaze is intense.

"I will not lose."

Once again, the two of us share the same simmering vio-lence of raw ambition. *I will win the Great Hunt for my family.*

At all costs.

My eyes flick up at him. "You can free your brother and give her the reward of immunity if you survive."

That's one of the prizes—a guarantee you won't be killed by the Allied Force until the next Great Hunt. It's how I'll free Evelie, Hucket, Rawley, Rabbit, Buckthorne. We'll be forced to work in the Allied Force, but at least we'll be alive until the next barrack selections.

Except Hazen lowers his voice. His tousled hair covers his menacing eyes. "I'm using the immunity for someone else."

"Who?"

"Myself. To kill my birth father." His mouth tightens.

My own mouth drops open. "For revenge?"

"No, to keep my mother alive." Hazen's warlike determination is palpable. "I accepted my adoptive father's last name, Creed. It will become famous in the military now. And before the rest of the nation finds out about my birth father's traitor wife's foreign husband and their abomination of a son—he'll make his move against her. I will stop him."

His eyes declare it all.

"I will win the Great Hunt at all costs."

I nod, until Hazen says something I don't expect.

"Coa, listen to me," he says. "Anyone who lured you into a public attraction as a child never cared about how you were going to turn out."

A slash of the machete sends a small colony of butterflies fluttering. They scatter toward the skies, inhaling fresher air. Hazen continues.

"He exploited children. Then he turned around and made you love him in order for you to stay. Do you understand?"

"What are you talking about?" I say. Furious as hell. "You don't even know Whitelaw. Did you listen to anything I said?"

"Every word."

I roar. Right in his face. "You didn't *understand* then."

"Coa," Hazen says as if he knows me, or my life. "If someone is willing to exploit you—you need to know that they're willing to harm you."

CHAPTER 40

"Exploitation is inherently harmful," Hazen continues, as if he knows everything. "You can't extricate harm from exploitation."

I snarl, "Shut your mouth already."

I sprint off, my nostrils steaming. I don't want to hear his crap—not from someone who ain't even *met* Whitelaw.

I told Hazen my story and he weaponized it against me. Which is the typical Arctic brute mentality.

But Bray rushes after me. It don't matter, 'cause I turn and shove right past him to get back to Hazen. "*You* wanted to exploit me when you saw the smoke. What does that make you?"

"We both agreed to use each other—"

"I consented for you *and* for Whitelaw to use me."

Hazen's lip twists, repulsed. "A child cannot consent. He exposed a child to public attention without even caring about the psychological repercussions it would have on them. It was intentional, since he studied psychiatry and he knew the damage of it, but his wealth mattered more. Anyone who forces—"

"You killed people, didn't you? That makes you worse." My voice is choked. "Don't ever speak on him. Not ever."

"Fine."

I fume. "Do you understand me? Never."

Hazen nods. We head to the shore in silence.

Hazen destroys a clot of hectically tangled vegetation. A wall of hissing, spitting, impaling ivy, overgrown tendrils, enmeshed withes.

I crawl through the opening Hazen created in the matted, entwined barrier. Bray clambers right behind me. Hazen heads through last. The killing field is spread out in front of us, as devastating as it was before.

Dozens are dead.

Hazen said snipers were expected to spare half—they killed *far* more than half of us already. My heart stops.

The bodies have been ravaged by insects, hungering vultures, starving creatures, and skeletal branches that still peck at them. Piles of victims are collapsed haphazardly. Bloodthirsty fruiting vines move, rooting themselves into the bodies, cracking through flesh, every element of Kaipo Island working in tandem to masticate the victims. Consume them.

Grief suffocates my chest cavity. I gulp back sobs.

There are no words. Only the overwhelmingly putrid stench and repellent reek of slaughter. Dozens of lifeless bodies. Simply *left there* to rot.

Hundreds of bullet shells are abandoned on Kaipo Island. Shrapnel. Residue. Chemicals. Desecrating the bodies. It's unspeakable. Hazen picks through the bodies, examining the ground for trip wires, avoiding any direct paths. Testing the weapons.

"We need to find cover." Now.

I gag as we trudge through a shin-deep expanse of skinned victims.

Hazen leads us through a territory of thicker vegetation, where he anticipates most of the covert snipers on the island will be spread out ahead. They will be located in the most challenging area that will excite vacationers. There's a reason he avoided bogs, mountainous terrains, high-altitude woodlands, and even deep valleys earlier.

Places people assume are the safest. Where snipers would target first.

We're keeping away from of sniper trails. At all costs.

Behind our backs, these snipers have been making record-breaking time. There are bodies everywhere, even as we spend the entire day and night searching for safer ground.

At this point, we must be among the last twenty-five survivors. Maybe less. And we didn't even know it.

Horror fills my body.

Almost all of the contestants are already gone. Dead.

Hazen warns me to forget the dead bodies. But I head off trail. A quarter of a mile away from him in the kill zone. I need to catch my breath.

I reach to close the eyes of someone covered in maggots, blood, and intestines. Except—a hand *grasps me*.

He played dead.

The barbarian from the electric rowboats. *He's alive*.

CHAPTER 41

A hand yanks me down to the earth.

As if I'm a rag doll, hefty fists slam me against a collapsed buka tree trunk. Thrashing me nearly unconscious. A scream would only expose my location.

Bright lights burst behind my eyelids.

Lurching with all his strength, he swings my body again. Cracking my bones against the harsh trunk. My teeth splinter. My ears ring, and blood runs down my neck. But he's ceaseless.

Aggressive. Barbaric.

"You stole my eye!" The barbarian's disfigured eye socket bulges almost out of his blotched, greasy face. Fresh blood blotted on his soiled body. "Give it back!"

I didn't rip out his eye. Czarina did—but there's no point in speaking to him. I charge my palm with lightning, still dizzy from the violent impacts. *He can't throw you again, Coa. He'll kill you.*

My mouth droops. Saliva dripping onto the grass with blood wet on my teeth.

Don't pass out. If he knocks you out—you're dead.

"Where is your pretty friend?" he seethes. "She dead yet?"

That snaps me out of it.

As soon as he clutches me again—I electrocute him. Gripping his wrist, hard. With his other meaty fist, he swings right at me. My sternum is smashed, my lungs blown out like candles. But I grip harder.

He pins me to the ground, coils his fist to bash my—

Swick!

With one swing, Hazen severs his head. He hurls his body, and it takes me a moment to realize he followed me. Then I notice the flood of people sprinting our way.

There are roughly ten of them—fleeing from a sniper.

Hazen has tossed the barbarian in their path, deterring them from our direction. A warning. Wordlessly, Hazen slings me beneath his arm and climbs a massive buka tree out of the incoming war zone.

The world turns black.

CHAPTER 42

DAY FOUR, NIGHT

Maximus tilts my upper arm, and I wince. A lick of golden hair falls in his diligent eyes. He examines me too closely, like a medical expert analyzing the slightest mark on my dark-brown skin.

"It's a burn. You need to tell me if someone hurt you."

Dragan surges into my mind, and I force a laugh. "Only my own clumsiness." I grin.

I bite down the truth: *My night terrors are debilitating now. I can't sleep. I keep burning myself by accident while cooking, while baking, while making tea. I'm restless. Mindless. I sent everyone to die on that island.*

Instead, I scatter kisses on his face. His knuckles relax after a full second and his joints fill with color again another second later. But my mind races. *We'll kill you, you spineless woman. Kunem ti se životom. We will all make your faithless blood run from scalp to feet!*

I swing my arms around him. "We need a holiday—a

respite somewhere." I pout. "Oh, I'm dying for one, Maximus."

"We are on vacation."

How is this a vacation to him? I flinch, thinking next, *Why is his skin frozen? It's over a hundred degrees outside.*

Maximus exits the bedroom to find me a medicated Välliance patch. But his hands are just as icy as the patch when he returns.

"Sorry, I will be more careful now. Sometimes I wish I could replace myself with a more mindful version of myself."

Maximus halts completely. "What?"

"Never mind," I mumble, but Maximus insists.

"Tell me. I didn't catch what you said."

I yawn softly. "I can't remember." Which is mostly true.

My eyelids flutter, but sleep is impossible. I can still see Dragan Blažević, a puddle of flesh, in my vision. If not him, it's a bullet-riddled Mikoš Volkov. If not him, it's Zaire's crushed cheekbones bleeding on the marble.

Maximus sits me down as if I might fall over. "Have you been speaking with someone?"

"No." I slip my fingers through his.

"You can tell me, Ife." He runs his free hand through my hair. "I want you to be able to speak openly with me."

"Can you cuddle me?" I murmur.

I'm astonished by how much I don't recoil from Maximus's touch while I'm exhausted, even though he's bone cold. Zaire couldn't reach me in time if anything happened, and we both seemed to grasp the horror of it. *I need protection.*

Pure anguish struck Zaire's blown-open eyes. I could practically read his thoughts. *This is too dangerous, Ife. Makarians believe you're a cold-blooded traitor. Now the Vraničarians,*

Hallowellers, and soon . . . every empire will be convinced of it. You need to get out.

Get out?

There's nowhere I can escape to where the Allied Force won't track me down, no nation they won't send soldiers to invade to return me. No continent is safe from their grip. And if Maximus hadn't protected me, and he'd let Dragan threaten me, what then? Would the world think him weak? Our love thin?

I've come this far. I only need to control Maximus. I glance up at Maximus, and his intense gaze lands on me. His face hardens in the moonlight, pale as silver, sickly as the bottom of a river. *He's ill.*

Despite being active and robust, he always falls sick right before his expeditions at the end of the month. His body temperature plummets. Icier.

The morning Dragan threatened me, Maximus's eyes shimmered with laughter, crinkling in the corners. His hands were warm all day. He seemed to be bursting with health. His bright, tanned skin was a nice deep gold. But now his movements are exact, deliberate, his eyes rimmed red. He's sicker than ever; even his breath tastes of . . . metal.

Vatrium poisoning.

Now thrill fills me, and my lips spread, reveling in it.

The eight-year-old in me who watches Maximus murder my grandfather every night in my sleep feels *giddy*. Not to mention Dragan and dead contestants in the jungle get well-deserved vengeance.

Maximus knows what it's like to feel weakened. He has vulnerabilities.

His eyes dart away from me now, as if to hide his pain. "It's nearly the anniversary of my mother's . . ."

My heart skips.

No, not sick. Grieving.

"I'm sorry." I sit closer to him. "My heart breaks for you. I'm so sorry."

Maximus murmurs, "This anniversary season haunts me every year." He's still not entirely accustomed to being open with his emotions. If you were looking at him now, you'd think he was strategizing military advances in the war room. "I couldn't keep her safe the way I can secure you now." One of his deepest regrets is not being old enough at the time to save his mother. The remorse has damaged him through the years.

"What was she like?"

Her warm memories always comfort Maximus. Except he doesn't smile now.

As if the memory is distant somehow.

"It's okay. Go to bed, kitten." He kisses my hair, my cheek. It's like a hailstone pressed against me; even his lips feel frozen. I wince. "I'll watch over you in case you need anything. I'm right here."

———

The razor-edged Great Hunt rages on. When it's time to prepare for the next island viewing, Maximus's enviably healthy again—as much as he normally is. Hearty. Hot blooded. His face is heated from the balmy island.

As if his earlier clear sign of vatrium poisoning was merely a brief defect in his system.

"Good morning," Maximus murmurs against my cheek. Kissing my throat. My navel. His lips claim every inch of skin. "I missed you."

I giggle. "Missed me? You held me all morning."

"Can't hold you enough in my dreams." Maximus smiles.

I roll my eyes, grinning. "Be careful flirting with me. Haven't you heard that my husband's a brute?"

"Is he very dangerous?" Maximus smirks.

"*Extremely dangerous*." I bite my lips, hiding a smile. "Menacing."

"I've never seen him around with you. What's his name?" Maximus asks conspiratorially.

"Sniper General Maximus Størmbane."

"Doesn't sound familiar." Maximus winks. "Let me steal you from your brute husband."

"*Steal* me?" I fake a gasp. "Are you trying to bait his fury?"

"Elope with me," Maximus murmurs into my hair. "Be mine completely. Surrender yourself to me."

"You're going to get us in trouble," I giggle. The resort screen begins to play the national anthem. The fifth day in the Great Hunt.

Maximus leaves for a minute to check on Thorsten.

Think fast. I know all about their mother, and I know how much he *loves* to tell me about her. Maximus keeps her alive through sweet memories and stories. It's strange he didn't reminisce earlier. *Is he already leaving his first family behind? Am I running out of time to stop this plan?*

Therefore, we invite you all to create a soldier today. The words of the rinder platz propaganda tapes still harass me, and I can't stop visualizing myself broadcast on their screens.

Maybe it was too painful, I assure myself. *He's not ready to speak yet. Even after all these years, it's still fresh at times.*

As he returns, Maximus reports of snores, nautical booklets, and a spaceship tucked under Thorsten's chin. Thorsten would've squirreled his way in our bed during the cataclysmic island storms last night, but the Hunt thrills wear him out. "Asleep for once."

"I'm glad. He deserves rest."

"How did you sleep?" Maximus smirks, pulling my thighs closer to him. "Need any help waking up?"

My teeth nip his ear. "Always. What do you have in mind?"

Maximus lifts me off the covers. "Hard exercise before duty."

But it bothers me—how Maximus barely sleeps. Thorsten is the same in that way. And when Maximus does sleep, combat rages in his head.

But when he wakes, he looks at me like I'm his happy wife. His escape.

As if he survived full-scale warfare and earned his prize.

Now, it's a hot morning, airless and damp. My cheeks sweaty, I slide onto my feet as Maximus starts a shower, and the water is heavenly. After we're done showering, I put on one of his dry shirts and watch the rain barrage the windows. The outside camp events are delayed because of the ongoing thunderstorm; there are warnings it might become a typhoon. Rain bashes the palm trees like medieval bludgeons.

"What did your mother used to do for the Hunts?" I ask, curious, when Maximus returns to the bedroom.

"She never attended," he informs me. "She couldn't tolerate . . . violence. She was always soft, warm, and affectionate."

I sense Maximus fears he'll forget her, what she sounded like, how she smelled, appeared. I suffered the same with my grandfather. At times, I can only picture his deep-gold eyes. Sometimes, I forget Thorsten was born through science, a harvested ovum—he never even met her. He only has her genetics.

I wonder what Vørian would've been like if he'd been

raised by Ølana Størmbane. How she could've changed his morality and ethics, taught him love and goodness. Better yet, removed her children from the Allied Force completely.

Maximus and I have raised Thorsten almost since birth. Thorsten and I have a pastry system—we lick all the sugar off our favorite treats while we watch action movies. We only care for frosting, sugar flakes, icing, and whipped dairy-free cream. Maximus, who's not fond of any sugar at all, will eat the damp remains so they don't go to waste.

Vørian's closest role models are all proud extremists and hypermasculine militants, and he won't indulge in treats at all. He insists on eating a fully carnivorous diet, hunting animals down to earn the meat. To him, a man trains his body, primes it for survival. As an initiate, he's deeply embedded in military training. In his view, why would you pamper your body with cream and soften yourself with sugar?

He believes no desserts should be allowed past the age of ten for young men. It's not masculine.

I never asked what happened to Ølana, but I can tell Barringer killed her to strengthen Maximus to be the leader Barringer needs him to be. It sounded like a wild, impossible conspiracy at first. *At first.* But it's as if Barringer will commit any heinous act to make Maximus as resilient and insensate as himself. His perfect successor.

It's common practice in the Allied Force military to kill a mother to sharpen the son. It's called *smithing*, like smithing a sword. Head General Størmbane's regime extracted Maximus's core humanity.

Which is why he sought it elsewhere.

As a result of the tragedy, however, Maximus Størmbane is more protective of his family than anyone I've ever met, completely intolerant of threats.

But I hope I'm wrong—for her sake.

And because I don't want to be next.

Maximus exhales, deep in memories. I lean against him, laying my cheek on his broad chest. "I wish I could've met her."

"You two would've been close friends," he whispers, his fingers slip into my hair. "She always loved foreigners."

"Really?"

"She spoke of them with high regard." He nods. "She named me Maximus for that reason. For her birthday, she had requested permission from my father to name me—she was convinced I looked like an ancient Roman legend."

"That's so enchanting, Maximus." I smile.

"I learned bronze sculpting for my final birthday with her, to surprise her, since she loved Roman history."

"You're so thoughtful, bear." It's a nostalgic memory to have, the opposite of killing your future wife's elderly grand-father on your birthday.

Inspired by Ølana's traditions, Maximus treats birth years seriously. Two winters ago, I received pink diamonds. Sixteen fleets of them.

All the fleets' inscriptions read: *Çircic'v anįa Ife.* Sun's gift Ife. As if the sun itself adored me enough to gift me my dark-brown Makarian skin hue—Maximus always says that dark skin tones are a direct favor from the sun. A sign of its obsession.

"So pretty!" I gushed fakely at the rain of pink petals that accompanied the present. General Van Raden, the head of Kilgrad, frowned at the extravagance. Meanwhile I tried not to think of the air pollution and floral waste.

"It's from the Former Oceanian Empire." Maximus laid a pair of earrings in my palm. "We uncovered it in the ocean wreckages."

Pale-pink diamonds are very rare, almost never recovered; it's too expensive to dive for them in the ocean's depths.

Maximus had the jewels excavated for me in bulk: necklaces, bracelets, tiaras, earrings. More diamonds than I could ever wear in a lifetime. Every time I thought I was done opening presents, a new jet would emerge, and he showered me with more. To men like General Van Raden, a kiss is considered an appropriately romantic gift for a wife each year.

Last year, Maximus outdid himself at night and bought three full constellations for me. That's not an exaggeration. Many lovers purchase a single star for their significant others. Maximus purchased extensive constellations. *My existence is the axis of your existence. You own the stars above my world, after all.*

He ordered the Warholm Space Institute to rename the constellations. I couldn't fathom the gravity of those three constellations.

The first—the constellation that was directly overhead at the place and time of my birth.

The second—the brightest constellation the night we met.

The third—the farthest constellation ever discovered, so no matter how far I explore in life, I'm always safely secured in his love. I accepted the official charts of them and attended the institute ceremonies—mainly out of shock. Trying to grasp the magnitude of it. He didn't just acquire a pattern of stars. He had the historic titles altered and recertified them.

He renamed them after me, and every scientific institution was forced to adopt the new names.

No one in Allied Force history had done that before.

All because once—only one time—I sleepily mentioned to Maximus how much I loved stargazing at night with him. Maximus responded, *I'd rearrange the stars for you*, and he did.

"Here. Show me your ears," Maximus says whenever I wear pink diamond earrings. "I love the way you illuminate them. My little princess."

My ikäninq, princess of all beauty. People gasped their last breaths across the world. Starving, nothing to eat but paltry remains, but I wore a fortune in my ears. I felt obligated to wear them every second of my life.

Soon, inside me, they became a symbol of how extensively the Arctic pays for my livelihood and expenses. At the cost of other human life.

CHAPTER 43

DAY FIVE, EVENING

My body convulses as I awaken over a day after almost being pummeled to death. *The barbarian! He'll kill me—*

Suddenly, I can't catch my rapid breath. I gasp. And gasp.

My body wrenches, vomits.

Hazen is talking to Bray. I overhear them.

"The bloodshed's real. There's a reason why there aren't many men like my adoptive father left in the Allied Force. I understand my military past. What acts I've committed. I am not a good man, but—" Now his eyes flicker to Bray. "But I permanently regret my contributions."

My body remembers itself. Healed from the barbarian's attack outwardly, from what could be nothing other than orún I might not have access to the next time. *There can't possibly be a next time, can there?*

Inwardly, I know I'll remain shell shocked and frozen from the near-fatal attack permanently, if I don't move on.

Seconds later, I force my legs to walk. One quaking foot-step at a time. Not trusting myself.

It takes me a few tries, but I manage to remember how to walk again on my coiled feet.

I sit next to Hazen. "What instructions did the sergeant give you?"

"Kill Kaiser Arcus."

"No—how to *survive* on Kaipo Island?" My voice grows desperate. How many more barbarians are pretending to be dead on the island? How many more covert snipers are there to run from? "Which areas will the snipers keep safe for you?"

"None. Arken offered no tactical advantages—only that he would keep my mother and brother safe." He asks, "How are you feeling?"

How am I feeling? I rasp, "W–We can't escape these snipers. We can't compete with this."

But Hazen's eyes are still determined. He already has a plan. "We can compete."

———

As if even the creatures know tomorrow will bring the full terrors, they sleep peacefully. Ready to have the rest of us dead soon.

A white-hot agony scalds my spine. I hold my knees as tight as possible, staring into an abyss.

Traumatized from nearly being bludgeoned to death.

But soon, it's time to keep moving. *Keep moving, Coa, keep moving. Stay on your feet, even if they complain.*

That's how I taught my bad foot to manage walking the first time.

Hazen's masculine jaw is rougher with mended wounds

and survival—he's even more of a man of the wilderness than before. His whole body is a living trophy, and I hear cameras zooming in. He tosses what remains of his dark shirt over his broad shoulder.

His sea-green eyes are focused.

"You were right earlier."

A rag from his shirt cleans away the smear of dried blood on his ear. A fraction of Hazen's eyelid is still missing, and I focus on that. Anywhere but the drone hover of cameras.

"I am a brutal exploiter. I will seize every advantage to protect my own family."

A silver drone whirs closer over his head, but he continues. Despite being recorded. Watched.

As if that part is necessary.

"In the past few days, I've seen the savagest parts of humanity—not as a soldier but as an outsider being hunted. I detested the Great Hunt before—yet I don't think I would've ever understood the experience of foreigners . . ." His words trail off, but he propels the rest out. "I've decided to spend the rest of my life restoring what my empire has destroyed."

Hazen hands me a rag to scour away the dead blood of Vraničarian elders left on my face, which is now five days old, practically part of my skin. He whispers near my ear. I can't rightly hear him on account of the blades whirring overhead.

I finally interrupt. "What are you saying?"

Hazen reaches for his machete resting beside my thighs.

"Why are you—"

Without warning, Hazen swivels his machete—destroying the drones idly whizzing over our heads. Lured closer by his speech, interested in what he had to say against his empire.

The cameras die a violent death as he hacks each of

them to pieces. Bray and I are each entranced as we watch. Numbed.

He's breaking the cameras open, extracting the trackers, biting through them. In his hands, all that's left are silvered spheres. He packs them into a makeshift rucksack. *What are they? Why are they important?*

"Why did you make that speech?" *Did he even mean it?*

"Because you were accurate in your assessment, and I wasn't afraid to admit it anymore," Hazen responds, as if it's that simple. But that's not it. He continues, "However, beyond that necessary truth, we needed the drone trackers."

"Trackers . . . ?" I repeat.

"We're approaching the snipers," Hazen announces, and I sit up higher. Panicked, I nearly choke.

Hazen specifies his plan. "*Bray* will be approaching them. A clean, eager young man." Hazen Creed winks. "A massively rich Great Hunt fan."

"What—"

"Likely tomorrow, the Allied Force media will send helicopters to rescue dead and dying fans, which means we need to seize island advantages early. Bray is going to ask a sniper to escort him."

It clicks.

An ambush.

We're going to kill the enemy before they kill us.

PART THREE:
THE FINAL HUNT

CHAPTER 44

"An ambush," I repeat after Hazen. Right after he wakes us up before sunrise.

I'm stunned—for what feels like the billionth time. I squint at Hazen in the darkness. I strain my ears, but I don't need to; his voice is direct.

"An ambush," Hazen confirms.

He makes sure we're fed and well slept. Then he prepares us for the ambush.

I hoped a full night's rest would wake him to the dangers of his ambition. In fact, I hoped he'd temporarily lost his sanity and would recover it.

Now I sit up on my rough elbows, still half-smothered by a fitful sleep. I spent the night sweating—certain the snipers would come barreling out of the bushes with rifles to end our lives or another barbarian might attack me. But Hazen appears determined to make it even *easier* for them than that.

"Wait. You were serious about this?" I ask.

Hazen's eyes meet mine. "As serious as strangulation."

Hazen is planning to *ambush* trained snipers. My heart pounds in deep fear.

Did he not see those blood-bathed shorelines? The ravaged woodlands?

Hazen packs the makeshift carriers he made for each of us. His plan's firmly situated in his mind. There's no parting him from it.

"Look—Hazen—thank you for saving my life. But this is not plausible."

He maintains intense eye contact. "It is."

Now, I get up. Nearly sightless in the moonless sheath of premorning dark.

I shiver. The strange tropical typhoon is imminent as eccentric weather roils the atmosphere. The usually balmy breeze has turned frigid. My breath is visible before my eyes in clouds of white.

Right now, we should be frantically, wildly searching for elevation or the safest locations, but Hazen refuses logic.

He refuses basic shelter.

Overnight, Hazen laid out a rough map of the terrain, as far as he's learned it, on the damp ground. As I drifted in and out of sleep, I saw him scowling at the areas he's covered and frowning deeper at the unknowns. He stalked from one side of the shelter site to the other, repeating routes to himself. His boots stained with blood and mud.

He went over numerous strategies and outcomes in his head.

Now, he scrapes his machete clean on his greenish-brown trousers. Pulls us to our feet and clears sleep from my face. Then dries Bray's closed eyelids with his shirt.

"Morning, sunshines."

My lips open. Alarmed, I attempt to remind Hazen of

the slaughter at the jagged shoreline. Only miles south from here. Exacted by these cold-blooded *trained snipers*.

"They're already coming for us—"

"Which is why we're heading to them first," Hazen explains, as though that were obvious. He appears entertained by the stark terror on my face. His heartbeat seems steady. Composed. "Before they hunt down every last one of us."

I swallow. Painfully.

What kind of self-destructive mission is this? I knew the military altered a man—but I didn't know it ripped out all your common sense.

"You're going to head to *their* territory?" I say out loud, to make sure he hears what he's proposing. "Where they've familiarized themselves with the area and reinforced their entire base?"

"Glory before fear."

I repeat, to make sure he grasps the ludicrousness of his mission, "You're heading into that base territory?"

"No." Hazen smiles, then swings his carrier over his broad shoulder. "*We're* going to head into their base territory. Together. Rangecroft." His smile widens. "Eat. I made breakfast."

I stand in his path. "Partners don't let partners traipse into their own murders. I can't let you do this."

In case he forgot, Bray has traceable technology on him that could directly lead snipers to me. The cameras have already captured us together. They could've studied me for hours. Days.

Hazen will put *me* in harm's way, if they use Bray to track me. I'm one of the last survivors. Hazen is *willingly* putting us in danger.

Yet Hazen seems to read my expression, and I can sense he feels the apprehension in my heart.

"I-I can't come with you. I can't do this and put my family's lives at risk."

"I'd never risk anyone's family here," Hazen assures us, aligning his boots. "But I can't sell any comfortable lies that you won't be possibly injured. Maimed. Mauled. Killed."

"Then you *are* risking our families. That's deliberate endangerment."

Hazen lands a hand on my arm.

"Which is why, if you trust me, you are going to be the most famous Great Hunt participator who has ever lived. As I said—glory before fear."

"That's what you want? What you care for? Glory—more than our lives?"

"You underestimate the power of fame and glory in the Allied Force, Coa Rangecroft."

No. I understand the essentials. During the mystic orún-soaked nights, the island dines on our memories, spreads them onto the dense air. At night, I hear his mother in my dreams; I laugh with his little brother in the mornings when I wake up.

I curl up to his softest home memories.

Each night, I grow up with him, year after year. See him age, strengthen, decondition himself from indoctrination, slowly slip back into it—and rely on his respect for the sanctity of life he learned from his adoptive father to survive the all-consuming Allied Force mentality.

Every night, I see him fight. A war for his humanity, if not actual war.

I've seen war through his eyes.

I feel a part of a family I've never met. I feel a lifetime with someone I didn't even know existed last week. I experienced a bit of what it's like to have a mother through his mother.

Growing up, I felt left out when everyone else was celebrating Mother's Day or Father's Day or Grandparents' Day and I was the only one who had to stand aside in my small class so they could get their group pictures or give their cards. Those are memories I can't forget.

It meant the world to me back then to run home, where Whitelaw would let us give him gifts.

Most gut wrenching of all, I know the person Hazen sees when he gazes at me, the feral fireborn that Whitelaw met in the wilderness and knew he could use to make a name for himself. I knew, deep down, Whitelaw's actions were never about me, but as long as I could pretend, I could feel important.

Someone worth not abandoning in the wilderness in the first place.

I should've burned Whitelaw alive for luring me and my kin into live shows, only I didn't know right from wrong at the time it was happening. I bought into the snake-oil lies. People told me all the time that those who love you tend to hurt you the most. But now I know folks who *truly* love you do everything in their power to not harm you, because harm is not love. It's damage. Right now, I won't apologize to myself for his cruelty; it isn't my burden to bear.

The younger Coa that needed his belonging, his sense of family, has one now in her kin—and she will do anything to keep them alive.

Anything.

"I'm going to keep us alive." Hazen's reading my expression again, and his voice is as close to a promise as we'll get. I try to hear him out.

'Cause as I read his expression, if we let Kaiser Arcus find us—*and he will*—no amount of concealment will save us without bulletproof gear that only the snipers possess.

"Bray will head into the sniper base. Alone." Hazen squints at the thick fabric of dark gray that swells the tumultuous skies. The tropical cyclonic storm is here—distant on the horizon. We might only have hours. Hazen walks us through the plan. He tidies Bray's appearance.

"The last helicopters will be on their way soon," Hazen warns. "Bray will ask for an escort and lure the sniper to us. We kill the first sniper."

"First?" I stammer, but Hazen continues and expands his plan.

"Once the sniper is dead, Bray will return to the sniper base and frantically announce that the island has killed the sniper. He'll claim deathly fear of heading out on his own again to the helicopters, and under the vigilance of cameras, the snipers will never let themselves be viewed as cowards. After, Bray will do his *absolute best* to get another sniper to us." Hazen's sharp eyes land on Bray to confirm.

My eyes leap to my right, and Bray's eyes are filled to the brim with vengeance. Determination.

"I gathered flumba powder. It's infamous for giving spiritual islanders invisibility."

"Snipers will have aquatic equipment. That should be useful as well." Hazen is already mentally ahead. "A murderous natural disaster is coming, and while Bray can be rescued, warm and coddled, like a beloved rich little citizen . . ."

Hazen and I will need high-grade breathing equipment. For survival.

Now it falls into place. "You should've led with that, Creed."

Hazen's mouth stretches to a crooked smile. "I wanted to watch you squirm, Rangecroft. I'll never tire of it as long as I live."

If you live, I think, but then Hazen's features turn solemn.

"There's grittier information. We will also need high-capacity weapons in order to kill Kaiser Arcus." His bold eyes are driven. "Make no mistake: he will not leave this island without our skulls."

If Bray is caught helping us . . .

Bray seems to sense the danger to his own life. "The war victims are human beings. Their people are my people." He speaks like a young man who's never *once* been to war—let alone seen it firsthand. "I refuse to hide from the dark truth of the world—or be hidden from it—any longer. My millions—"

"Your *family's* millions," I interject quietly, so he understands what he is signing up for, "and you will destroy them in this. You need to know that. All of the resorts, any modicum of *wealth*, all of it will be forfeited because you want to play hero on-screen."

He needs to hear the hard outcome of this. A wisp of filthy blond hair sticks to my temple.

"Coa. I want to make a difference for once in my life. I don't care about saving the day." Bray's eyes bloom red with tears. "There is no day left to save for these victims. I have a chance to make all these people's deaths count. Who am I if I had a chance to not let them die in vain and I spat on it?"

"They will kill you if they find out what you've done." My voice trembles now.

"If I die for seventy-five people, so be it. I lived for something," Bray replies, determined. He's inseparable from his resolve. "My face will mean *something* to the Allied Force homeland. They will know my face could be any of their sons, nephews, grandchildren. And my family may be affluent, but they will revolt ferociously over what will be done to me. Whatever happens, they won't act civilly."

I know how I sound. I hear how vile my words are, deterring him from avenging the dead tribesmen and past victims, but my family's lives are on the line. And if he's unconvincing to the snipers at any point . . .

All of this, each gritty day and night of survival, was for nothing.

But Hazen almost reads my mind. "Evelie," he whispers, like a stab to my rib cage. "Rawley. Hucket. Rabbit. Buckthorne. Those are the names you mumble out in your sleep."

"Don't you dare—"

"Coa, we can hide as deep as we want," Hazen cautions, undeterred. He reminds me, "But if we don't secure any weapons that even come close to protecting us from Kaiser Arcus—it's over for your family."

His hand takes hold of my arm to display my own scars from punishments in the fields.

"And you cannot hide from the Allied Force. That is the entire point of the Great Hunt. *We will force you to hide like rats, and we will come for all of you—no matter what continent or region of the world you live in.* If you haven't learned that yet—the war taught you nothing."

The Allied Force will kill you, his eyes warn. *There's nowhere to escape to.*

This entire Hunt, the snipers have been biding their time. Murdering us in front of tourists by the dozens and saving the most anticipated kills for last.

The participator who can be exploited for the most entertainment value—Hazen Creed.

And the girl who they should've killed the first minute she stood onstage and refused them.

They've been waiting days for this. The entire Arctic audience knows it.

The sergeant knew he wanted to punish me for my defiance and plunge the knife in deeper than it ever would've been otherwise. He wants to let me think I've survived six days on my own, and I am so close to saving my family, only to take it all from me.

They could've hunted me down at any time.

I'm supposed to be broken by now. Sobbing uncontrollably in the yanyan bushes, delirious with suffering.

I am *supposed* to be humiliated.

I am *supposed* to be shattered. Ruined by them.

I was the young foreign woman the audience was supposed to watch fall apart. They expected to relish my destruction.

But I am steady on my feet. Smoke is expelled from my nostrils right now. Lightning catches in my eyes.

If Hazen were only thinking of himself, he would've left with Bray while I slept. He gave us the chance to fight for our families and our morals. Together.

This is our last chance to fight back with everything we have.

"Let's kill them."

CHAPTER 45

IFE STØRMBANE

DAY SIX, NIGHT

Kateri is missing.

She's always punctual every morning she's scheduled to come. But she's an hour late now.

Laborers have been getting kidnapped from their work lines, canteen workers have been chased by reckless teenagers into the rubber fields, and sugarcane workers were harassed in their barracks by tourists. Found dead shortly after.

Meanwhile, Pacer's composed. Collected.

"A family emergency," he keeps saying. Almost like a script.

But it doesn't settle right in my stomach. She's gone. I tug at my hair ends.

Did they send her back? The Allied Force wouldn't charter an aircraft over the Atlantic for her alone to return to the Kilrød. I provided her with a security unit myself.

They would've—should've—notified me.

None of it fits right. Kateri wouldn't abandon her family

in the Kilrød and escape the island to go anywhere else. There's no escape from Traeger Island—I gasp.

I haven't seen Kateri since before the nationalist rallies.

——

"Zaire, I need you to find someone for me," I say quietly, beneath my breath and behind a dark-sheened bull due in the bullring soon. Pacer guards the entrance of the primitive-creature stables.

These stables reek of animal scat, aged ropes, and rusted doors.

"I'm *grand*. Thank you for asking. Perfectly fine. Not for lack of your savage husband trying," Zaire seethes.

"Sorry—are you okay?" I squint in the dark. A bull snorts, pawing with its forefeet and sending dirt flying behind it. I make sure to keep the island cuisine I brought Zaire out of the flying dirt, the iced spritzers chilled in a cooler and his meals still warm.

"Your cold-blooded husband *nearly* removed my internal organs, while I was awake and alive, but other than that, I'm stellar. Why are you here other than to check on me when you shouldn't?"

"My hair designer is gone." I swallow a lump in my throat. Force myself to speak my agonizing thoughts. "I think she was abducted."

"Abducted?" There's no space Zaire can't get in and out of. He has a thief's smile, but really, he's a tribe hunter, one you wouldn't even know was there. Zaire used to spend summers hunting with the hunt king himself. He could find Kateri.

"The Arctic renamed her Ekaterina. But her name is Kateri—"

"Any foreigner taken is already gone."

Our made-up language is gibberish, so it takes me sixteen confused seconds to decipher his last words. That's what I tell myself, instead of admitting to the wash of despair that hits me.

"The Arctic is deadly. Ìfẹ́—we leave *tonight* on the rafts."

I declare, "I'm not leaving without Kateri."

"Is she worth your life?" Zaire demands.

As he enters the moonlight, my anguish escalates. His face is brutalized. The enforcers fractured his nose, exposing the bone. His high cheekbones were mutilated, and the flesh over his right eye is distended. Half his vision is obscured by beaten flesh.

He can't heal himself without the Arctic discovering his Kōn heritage, which was the intention.

Zaire repeats, "We leave. Tonight."

"Even *with* Kateri—I can't leave." I take in a jagged breath. "They're going to follow us and kill you. I will never let that happen. I *refuse* to leave until they're all dead."

Zaire exhales. Exhausted. "I knew it."

"My espionage is crucial—"

Zaire interrupts, "It's not espionage—it's *naive*. This is not calculated espionage."

"It is well calculated," I insist, removing my useless high heels and heading over to retrieve my container of medical supplies. I had a gut instinct that he'd be injured, despite the Allied Force having the advanced medication to heal him properly and making a show of cleaning him up in front of me before he was escorted out of the resort. "I infiltrated the war room. The Allied Force is going to expand their war with the North Transatlantic Empire. I obtained the dates of the first critical deployments, the combat zone coordinates, the target locations."

"*Maximus* obtained these details," Zaire corrects.

I fix my eyes on him. "I have his access."

Zaire counters, "You cannot realistically collude with the North Transatlantic Empire. At best, they won't believe you. At worst, they will take your information and start another war—"

"I'm willing to take that risk." The Allied Force has a track record of consistent genocide. There's not an army on earth that won't need preparation for large-scale war with the Allied Force. All the inside details they can acquire.

"All right." Zaire feigns playing along. "What will happen when the Allied Force realizes that their enemy *too accurately* predicted their onslaughts, military invasions, and offensive strikes?"

"The Arctic generals will be pitted against each other."

Including Maximus—he can die for all I care. Zaire grimaces as I gently soak his ear with a medicated cloth. "Implausible. What happens when they *alter* their plans?"

"I will infiltrate again," I reply, dabbing his skin gingerly. "As many times as necessary. The North Transatlantic Empire will smell the danger ahead. They'll remember my kindness."

Zaire spits in sarcasm. "Right! Because the British are *famous* for returning their favors? The Americans are *acclaimed worldwide* for never betraying their own allies? Setting them up for mass death?"

Blistering fury spreads through my lungs.

"If they dare—they will all burn." I punch one of the steel barriers between the cattle. "I won't spare them."

"You've never killed anyone by yourself," Zaire reminds me, in broken gibberish. He opens the cooler of chilled champagne; it's the best I had last minute. "When the Americans corner you, restrict your body, force a gun to your trachea—how will you defend yourself?"

My head tilts. "I won't ever be in person with them."

Zaire smirks, as if I fell right into his point. "Why would they trust someone they've never met—*who lives in the Kilrød?*"

He interrupts me before I can respond.

"Who sleeps beside the sniper that holds the world record of confirmed kills—"

I fume. "I'm clever enough to field their questions. Mind your business." I remind him, "I was born in war."

Zaire chuckles, crushing a cube of ice between his teeth.

"The Allied Force military controls three hundred fifty million soldiers trained from birth for warfare." He laughs. "But ah, yes! A sixteen-year-old *child* will kill them all."

"I am not a child."

"You are not an adult. You are in the costume of one."

He rakes a hand through his blond-brown curls. His verdant eyes are heavy with sudden fatigue.

"You are not prepared for war, Ìfẹ́."

"I survived war."

"Not by your own protection."

"I am resourceful then."

"You are a danger to yourself." Zaire taps my forehead. "Your undersized brain can't recognize itself. That should tell you everything." Zaire shakes his defeated head and dampens a cloth with medicated wound-dressing liquid. "Let's pretend they believe you, right? Which is improbable. The whole world will be lit on fire, Ìfẹ́."

"My contingency plan is Kòng Zhì. Kòng Zhì is the third-largest empire territory." My breath is rapid. "They have secret armies no one's ever seen. We can make allies of Kòng Zhì."

"Kòng Zhì *collapsed.*"

I gasp. "When?"

"Three years ago. Did the Arctic forget to brief you? Were you not first on their list of important informed military affiliates?" Zaire's golden head drops in frustration, and his vexed voice fills the fusty bull stables, full and resonant.

He smells of the exhibition bullring, but I can also smell plantains and mangoes on him. And home.

"The Tirean Empire—"

"Tirean is a dead zone," Zaire tells me. "What aid did *Tirean* deliver when thirty thousand Makarians were killed per day? How many soldiers did Cheon send to defend our borders instead of their own? All of these extended subsets of Alvorada, where were they all?"

I frown. "Zaire—"

"No one. No one will help you." Medication drips from his neck. His eyes are brutal. "Listen to me: *Not one empire* will ally with you. All of them will watch your new nation kill you." His hands clutch my arms. "I am trying to *save* you."

"It's cowardice to run."

Silence.

"Cowardice!" Zaire roars in my face, coming up close enough that his harsh breath lands on my forehead. "No. It was *cowardice* not hunting you down since you cluelessly decided to surrender our empire. The hunt king himself punished *me* for it. I located you to conceal you."

Air drops out of my lungs. "What?"

My blood roars in my ears like a chainsaw.

"You don't think I've known where you were this whole time? I detected you in three months. How did you *think* the hunt king would retaliate against us for surrendering his region? Leaving his children open to slaughter?" His fists grip my arms. "The hunt king's men burned each of my fingers, each bone, all the way up to my jawline; he didn't care that he used to think of me as a son. Since I was a rainborn, they drowned me with gallons of órrò—sacrifice blood. Do you know what that torture did to me? Do you know how much thicker coagulated blood is to choke on? *Then* they sent me to kill my own."

He could've killed me.

He's still tortured. I can see torment in his eyes.

"Sorry. I'm so sorry." I falter, nearly losing my feet under me, needing to clutch onto the steel partitions. "*No.* I didn't mean for this to happen—"

"If I thought you knew what would happen, I wouldn't be here." His green eyes are as livid as the sun. "But you married the bone king's killer. The hunt king's brother's killer. Did you not anticipate his wrath?"

I tear diamonds straight off my tiara, yank diamond bracelets off my wrists, thrust anklets at his chest. "Take these. Run. There are at least fifteen dozen bags of Axer diamonds in my safes. A billion vikęs per bag, if you—"

Zaire scatters my diamonds across the ground. "Don't insult me. You're becoming more like them every day; compensate someone else."

Pure rage fills my chest. "You take that back. I am nothing—"

"The Allied Force—"

I spit, "Take that back!"

"The Allied Force killed our bloodline. You want to give me their diamonds for it? *To run?*"

"Our diamonds! These were ours first. On *our* land!" Tears scorch my eyes now. "These are Makarian diamonds.

They will always be *Makarian* until we die. I will do what I want with them."

I glare, my blood now explosive with convulsive anger.

Zaire's voice turns cold. "Your husband killed my grandfather, and I have to stare at him every time I track you. Your escape means nothing."

"Listen. *I* am trying to bring back our empire." My voice ruptures. "I am *alone.*"

"Because the rest of the world isn't trying? Correct?" Zaire snarls, his tone vicious. "Only you *alone* are trying to stop the Allied Force. No other nation with armed forces and significant manpower is defending itself against extermination."

A corrosive silence sits in the room.

"The Allied Force is killing everyone in sight, Zaire. This is a long revenge."

"Revenge?" Zaire repeats. "All of this is vengeance? Not an infiltration mission to stop the Allied Force?"

Zaire's eyes are like hell itself. His pinched nose meets mine. "Every action you take affects us all. Learn what you want, sneak into every war meeting on earth, but war is oblivion, quickly, and if you make a mistake, we all go with you."

All of us go with you, his burning eyes say. *Billions. Even me.*

My eyes release hot tears. "All of these Arctic men stole my innocence. My childhood."

Of course I demand vengeance. I won't accept anything else.

His eyes remain severe. "You can kill a million Vikarian men—and it won't return your innocence to you at the end."

"Abandon me." I push him. "You don't understand."

"These men that stole your innocence as a child stole mine," he says, his voice strained. "If anyone on this earth will understand you, it's me."

I plead, "Go home, please. Tell everyone you rebuke me. Don't follow me, Zaire, because I will die for my country. I've been dead for eight years."

"I'd die with you before that happened," he grumbles. "Why do you think I'm here?"

We'd both die for each other. We love each other too much to have any other choice. We hurl insults and compete to call each other crueler names, but deep down, we'd die for each other a million times. Then a million times more. There is no death that could stop us from trying to rescue each other. I'd lay down my life for my country.

I'd exchange my soul for Zaire.

Zaire mutters, "Your life is exactly why I'm here, if your small brain forgot." He dries the agitated bull's sweaty withers. In honor of Spain's several genocides against innocent natives and its tradition of bullfighting, the poor bull is isolated in the dark from its friends. No food or water is permitted to the bull, per tradition, and it will be tortured mentally and physically for hours. Anxious and distressed, the bull will only be pardoned if it provides a spectacular show for the Arctic tourists. Otherwise, it will be ceremonially killed in front of everyone.

The sergeant explained everything in detail.

In the Spanish practice, before the match, the bulls are deliberately burned excruciatingly with a metal brand or disadvantaged with a harpoon, making it bleed on itself before it's unleashed into a bullring to eager fans cheering for its slaughter. A dark fate would've befallen the rubber-field workers chosen to fight this bull tonight—and the bull itself would've been killed—but I invited the sergeant to dinner with the Størmbanes, on one condition.

The bullring should never again honor Spain's violent

history and sport. The sergeant arrived for dinner with the scheduled bullfight permanently replaced with exclusive footage of the Great Hunt.

Now the bull gives a grateful snort as Zaire and I cool it down with chilled water. But I can tell Zaire is still pensive. "That tiny head of yours is so thin with air and impracticality." He forces a smirk. "You're lucky one of us remained practical."

I smile, sniffling. "And yet, somehow, I'm the one who got this far." I wipe my face. Swipe my gross, embarrassing tears.

I detest crying in front of anyone, most of all Zaire.

Zaire snorts and embraces me with his better arm. "Yeah, if only I'd been born less intelligent, I might've taken the same risks." He smiles as if he's proud, as though he knows that if I have a plan to save our empire—at least I'm willing to die for it.

"You'll be electrocuted for me?" I ask now. "That might be the cost."

"Does it have to be so gruesome? Three hundred lashes?" Zaire asks. He thinks it over. He comes up with: "I'd take one bullet—*exactly one*—to the kidney for you. Maybe even the right side of my chest after, and only eleven electric lashes, not one more." He smiles. "But I could get us out of here before it comes to that."

"You know the exits?"

"You think I'd go anywhere I *don't* know all the exits?" Zaire gives his signature tilted smile.

He throws his knife, and it cleanly pierces the dark eye of the towering statue of Barritus, the founder of the Allied Force military, overseeing the fields.

I hate how perfect Zaire's aim is. It's precise.

His smooth lips quirk. He will never change.

But my pulse pumps in my throat, and I try not to imagine Zaire dead—or Kateri. Shot down by one of Maximus's soldiers. I nudge his shoulder. "You'll find Kateri?"

"I will try," he responds tensely. "But right now—stay focused. The direction you're headed, you're going to start an empire war."

CHAPTER 46

DAY SIX, MORNING

Bray's excitable voice approaches the ambush location with a sniper.

Right now, I'm Hazen's eyes, ears, even his nose—he's high in the thick canopy of trees that scrape the clouds. On my signal, he'll strike. We've timed it so the sniper won't have more than seconds to signal for help.

I'm not muscular enough to tackle and pin the man with my lanky arms and legs. Especially not a man as burly as the one slashing through the vines with a serrated knife.

Besides, in the time it'd take me to even try, he'd shoot me dead between the eyes.

An automatic rifle's strapped across his chest. The rifle is situated within reach of his dark gloves, which bear the Vikarian flag.

Hazen told me that in previous Hunts, Allied Force snipers tended to keep their rifles slung against their backs, not in their hands, to show they felt no fear. They thought it appeared weak to clutch their rifles to their chests, so they secured the guns to their backs.

But in those Hunts, the landscapes never retaliated.

This sniper's likely tense. Trapped in the heavy, dense air. Aware of the chaotic, devastating typhoon that is imminent—also likely unnerved by the belligerent, combative creatures.

A fast-moving layer of blackened clouds is blanketing us in bone-chilling rain. I swipe my eyes clear.

If I move *too* far, if I dare rustle the chuko bushes, this sniper might riddle them with bullets. *No sudden movements.*

But Bray is gushing as if he won a world championship. "*Awesome!* Blood drips from tree leaves!" he says, acting astonished. "Did you hear the gullbar lemur cries last night? Did you know they can accurately mimic a child's cry to lure prey?"

"Tighten yourself up." The sniper is not amused. His boots squelch in the mud. "Straighten your spine when you step. This is a hazardous island, boy."

"Good call. Did you know—"

"Assume that I do know." The sniper cuts him off, impatient. "I don't want to hear about this damned island or its filthy creatures."

Bray nods. "Sorry, sorry—I know. It's barely eight in the morning and I'm jabbering your head off. But do you mind—"

"I mind," the sniper snips. "Whatever it is, I mind it. *Entirely.* Rabid fans like you cost us the greatest history-making trigger areas on this island. Traps that I spent weeks devising. We couldn't lay half of them to protect random *civilian* miscreants from dying gruesomely on a screen in front of their parents."

"Sorry," Bray mumbles, and he nails the apologetic cadence, the disappointment.

The sniper points. "See that field? Ahead, northeast? There's not more than a mile left—"

My heart hammers. *Thirteen more steps.* He needs to tread thirteen more steps forward, and he'll hit my rabbit fence. Bush rabbits back home got used to sensing my fences, but the average person won't notice it in all this drizzling rain—let alone have any idea what they've stepped in. It looks nothing like a trapper sniper's snare.

Now, the sniper is eleven steps away. But he stops. Points north with his dark gloves. "Once you hit the field, the helicopter will be here in two or three hours. Don't touch anything. Don't *provoke* anything. Don't *invoke* anything."

"Is this the last helicopter run? Only saw one yesterday."

"Yes, it's the absolute final one. Don't miss it."

"Thank you. Victory to the Allied Force."

"Victory."

No! Come back. Come back.

I gesture frantically at Bray. He bobs his head at me, watching the sniper retreat the way they trudged into the involute, knotted labyrinth of bushes. About to disappear.

In the sullen rain, a glint of light catches his aquatic equipment. I reckon no sniper would be caught dead without it at this point. The typhoon's almost upon us.

"Sir!" Bray shouts, an impressive amount of trepidation in his voice. "Glories—sir! Sir!"

"Get a hold of yourself. What is it?" the sniper snaps, turning his head but not coming nearer. "What are you screaming for?"

"I thought Banza and its mate were a myth. Do—can you hear them?"

Two Banzas. It's a nice touch, because color leaches from the sniper's bearded face. As if he's witnessed something beyond his comprehension. He even removes his earpiece, as if he couldn't have heard Bray right. "More than one?"

"Banza and Kwena," Bray lies fluidly.

Banza *was* silent all last night. I thought it was something to be relieved about until I realized later that Banza might be saving its strength to hunt.

Banza alone is petrifying to imagine. The thought of two of the serpents on this vulnerable, small island almost steals my breath.

"Am I hearing things?" Bray lures him one step north. Three steps. *Keep coming*. "It's strongest here. Please, tell me I don't have to go through Kwena to reach the field?"

"Move out of the way," the sniper orders, sweeping Bray back as he passes him. Listening hard to the eerily silent jungle around him. Nothing. *Eight more steps*.

"You hear it now?"

"Yes, sir. Faintly approaching."

"*Approaching?* Don't stand there—shield your eyes. It can kill in one glance."

Bray takes another four grass-soaked steps. He looks so certain he hears something that even my ears perk. But I'm alert.

"Where can I hide?"

"Stay calm. I'm contacting—"

Four steps. That's it.

Bray takes in a sharp breath.

"What are you hearing, boy?" The sniper adjusts his earpiece. *Three steps. Two steps. One step.* "My detector—"

A machete is hurled at the sniper. Faster than I expect.

I expect him dead, brains splattered, and my nose wrinkles.

To my horror, he must hear the whistle of a blade through the branches just in time.

"Move back!" He barely finishes his sentence, grasping

Bray and forcibly tugging them both out of harm's way. Hazen's machete lodges firmly into a tree. *Crap. He's alive. He survived.*

Bullets spray from the automatic rifle. I hit the ground. Lace my hands over my scalp, as if thin fingers can shield my skull from bullets. Exotic birds scream, dropping from the sky, lemurs explode from gunfire, and white-tailed monkeys drop dead onto the ground as the sniper shoots in the direction the machete came from.

No bodies collapse to the ground.

He might run. He might take his breathing equipment and his weapons at least to a distance where he can secure the area, set his scope, and properly kill whoever tried to kill him first. I almost bolt out of the bushes.

"Boy. There's—"

Hazen's second machete finds a home in the sniper's jugular, right as he slings his sniper rifle onto his shoulder, grips Bray, and attempts to sprint with him away from danger. But Bray doesn't move. Bray glares in cold hatred.

We wait until the sniper's gloved fingers stop twitching.

I try not to watch the light drain out of his eyes.

In minutes, Hazen's boots hit the softened earth. Rut leaves scuttle away and vines prepare themselves for more warfare as Hazen takes the rifle from the sniper.

"One down. Two to go."

———

All Bray needs to do is keep it together.

He did excellently the first time—but witnessing murder in person has made him lose his nerve. *Burying a sniper* has robbed him of his composure completely.

His soft whiskey-brown eyes bulge. He's shell shocked. He saw, firsthand, a man's jugular vein being severed right in front of him. Blood is splattered on Bray's jaw, his cheeks, likely sticky on his hands. Still warm.

Every other quarter mile, he stops to vomit in the drer shrubs. "I'm fine."

"I believe you," Hazen says, but we share a glance at each other. I finish ingesting the invisibility flumba concoction.

"I'm fine."

"Sure," I tell him.

After the third time Bray's breakfast decorates the vines, Hazen halts and secures the breathing equipment to my body. "In case this is all we get," he says discreetly to me. "I'll take the weapons."

He divides the spoils, giving Bray some of the weapons. But Bray can't bear to even look at them.

"He would've done worse to us," Hazen reminds him. He doesn't need to bring up the depraved forest of victims. "He would've gained fame by killing us."

Bray sinks to his knees. A hover camera is monitoring the region—it'll be close to us soon. Bray's adorable features, silky hair, friendly eyes, "rich citizen" appearance—all of it will be intriguing to cameras. He sticks out in the gritty atmosphere.

He's a living wealthy advertisement of the lush expeditions of upper-class tourists. The elites embarking to experience historical events. Clean boots. Excellent uniform. Darling exterior.

He's going to be used by the media for a new commercial advertising the next Great Hunt. *Join us again soon!* They will not let his screen time go to waste.

But it's going to be a problem that he's involved in the planned murder of a sniper.

His life will be threatened.

Bray wrenches his hair.

"Everything will be okay," I promise him. "You'll be on a helicraft soon—safe and cozy in bed. I get it; these were your heroes—"

"They were *not* my heroes!" Bray snaps out of it. And I realize he's not even thinking of the sniper or his own life. His eyes are enraged. "I can't leave you guys to die out here. I can't get on that helicraft and desert you. There's no way."

"Desert us?" I ask. Bray's not even a participator. "Bray, listen, you have no obligation to us. You need to leave."

"*Obligation?* I'd never forgive myself if I left my friends behind." He cleans his dampened face with his sleeve. "And I don't care how weak and tenderhearted it makes me seem. But I see you two as my friends. I don't give a damn if the world knows it. There's no way I'd leave my own friends behind in this. Not on my life."

He's worried sick over us. Literally. It's strange to see someone who never grew up with me so distraught over my life. Viscerally pained that I might be hurt.

But I don't easily forget that Bray sees our families in his dreams now. He visits our childhood memories in the early mornings between night terrors. Before Bray's carefree ignorance was ripped from him, Bray's life was idyllic.

But now is not the time to grow sentimental. Except it's heavier for Bray than that; he feels emotions more deeply than most people do, I reckon. He sparks genuine friendships because he can't help it—he doesn't even need to try. He just cares with all his heart. He's always had the safety to.

Bray wipes his hands on his trousers. "We're going to survive this. Together."

I warn him, "You'll get killed—"

"So be it." His eyes are incandescent. "At least I'd be killed for people I care about."

He's not thinking straight.

Bray Rainsford is his parents' only child. He's their whole world and all they truly have. You can replace money; you can't replace a child you waited over nineteen years to have. But an overwhelming respect for him kindles inside of me.

Bray has heart—more than most would in his situation.

I squeeze his shoulder. "I swear, after this, on the outside we'll find each other. Hazen and I will find you. We'll all be actual friends." I soften my voice, doing whatever it takes to get him back on track and inside of that sniper base and on the helicraft straight after. "Take the helicraft. We'll meet you on the outside."

Raindrops sprinkle my nose as Bray smiles at me in the drizzle. My long blond hair is plastered to my lips and spine. My freckles spread whenever I smile, and it can be charming when I want.

His deep dimples split his handsome face. Pure happiness like a puppy's takes over his eyes.

I glance at Hazen, waiting for him to convince Bray to finish this. We need to get started.

"Nice work. Your assistance was crucial." Hazen firmly shakes Bray's hand, as much of an Allied Force man as ever.

I roll my eyes as Hazen continues. "If you need to cry and pour your heart out, now's the time." *Say something warmer to him.*

But something in his eyes speaks of deep-seated, hidden rage.

Bray Rainsford gets to go home to a nice, warm bath to get rid of the grime, receive a therapeutic massage in hot oil, and snuggle into bed, while Hazen will have to die knowing his mother and brother will lose their lives if he doesn't win the Great Hunt.

Bray can live whatever life he wants.

Hazen needs to kill to survive. Like a carnivorous animal.

They will never be friends.

Hazen's life will forever belong to the Allied Force. The military. He's their property.

Bray can't possibly understand.

"Safe journey back." Hazen's smile betrays nothing. He's single minded. Determined. Whether Bray makes it out alive or not is of little consequence to him. He moves on. "I appreciate your sacrifices. Sorry there's no tears; I destroyed my tear glands. But my gratitude knows no bounds—"

"Wait," Bray exclaims. "You *destroyed* your tear glands? That's real?"

"Soldiers insert engineered chemicals into our tear glands. It tests your discipline. Endurance. All soldiers must permanently damage them." He gives a wisp of a smile, visibly amused by our appalled faces. "It gives you an indestructible mind under pressure."

"No way!" Bray leaps back, as if physically repelled. "I don't believe you."

"Did it hurt?" I can't help but ask.

"Agonizing pain. But that's the cost."

At least we're on the move again, but Bray stammers, "Can't it deteriorate your vision? Not to have tear glands?"

I chime in. "What about soldiers that mess up?"

"No one in the military goes to waste. Even the permanently wounded are used," Hazen explains. "Or *reused.*"

My mouth gapes open. I wait for Hazen to admit he's joking about all this—there's no way any military could do this legally. But I realize it's true.

"Aren't you infuriated?" Bray asks, astonished. "Aren't you *angered* at what they've done to you? I'm furious *for* you. They mutilated young men to ensure they never cry!"

Hazen stares him down. "It's incorrect to believe that the purpose of destroying our tear glands is to never cry. It's about the *experience* of crafting your own strength, to remind young soldiers that once their nation asks anything of them, even to damage their tear glands with their own hands, they will commit. Afterward, they realize they have been through one of the most excruciating mental experiences possible. The soldier will know no matter what arrives in his life, he will survive again."

Hazen goes on, "There is always a purpose for every exercise in the Arctic military, from training for a steady hand to preparing a fortified mind. It's one thing to believe you are capable of anything—it is another to prove it to yourself."

Bray refutes him adamantly. "There are three hundred fifty million Allied Force soldiers! We outnumber *every* nation's army; it's not even necessary!"

"It is *absolutely* necessary," Hazen responds, cold. "A kill might stay with you all your life. Every soldier needs mental preparedness."

"That's *still* sadistic—"

"That is the least of my concerns. You don't seem to understand that—and it doesn't surprise anyone. You were raised with everything, *Bray Rainsford*," Hazen says, bristling. "The rest of us hardened ourselves. While you enjoyed chocolates, winter sports, and girls."

"It's better than maiming my eyes to build strength!" Bray erupts, as if he can't grasp that Hazen doesn't want to avenge himself. As if Bray can't tolerate even the *lightest* atrocities the soldiers commit among themselves, which is understandable, but I don't pity a single one of the soldiers.

And Hazen is not interested in exploring his own trauma. For a reason. "Enough."

"Have you ever had a single romance in your life? Have you ever kissed anyone?" Bray exclaims. "Have you experienced life beyond the military?"

Dark circles appear underneath Hazen's eyes. "I was engaged. She was my life."

Wait. *Hazen was engaged?* He never mentioned that. "What happened?"

"The torture unit did not permit marriage any longer. My engagement was effectively terminated." Hazen glares at the sun. "She was given to me as punishment in the first place. But I imagined my life with her."

I repeat, "Punishment?"

"Due to the fact that I did not privately report my adoptive father's foreign blood, the military publicly arranged my marriage to a foreigner as a humiliation." Hazen concludes, "Without her, I will never marry as long as I live."

I can't imagine falling so deeply for someone that I'd discard marriage permanently if it wasn't with them. But Hazen doesn't speak one more word on it.

He heads over to Bray. "You have no idea the value of your own life. What it means to fight for your life. To earn it."

"Life is not earned; it is given," Bray says. He opens his lips wider, but Hazen continues and squeezes his shoulder. *Let me finish.*

"I lay down my life in battle—so civilians never know what it's like to fight for their lives."

"You shouldn't have to."

Hazen chuckles. "Trust me. There are times I don't want

to." He continues, "But I admire civilians like you, Bray Rainsford. There are men in the military in it for glory, rank, prestige, who would never have half the courage you have. Men who put their bodies in the line of fire."

Hazen smiles, as if he's proud of us. This completely unlikely triad.

"I will always respect those who back up their words with their bullets."

Bray embraces each of us. Hazen's mind is already prepared to forge on—I can feel it. Only one sniper is dead.

We need to kill another sniper.

CHAPTER 47

IFE STØRMBANE

DAY SIX, MORNING

Kateri.

She draws open my door the next morning—her whole ear missing, ripped off. My blood drains out of my face completely.

I haven't seen her for days, but it feels like years.

She appears ravaged; it's clear she's been tortured. Brutally. Her skin has the scoured, harsh appearance of wounds recently healed by advanced Arctic medical technology. Purposefully not fully healed to send a clear message.

Who's trying to send me a message?

Head General would've never kept her alive.

Maximus does not torture women.

Vørian demands an audience.

Who did this?

Her once-bright brown eyes, intelligent and dynamic, are dulled. Her poppy-red lips are smeared. Her silky dark hair's shorn bluntly at her ears.

Her scalp's bloodied with a gash.

I almost jump out of my skin, mortal fear escalating in a wave of panic. I leap out of bed. "What happened?"

Kateri's eyes dart away from me.

I swallow a breath. I've seen enough detainment footage to know the results of interrogation when I see it.

"Everyone out!" My voice vibrates, enraged. My body is shaking; I can't make it stop.

I could kill someone.

"My ikä?" Valeska lurks at my door. She warns me, "We cannot be late—"

I roar, "Get out!"

Even Pacer is exiled. He was the only other person there the day Kateri vanished, but I don't want to think—I can't envision him betraying me. Ever.

But they gave Pacer to me. Maximus renamed Pacer himself and never bothered to inform me of Pacer's birth name. Pacer is still theirs.

I call back four helpmaids so as to not be too suspicious, and I invite them all to my resort gardens, slamming the glass doors behind us. Baby shower decorations are being set up, and a sinking feeling runs down my ribs, but I keep moving. Fast. We travel deep inside the garden, taking the winding ivy stairs. The blooming, leafy walls of the botanical maze swallow us.

The floral aroma's so overpowering I'm choking, but I chose this path with intention. Even if an Atkan like Pacer follows me, I'll know about it, as the bushes are thorned with red roses and Makarian orange pellums. Sharp as knives. I had the botanists select thick and cutthroat pellums; I will be able to tell if anyone is following us, as they'll be impaled on the flowers, blood spilling down their skin.

When I asked Pacer to stay back, I claimed it was for Zaire, but his face twitched. As if he knew, when I saw Kateri, I would discover her noticeably changed.

I want to trust Pacer. *But is Pacer in on this?*

I make the other girls stand just out of earshot.

"What happened to you?"

I grip her. Kateri doesn't look at me, frozen in despondence. I wave my trembling hand in her face.

"What? You were abducted at a rally and never—"

"They know."

My heart drops. My mouth feels like I ate cloth.

"Know what?"

Kateri dips her head, scratching the raw pink flesh where her ear used to be. She turns away, as if she doesn't even want to show the resort windows her lips. She picks up baby shower flowers, and I expect her to rage, spit, lash out against me, to curse ever meeting me. *Anything.*

I need it. I feel so guilty for bringing her here I'm shaking. "They know what?"

"About you. About your brother." Her eyes flick up. "That you want to know all you can of the Allied Force. You went into the war room without the sniper general several times."

Her dark eyes watch me.

I try not to collapse, gripping the hedge so hard a thorn tears open my finger. Blood drips down my French tips. "And they tortured you to get it out of you?"

She could've easily turned traitor to get out of the interrogation. Zaire might need—Zaire! Overwhelming alarm jolts through my bloodstream. I fear for him like I never have. *He needs to get out, now! Right now! Get out!*

My heart thuds rapidly. Frantically.

Kateri's voice cuts through my buzzing thoughts. "It wasn't an interrogation. It was a reeducation." Her words are frosty. Sarcastic.

"I—what?" Then it hits me. "You stole fudge ice cream."

Kateri keeps selecting roses and nods. I rush to pick flowers too.

I swallow.

"I'm so sorry."

"Thievery."

An act as tiny, as insignificant, as stolen *delicacies* caused her to be brutalized. Fury sings in my blood.

Her voice drops. "I'm sorry too."

Horror fills me. I can't blame her for whatever she had to expose to make it all stop, but I still clench up with anxiety. *What did she reveal? When will I be killed?*

"What did you say to them?"

Her lips twist, as if she can't say it out loud, shaking her shorn head.

I drop to my knees. Pellums spill out of my hands, and I bend to pick them up, tie them together, make bracelets, necklaces, whatever I can. My hands are slippery with terror. "Tell me, please."

My brother is at stake.

A heavy silence.

"I told them . . . that . . . the hunt king made you ferret through their war room. His men's spell led you to pick his brother's island, and their dark orún held your spirit captive." Her voice, smothered with shame, cracks. "T-That it's the hunt king that wanted to access restricted records to breach the Arctic."

The hunt king, Oringo, announced my death warrant worldwide. It'd be petrifying to have Oringo's men control my body. He has some of the rarest darkborns, men capable of mind possession and communication with spirits, gifted to him by the sun king.

The darkborns crafted the forbidden art of dark orún.

Kateri's voice wavers. "I-I told them the only time the hunt king's men let you free is around the sniper general. Because he knows you too intimately." Her eyes fill with regret. "I just couldn't think! And now they plan to find and execute the hunt king's men, and I'm so sorry. I didn't mean—I was so scared that—"

"Kateri—"

She dissolves. "You already lost so many family members—"

She shivers, and I wish I could hug her.

"Forgive me. Please—"

"They can never make me hate you, Kit." Even in the depths of torture, she still threw the Allied Force off my scent for my sake. We both know I mean every word of it. "They could never make me blame you for any of this."

I want to end the hunt king's men too. Not because the hunt king isn't my family, but because he tortured Zaire. Then sent Zaire to kill me. But if Oringo catches wind early . . .

If the war between us needs to be *now*—so be it.

I was born in war.

For my brother, I will be war itself.

Wait.

It finally dawns on me that when Head General warned me at the reception, it wasn't because he was onto *me*.

Remember, you can't bite into something poisonous and expect survival.

He was sending a message to Oringo. *I'm watching. My men will kill you all. Without effort.*

He was warning me to select a side. *I want you to be strictly as I dictate.*

Even before Kateri said anything, I'm sure Barringer anticipated the orún darkborns' infiltration. I rarely displayed interest in Allied Force politics before six days ago. It's too drastic of a behavior change to be natural, and now Kateri has involuntarily confirmed that.

This is a setback, not a death sentence. I can even claim Zaire breached the Allied Force territory to warn me of the darkborns' infiltration.

I drop the pellums, almost shouting with hope. I can't hug Kateri like I desperately want to. I just thank her profusely.

"Does Maximus know?"

The gates bang open, and we're out of time. Soldiers advance, and I act like Kateri didn't tell me anything, like I still don't know what's wrong with her. Right now, the Allied Force probably thinks she'll be loyal to it out of fear; I won't jeopardize that.

But it's delicious that they're depending on the girl who bitterly loathes them. I can't help smiling.

I repeat, "Does Maximus know?"

"He was the first one to believe me," Kateri remarks. "When he arrived, he had the enforcers release me; he never authorized the punishment."

My shoulders drop as relief spreads over me.

"But he was also the first one to suspect you."

I stop breathing.

"What?" I slap my hand over my mouth. My world tilts, time suspended. *What?*

I can't go back to the resort without wanting to tear his face with my nails. *Why is he complicating everything?*

Kateri glances at the subtropical resort, where guards are swelling into the gardens, and I nod.

I wipe my face clean of emotions, calling the four girls to dance with me. Still the vapid, foolish little girl above all. I motion, begging Kateri to join, but my eyes scream: *No. Don't do it.*

Kateri acts too self-conscious to join.

The guards escort me inside.

I'm an amateur, and I'm going to get us all killed.

CHAPTER 48

A grim fear balloons across my lungs. *I need to confront Maximus Størmbane.*

Night air soaks into our resort suite. The pristine arch of the Rainsford Resort is entrenched by a sludge of dirt roads. The road outside was left authentically bare to give the full experience of the forced-labor camp, so Maximus had to carry me into the resort to spare my heels. However, the threat of dark tension intensifies the atmosphere inside. Maximus removes his tuxedo jacket and his custom-made watch and sets aside his silk bow tie. He drains a shot of køvma from the gold bar cart.

"Your hair designer was located." Maximus swallows another shot.

Poisonous words twist my tongue. But I refuse to air them until they're smoothed and laid out straight like iron, instead of lit with electric wires and gasoline.

"Thank you. I was worried sick, bunny."

Rain assaults the glass, but I open the balcony anyway, letting in gusts from the violent storm splitting open the sky.

Rainwater spits in my face; dangerous and furious winds tug at my nightwear. This island weather is implacable, injurious, a feat of nature. The water floods over my feet, washing right up to my shins. The storm is daring someone to risk entering it, and right now I want to throw myself in, shove myself into its howling wind, its whipping air, and disappear. Get lost.

Stop breathing.

My bare feet scrape the railings of the top-floor balcony before I realize where I'm standing. But it feels too good to stop climbing. I head onto the alabaster roof, like I did back home, where I could escape into the rainforest skyline and *think*. I smear my damp hands on my velvet night slip to get a better—

Hands pull me inside, and I feel Maximus's calloused fingers grip my collarbones. Hard. Fury explodes in his fierce blue eyes. "What are you doing?"

I'm going on the roof. I blink. "I'm climbing."

"In the storm? There's a hurricane watch for the entire sector." His voice is livid, and he's trying to hide it.

There's his fuse. I free my shoulders from Maximus's hold and reopen the balcony doors. But he follows me outside.

My straightened hair frizzes. Then curls.

Pink hair that took hours of pain to style is now glued wet to my skin. My face. I am *not* the Arctic ideal. My clothes are drenched and cold instantly, and Maximus snatches my elbow, then my upper arm.

My breath's barbed with ferocity. "Why can't I do what I want?"

"You *want* to climb a building in this—"

A scream stops us both. A human scream.

It's not my own.

Who are the enforcers killing this time? I want to hiss at him, unleash all the anger inside of me. *How many foreigners need to die?*

Maximus doesn't flinch. He doesn't wait until the screaming ends to drag me inside and yank Välliance towels out of the electric steamer, which senses the room's drop in temperature.

He doesn't even care that someone—a diplomat most likely—is giving a tortured bellow, having been invited here to die at the hands of an aggressive enforcer.

Heat slashes my face.

"You're brutal," I say. I can't even chase after the scream and help, not without forfeiting everything, and *Maximus* never has to grapple with that.

"Brutal?" Maximus repeats. "I won't let you thrust yourself into a rampant hurricane and I am brutal? I am a tyrant."

"You're brutal because someone is screaming and you don't care."

He towels my hair. "You don't know what they did."

"Don't laws and trials matter to this island?"

"We should waste resources *and* time, if it's urgent?" His eyes flash. I've almost never argued with him, and I've rarely spoken back or out of turn.

I could count on one hand the times I've opposed him on anything in three years. An ill-considered outburst will expose my deceit, so I murmur, "I'm just not used to it. This feels different than at home."

A knotted knuckle caresses my cool cheek. "I know. I'll turn on the sound isolation."

But that doesn't *fix* anything. We're leaving them to torture.

I soften my voice. "Why do you always assume they're wrong?"

"Why do you always assume they're right?" Maximus dials on the sound isolation on the metal doors, giving us privacy. If I shriek at the top of my lungs, no one will hear it.

I grasp a new Välliance towel. It evaporates water instantly, steaming over my neck, further curling up my hair. "I thought you loved that about me: my 'inexhaustible goodwill.'"

"And I thought you would tell me everything about you, Ife. You're hiding something."

My stomach drops. "Like what?"

He's too sharp to preemptively inform me of what he knows, so I break my voice, a painful crack that makes the air wince. "Like what?"

Maximus closes his mouth. I need to dig deeper.

I climb into bed, dry and warm. *Think. Think.*

I hate when I can't protect Zaire. I hate that Kateri was tortured because she wanted to comfort me. But there's no running away from it now; I have to win this, on my own.

"Maximus." My voice is as gentle as air. "Could you come here, please? How could you say that?"

When he remains standing, I quaver, "Please."

He exhales. We aren't good at arguing with each other; too much heart is involved. We don't have any practice in it, and Maximus's treading closer, so I need to build emotional momentum. Now.

I shatter.

A mess of sobs and tears spreads throughout my voice, and I grab fistfuls of tissues. "Have you ever thought I–I *have* to hide things from you?" I don't even look at him, as if my heart will implode if I do. "D–Do you have any idea what it's like to be foreign here?" My hands tremble.

"So you brought someone from home. Your brother. I know already."

"What?" I gasp. "You know?"

"We compared his DNA with yours."

You have my DNA? But I look around—hairbrushes, toothbrushes, pillows—and throw the surprise away. I force myself to sniffle, my mucus wet. "I felt so alone. Y-You're gone for days or weeks on international campaigns." Another sob bubbles out.

"I know." He sits next to me, and the mattress sinks underneath his weight. "But my closest komrades died in war campaigns. I'd never take you or Thorsten with me." Maximus squeezes my hand. "Never. But I want you to be happy. I don't care that he's here."

"But you suspected me?"

"I knew something was off. You . . . changed with me." *Less bouncy, flirtatious, airheaded.* That's what he's obsessed with, the fantasy he fell in love with. I broke the fantasy when I screamed at him to stop letting his men attack Zaire. A carefree wild spirit, easily excitable, something almost unreal. A freedom he can witness, feel, like a fresh breath without war. I risked it all for Zaire.

I mumble, "I believed you'd refuse him entry. I'm sorry."

"You don't need to hide anything from me." Maximus's calloused hand pushes my hair back. "Chief Prince Zàirẹ can visit you at any time—know that. He's my brother-in-law."

I can tell Maximus tried the last part out on his tongue and didn't like the sound of it. He had never met Zaire outside of what I'd told him, so Zaire is an unknown element to him.

Tears fill my eyes.

"But Maximus, your men tortured my hair designer. Why?" My voice is strained. "Why would anyone allow that over stolen ice cream?"

"Theft is an indication of escalating illegal activity, but

that wasn't the reason. She lied to you if that was what she told you."

Kateri lied to me? "What happened?"

"She disclosed classified information. She'd already been interrogated by the time I directed a search." His warm hand leaves my hair. "The person who turned her in had ordered that the ear be cut off and hair shorn. She was initially caught for the delicacies, but the person who caught her briefed the sergeant that she revealed classified material. I released her after my investigations. There wasn't any need to kill her, but by regulation, she would've been killed. Classified details are never to be released without authorization."

"Who turned her in?" Anger fills my face. "Pacer?"

"Does it matter?" Maximus sounds furious. "She broke protocol. She cannot disclose classified surgical practices. Several good soldiers require confidential surgeries to survive," Maximus states, revealing a note of personal anger. "My closest komrade had lifesaving surgery, and if any foreign opposition had discovered it, they could've effectively ended his life. Permanently. There are measures to keep soldiers alive, and they cannot be exposed. Not to anyone."

Kateri? Telling me about surgical measures for soldiers? When? The only time Kateri mentioned any surgery was when she taught me how to kiss. I had no idea how to do that at first. As a close friend, Kateri taught me, slowly, passionately, in the dark. *Just mimic this. Here, put your hands there.*

Lower. Kiss him slower.

Good. Kiss a little softer, right here. Tilt your head; open your lips.

It's surgical—but it should never feel that way. It needs to feel natural, loving. You'll catch on.

Kateri is from the Asiatic seas, birthed on one of the

islands, and all the girls there were used to pirates, men, liars. She knew I was inexperienced before I even spoke a word.

I ask again, almost demanding, "Who turned her in?"

"Valeska Van Valken. She overheard your hairstylist informing you of neurological surgeries."

I gawk. *What?* Kateri never mentioned actual surgeries. What was Valeska talking about?

Maximus continues, "Kømmand Sergeant Arcus recommended the woman be sent to the Execution Range, where prisoners' heads are shaved before hard labor. Their right ears are removed to mark them." He explains, "Pacer recommended we release the woman with a warning, as enough was committed. I agreed with Pacer and discharged her."

I'm speechless.

Valeska. That filth. My nose pinches. "Valeska's a liar. I want her permanently banned from the premises. Fired. Escorted from Traeger Island—"

Straight to hell.

"For eight generations, the Van Valken family—"

"Valeska lied! Kateri never told me about neurological surgeries!" Hatred scalds my heart. Real and fresh. *I am going to destroy her. She will not survive this.*

"Van Valken's father is the head councilman of West Kilrød." Maximus frowns, as if I don't understand the Van Valkens' political history and importance in the unification of the Kilrød. "The investigation is already concluded. The woman was already injured when I arrived, and she did not receive further punishment under my watch. Everything is resolved."

"Valeska lied." My voice cracks. "Kateri knew something *else* unknown about me."

His eyes narrow. "We know. The hunt king's men."

My throat catches.

"You know already? That there are times when I'm not myself? And I can't be myself—" My head slumps, full of shame, and I let my eyes brim with tears. Hiccuping. "Maximus, I'm so sorry—"

Maximus doesn't move.

"I'm scared." My throat closes. I gather up my silks in my shaky hands. In the role of a docile, clueless wife, I need to sell this act exactly right. The "how could I possibly know any better?" act is crucial in every wife's arsenal. Her life depends on if she's good at it. Now, I never attended a day of school, but I graduated top of my class in being a birdbrain wife to an Arctic man. "You have no idea how deeply afraid I am. I thought my brother could help; he knows more about mind possessions and resistance."

Silence refills the air. This time, a tight tension rises . . . slowly.

For good measure, even though I've sold the first taste of it, I hiccup again. Wet and full. You always want to sound authentically hopeless, *almost* destroyed beyond repair by your actions, as if you're on the *brink* of collapse, to men like Maximus.

Suddenly, I feel his warm thumb smooth away my new tears. Maximus, as always, gets absurd when I cry. As if he can't stand to see it.

"I know." His voice is contained. "But you shouldn't have held it to yourself. Not that."

A painful cry. "You don't understand—I can't control it. They get into my *mind*. They're never supposed to do that."

"I know."

I shake my head. "You *don't*. You can't know what it's like—" Bent over, I gasp heavily, sounding like a knot's in my chest. This part of the act is crucial; the broken whisper is an art form. If it's ruined, the entire bit could fall apart. The perfect broken whisper is a tragic murmur, so soft and vulnerable that it forces the other person to lean in deeper toward you to hear it. "You can't imagine. What it feels like."

I pretend as if I've spilled the contents of my heart between us. I've created the perfect product, and now all he needs to do is believe it and *buy it.*

However, Maximus's knuckles are white. "We anticipated they would infiltrate. It made little sense that the hunt king would order your death and never act upon it." He looks down at me. "We just needed confirmation that his men breached the surrender terms." His voice is lethal. "They violated my family. It means that we will respond in turn."

"Maximus, I don't want to betray you—even by accident. Maybe you should . . ."

Tears sprint out, slide over my lips. He doesn't catch them.

He stares at me. We're only an inch apart now, skin brushing, chest to abdomen. Maximus looks at me as if considering something unspoken. His gaze makes me feel naked, so intense that I can't breathe.

"I need it to be you who does this to me." I tremble. If all else fails, you risk your life. You cede the power of your life into his hands. In most situations, that's extreme, but given what's at stake, I can't afford to dictate. "You can end me, and that way, they never take over my mind when I'm with you. The Allied Force military won't be breached."

My shoulders quiver. *This is a huge risk. He could actually kill me.*

"I'd do this a million times again, our marriage," I say quickly, as sobs trample my lungs.

Maximus does not speak a word. He does not move an inch.

My breathing doubles. My voice sprints at its fastest. "I love you, Maximus, only you in life. I'm ridiculous for you, and it hurts to be a hazard. *I've been the military breach this whole time.*" I lean up and kiss each warm cheek. "Can you accept my final apology? I want to end this."

"Don't apologize." Hard blue eyes break away. "Everything is new for you. It's nonsense to hold you to the same standards as everyone else." Maximus stands. "It's their end, not yours. The orún darkborns committed an act of war—and we executed indiscriminately."

I cover his mouth. My fingertips damp. "Maximus, stop, you can't say stuff like that. Those darkborns belong to the hunt king. Ancient—" Then it hits me what he said.

We executed indiscriminately. They're already dead.

I can't breathe. "The hunt region will need firm leadership—"

"His region will have you."

His eyes are serious.

"I . . . *What?*"

"You will be the official recognized leader of East Makari."

I whimper. "No, you'd have to . . . *kill* people. All of the old council, the remaining kings; they'd never let me ascend to power. No one would want that."

But that's the punishment.

This would make *Maximus* the sole leader of East Makari by extension. Head General undoubtedly strategized that killing blow.

This is the perfect excuse to decimate the rest of Makari, even though in our marriage agreements they swore they'd keep out of Makari. Completely.

"Maximus—"

His eyes drop down to my messy face. "You're very resilient." For a second, I almost think he can see my mind racing. But he concludes, "I trust you over anyone in Makari."

"And the village generals? If people find out what happened?" I gasp. "If they target me? You don't realize how thoroughly they can conceal themselves."

I'm even more of a target now.

Maximus stands out of the chandelier light. A savage breathes in front of me, burning with rage, brutality stealing over his features, over his softness.

My lips part. He looks dangerously like Head General.

Younger.

More passionate.

His blazing eyes hold mine, and the adventurous explorer dissolves. The experienced commander appears. "Whether they hide in the heavens or on the earth—I will find them. I will bleed their ancestors out of history and drain their bloodline from existence. I will accept their obedience or I will accept their blood."

My pulse calms. This man will never let anyone hurt me. Not even an empire.

CHAPTER 49

DAY SIX, MORNING

"Son, son—calm down," a new sniper orders Bray. Hazen and I are inside of the sniper base, ten feet behind Bray, invisible to the snipers. "Speak slowly. You're hysterical."

"Not hysterical," Bray gasps. "The island! The island killed him! The earth swallowed him right in front—right in front—" Bray nearly collapses, as if he'll disintegrate from what he's witnessed. "It dragged him underground!"

His voice rises. Trauma in his eyes.

Sweat plasters his caramel-brown hair to his pale temples.

"I grabbed him—I held on as hard as I could—but it swallowed him alive!"

The sniper base freezes. The entire base is heavy with weapons. Men. All of them pause—watching him announce an eerie death that's unnatural to the Arctic.

But now their new normal.

"Told you I hate this island," one of them seethes. "It was Säger, wasn't it? He escorted you, didn't he?"

"Damn island didn't even give him a chance to contribute his finale."

Someone checks his wristchip. A grim line is etched on his forehead. "Säger. Dead," he confirms. "Time of death estimated two hours past."

"Stand here."

But there's something unexpected . . . Despite the disgustingly efficient setup of their constructed base, not many snipers are left alive. The base has been emptied of manpower. Kaipo has ripped through with vengeful slaughter.

The typhoon's wind is already pulverizing trees—the strategists of the Great Hunt vastly underestimated the inhospitality of the hexed island.

Allied Force soldiers prefer to stalk their prey, learn everything about it, to ensure they have every advantage. Their strongest belief is there is no such thing as too much preparation. No obstacle is insurmountable, if it's well examined.

Someone selected this hazardous island.

Someone's head will roll for this. *People's* heads will roll.

These snipers are celebrities more than they are the top-ranked snipers in the military. The Allied Force would never send its absolute best to die in a tourist attraction.

But that doesn't stop them from being highly dangerous men.

The sound of a hound barking fills me with terror. "Let me see the boy?" a composed voice asks. It's not Kaiser Arcus, and to my perplexity, confusion warping my brain, this man is wearing the head sniper's uniform.

Is Kaiser Arcus dead? Gone?

I'm compelled to turn my head to stare at Hazen. We're meters inside their base, invisible even without the flumba powder's enchantments, due to the dense jungle.

"Child, you must be very scared," the new head sniper says calmly to Bray. "Please, sip warm milk and indulge in a light dinner."

"May I sit?"

"It won't be necessary," the man says. There's a sinister calm to him. He has an aristocratic air. He doesn't seem eccentric, but he's the type of dignified, highborn man to have bought his way into the Great Hunt to murder. Unrestrainedly.

A contributor not from the military. Which makes him an unknown factor.

I swallow. Hard.

"Not necessary?" Bray repeats, and I have the overwhelming urge to get Hazen to pull him out of there. Get Bray to run as far and as fast as he can. My heart thrashes inside my chest.

"The helicraft will be here shortly. You wouldn't want to miss it, would you, my child?"

"Oh. No," Bray rasps. "Are we too distant—"

"Not at all. May I see your boots, my boy?" the head sniper asks.

Bray nods. "Of course, Lieutenant—er. General—um—"

"Oh. No, I am no military man." The man waves the title away with his hand. Confirming my suspicions. "My boy, in fact, we have much in common. We share a taste for the extreme, the grisly, the dark. We enjoy the finest sports."

"You know what I enjoy?" Bray squints in the drumming rain, studying him, as if trying to piece together if he knows him. But the rain and thunderclouds render the area dark and murky.

"You must have an appetite for darker sports. Surely you would not breach this island without a craving for blood." The man chuckles. His hunting gloves are a black, old-fashioned pair. He chortles. "The Great Hunt is not known for its gentle viewing!"

He waits for the men to laugh, and obligingly, they chuckle.

"Sure, I guess," Bray agrees, inching back half a step. The man advances half a step nearer to him.

His angular figure is domineering, imperious. "Please. Explain everything."

"I'm sorry?"

"Explain what occurred, my son."

"Sorry. Mentally, I can't—"

"A young man, not yet forty, is dead." Another step closer. "Surely, in order to bring peace of mind to his loved ones and safety to the rest of these men, you can recount your experience?" The man lays out a meal, attempting to let Bray nourish himself, since the boy's visibly paled. But he does not let Bray sit.

Not once.

His hard black eyes are focused on Bray's boots. Bray finishes every morsel on the plate, and the man asks, "Are you feeling better now?"

"Hardly," Bray rasps, still acting. But now performing as if his life depends on it. "Can I recount it on the way to the helicraft with one of the snipers?" *Smart.*

We only need one more ambush—

"One of the men?" the new head sniper repeats.

"It's just—I don't want to miss the aircraft, and I'm terrified of this island," Bray squeaks. "Truthfully."

The man lets Bray's words die a miserably loud death before he responds with one word. "Interesting."

"Sorry?"

"My boy, your boots, they interest me very much—" The

head sniper taps an electric cattle prod against Bray's boots. I grip the handcrafted spear in my sweaty hand. Gulping down fear, I can practically feel Hazen frown before I see it. Hazen narrows his eyes.

Something is wrong.

This man is insidious.

The electric cattle prod, used as a cane, is insidious.

Bray needs to get out of there. Now. "These? My boots are souvenirs from old Hunts. I bought them for the experience."

"Of course," the man agrees, but he scowls slightly. "Except that's not why they intrigue me. You stated the *island*—the earth itself—swallowed this sniper?"

"Yes." Bray straightens.

"And you were standing near him? About as close as I am to you?" the man inquires. "In your own words . . . you held on to him as hard as you could?"

"Yes."

"And yet the island did not swallow *you* alive with him? Though you were mere centimeters away—right beside him?" The head sniper prods the boots again. "Blood is etched onto your person, yet you have no wounds yourself? Your beloved boots show no sign of struggle, no crease of effort, not even from attempting to unbury yourself or fighting half to the death to free the sniper, as you've implied?"

Bray inhales. "It all happened very quickly."

"Explain the blood."

"His weapon discharged; birds were killed by the gunfire," Bray says, exactly as Hazen instructed him. "Here's the rifle. The metal—"

"Ah, perfect." The man examines the firearm. "Precisely as you've said."

He hands the semiautomatic rifle to an extractor sniper.

"Right, the island is fickle. I don't know why it didn't kill me." Bray audibly breathes.

"I'd imagine," the head sniper says as one of the trapper snipers rises. But an extractor sniper picks up an equipment carrier and a heavy body bag for Säger.

The extractor speaks. "Typhoon or not, someone needs to take Säger home. I'll unbury him. Some excavation equipment, grappling supplies, and solid rope won't make it difficult as long as the earth gives." He turns to Bray. "I'll escort you to safety after you point out where I can uncover him. Let's move—" But the head sniper dismisses him with a discreet shake of his head. An impossibly warm smile stretches across his older face.

"No. Allow me to escort the boy myself."

CHAPTER 50

All three of our heartbeats are propelled by adrenaline, I reckon. Tense. Rapid.

Hazen and I have no choice but to abandon our hiding place and trail them. Soundlessly. Which is practically impossible when you're as petrified as I am right now. My heart drills into my chest, hammering against my insides. Hazen squeezes my wrist to keep me steady.

He remains focused. As if he knows the two of us, both Bray and I, need him to be the composed one. As coolheaded as always. Prepared.

But none of us expected a new head sniper—let alone one not previously introduced in the sniper parades. An affiliate who's not even *in the military*.

"Sir—"

"Please, you may call me Walden Richter."

Hazen stiffens. But he appears alert for a different reason—as if he can feel something. Someone watching us. Stalking us.

I don't risk a word within earshot. We keep trailing them.

I try not to slip.

The drones hover over our heads. Near the dense canopies

flooded in mist—but I can hear their faint whir. Likely they're zooming out on the entire territory.

Bray halts. His muddied boots pause in the ankle-height white fog.

"Um. Sorry. We're headed in the wrong direction." Bray points toward the path he took before. "This isn't the helicraft route that the sniper escorted me through earlier."

"He led you?"

"Yes. Escorted me northbound, veering eastward." Bray's practically a human compass. He's memorized every navigation tactic.

"You seem highly competent with directions," compliments Richter, patting Bray's arm almost condescendingly. "But sorry, I must ask again—he led you?"

Why is he asking? My brows knit.

"*Yes*," Bray retorts, nearly annoyed. "A sniper wouldn't have let me lead him." Bray states this as if it's obvious, as if he doesn't understand the weight of Richter's question. The repetition. I don't either.

But Hazen's heart rate accelerates slightly. His apprehension is readable in his expression.

And thankfully, Richter ceases to push further for a moment. They force their way through the wind-driven debris of vegetation. Howler monkeys with backward-facing ears stare at them.

Meerkats observe, their fangs twice the length of their heads.

Richter is undisturbed. "Yes, I don't suppose a sniper would've wanted to be led," he allows, but I can tell the underlying message is, *You will not lead me into a trap, either.* Yet on the surface, his voice is still warm. There's only the dark, untamed fury underneath his corneas.

Otherwise, he has kind, winter-blue eyes and frost-white hair. An eccentric old man allowed to contribute to the Great Hunt.

He chuckles, amiable. "Certainly you don't expect to retake the same path that led to disaster—if there is a mystical sinkhole or man-snatching terrain ahead of us, why risk it twice?" He lets that sit. "Trust me, this is a fine path to the helicrafts."

"What about the sniper's body?"

"You'll see."

See what?

Something crunches behind us. But I'm engaged in the scene ahead.

Bray will be led into the convoluted pinelands if he doesn't end the route right here or shift the path—he'll end up miles from the last helicraft and miss his last chance to escape. I refuse to abandon him to Walden Richter, whose very presence exudes gruesome intent. A macabre feeling.

"Believe it or not, people compare me very often to Head General Størmbane," Walden Richter divulges, as if it's the highest compliment ever paid to him. His dark-gloved hands are clasped behind his back. "Please, ask me why that is."

"Why is that?" Bray's voice grows thick. But instead of fear, there's rage seeping from his tone. Defiance. As if he knows what's about to happen.

As if he refuses to run for his life. The longer he walks, the more time Hazen and I have to run away—but neither of us does. We tramp forward. Together.

I watch Bray's fists clench.

Richter detours right into the middle of a ragged field of tall grass encircled by trees broken by the wind. Volatile winds crack ancient bark, snap apart prehistoric tree limbs with tremendous velocity.

The temperature sinks to a few degrees above freezing.

My breath is white. Visible.

Richter halts. "But first, ask what I do for a living if I'm not in the military." He meets Bray's eyes evenly.

"What do you do?"

"As a retired expert—I trained panthers, jaguars, cheetahs, leopards," Richter informs him. Casual. "Lynxes. Even the fire-breathing variety."

"Right."

Another heavy crunch, splintering twigs and leaves. A hefty paw lands in the wet, sucking mud. The dark rain persists.

Eyes with dilated pupils are luminous in the dark.

"Rainsford," the man says, disclosing he already knows Bray's name. "Your parents miss you very dearly. I'm sure they're absolutely beside themselves about your imprudent decision to enter the Great Hunt. I'd very much like to return you to them, alive and well."

"Are you threatening me?"

Richter maintains his warmth. Bray has a few inches on him and is younger, so he likely has better stamina and agility, but Richter does not flinch under Bray's most hostile glare.

Don't even try it. I squeeze my spear tighter.

Due to the flumba powder, anything in my grip is invisible—until I release it. As much as I try to forget the first day of the Great Hunt—I would repeat it to save Bray's life. I will spear this man's throat.

My fingers squeeze harder.

"Threats are not beneath me; I do find intimidation very effective. Which is why I was deliciously drawn to your friend Hazen Creed. A very intimidating look about him, indeed." My world shifts as Richter turns in our direction. "Hazen. You're here, aren't you?"

Silence drops.

Right now, Hazen and I are completely invisible. Even animals can't sense us—the flumba powder hides our body heat and scent.

All Hazen needs to do is remain silent.

"An intimidating man, truly. Do you believe he'd risk his life to save yours?" Richter asks Bray as the cameras descend closer. When Bray doesn't respond, Richter smiles slightly. "Surviving a deeply traumatic event with someone can concoct a ferociously potent bond. Almost unlike any other."

Bray cuts him off. "Can't see why that matters."

"Very well." Richter straightens his boots. "I will only ask you this one time, and then the animals will be unleashed on my command. I'd like the truth."

Prematurely, a battle-scarred panther leaps into the drenched, high grass. Its talons are sharp, as long as a small child's foot. Its body is the width of a small car.

Its mouth froths for blood.

These aren't normal wild predators.

"This is my largest. Wyoni," Richter introduces. "Its tongue alone can scrape the skin off your flesh with ease."

Bray needs to get out of here *now*. Frozen, he stares in the rain at the creature. Fog rises to their shin-length black boots. Richter knows the cameras are listening—watching. He knows professional snipers are beloved. Bray can never— not once—return to his homeland, his normal life, if he gives away even the slightest indication of what we did. *Run.*

But Bray's boots straighten on the muddied ground. He widens his stance in clear preparation to fight the man.

"Will it be one question?" Bray asks.

Please, run, Bray. Please.

He ignores my mental pleading.

"Are you afraid of being asked several?" Richter raises his brow.

Bray reminds him placidly, "The helicrafts will leave."

A jaguar the size of a bear appears through the mist.

A lynx approaches from the opposite end. *We're surrounded.*

"I'm grateful you're aware of its departure. Which is why this time pressure is very necessary, I'm afraid." Richter stands nearer to him. "Will you answer?"

"I will." Bray doesn't buckle or waver as Richter's winter-blue eyes slowly narrow.

"Excellent. Did you kill those snipers?"

CHAPTER 51

DAY SIX, NIGHT

Maximus cleans his firearms.

"Ramverstad is a militarized location—but it's rugged and challenging. Perfect for rearing robust sons." He smiles. "Either that—or we could relocate to Vünger, near Mount Ivkør. Thorsten's mountain training station will be close in proximity to us. He'd love that."

Tears fill my eyes, threatening to escape down my cheeks.

There are only six laborers left in the Great Hunt, none of them expected to survive the final night. As a grand show of his ingenuity with snares, one of the snipers devised a minefield of explosives. The explosions, upon detonation, become celebratory fireworks brightly visible to the island here, exhilarating fans each time a poor, suffering laborer—

"What's wrong?" Maximus sets aside his antique.

"Nothing. I didn't . . . mean to interrupt." I sit in one of his vintage vacation shirts, his scent all over me. *It's my fault. It's my fault. I am a war criminal now.*

"You didn't interrupt." Maximus's dimples show deeply. "Alkenheim is an impressive option; the winter combat sports are exciting for young boys—"

Is he trying to torture me? Acting as if this is all a standard tourist experience? Another firework blasts across the starless night sky.

"Excuse me." I rush to the sink to splash my face with cold water. My infuriated shaking worsens. I grip the basin so hard my fingernails bend. I need to scream, but I can't.

Don't you dare give into wrath. You've come too far, ìfẹ́mi. My love.

The Allied Force needs to have control over me, and I play my part. But I'm sick of having to keep up *this* act, where I can't lash out at Maximus. Where I can't command him or argue with his decisions. Where I have to bury my grief.

Heavy footsteps approach. "Vünger is remote—"

"Vünger?" I steal a deep breath, steadying myself. "You were trained to kill the bone king in Vünger."

There. It's out. It hangs dangerously in the air. I tried—so hard—to rid my voice of violence, of pain, but I didn't. "You killed him, right?"

Silence drops between us.

I didn't forget that night. I've never forgotten how old I was when I witnessed the act or how old he was when he committed it. Maximus was born on the eighteen of Markẹn—May. I was born a few years later on the fourteenth of Decżem—December. I didn't forget how the Allied sergeant called him over for his *destined glory.* He was eleven. I was *there.*

Right now, Maximus stands at the doorway. I'm under five feet tall, tiny compared to him. His six-foot-four, strapping, muscled body stands over me and takes up all the space. He could be capable of anything.

Maximus responds, "Another soldier killed him in my place. That morning, I was allotted six hours to make final peace with my mother. My best friend, Rainer, and I were physically identical growing up, and everyone always confused us. I can't apologize enough that they did that to the bone king." His voice is clear. "I never killed him. But I regret his execution."

My body freezes.

"I don't believe you." I want to spit out worse. I've spent years hating him. It needs to specifically be *him*, not someone else I've never met. I've vomited every night we've been married, loathed him, spewed hatred in every kiss, every smile. I've ingested *herbal poison* to keep from bearing his children. All I've fantasized about is his death since I was eight and a half.

It *has* to be Maximus Barringer Størmbane.

He was a child himself when it happened, but I don't care. Nothing lets me forgive him. *I* was a child—what about me?

Maximus wouldn't have been killed for refusing to kill my grandfather, and I would have been killed if I'd intervened. For blood's sake—my grandfather was *elderly*. Even children know right from wrong, mercy from murder.

It's one thing to kill elders, but it's another to kill our bone king. As a *child*, no less.

Maximus disgraced us.

I grip the gold basin. Raw flames of wrath lick through my heart, threatening another explosion.

"Come here." His voice is lowered.

No, Maximus, I want to snap, but I dissolve to the floor and slam the door to the bath on him. My first real defiance.

I visualize young Maximus, examine him in that smoke as he removes his facial shield to look at my bleeding grandfather, then at me. Indifferent. *That* made me detest him more—he didn't even care, so uninterested you'd think he'd been dragged to a formal banquet instead of a live execution.

That general was just as sick as the village warlords, corrupting children, forcing them into labor and genocide as soldiers. Those children witness atrocities and never recover.

All Maximus has been trained to do is kill and seize—That's all he knows.

It hits me, painfully. Maximus was a child soldier taught to murder proficiently since he was six years old. The Kilrød permits no humanity. Could Maximus have *ever been* humane?

Beyond that . . . at what point does it become the child's fault? Is it ever the child victim's fault? *Is Maximus a victim?* Can I pin blame on an eleven-year-old youth? Any child victim?

A cold wave drowns me, freezing and all-consuming. Breath is unable to enter my lungs until I can think. But I *can't* think.

I wipe my mouth and get up, swallowing the acidic malice. I force open the door, gripping the pure-gold handle, glaring up at Maximus. Ready to witness the killer inside of him. His boyhood was extracted a few years after birth. The child is gone.

I prepare myself to see the genocider.

Instead, a mature gaze scans me, reading my emotions with almost expert precision. Searching for the love for him remaining in me.

The committed, bloodless soldier is positioned in front of me. A man who's killed too many. A war-damaged general who is still insensate, still unsentimental about his achievements. *The bear is not saddened.*

That's the most terrifying part right now. Deep down, I can sense he still feels . . . nothing. And he knows it.

He's indifferent to the murders of foreigners. Even after all these years. Maximus has zero capability to *humanize* outsiders in him.

Except Maximus *wants* executions to disturb him; I can sense it. He *wants* his humanity. But he still doesn't have it; it's still out of his reach.

Killing is a duty for him. It has never been a horror, only a task, as he was taught.

Maximus was inducted into the special forces of the military. His assignments spanned years—not months.

The soldiers endure constant war with no break or pause. They can't be reintegrated cleanly into society. The war-conditioned mindset of their society is another battle zone.

Maximus was on tour for years on end, amassing bodies and political war trophies.

My throat's too tight to even voice the truth—that even if Maximus regains his humanity, there is no room for it in the Allied Force. He cannot stop their decimations.

Maximus is the same exploited tool that I am. We both watched our family die. Watched war criminals create children like Vørian and radicalize them.

Not to mention—I have now sacrificed parents, daughters, sons, field-workers, canteen workers, rubber laborers. I sent dozens to die. Who have I become in war? Who am I now?

I slip to the marble floor. I sacrificed people for my empire; Maximus was forced to kill for his empire. We're more crushingly alike than I want to admit. My fingernails sink into my hair. Wanting to wrench every strand out. *We're both war criminals.*

How did this happen? How did the world let this happen to children?

I can't look up at him. I can't confess my war crimes out loud. *I sent victims to die.* I feel my sanity slip out of my grasp—and I realize Maximus is the only one who will understand.

Not Zaire, not Kateri; neither of them would ever forgive me if they knew. Maximus can shoulder the burden with me.

"I-I killed those people."

"What people?" Maximus questions without judgment. He doesn't even ask about the killing itself, only who the victims are. I know he will eliminate the evidence and take responsibility; he's diligent and devout. His loyalty is embedded deep in his core.

"I chose . . ." I confess. "I *knew* the island was cursed, and I-I killed them. I didn't mean—I didn't think—"

Remorse, as deep as oblivion, overwhelms me.

"I'm sorry," I whisper. My head falls. "I'm so sorry."

"For what?" Maximus sits next to me on the marble. "The snipers are sent to end as many foreigners as possible for tourists. The location never mattered. You didn't kill them."

Foreigners would've died anyway. But that doesn't absolve me.

"It was still my selection. I'm sorry," I whisper. My remorse is for the laborers.

"Don't apologize. You needed more preparation than I realized." Maximus starts to gather my hands, but he stops himself. As if he knows I don't want to be touched. Deep down, I envision the good-natured person he could've been in another lifetime.

I don't have the heart to tell him that his love for me is unrequited. That even if it wasn't him who shot my grandfather, it's still not in me to forgive any of the Allied Force men, and that is why Hazen and I could never work.

Hazen sees me without trying. Worse, Hazen sees me for who *I am*—he can see right into the darkest, most unlikable, most vengeful, most incurably arrogant corners of me—and he still *loves me anyway.* It took twice the effort to convince him of my naive act.

Hazen could tell his love for me was unreciprocated immediately.

It's why I married Maximus instead. Except Maximus *knows* me for who I am, even if he doesn't know why he knows, even if he can't explain to himself how his heart can sense mine—his soul recognizes mine. After all the trauma I've suffered, Maximus still knows the innocent parts of me like the back of his hand.

And I feel sickened, knowing I'm going to exploit Maximus, exactly the way everyone around him is using him. War is personal, but this isn't. I want to make a sliver of us real, every little moment I can now.

"I'm sorry your mother passed," I say. "I was close to my grandfather. The pain is excruciating, like nothing I've ever felt."

"I know. I apologize that your loved one was killed."

Not *I'm sorry he died* or *I'm sorry he passed. I'm sorry he was killed.* He said it out loud.

A choked cry escapes me. My throat tightens, but a gulping sob combusts in me, and the air cracks with a broken echo. Hot tears splatter my skin. My heart is wrenched apart.

I wish, in this moment, we could be friends. *Allies.* Not husband and wife, not political opponents, but real friends. I wish I could undo the war crimes.

"We still have the island viewing." I clear my face and pull up my knees, wrap my arms around them. "Can we eat together first? Right here?"

He swipes his thumb across my knees in comfort. "Sure."

I need to be perfect, as close to the Arctic ideal as possible. I'm not close enough. Not yet.

But Maximus smiles warmly at the roughened, hyper-pigmented birthmarks on my thighs.

"They're a map of your body," he responds, like he never needs me to be perfect; he'll only see me as perfect anyway. But I can't let myself see what he sees. It's too great a risk. "You look like me."

I don't resemble him at all—my scars are internal, and his physical scars are *violent* and intense. His muscular back is a mass of traumatic combat scars. But slowly . . . I understand his meaning. We both have battle scars—together.

"There's a saying," Maximus remarks. "'A man can endure anything as long as he has a cause.' I'd endure anything and everything for you. You're my cause. My purpose in life."

My heart pulsates. He gazes at me, and the eye contact alone is intoxicating.

Maximus lowers his voice. "I used to talk to the stars at night as a younger deadeye. I would wonder at their view of history, asking to see all of the heartache they'd seen, and I'd compare it to the heartache I caused. Hoping I was less callous than those before me. Then you came, and you breathed fire into me. I didn't understand you at first; I couldn't comprehend your affection, the lack of cost, how freely you gave yourself to everything you loved. Military initiations numbed me beyond recognition. With your love, I felt alive, and I felt desperate to warn the stars above that one of their own had fallen to earth." He smiles. "But I never did. I kept you for myself. I could never return you to them."

He brings my fingertips to his warm lips.

"I love you, Ife. More than the stars would understand."

CHAPTER 52

DAY SIX, MORNING

"Did you kill those snipers?"

I don't let Bray answer Richter.

Almost before Bray's lips can open and end his life, end all of our lives, I send ferocious strikes of lightning into the woodlands. Enough to scatter half the creatures.

But at least one bolt straight at Walden Richter.

Richter avoids it, barely, but enough.

"Fireborn!" he exclaims. Audibly, he swallows shock. "Right in our midst. The girl, perhaps? Drones recorded your gruesome kills of the tourist youths."

I labor for air. My lungs are scathed.

My knees hit the ground.

"Aim is everything—and given that the foreigner trailed us with an exquisite opportunity to hit me very directly, I take it that aim is her weakness." Breathing heavily, he squints into the increasingly dark rain. His eyes are ruthless.

It's still morning, but the typhoon's morbid clouds repel almost every puncture of light.

It might as well be near night.

"My lynxes are very protective of me," the head sniper warns, but in an amused voice. "Strange. They didn't detect your scent."

I don't dare move.

I breathe only through my nose. Silently. I utter not one word as his creatures stalk around the pineland, unleashed by a single wave of his palm.

Halted by a single whistle between his teeth.

See? he seems to say. *See how well I can control them?*

"But I shall enjoy hunting you, myself, with the beasts." It's a savagely intelligent threat. He *wants* me to move right now. Run. Sprint for my life and be eaten alive. He allows me to *think* he's letting me slip away free for now.

I dare not move an inch.

"Hazen Creed, you're too clever by half," Richter compliments, shifting targets. The snarls of the lurching lynxes thicken in the rain. "It appears you stole the drone camera trackers, didn't you?"

Rain patters the ground. Insistent.

"There are about four in one place right now in these very pines. Yet they do not appear in the sky—they're nowhere to be found. Footage is missing. Who would've thought to do that so cleverly?" He sounds very impressed. He delivers his theory of what Hazen has planned. "You *wanted* the entire fleet of snipers to pursue you and be obliterated by a trap that you set deep in the jungle. After their deaths, you would've had your pickings of their weapons and breathing supplies."

The rain intensifies.

Hazen didn't inform me about setting any physical traps

for snipers, but I can tell he did as a final resort. Still, I don't avert my eyes. I fix my gaze on Walden Richter.

He metaphorically throws Hazen to the wolves. The Arctic wolves.

"Hazen, I heard that you harbored filthy blood in your own home and did not report it to the military?" Richter inquires, casual. "Was that your restricted military file I read? Kømmand Sergeant Arcus went to extreme lengths to conceal your information. Perhaps if you come with me to make better use of your intellect, I might decide I'm mistaken and have the footage erased."

Cameras—humming, buzzing—float closer.

But Richter, by now, realizes he hasn't quite hit the right nerve. Hazen isn't seduced by the idea of collaborating with the Arctic. Even though the offer to be saved in the Great Hunt is unprecedented. A first. It's almost unthinkable that anyone would be spared during a Hunt.

"Well?" Richter asks. Patient. "I assure you, if you are concerned that this isn't a real offer of well-earned amnesty—it is." They want to find out what Hazen is capable of. Richter's face lightens. "Hazen Creed, I hope to view you as a son of my own. A young man more strategic, more boldly cunning, than the average field soldier."

Hazen Creed has the luxury of his mother and brother being alive.

Unlike the rest of us, he still has a home. His nation is still alive.

"Final offer."

Silence.

Richter stabs deeper. Insulted by the stretch of quiet.

"As you wish. You are a traitor to this nation. A traitor to your very countrymen."

My heart spikes against my chest. I pray Hazen doesn't explode into rage—lured to take the bait.

And even Richter finally seems to sense it—Hazen won't capitulate to him. He won't expose himself. He's entirely disciplined and collected.

"It is very terrifying to me, a young man so painfully exceptional who could love his own family this greatly. Above his nation."

Richter turns away. As if he's departing at last so a larger animal can attack and eviscerate us.

"But alas," Richter states, "I had a sense that you might've set traps. Of course, I'd never risk world-famous snipers just to prove myself correct. You and I are both too astute for that. So, therefore, I came alone. And make no mistake, he will hunt you down."

He. He will hunt you down.

It hits me—he's leaving us for Kaiser Arcus to kill us. He knows exactly where Kaiser is, and by now—it's too late. Kaiser's coming for us. I gape at Hazen. *What do we do?*

What trap did you set?

Walden Richter finishes his speech, wincing at his electricity wounds, examining the damage to his burnt ribs. I realize I *mostly* missed. Mostly.

My aim is not as weak as they think.

"I rarely permit many circumstances to infuriate me," remarks Richter, his voice pinched with fury. "But it deeply *angers* me that a mind like yours is squandered on foreigners. You will regret this very deeply."

Walden Richter's humiliation is tangible. He's deviously intelligent but also imperiously prideful, so not for a hot second do I believe he's fixing to leave us for dead, as he seems to change his mind after staring prolongedly at the cameras, which now record him speaking to himself at best and being flagrantly rejected at worst.

He plans to indulge in the enjoyable sight of his animals dismembering us.

He reaches for his weapon belt.

He wants this honor.

"Hazen Jürgen Wargrave—son of Jürgen Wargrave himself—I conclude that glory is *not* destined for you."

CHAPTER 53

IFE STØRMBANE

DAY SEVEN, BEFORE DAWN

Hot, heavy rains barrage the windows—another menacing storm. Yesterday, under the gaze of a full moon, all four of the hunt king's darkborn men were located and killed.

Right now, Maximus hands me a mug filled with a hot pumpkin-caramel blend. He hunkers at the edge of the silk mattress next to me.

"How are you feeling, kitten?"

The hunt king will declare full-on war, but the deaths are pure relief for Zaire and me. I bring my knees up to my chest and gently wrap my arms around them, laying my cheeks against my smooth skin. "Not perfect."

"I know." Maximus runs his scarred palm over my hair. "I'm sorry."

He moves, and I feel the mattress sink behind me as he envelops me with his right arm. His skin's freezing, but I try not to shiver as he brings the mug to my lips. "Here. Drinking this always made me feel better as a kid. I know it's nothing compared—I know it's not fair that—" He tries to locate the right words.

"It's okay, Maximus." It's better than okay. Everything will finally progress. According to the footage, the laborers are hunting *snipers*, and if they succeed with defeating the snipers for once, it will make Great Hunt history.

Part of me likes to think the island's flumba orún kept them alive. Gave them a fighting chance.

But the rest of me knows those watery deaths and creature kills were my fault.

Sugary warmth wafts into my nose, rich with pumpkin, and Maximus kisses my shoulders. I always drink steamed apple juice with caramel and cinnamon, but this immediately becomes my new favorite. Warmth gushes through my insides, and I take another deep sip. "Thank you."

"Did they make it right?" Maximus asks. His broad jaw rests on my shoulder. Another kiss.

My lips twinge. "It's a little too hot, but I love it. Do you want to try some?"

Maximus shakes his head. He wraps his half-frozen right arm higher around my ribs. Locking me in. "No, that's okay. Finish it."

I drink as much as I can and set the mug on the table. Resisting the urge to stretch, I get up to take a bath.

"I'm going to—" My eyelids droop, suddenly feeling heavy.

"You're going to?" Maximus asks.

My tongue feels thick and heavy in my mouth, like I can't lift it. "Bah . . . bath . . . I wan . . . thu . . ."

My knees shake, and I stumble into the nightstand. I knock over the mug, and it shatters across the marble floor. Blistering-hot liquid spills, pooling around my feet, scalding my toes.

The darkborns survived. They're going to possess me. Kill me.

I hear the bed creak behind me. Distinct footsteps.

"I'm sorry it had to be this way." Maximus's voice drifts to me.

What?

My eyebrows, too heavy to crease in confusion, struggle to rise. My legs wobble as I claw for the walls and clutch them as tightly as possible. My nails bend from how hard I'm trying to hold on. My heartbeat slows. I can't let go of the wall. If I do, I'll collapse.

I try to scream, for Pacer, for anyone else, but my vocal cords are completely relaxed. I'm falling toward sleep.

I fumble for the wardrobe, hitting it hard with my shoulder, but I can barely feel the pain. Escaping is impossible; even the door seems a million miles ahead.

My mouth's so dry it's like I've swallowed pounds and pounds of cotton. Sleep comes close, so temptingly close, and as my body leans forward, my eyes fight to stay open. My knees give out, and I crash into something hard that catches me. Strong arms wrap around me.

"I'm sorry we don't have magic to do this," Maximus murmurs into my hair. "I apologize for how painful this will be."

I gaze up into his eyes, expecting dark gold, a sign of soul possession by darkborns.

But his eyes are as blue as summer. It's him. He's killing me.

"Max . . . please . . ." My mouth talks on its own. I hear it, but I can't control it. I want to cry. Not out of anguish but out of rage. Alarm instincts fire but fail as quickly as they start. *"Please . . ."*

Please, don't do this. My lungs are weak. I'm so tired my hand can't even curl into a good fist, can't grab a handful of his clothes. Maximus lifts me over his shoulder and lays me on the bed. I stare, my eyelids half-mast, at the ceiling. The resort chandelier hangs above with luminous champagne-colored crystals. Luxurious. Indifferent.

"You'll always be my first wife," I hear from far away, as if Maximus is all the way across the room or halfway across the globe. "Take comfort in that."

"Wha . . ."

I feel two pats on my knee. He's next to me. I roll my head over and see him. Maximus's hair is almost light brown in the dim, rainy sunlight. Humidity surrounds us.

"You survived so long because your love is so consuming, so effortless. So giving. I'll miss it." Lies wrap his voice.

I feel a sharp pain behind my ribs, and I don't have to guess what it is. Poison. He poisoned me. I'm dying.

Toxins burn through my toes, shoot through my legs, charring every atom, every fiber.

"Max . . . ple . . ."

"It only hurts the first six hours," he assures me, his voice steady. "I'll stay with you for all of it. The last two hours will be excruciating, but your body will survive it."

He kisses my limp fingers.

"Wh . . . why . . . No . . ."

Emergency fight or flight surges for a final time. It's a bolt of energy, enough to whip me out of bed and let me make it three sluggish steps before he effortlessly picks me up with his right arm. As if retrieving an ammunition pack that fell on the floor. I weigh nothing to him as he lifts my entire body with that arm.

I never stood a chance against him.

"Pacer adamantly argued on your behalf. He always argues on behalf of women. Did you know that?" Maximus sounds amused. He moves a stray piece of dampened pink hair from my forehead. "The entire war council resolutely agreed with him. They fought me on this."

"Wh—"

Maximus's face hovers over mine, and I see a barbaric coldness in his eyes that I've felt intermittently in his hands since our wedding day. He wraps a blanket over me. I'm shaking; I can't stop.

"Pacer swore Makarian girls are rarely so willing, and he promised you and your brother would be simple to control."

Zaire!

I try to sit up, but it feels like an eight-hundred-pound caiman is crushing my chest. My blood pumps the venom faster as Maximus slides a cool pillow under my head and lays me back down. I feel like I can't breathe. Sweat pools at the base of my spine.

Finally, my panicked energy is all gone. Evaporated. I can't move.

Maximus sits back and shakes his head in thought. He swipes a rugged hand over his jawline. "Pacer has a full heart. A good one. He firmly believes you're too young to replace. Not now. Not yet. Let you live, have memories, mature. Give you a real chance to prove yourself."

My brows can't move, can't even push toward each other; my mouth can't twitch. But my ears hear him.

"Except my father ordered you to control your emotions in public view—and you defied him at the execution." Hatred burns in his eyes. "He issued you a last warning at the Interrogation Department, which was a rare gift, and you did not heed him. Therefore, your replacement operation was scheduled."

Vørian was never who I had to fear. It's been Maximus, the whole time.

Sniper General Størmbane.

My breath becomes shallow. "Max . . . please . . ."

"Do you know who Rainer Van Valken is?" He gets up and removes his shirt, revealing his tan broad back and its deep scars.

I can't even fully shake my head. *Valeska's brother?*

She's only mentioned him once or twice. That she's significantly older than him and he died before his time. But what does he have to do with me?

"You killed him. Not *you*, your Makarians. He was my best friend, and he lost his head under darkborn possession and almost killed me because of your people. His death anniversary is tonight."

"Please . . . Max . . ." My voice cracks. Tears gather in my pleading eyes. *Please, have mercy, General.*

Maximus holds my hand, and ice expands up my skin. "A Vikarian girl will rightfully be in your body, Ife—but the genes will be fully yours. Our kids will bear your face, your smile maybe. Your green eyes—they were always your best attribute."

You won't get to see them, he's saying, *my children.*

"Just . . . divorce . . ." *Can't he divorce me?*

"I would never fail at marriage. Never." Maximus refuses to be a common man. Dedicated to his own lineage. "Your mind will be scientifically replaced when the time arrives."

No. No. No. The Allied Force is going to replace me. They're going to use their technology to implant someone else in my body. *My body.* A chip lodged deep inside me with another girl's thoughts, her loyalty, all the while keeping the bloodline of the bone king fully alive. Maximus has already arranged my future. He explains, "You are expected to bear one child per year. For fifteen years." *My body.*

His judgment is merciless.

"I have zero confidence in your ability to raise Arctic men," Maximus explains. "However—your blood will be used to make our men invulnerable to vatrium."

The Allied Force wants my skin, my orún genes, and its capabilities, but they don't want me. Not alive, at least. Faintly, I hear a guard brashly speaking outside my doors.

"Scream, and it's over." Maximus's eyes are threatening.

I scream. As loud as my deflated lungs let me. It's my only hope.

His hand slams over my mouth, but not painfully. I realize he won't physically harm me—he can't. My body is now too valuable to him if he has vatrium poisoning. But he smothers my mouth. My voice.

"You . . . mother?" I ask. "Your . . . mother . . . in . . . meh?" *Your mother in me?* I can barely manage the words. My body insists on shutting down. Frustrating me.

Maximus tilts his head.

"No—no." His eyebrows are furrowed. "Why would it be my mother inside you? I wouldn't have kids with my own— Ife, my mother is dead. I never lied about that."

I tremble. "Va . . . leek . . . Vales . . . ka?"

I remember her words now. *Stand straight! The second I can, I will replace you with a sharper woman. There's a twenty-year career on the line.* Valeska knew this entire time. She even framed Kateri for the neurological-surgeries leak to get an opportunity to speak with Maximus alone. She sacrificed a foreigner without a second thought. Did Valeska plot to marry Maximus?

Disgust contorts his darkened features. "Valeska is like

a relative to me. That's reprehensible." He lifts my chin so I can look at him. "You need to ask more perceptive questions. For example—how many bullets it took to kill the sun king. Where I buried the hunt king."

Fury rushes through me. I try to grab him, and Maximus cages my fingers. "Kaipo Island killed good men, and as soon as we located the sun king, I killed him." His voice is pitiless. Critical. "The hunt king was on his knees as he witnessed his younger brother die before I killed him after."

Rage shoves me. I need to find Zaire before they kill my entire family—

As if reading my mind, Maximus remarks, "Your brother escaped the island—with the stylist. No need to grieve. Neither interest me."

"*Lia . . .*" *Liar.*

"I canceled their executions."

He's lying. Maximus's execution orders are never rescinded. Maximus is tracking Zaire with the expectation he'll be able to find the rest of our family.

Right now, I'm not going to cry. I'm set on that as he studies my face. Hell bent, in fact. My fists tighten, and I refuse to cry.

I raise my chin.

But tears sting the corners of my furious eyes. I am getting my family members butchered all over again. I could get Zaire and Kateri killed now for my amateur mistakes. Deep down, I crave the impending sleep just to end the suffering. *I failed.*

Maximus is, above all, an Allied Force man.

He took everything. My girlhood. My childhood. My muscles loosen. *My body. My family. The Arctic seized it all.*

I cannot seize it back.

As desperately as I tried, I cannot end the Allied Force.

CHAPTER 54

COA RANGECROFT

"Hazen Jürgen Wargrave—son of Jürgen Wargrave himself—I conclude that glory is *not* destined for you."

Richter draws an antique firearm. Hardly the size of his fist, but deadly.

He can only aim at one of us—and the only visible one is Bray. But Richter does not know that although Bray turned in the dead sniper's rifle, Hazen took the spare semiautomatic handgun from the dead body right after he thrust his machete through his neck.

Hazen hits Richter's throat with two direct shots, even in the destructive rain, but Richter remains on his feet. *Impossible.*

Collapsed bullet shells plummet into the mud.

"Did you think that I would arrive defenseless, without armor, Wargrave?" he roars over the thunder of Hazen's bullets. "Do you believe the Makarians are the only ones capable of invisibility? Has your clever—"

A hand grenade. Hazen does not even hesitate to throw it.

Walden Richter's eyes blow open wide. Terrified.

He flinches. Luckily for him, his invisible armored defenses *are* highly resistant, but as Hazen empties the magazine of bullets, they're sustaining critical damage. Hazen doesn't relent—using every grenade found in the dead sniper's arsenal.

Assaulting my eardrums. Painting the sky red with gunfire. Explosives.

Hazen's wearing him down, and soon Richter's armor will break—therefore Richter needs him distracted. I can practically read his calculations. But I refuse to give him the chance.

We're a team right now. A unit.

I crack a bolt of lightning directly at Richter. Several strikes, one right after another, unceasing and unyielding. Burning my own lungs. Rapidly my lungs are losing air. Orún fire itself smokes through my lungs.

I collapse. Panting. Spent.

Richter's bloodlessly fast.

He couldn't dodge the electricity, nor the ammunition, barraging him from all sides. But in this brief millisecond, he shoots at Bray twice, and each bullet hits Bray's body. With resounding force.

Bray crumples to his knees, desperately trying to save himself. His wounds are far worse than Richter's. Fatal. Bray knows Hazen will be distracted. "Keep shooting him!"

Helplessly, Bray presses the entry wounds on his body, as if he can stanch that much blood. An onslaught of blood.

A crying gasp bleats out of my scorched throat. My limbs shake uncontrollably, unable to even move, my trachea suffocating on its own smoldering tissues.

So I crawl on my forearms. Dragging my useless deadweight body, grasping for Bray. "Bray . . ."

Sadistic, Richter shot Bray in body parts where the wounds will not kill him instantly, extending his pain as long as possible. But he marked Bray for death.

My eyes sting with tears.

I want to boot Richter down to the ground, pin him like an animal, ensnare him with fire. Growling like a beast—flames in my teeth—

Ferocious smoke, dark as charcoal, obfuscates my vision. Even my nostrils are expelling smoke. Darker than ever before.

I summon lightning onto my palm, but it dissipates. Not even a crackle.

This is what Richter wanted.

Hazen rips me backward suddenly to keep me from being shot in the skull. I realize Richter estimated my location using the tracks in the mud that show my movement. Even though he can't see me, his bullet grazed my head. My scalp is scorched as inches of my hair are torn away. Hot blood trickles down my forehead. Bone chips rest in a bloodied mess of hair. *He shot me. He shot me.*

Richter *grazed* me.

But that bullet's graze vaporized centimeters of my scalp.

My primal scream of agonizing pain exposes my location. I can't contain it. It's pure torture I've never felt before.

Graciously, the ravaging storm thrashes heaps of torrential rain down onto the island. Skull fragments, tiny pieces of broken bone, roll down my head. *I'm going to die out here.*

If we can't kill Richter, I'm going to die, and Kaiser Arcus is still out there.

My knees are swept out from under me as corrosive vines stab through our shirts, drag at our limbs. Attacking everywhere.

Forcibly, I'm wrenched away from Bray's reaching hand. We grasp for each other but miss by inches.

Disoriented with blood loss, I navigate the rising floods to catch myself on Bray's damaged shoulder. I cauterize his wounds—with the very last of my orún fire.

But I notice a gore-covered tree in front of me, which a naked man is tied and bolted to. Not just any man, a *sniper.* Every Vraničarian victim's name is carved into his skin.

Across his dead chest in Vikạrian: WØLVENSTARKER. Sniper.

It hits me. Walden Richter did not ask Bray, *Did you kill that sniper?* He asked him, *Did you kill those snipers?*

Someone else hunted the snipers. Walden Richter led us back to these coordinates.

Worst of all, I sense who did it. Six metal crossbow arrows pin the sniper to the thick kapok tree. Execution-style.

Alina Volkova.

She did not ambush that sniper simply for the Allied Force to view across the forced-labor camp. She hunted the sniper down for her homeland.

My heart crashes against my chest. The body's fresh. She's nearby.

A crunch steals my attention. With a jolt of panic, I realize cauterizing Bray's gunshot wounds cost me precious seconds. Walden Richter's alive. A threat.

I try to summon lightning again into my fist—but my fingers scrape nothing but air. My blood spills into the earth from my graze.

"There you are. Foreign filth—"

We strike at the same time.

A cry explodes from Richter's voice.

My lightning, I think, *my lightning finally killed him.*

Richter hits the sodden earth.

Horrifically, my hand is *still* bare. Regular human skin. Unforgivingly vacant of orún.

Richter only missed because in one wrench Hazen—bare handed—ripped off his critically damaged armor. Weakened by artillery. Fractured by the hand grenades.

Hazen does not grant Walden Richter the mercy of being shot to death. Hazen does not even give him the audible response he practically begged for.

His machete plunges into Richter's spine. Hacks through vertebrae, razes through muscle, until it reaches the outside of him. Impaling him. Completely.

Richter is dying from only a makeshift machete—that Hazen crafted himself. Within hours.

Richter was right about him. A young man painfully exceptional.

Blood gurgles from Richter's mouth. "Potential. Wasted . . . squandered . . ."

"You can cry over it to my uncle—after I kill him tomorrow."

CHAPTER 55

DAY SEVEN, BEFORE DAWN

I drift in and out of consciousness.

As soon as I sense Maximus coming close, as if to give a last kiss goodbye, the urge to vomit is so overwhelming bile rises.

Maximus lightly kisses my cheek, but it's enough. The bile surges up my throat, almost choking me as I lie on my back. I'm grateful my throat is too relaxed to cough. I feel something more cold blooded than him slipping over me—determination.

Maximus holds my fingertips in his polar grasp. "You'll be our first official test. Arctic men will not live a mortal fifty years on this earth; we will reach immortality in our dominion. With the orún power of Makarians and an Allied mind, we will change the fate of mankind."

———

I vomit on the sheets as soon as Maximus's footsteps disappear.

He'll be back soon. I force myself to lift my impossibly

heavy upper body and throw up again. Poison splashes the floor. Maximus only kissed my cheek for half a second, but that was more than enough. Even thinking of him is enough to repel me.

I retch until my stomach hurts, emptied out. Then I retch *still*. All the herbal concoctions I've swallowed for contraception have built up my resistance to this poison that's supposed to kill me, and it doesn't even hurt as much as it should.

My whole world spins, dizzy, nauseous, and I wait for the room to slow down. I clutch the fresh sheets until it finally stills and blurred images become one. I dive under the bed to replace the sheets. I wet the bed so often as a child, believing the Allied Force was aiming to murder me in my sleep. I still make a habit of keeping a second set of sheets under my bed at all times, just in case.

I replace the sheets as fast as I possibly can.

I whip the fan settings to blast, whirring away the stench of regurgitation. I spray an obnoxious amount of lavender perfume, then wipe saliva from my mouth in one clean sweep, resisting the instinct to use my sleeve and instead smearing the slaver on the used sheets, before burying the silks where Maximus never searches: my makeup drawers.

I will destroy your entire genocidal empire. I swear on everything. I catch my greasy face in the mirror, my eyes bloodshot, watery, dragging with drugs. My soft skin's once-dewy sheen is slathered with heavy sweat. My mouth hangs open, panting out loud. I rinse my mouth in the bathroom and drink down fresh water until my organs threaten to burst—and my mind clears.

Weapons.

I need weapons.

I always make my hair clips like knives. If you ever need them, use them. Dozens of political leaders are suspicious. Kateri is a genius. The gilded clips in my drawers are also sharp blades. I test one out on a dense pillow, and the seams immediately burst, spitting out feathers. *Men can have their strength. We'll have brains.*

Kateri saved my life.

I hurry to the bed and remember something the bone king taught me when I was a little girl. *The night you get married, steal your husband's breath, his spit, his blood, his hair, his skin. Keep it in your ór'rù'ta jar and mix yours with his. Don't dare forget. Travel with it everywhere.* The Eternal Ritual. Necessary among kings with our sacred blood. *Use kakru salt with my magic. If your husband kills you, he will also die.*

I was too foolish to complete this ritual when I got married. I never suspected Maximus would ever kill me. *Maximus?* The man who always fawns over me and acts like I'm his own soul? The prize of the stars? The breath in his lungs? *That* Maximus? Never. I was his little princess, and he was a protector dead set on killing any enemies that came for me.

I always assumed it would be his enforcers, his father, Vørian, an assassin. But now, I drag out my grandfather's kakru salt and scatter it over the marble floor. I cut my hair, spill my blood, spit, and rub dead skin off my knees—mixing myself with Maximus. The kakru salts turn dark gold. On our wedding night, I stole his being—breath, spit, blood, hair, skin—and bottled it to appease my distrustful grandfather. An act of honoring him, since I'd run away as a thirteen-year-old to live with Maximus and rushed into a wedding at fifteen.

The man who I thought killed him but who instead killed his dearest brothers.

But now, Kōnkon's saved my life as well. *Grandfather.* As

if he always knew I'd marry a monster, that I was attracted to challenging them. Head on.

The darkened salt runs through my palms, and I smear it over my skin and face, through my hair, and swallow as much as I can. Orún pulses through my body. The bone king's orún. The bone king before him, and the bone king before him. A whole lineage.

I still won't possess real orún of my own, but once they know about it, it'll be enough to keep Maximus or his enforcers from murdering me. Ever. My mother never had to use it. My father's been wildly in love with her since they were twenty. He would die for her.

Now, Maximus will die for me. If he kills me, he'll die *with me.*

And I refuse to die before seeing my empire revived.

The kakru salt sinks into the marble floors, vaporizing, and I rush back into bed, setting myself down exactly as Maximus left me.

If I were being closely monitored right now, the resort would've flooded with enforcers. Instead, Maximus poisoned me and left me to suffer. Fatal mistake.

I hear clicking footsteps. Like heels.

A girl's voice. High and young. "Is Head General Størmbane going to let him choose his next wife?"

A woman. Older and stern. "Why not? Sniper General Størmbane doesn't care for it. But I doubt he's in any rush to get remarried. He's a teenager, nineteen soon. They fall in and out of love."

"Is it ridiculous to hope it's me?" The girl giggles.

"You'd give up your body to live in a *Makarian*?" the older woman snarls.

The girl hushes her voice as they enter my room. "For

Sniper General Størmbane? Yes. I . . ." She swoons. "He's the man of my dreams. I offered four times. They're rewarding their pick with billions for their lifetime of service. It would mean everything for my family."

"I could never," the older woman dismisses instantly. "It's too vulgar of a sacrifice having to be inside one of them. A rich Vikarian girl will secure it; she can avoid looking at herself. She understands duty and societal responsibility. But think of the poor general. He'll have to share his bed with that Makarian body his whole life, present himself in public with her, use her vessel for his children. He's the one who will suffer for our country, and we must support him."

"He picked the prettiest foreign bride before . . . I mean, I was surprised—I thought he'd like . . . plain girls. Maybe he wants one now."

"Like you?" the woman responds, suspicious.

"Oh! I only meant . . . Never mind . . ."

"She's every foreign girl, senseless and promiscuous. She attracts men. He was baited. Do not compare yourself to nonsense."

"You think so?"

Gloves snap. "Absolutely. She desires attention from men. A seductive slevt. How many women do you see her associated with? Isla Moon invited her to the women's soiree, and she *spurned Isla Moon.*"

"All glory, I noticed that." It dawns on her. "She sat exclusively with the men—mostly Sniper General Størmbane—the whole event. I don't think she likes other women."

"She doesn't like to compete. Afraid of sharing any flattery. Sniper General Størmbane requested a mature woman this time." The older woman reeks of antiseptic and balm when she sits next to me, leaning over my body. She slathers a frigid serum over my toes. "He's requesting someone with at least thirty years of life behind her. I think her youth scarred him."

"Says Head General Størmbane?"

"No. Says me." Maximus's voice enters the suite, and they stand at strict attention.

"Sniper General Størmbane, I didn't realize you were here!"

"Thank you so much for your sacrifice, Sniper General Størmbane." The girl bows, deep. I can barely see her auburn fishtail braid through my lashes.

"It's not my preference to kill," Maximus discloses, as if he hadn't just been amused by it earlier. He's now wearing a pure-white vintage watch, his tanned, rippling arms finely displayed, paired with a crisp rifle club uniform and leather hunting boots. As though he just stepped off a Kilrød hunting range. He steals a close seat, and his face feigns regret, but only I know inside he's celebrating. *Do you know who Rainer Van Valken is?*

The death of his friend finally avenged.

Maximus drains a dark läkøn into his smirking mouth. "Excuse me for needing something . . . heavy to get through this difficulty. I don't wish to do this."

You outrageous liar.

"Not at all! Anything you need, Sniper General." The girl giggles again. "My assistance is my pleas—"

The older woman elbows her and bows. "We wish you blessings. We pray you pick an agreeable wife."

My skin rises just *feeling* him near. I can kill my way through two women, *maybe*, but he's much stronger than me, and I'm still weakened from the poison. My organs are screaming, my movements slower.

Leave, Maximus. I'll deal with you soon.

But he sits right next to me, holding and kissing my palm, promising that he loves me. But he doesn't trust these women exactly like I don't; they could easily expose to the world he doesn't love me, and outsiders *will* detect it. They'll unravel everything, knowing the Allied Force replaced me.

A reminder no world leader is safe. No matter what the Allied Force declares. Stirring a deeper resentment among the remaining empires.

I can manipulate that, insinuate that the Allied Force coerced me, and I save it in the back of my mind, locking it in the fiery heat of my skull, as I feel the nurse's clammy hands slip up my thighs, under my arms, around my neck.

Staying still's impossible. My knee twitches.

Maximus presses me down. "How long does it usually take for them to go to sleep?"

He cracks open another läkøn bottle. Presses it against his lips.

"Her final rest should be in a few short hours, General. Makarian skin is thicker."

That's not true, and he knows that, but he nods. Hours spread. The stifling air grows hot. Insufferable. When Maximus leaves, finally, I spring forward.

"Nurse Stolt, do—"

I lunge forward with the razor-sharp clip against the younger girl as she speaks, plunging it into her chest—deep and hard. Her eyes burst wide in shock. I kick her off my bed, racing for the older woman. She hurls her medical cart between us and dashes for the door.

"No, you don't!" I growl.

The floor is slippery with pooling tonics from the cart, but I gain on her.

"Enforcers!" she shrieks. "Enforcers!"

I leap over her cart, and she throws open the double doors. I shove them shut with my shoulder, then whip and lunge at her.

She dodges, scrambling along the floor. Gasping. "You beast!"

Oh, it's fine when men are beasts, but tides forbid a girl get rough.

She rushes for the help buttons along the walls. The girl gurgles behind us.

"Enforcers!" The woman darts from me, but I'm faster. Swifter than her.

She grabs a fistful of something from her belt pouch. Powder explodes into my eyes, making them sear with pain, reeking of talcum powder. I fight through the burn, clawing the air. Sightless. Thorsten and I have play-wrestled Maximus for years, adapting after each defeat. I've learned echolocation. I just need to hear her voice—track her down—

"You will *not* kill me, you filthy—"

There. I catch her voice, swinging wildly, my clip tearing into clothes, skin. I don't stop. She yelps from my fifth swipe. It makes contact, but so does she.

Sharp pain pierces my thigh, ripping a scream out of my lips. My heart spikes.

Visionless, I graze her again with my blade and she scrambles away from me, knocking everything over. Something's lodged inside my thigh. Her shrieking barks almost tear through the heavy doors. "Enforcers! Guards! *Security!*"

I gaze down, my eyes stinging. *Medical shears* are lodged deep in my thigh. It hurts so badly that I can't think for a full second.

My whole brain buzzes with raw pain. *Run after her!* I

suck in a breath and tug the shears out, biting my inner cheeks to keep from screeching out loud. I've been through worse, *much* worse, but it's been so long since I've been stabbed or injured so deeply, and it feels unbearable. *Snatch her!*

Nurse Stolt runs, and I'm after her. I grasp her at the door and toss her down by her medium-length asymmetrical haircut, then pin her.

"Not so fast." I smile, feeling a new wave of adrenaline. Control. Zaire practically smirks in my head. *I need a wickedly historic line right here.* I see the woman who was going to kill me, now in panic for *her* life. "Want to find out how perfect my aim is?" My grin widens. "Scream or move again."

I could've done better. Zaire would have killed it. But her brown eyes bulge nonetheless, her gaze flying toward the door. Her thoughts are too obvious.

Strands of her gutter-blond hair are stuck to my hands with blood.

She wrenches free and flounders onto her feet, then sprints. I sprint after her. My limbs hurt, but I power them anyway. My hands grab her hair and plunge the clips toward her neck, before she suddenly propels me in front of her. Sending me right over her shoulder, slamming me hard into the marble. My spine hits. I gasp for breath.

Spitting more of the poison up.

"You'll *never* kill me, you dirty slevt!" She rushes for the bloodied shears at the same time as me.

I let her snatch them first and plunge the clip through her throat when she whips forward to attack with the shears. Her eyes pop. She catches me in the cheekbone, but I deepen my thrust in the middle of her throat.

Then I slide off her. Panting.

My cheekbone stings, torn open. *You'll never kill me, you dirty slevt!*

I smile. I don't have to kill her.

———

I think of being uncontrollably dramatic when Maximus returns, awaiting him in my bridal dress, marital robes, or something equally iconic, dripping in blood, and laughing maniacally. *Anything* that would make sure he never forgets what he tried against me. But I've worked too hard to let him make me slip now.

I need to play this right. Exactly right.

Savor my new power. *This is only the beginning.*

Maximus cuts open the doors and sees the two women slumped over, direly injured. But I'm wide awake on our bed, in a frilly nightgown, covered in blood, crying hysterically. He freezes.

I *intentionally* wore stark-white clothes, contrasting with the bright, overpowering red blood.

I can't help but glance up, and I don't think anything can be more delicious than the astounded shock on his face. I drink it in and quickly return to sobbing inconsolably into my palms. He calls for the enforcers, just as I need him to.

"How could you do this to me?" I shriek in front of them. I scream at him. A wild girl now. "How could you!"

Maximus glances at the two dying women, his Arctic people, the struggle, the *blood*. Syringes and containers are scattered everywhere. Välliance bots rush in alarmedly, lights flashing. Before Maximus returned, I made *certain* to knock over vanities, nightstands, and paintings, smear blood on walls. I made it appear like a real fight, like they almost won. As he steps over the debris now, he heads directly to me.

Maximus's jaw is clenched with fury that I survived. He probably *detests* that he doesn't have his trusted enforcers with him—only the standard ones who patrol our resort floor, too oafish to trust with his real plans for immortality, which would start a frenzy of every man hunting for his war trophy. He comes close, yanking back the silky canopy curtains from our bed, but he knows better than to come too close. Maximus stays back from me, inches apart.

"What happened?" His voice cuts. His face is fuming.

Sobbing, I splutter, "Do you realize what I had to do to *save* you just now?"

"What do you mean?" His eyes focus on me, searching for injury. Finding my face slashed, my bleeding thigh. "Ife, what *happened?*"

His fresh rage is real. I wasn't supposed to get injured in the process. *Ever.*

These women ruined his merchandise, his war prize. I was meant to stay flawless.

These careless, reckless women attacked an expensive artifact that cost human lives and trillions of vikęs in infiltration, resources, and acquisition.

More than that, Maximus lost at least a pint of my needed blood. He's patently irate. My eyes shimmer, glossy with tears. He comes even closer. I think it's the stunned shock, the fact I shouldn't even be *alive*, that almost overrides his own self-preservation instincts and makes him dare to venture close.

But Maximus is not senseless; he holds my shoulders, hard enough to prevent me from retaliating. Even if he'd never strike me, I have every motive to kill him. His hands shift downward, and he grips my arms, my wrists. "Ife, kitten, what happened? Are you all right?"

I want to lunge right now, bite off his nose, but it would expose my deception. *What do you think happened? Do you think I'm all right?*

"Tell me," he whispers instead of *I'm sorry*, instead of *I'm a traitorous, murdering husband.* As if he thinks I'm artless enough to admit to near murder in front of these guards.

"Assassins came," I gasp, crying. I suck down a wet breath. "And they were—they were dressed like nurses. If it wasn't for my orún, I'd—"

"Orún? You don't have orún." Maximus's face scans mine as if he's thinking, *Do you?*

"You thought I *didn't?*" I catch the surprise on his face and savor it. Bawling harder in heartache. "I-I just wanted you to treat me as a normal girl. A normal wife. And I had this horrid nightmare that you were trying to kill me—"

"Ife." Maximus shoves my face into his broad chest. "Stop. You don't know what you're saying. You're in shock." He pulls my head back and edges his thumb over my lip. "I would never."

Liar. I rip away from his thumb, his body. Resisting the urge to bite him all over again.

"I know *you* wouldn't, Maximus. Because anyone who kills me kills *you*," I quaver, as if struggling to keep from breaking apart. Sniffling. Gulping. "That's what happens when you marry the bloodline of the bone king. Our lives— *our bones and flesh*—are intertwined forever. By eternal orún."

His face completely stills. Blanching.

"What did you say?"

I take advantage of the quiet as the enforcers slowly stop moving. They briefly halt their arrests of the groaning women. "That's—that's why I always knew I'd be safe with you and all—all the guards. That's why I fought so hard, so these women wouldn't kill me and end up killing you by mistake."

His eyes narrow. Intense. "What are you talking about?"

He takes my chin, forcing me to look up at him, at his fear. "What are you talking about, Ife?"

His eyes widen as he sees my new face. Not some slobbering, crying, betrayed girl. But a face of fury. A surviving wife. Who breathes only fire and survival, in full control now.

"What did you do?" Maximus demands.

The real Maximus Barringer Størmbane—willing to do anything for *his* empire, even kill his own wife—stands in front of me.

He enters the canopy, pulls the curtains shut, and holds me down. When I knee him, he crushes his knee against mine to trap my limbs. Weighing down on me enough so I can't move. I can't harm him.

"Explain this. Now."

I lean up. Whispering so low even the Välliance Megacorp medics that swarm the room, ready to start tending my injuries, can't hear.

"You married a sorceress, *Maximus*." I clutch his clean shirt in my bloodied hands. "I have dark magic, *real dark*. And if you or your nation ever attempt to execute Zaire or Kateri again, if you even harm a follicle on their heads, I'll slit my own throat to kill us both. I'll end us completely. One day, I'll do it out of spite, simply because I can. Know that at any time, if I die, you're dead with me. *Long live the Allied Force.*"

CHAPTER 56

Maximus sits with me for breakfast. His glare is heinous. But his face tightens when his father arrives, and a small grunt of frustration tugs from his throat. Barringer seems surprised to see me alive.

I *feel* alive. My hair is all over the place—wildly curly. Gorgeous.

I did it myself.

My pajamas are a pink half shirt and satin shorts. I'm completely relaxed, slouched, showing off my new scars, leisurely scooping up peanut butter with my fingers. I sit on my bare legs folded on the tufted chair. My glossy pedicure is fresh. I love my body. I appreciate every inch now. It's survived *everything* and brought me this far; I have nothing but deep respect for its resilience. I'm grinning.

Oh! I also have a new scar on my cheek, and I don't plan on getting rid of it. Ever.

It's *my* war trophy.

I'm triumphant. I don't plan on letting them have *any*

control over me anymore. I have the power now. I am the leader of Makari. The only.

This morning, Maximus finalized it.

"Ife, you look healthy." Barringer kisses my temple. His hands are calloused, large enough to split my neck.

Barringer glances at Maximus for information, but he gives him nothing.

Barringer's mouth sets. He has my usual papya pulp poured, with a few slices of mango next to the full glass, but I stop the attendant, insisting I pour my own hand-squeezed drink. Only one for me and Maximus to share, together. Same beverage.

We will share meals and drinks from here on out. I let Maximus sip first.

His eyes avoid his father's brutal gaze.

"Thank you for the compliment, Viker. I'm so glad you think so. You look healthy as well." I beam, relishing Maximus Størmbane's refusal to update his father on how he failed.

As the sniper with the highest kill count on record, he cannot stand his target remaining alive.

But now his own life is involved.

"Oh, Head General!" I put down our fork. "Maximus is *dying* to tell you something."

I love messing with Maximus. I don't even have anything for him to tell his father—not really—but watching his rough blue eyes glower at me is too *absolutely divine* to stop.

His very life is inseparable from my survival. Forever. I'm exceptionally lucky for that.

"What is the information, Maximus Barringer?" Barringer's right eye now looks at his son.

Vørian's out hunting, but I almost *wish* he could witness

this moment. Thorsten sneaks some of my peanut butter to add to his hard-bread pakaen, oblivious. Smiling sportively.

"Pressing news, Vikęm." Maximus rubs the back of his neck, glancing at me for my ransom, any hint as to what I want. As if his bloodline is held hostage.

Time smears. I smile innocuously behind our glass, eating from his plate, with his fork, enjoying his guaranteed-unpoisoned pakaen. Which will be our new favorite this week.

Meanwhile, seconds spoil in silence.

"Maximus, don't detain your words." Barringęr's mouth tenses as he polishes off his steak knife with a serviette. "What is it?"

"I . . ." Maximus straightens. He surmises what I want. "I want . . . to marry Ife again this summer."

"You married her this past winter. Why another wedding?"

I almost burst out in laughter. *As if! I'd eat an entire armored vehicle without water before I marry him again!*

But I realize what I want.

"No, honey bear, the other thing," I murmur, tracing tiny circles in his palm.

"*What* other thing?" Maximus locks his palm tightly over my fingers.

I announce, "Maximus had the brilliant idea of enriching my childhood village. The entire valley region." I perk. "He wants to bless everyone there with a very generous donation of *ten million vikęs* to each of them. Tonight!"

His mouth hardens.

"Best part—all from his own funds!" I smile up at him, caressing his flushing cheeks. "He's so kind. My sweet husband."

I take a sip.

"I was so shocked I just about *died*, right, Maximus?"

His fingers release mine. I wait for him to refuse, to admit his dire situation. But pride coats his eyes. He brushes my fingertips against his lips, kisses them. "Anything for kitten."

Head General watches, his eyebrows lifting. "It's possibly a wise donation."

Barringer examines the potential tactic. A false peace offering to Makari after the fresh murders. Maximus will make the millions back in mere moments.

"Maximus Barringer, see that it's done," Head General decides.

Maximus nods. "Yes, Vikęm."

I leap to think of the next thing to torture him with, but Maximus coughs suddenly, wet blood spraying over his palm, onto my nose. My first thought is *poison*, and I prepare to disgorge my own stomach acid just in case, but Barringer's reaction is too detached.

"Warholm war strategists have arrived to examine the island themselves. The orún might prove itself useful for adapted ammunition without the need of vatrium." Head General speaks as if it's normal. Maximus's coughing. Wheezing. Rasping.

Vatrium poisoning and lead overexposure are rampant in the military. If Maximus has severe, critical vatrium poisoning—he will still execute his duty without alteration. But I act concerned, patting his back, rubbing his blond hair.

"It's okay, bunny bear. Are you all right, Maxi . . ." My words die. My fingers feel something corrugated. Hard.

I move his hair aside from the nape of his neck and see a metal implant that makes me gasp. *RA NER*. It's old and weathered, gray and rusted, like it's been there for years. My hands have palmed Maximus's hair all over before, but he has rigid, coarse combat scars, and I assumed I was feeling them.

Now, I smooth his dark-blond hair back into place, and it's impossible to keep shock out of my face. *Do you know who Rainer Van Valken is?*

You killed him. Not you, *your Makarians.* My blood freezes. *He was my best friend, and he lost his head under darkborn possession and almost killed me because of your people.*

My lungs tighten up.

You'll be our first official test.

I can't breathe.

Official test.

I wasn't the first test.

He was.

CHAPTER 57

I slam the door to our bedroom shut. "Who *are* you?"

Maximus—Rainer—whoever this is—seizes my mouth so fast my whole world whirls. He tightens his abrasive hand over my nose and mouth.

"Do not speak."

I kick against his knee, but it's like striking steel. I claw at his arm, but it's like scraping ice. He moves differently than Maximus usually does. More brutally.

"Listen to me, right now." His breath lands roughly against my skin. "If I let you go, you do not disobey me and *you keep your voice quiet*, do you understand?"

I nod rapidly. He releases me.

Air floods my body.

"Maximus is dead?" I whisper.

He's terse. "Who told you that?"

"My orún tells me; I know it." I swallow. "I . . . don't sense him. Who are you? . . . Rainer?"

He captures my upper arm and drags us into our private bath, running multiple showers. A Sestina bot floats up and aromas of warm jasmine and chamomile fill the space. He rams the glass door shut behind us. Mist rises. *"Thank you for choosing Sestina Megacorporation. Please rate this experience—"* He holds me by my dark-brown shoulders.

Temperature-perfected shower water falls over our clothes, our faces, our lips. It slips down his airy shirt, my bare feet, but I can't even move. Inches from his chest. Steam spreads, almost masking his steel-set mouth.

"Are you inside our head?" he demands.

Our head?

Oh no.

"You're in his body." I slap my hand over my mouth, pure shock vibrating me. *"With* him."

A shout is trapped in my chest. Now it makes sense, the sudden murder plot. The cold-blooded gaze in his eyes, him wanting to kill me. *He* detests me, Maximus's best friend, Rainer. He's inside Maximus, right now, in control.

Rainer Van Valken's real body was killed. Valeska's brother is alive.

But is the actual Maximus . . .

"Maximus isn't dead." His body leans over, caging me in. Even his breath is different, coated in mint, but I detect the dead underneath. Notes of a corpse. I've inhaled it before.

I stammer, "He kept you alive. In a metal implant."

"Inside him, yes."

Barringer doesn't know. If Head General Størmbane knew someone else was living inside of his oldest surviving son, even in alternating turns, he'd remove the implant. End Rainer's life, permanently.

Rainer grips me, but I probe deeper.

"Makarian darkborn soldiers possessed you and killed

you?" I gaze at him. *No, no. That's not it. Maximus wouldn't have been able to get to him in time.*

Makarian darkborn soldiers sever the brain completely, irretrievably, if they make the kill. Maximus killed him. He must have.

I figure Rainer's body was already possessed, and they couldn't salvage it, so of course, Maximus would be overcome with immense regret. He'd feel the need to save him, offering his body in exchange.

When did it even happen? How? Rainer probably attacked him, possessed. They fought, and Maximus killed him before retrieving Rainer's brain, saving it in a head implant, inserting it in himself, and resuscitating him. I can imagine Maximus committing to that. *It's their end*, he seethed to me, without hesitation, about my own government leaders. *Whether they hide in the heavens or on the earth—I will find them.*

And instead of delegating the task to someone else to have it grate on their conscience, after the leaders were located, he shot them all himself. Maximus is intensely loyal to people, and that, ironically, almost got me killed.

I forge ahead to see if I'm right. My head spins. "They managed to spare your brain, sustain you inside Maximus. Allow you control of him every so often."

He glares at me. Rainer's eyes are vicious.

You are art everlasting.

"Which one are you?" I ask. "The one who said I'm art everlasting? That you love me more than the stars could understand?"

"What?"

Not him. I quickly cross that off. I still have to pretend I'm wildly in love with the real Maximus. But when is *Rainer* in control? I flick my eyes up, refusing to look away. Determined. "Which one of you killed the sun king?"

Rainer's mouth hardens, and his eyes hold mine. "I did. Kaipo Island killed eleven soldiers. The sun king got a clean kill, honorable."

I shove him, hitting his chest. "You killed a king who did nothing to you! You barbarian!"

He restrains my wrists. "It was necessary; he committed the first aggression."

"You violated *his* island! It was defense!" I knee him, and he catches my knee with his cold hand. He corners me against the moist shower walls. I scream, and a resort guard barges in. "Are there issues—"

"Get out!" Rainer demands.

The guard salutes in apology and departs. Just like that. The automatic door slides shut behind him without his giving a retreating glance.

Locking me in with Rainer.

No, come back! Don't leave me with him!

Rainer glares down. "Your sun king refused to surrender the island and deliberately assailed our men—"

Wrath rises inside me. Seething.

"That's war," Rainer snaps. "We answered his threat and delivered his body."

I should've known. Not only did my senseless selection of Kaipo Island trigger its invasion by trespassers, but I caused his execution. I never anticipated the Allied Force would track him down for the deaths of eleven intruding snipers. My sharp attention was distracted.

I won't make that mistake again.

"When is Maximus . . . himself?" I dare to ask, feeling like a hare under the gaze of an expert hunter.

His hair darkened with purified water.

Rainer, by himself, is too savage, harsh, and unforgiving. He's *infuriated* that he was killed—I can smell his hatred on him. Profane rage radiates off him.

I wanted a fight for freedom, and here he is, alive in front of me. I spoke my lies into existence, except instead of the darkborns controlling my body . . . Rainer occupies Maximus's body. And Rainer clearly isn't over his grudge for being murdered.

"When will I get to see my . . . Maximus?" I ask. "My husband?"

Silence presses the air.

"Every nightfall?"

Rainer opens the automatic glass doors, but I follow him out. A Sestina bot bounces up and I kick it away. Cold air runs over my skin. My palms are still wet, but I grasp his biceps.

"Every time war trauma pushes through?"

"Leave it—"

Epiphany strikes me. "The implant has an internal timer."

I only need to figure out what triggers the internal timer.

For three years now, I've daydreamed conspiracies to explain why Maximus's hands sometimes feel hypothermic on me, freezing cold—and I've imagined him as an Arctic wolf in the night. It was almost as if he was another person. I never realized how close I was to figuring things out.

"Ife—"

"I'm right." I hold his cheek, acting as if I'm having a vision with orún. I even close my eyes like a fake oracle, but Rainer walks past me. "Don't worry, Rainer. I won't tell anyone. Despite everything, I love you. A friend of Maximus's is my friend."

His mouth twists. "We are not companions. I'm not Maximus."

I swallow.

"Maximus can't even hear you," Rainer continues. "He and I communicate by writing, but he can't fully see you. He's in . . . a darkened area."

Where Rainer goes when Maximus's in control, and where Maximus goes when Rainer's in control. That's why Maximus always tells me *I missed you.* Why he means it so intensely. He actually does miss me. *I'll always come back to you. It's only a matter of when, not if.*

Rainer can't stay. I'm not living with two men. And now that I know about this head implant, I can extract it when Rainer's not here.

But Rainer catches me glancing at the nape of his neck. "If you remove the neural implant, you'll kill him, and I will not let that happen."

"No, of course not." I twist my fingers behind me, like I wasn't just scheming to kill him. "I'm only curious. Why did you want to kill me? Did you really mean to?"

His animus–filled eyes make it obvious. I'm a Makarian. As if there's no reason above or below that.

But then he explains.

"Each day your crisis is what nail colors you prefer, and the conflict of my day is deciding the number of men I will sacrifice. You are not fit to raise men."

My fake vision of our sons.

My gut wrenches. That started everything.

"You cannot birth men in the sniper general's family on vegetation alone. You are a glorified expense—a weak, over-feminine, highly emotional, glorified expense."

A glorified expense?

I grit my teeth.

"Maximus refuses to confront his vulnerability." Rainer can hardly speak through his own constricted jaw. "A majority of his family is dead, and he cannot restore them. You, least of all, cannot regain him the glory that was lost to grand history."

Rainer is remorseless, practical.

"Someone should've been inside you, accountable for your duty. I waited too long."

I realize now Maximus almost always calls me his little princess, his little wife, his ikäniną. But Rainer calls me *kitten*—a tiny, vulnerable creature. Destructible.

But it's more than that.

Rainer seems to think that just anyone could fake my voice, mannerisms, verbiage. But I could win *awards* for my acting. No Vikąrian girl can behave as moonstruck, heartfelt, sugary, as I can. It's a damn science to me.

A spine of regret comes out in his roughed voice, and I realize his pain. Rainer's only alive, stealing hours, days, weeks, from Maximus, because Maximus cares for his best friend. Maximus is loyal above all else. Now Rainer is taking it out on *me*.

Rainer's metal head implant won't survive forever. Eventually, it'll degrade or short-circuit. He plans to live to see the final objective of world dominance secured. *That's* why time is crucial to him. He's finite.

Rainer permitted Maximus three years with the dream life and dream exotic beauty he always wanted, before he acted against me. But now Rainer aims to achieve the Allied Force's destiny.

I open my mouth to comfort Rainer. Ready to play a new part. It would gain me secrets, leverage—

The resort screens blare the national anthem for the final Great Hunt day. The closing ceremonies will take place soon.

"Maximus bought this for you." Rainer lays out a sundress. It's a ribbon dress with pink bows all the way to my waist. It's outdated. I recoil.

"I . . . love this."

"Put it on. Maximus wants to gift it to you for your closing ceremony appearance." Rainer mutes the screens after the anthem. "Get dressed."

But he cautions me, "Several snipers died on that island, *sorceress*. There is more to ancient Makari than you've ever informed us." He heads over to his arranged firearms and rifle club uniform. He slides his hands into carbon-black hunting gloves after he's dressed. "Your genes will deliver the Allied Force new weaponry."

My jaw drops.

Before he can stop me, I swipe his hunting knife from his belt and slash it right across my palm. He grimaces, grunting, his own palm instantly gashed. It's wet, bright red, and blood spills onto the white marble floor.

Our blood patters on the ground between us.

It stings like hell, but I don't care. I am Chief Princess Ìfẹ́. The leader of Makari.

Maximus's best friend is never going to order me around when he's not even an *heir* to the empire. Rainer survived because someone *else* saved him. I saved myself.

Zaire would urge me to shut up, lie low, escape this savage. Rainer has been in Maximus's brain before Maximus even was engaged to me. The date he died was written on the corroded head implant. Years ago. Yesterday.

I was eleven when Rainer died. His military glory was ended in his early teenage years. But that is not *my* destiny.

I am my own leader. *I* decide how much information the Allied Force receives. Not a barbarian that murdered my grandfather and his brothers. I've come too far to secure my new power.

I know Rainer is going to keep me right here, closer than ever, under his direct watch. But I *will not* surrender my status. This gash on my hand is only a reminder that I could execute all three of us when I want to.

Rainer's nostrils flare. He comes close, and mint wafts over my wet hair.

"My ikä, tell me, which one of us do you actually think you married on your wedding night? Me or Maximus Størmbane?"

My brain freezes.

"Who do you think planned it that way?" Rainer glowers down at me. "Me or Maximus Størmbane?"

I can't breathe. My lungs tighten.

"You will complete your duty this year as I declare it." Rainer holds up my chin higher, forcing eye contact, ensuring I understand this time. "You are my wife and the mother of my future children. You belong entirely to me." His eyes are brutal. "In this as in all things, you will remain obedient. My authority defines your existence. You will be submissive and dutiful to me as my wife. As I will protect the vessel of your body as your husband. Do you understand?"

My skin prickles.

Elope with me. Let me steal you from your brute husband. Be mine completely.

Maximus never married me. Only his body did. His name did.

Rainer married me. Swore every vow.

I swore to Rainer Van Valken.

If I remove the neural implant now, Maximus could die. My most powerful ally inside the Kilrød. I clench my teeth. Rainer is a firm traditionalist—the kind that considers a wife his property. He plans to get his death's worth.

He is the kind that's hardest to kill.

There's no compassion in him. Rainer knows what it's like to die and he still tried to kill me. This whole empire will know what it's like to die. I swear it.

Makari will rise.

Apoyê. That is war.

CHAPTER 58

DAY SEVEN, MORNING

A radio crackles. *"Keger—come in."*

Kaiser Arcus's voice. Abrasive. Corrosive over the comm radio. Hazen squeezes Walden Richter's radio tighter. Waiting.

Kaiser repeats, *"Keger, come in. This is Alphøx—send Hazen Wargrave's coordinates."* A guttural grunt. *"He's still invisible on the radar. Come in."*

A buzz of electricity on the comm. A distant gunshot.

"I don't have all night, Keger. These creatures are eating us alive—shoot one and a dozen keep coming—"

I ask Hazen, "Keger?"

"The Execution Range," Hazen explains. He glares at the rugged, malignant horizon. "The coldest glacier on earth. Richter named himself after the deadliest execution range."

"Aren't all execution ranges deadly?" I remark.

Hazen does not respond. As if I don't want to know the actual scale of human atrocities that the Allied Force has committed. He reinforces his bandolier of ammunition in the meantime.

Rain batters the typhoon-devastated island. It took hours for the brunt of the storm to pass. Mudslides nearly took our lives before the gale-force winds tore at our flesh.

There's a crackle of lightning. Another typhoon might hit us.

Hazen concentrates. Waiting another minute.

"Keger—I have zero visuals on you. I deployed another set of drones. Are you injured? Do you need extraction?" A beat of vitriolic silence. *"If I find out you're harboring Wargrave to recruit him, I will sever your—"*

Now Hazen speaks. He raises the bloodied comm to his mouth.

"No need to sever anything, Kaiser. He's already buried." Hazen smirks. "You're next in line."

Kaiser's animalistic breath barrages the speakers. *"Reveal yourself. You're petrified of me—admit it."* Kaiser gives a blunt laugh. *"You're cowering on the island. But don't worry. I will find you."*

"You'll *find* me?" Hazen chuckles. Sharpened with hatred. "*Find* me then. Send every last drone to capture your own death. Hand-deliver my glory on a platter. If you don't—I'll find *you*."

"Send the coordinates then. If you dare."

Hazen lifts the comm to the roaring cave. Darkened water gushes past Hazen Creed, which renders his features almost unholy. His stolen uniform is drenched. "Triangulate. Locate. Need assistance?"

A beat of static. Hard listening.

"Waterfalls. I know where you are."

"Perfect. I have a gift prepared for you." Hazen can't help

his mocking, cocksure confidence. "By the way—Thorleiv sent me to kill you. Even *Arken* knows I'm of higher caliber than you ever were."

Kaiser should shut his yapper. He doesn't even realize what Hazen plotted. Kømmand Sergeant Arcus didn't leave Hazen instructions, yet Hazen survived on his own, hardened by the island.

Without the same pampering of preprovided ammunition that Kaiser relied on, Hazen acquired it all himself. Resilient.

But Kaiser's caustic voice growls, "*You think Thorleiv is the butcher? When I'm finished with your abhorrent, mongrel abomination of a half-breed brother—*"

A sizzle of incoherent audio. Fracturing in Hazen's fist, the comm complains. I expect Hazen to not even dignify Kaiser Arcus with a real response, only another detached chuckle. But Hazen violently growls right back at the mention of his half-foreign brother.

"Your father won't even *recognize* your body in hell when you next see him. Get ready to die in front of your nation. No more words."

———

Adrenalized, I pack light. Bray coughs, weakened.

"For me, it's done, but you owe Kaiser Arcus nothing." Bray's pallid face is bleached of color. "He's dangerous. More than you believe."

"Don't speak like that." I'm sick to death of Bray repeating everything he wants us to tell his parents, his friends, his loved ones. His final goodbyes. I ignore Bray's defeated attitude. He will survive this. "You will live."

Bray exhales. "I won't. Coa, tell Ife . . ." I expect him to gush about how much he loves her. I cut him off.

"Save your strength—"

"Tell her the truth—about everything here." Bray draws a ragged inhale into his orún-battered lungs. The unforgiving island has no longer allowed us its healing properties since the typhoon tore through. We barely had enough herbs to treat the heaviest of our wounds. "Vow to me that you'll tell her. No matter what it means, she needs to protect herself— and she deserves a warning of the true Arctic. Don't spare her descriptions or gory details—expose everything to the world." He coughs.

Hazen's ears perk at the mention of Ife's name. An unmistakable expression emerges on his face—I can't decipher it. I ask, "What?"

Hazen says, "Nothing."

For a moment, Bray stares at Hazen. I don't comprehend the unspoken interaction in their exchange. Fatigued, Bray coughs blood. "Of course. She was yours. *Of course.*"

I balk. "*The ikä* was your fiancée?" *What?*

I try not to imagine a world where Hazen Creed would've been the one sending me into the vicious jungle to my death instead of Maximus Størmbane. Repulsed by me and married to Ife with authority over Makari-Africa.

Without her, I will never marry as long as I live.

My memory of Hazen's words slams into me, and I'm unable to meet Bray's heartbroken eyes. Bray whispers, "Would you have taken care of her as her husband?"

"She still means everything to me." Hazen holds direct eye contact with Bray. Delivering every word—even if it hurts. "You need to stay here. Kaiser Arcus is lethal—"

"I can't *stay here* if foreigners are dead *out there.*" Bray gazes at him with fury. As if Hazen and I can't possibly understand his nascent cause—too obsessed with ourselves and our families to comprehend sacrificing our lives for a greater good. "These victims need vengeance. If I'm killed out there—it will matter to the masses. Word will *spread*."

"For a month. Maybe a year." Hazen sounds incisive—honest. I realize, belatedly, that over the course of the Great Hunt, something altered inside of Hazen Creed. *Everything* altered. He's turned against his own nation; there is no longer an in-between. "If you want to create a significant impact—*stay alive*."

I agree with Hazen despite myself. "Tell the world yourself. In your own words."

Hazen continues, "I will kill Kaiser Arcus in front of our own people. I will end him as a symbol of what we were forced to do to each other and for what they did to these victims."

Victims. That's the second time Hazen's said *victims* in this context. His voice has deepened with remorse, hatred, and vengeance. "They will watch their greatest die on the altar of his kills."

Bray's voice heaves with effort as he forces himself to remain standing on his torn boots. "If you mean that—you'll let us all kill him. You'll let each of his victims take him down themselves, not seize the honor of it for yourself."

Hazen fumes. "It's not *for* myself. It's for my mother, my brother, and the dead."

"Then prove it."

Hazen visibly considers it and then at last nods, agreeing on the right avenger to kill Kaiser.

Bray stays determined. Strong willed. "Prove we do not

forget the dead. We do not abandon the forgotten. We fight for the endangered. We war for them all."

———

Kaiser Arcus.

That coward.

Earlier, Walden Richter arrived with armor and weapons on his *body*—but now Kaiser Arcus approaches with an armada of utility vehicles. Automated all-terrain vehicles reinforced with the sole purpose of providing him with ample ammunition . . . simply to take on Hazen Creed, who killed competitors, a barbarian, a sniper, and Walden Richter himself.

We're concealed in the kapok trees for height advantage.

The wild grass plains below us are scattered with damaged tree limbs, wind-struck evergreens, rattans with their exposed roots desecrated by unnatural disaster. The sun's sunk almost completely beneath the rainforest canopies, its hot breath bated.

Down below, the vehicles rumble, their massive wheels ripping through the jungle carpet. Disrespectful of nature, of Kaipo's territory.

Alina Volkova stands squarely in the blanched mist.

Patient.

A woman is prepared to kill Kaiser Arcus. She challenges him, standing in his trajectory, refusing to remove herself from his path. An insult he won't ignore. He's careless right now of his surroundings, certain of his weapons and defenses, and he halts the foremost utility vehicle, grinding it through the dirt. As if it's a pit stop.

Her mountain-blue eyes are fortified.

His hulking boots descend from the vehicle.

Kaiser darts a cautious glance through the trees, momentarily nervous of enemies.

There are four.

Two on the ground level. Two at high altitude.

Alina Volkova steps forward.

"Kaiser Arcus, you will meet your death—" A gunshot.

Kaiser shot directly at her skull.

Undeterred, Alina Volkova reaches for her crossbow, an act Kaiser does not yet know to fear. Kaiser is unaware of how her crossbow has been modified by Hazen Creed himself. Alina marches ahead toward him. Indomitable. "You will suffer for the murders of Vojislav Vulović. Leslaw Skarżyński. Zlatka Delčev. Vice President Václav Vengerov—"

A barrage of gunfire.

Rapidly, smoke spreads through the air.

"—Mikoš Volkov—son of President Emil Volkov and Iskra Volkova. Brother to Alina Volkova—"

Nose pinched with fury, Alina emerges from the gunshot fumes. Walking right into his gunsights.

Kaiser reenters his vehicle, and this time, he snatches heavier artillery. Setting a powerhouse firearm on his right shoulder.

Alina remains dead set.

Her invisible body armor sustained life-threatening damage from his onslaught of ammunition. But she aims a single crossbow at his massive chest. Primed.

"I am Alina Volkova, your kill commander."

Now Kaiser smirks. Responding to her with dark laughter. "My kill commander. Worthless woman."

Alina does not return his laughter. She does not humor him.

She knows Hazen Creed's vantage point—they agreed upon it as Hazen orchestrated this ending.

Her ending.

The Allied Force never planned to allow her to live—she knew that. When we approached her, cautious of her crossbow, I remembered her warning. *If you ever think of setting foot in my path again, I won't care that you're young or a war refugee. I will kill you the same way I did all of them.*

Hazen did the talking, and Alina wanted nothing more than the honor to humiliate Kaiser Arcus. She had planned a speech for the drones. Now, she has one for him.

I prepare for my lightning strike—with the understanding that I've never generated this volume of electricity before. It could end my life. Will likely end my life. But I've said my prayers.

I'm ready.

But Bray is at ground level. My eyes sting with tears as I see him strapped with explosives. He is invisible behind Kaiser. Alina will not shoot Kaiser—she's shooting Bray Rainsford.

We only have one shot.

In six seconds, the jungle in this area will be obliterated. Hazen has planned the confrontation down to the *millisecond.*

As if the behavior of Allied Force military men is his area of expertise.

If I survive this, which deep down, I know I won't—I plan to search the jungle for Czarina. A part of me can feel she's still out there, a clever and quick girl. I'll stick by her side until the end, if fate lets me.

But right now, all I can think of is the sergeant's earlier words to me. *Your rank's lower than expected ... We will kill you. Shoot you straight to death. You understand that outcome, right? ... I'd hate to harm any of the livestock.*

I did not die the first night as expected. I am not livestock and I will never be livestock.

I am Coa Wildflower.

With finality, Hazen has Kaiser Arcus in his gunsights. Disciplined. But Kaiser spits, "Any final words?"

Now—of all times—Alina mocks Kaiser. She ridicules the entire Allied Force in her last words.

"Glory is destined for me. Ingloriöt."

She nods at Hazen. *Kill him.*

In deadly synchronization—all of us strike Kaiser Arcus. Precise. Ballistic.

An explosive shock of light. Detonating hard enough to make the earth tremble.

Destructive enough that Kaiser Arcus, Alina Volkova, and Bray Rainsford are eliminated from the earth first.

ACKNOWLEDGMENTS

Dear reader,

Thank you for reading this book. Whether you buy it, borrow it, or steal it, it truly means the world to me as long as you read it. If you pirate, please consider leaving a rating and review on Amazon and Goodreads as a fair exchange. We'll still be best friends!

When I initially wrote *The Empire Wars*, I was only a sophomore in high school, sitting in my room and reading "The Most Dangerous Game." Simultaneously, for homework assignments, I was learning about world genocide in depth for the first time in textbooks. It rattled my existence. As I read about Belgium's blood-soaked history of killing a reported twenty million innocent Congolese, I pictured a girl working in the rubber fields and what it must've felt like. The first iteration of *The Empire Wars* was born.

As a kid, I wasn't allowed to read *The Hunger Games*, because my mother thought the idea of children killing each other was too intense. This felt painful to me since another family member of mine had been pulled out of elementary school to fight in a genocidal war when he was young, and

I knew then how real violence against children was in the world. I knew my counterparts deserved to be learned and remembered.

Years before the first draft, I sneakily checked out *The Hunger Games* from my school library and stuffed it in my backpack, and I streamed *Battle Royale* soon afterward. The second iteration of *The Empire Wars* began with those iconic books in mind.

This book is deeply personal to me, and above all, I want to thank Jesus Christ. Without God, this book wouldn't have been remotely possible. It truly consumed my life. Further, I'd love to thank one of my literary agents, the amazing Lynnette Novak, who championed this book from the start. Any author is absolutely lucky to have her in their corner—she's incredible! Additionally, I am forever grateful to my second literary agent, Nicole Resciniti, for believing in my book and being absolutely wonderful.

Furthermore, I need to express my deepest appreciation to my editor, Daniel Ehrenhaft. Without a doubt, he is truly one of the most gracious, kind, and intelligent human beings I've ever met. His editorial perspective and expert opinions were invaluable and infinitely improved the book, making it what it became.

To Riam Griswold, you are a complete genius. You are the brilliant, sharp, incisive copy editor that thoroughly transformed *The Empire Wars*, and I am in awe of you. I cannot possibly thank you enough.

Also, I would like to thank the entire publishing team at Blackstone Publishing. Special thanks to Sarah Bonamino, Francie Crawford, Nikki Carrero, and Nicole Sklitsis. Thank you as well to the artist of the phenomenal book cover.

Deepest thanks to my film/TV team at the Creative Artists Agency, Rukayat and Uzi. You are greatly appreciated.

A heartfelt thank-you to Brenda Drake, Beth Phelan, Stephanie J. Scott, Erica M. Chapman, and Tomi Adeyemi for helping me at the start of my journey. I was so thankful then, and I am still thankful now, more than you will ever know.

Thank you to Angie Thomas for being one of the greatest writers of this generation. Thank you for taking the time to blurb my book; it's literally a dream come true.

Thank you to Madeline Miller for changing my life by writing *The Song of Achilles*. You are a supernova. Thank you for writing my favorite book in the entire world, shattering my heart with your prose, and inspiring me with your legacy. You are amazing.

Cindy of *Withcindy* and Rachel of *Reads with Rachel*, you are some of my favorite people on the internet. Ever. You are beyond exceptional, powerful, and unbelievably talented. You are carrying the entire book community on your backs. Your works are going to revolutionize the book world, and we don't deserve you.

To my #DVpit Twitter buddies, Anthony Nerada, Pamela Delupio, and Tamara Cole, you are all awesome.

Kindly, I'd love to thank Infinity Ward (*Call of Duty* creators), Hideo Kojima (*Metal Gear Solid* creator), Madeline Miller (*Song of Achilles* author), Suzanne Collins (*The Hunger Games* author), Koushun Takami (*Battle Royale* author), Richard Connell ("The Most Dangerous Game" author), Gillian Flynn (*Gone Girl* author), David Fincher (*Gone Girl* director), Christopher Nolan (*Dark Knight* trilogy director), Ryan Coogler (*Fruitvale Station* and *Black Panther* director), Jordan Peele (*Get Out* director), Quentin Tarantino (*Inglourious Basterds* director), Ava DuVernay (*13th* director), Shonda Rhimes (*Scandal* creator and *How to Get Away with Murder* producer), Yeon Sang-ho (*Train to Busan* director), Hwang

Dong-hyuk (*Squid Game* director), Hiromu Arakawa (*Fullmetal Alchemist* creator), Hajime Isayama (*Attack on Titan* creator), Gege Akutami (*Jujutsu Kaisen* creator), John Green (*The Fault in Our Stars* author), and all the innovative creatives that inspired me future and past. Huge thank-you also to Beyoncé, Billie Eilish, and SZA for your motivational and impactful music.

My heart goes out to every survivor and victim of genocide. May all oppressed people be freed. May Congo be free at last. Thank you to those who have risked their lives and mental health to report, examine, and document genocide.

My prayers are with Henrietta Lacks, a Black woman whose stolen cells led to medical discoveries, saved the world and countless lives, and became the first immortalized human cell line. The world infinitely owes you.

Last, but never least, I'd like to thank my own family and friends. Your encouragement and endless support throughout the years sincerely saved the book. Thank you, thank you, thank you. Ohana forever.